WHAT SHE WALKED INTO

TAYLOR JAKOVINA

UNQUIET QUILL PRESS

Cover design by Taylor Jakovina

First edition, 2025

ISBN: 979-8-9994767-1-5

DEDICATION

To my mom and my husband—thank you for letting me read this book out loud to you again and again (and again), and for listening like it mattered every time. Your feedback, your patience, and your presence helped me hold the emotional center of this book, even when it got overwhelming.

Mom, thank you for your quietly profound influence on my life. For teaching me how to survive what feels impossible, how to honor effort without losing balance, and how to trust my own footing when the path wasn't clear. The shape of this book, and the part of me that finished it, both start with you.

— • —

A Note From The Author

What She Walked Into explores themes of grief, trauma, emotional ma-nipulation, and death. While the story avoids graphic violence, it includes elements of gaslighting, psychological abuse, and institutional failure.

I approached these themes with sensitivity and care, always keeping the emotional truth of the characters at the center. If any of these subjects are difficult for you, please take care as you read.

1

— · —

October 26, 2024, 2 AM - Sophia

1 Day After Julie Went Missing

The first thing I noticed was the cold. Not the crisp October kind. Something deeper. Sharper.

A marrow-deep chill that settled in my bones, like I'd been standing there for hours.

Then came the silence.

Thick. Suffocating. Like the air had been emptied of sound.

I exhaled sharply. Too loud. Like I was interrupting something.

A gust of wind stirred the trees, dead leaves scattering at my feet. My head throbbed.

Where was I?

I blinked hard, trying to orient myself, but the trees stretched endless and unfamiliar. Even in the dark, I should've known this place. I'd grown up with these woods behind my house. But standing here now, they felt... different.

As if I wasn't the only one out here.

And they weren't quite my woods. Not exactly.

Heart pounding, I turned, eyes darting past the trees. I saw the faint outline of a house through the dark. Not mine. Six doors down. Mr. Linworth's house.

When I finally took a step forward, my legs were sore and wobbled, like I'd just been running for an extended period.

My pajama shorts were frayed. Scratches lined my thigh, thorn marks. My arms ached. Dirt clung to my fingers, caked under my nails, streaked up my forearms.

Dried blood.

My breath stuttered.

Not just dirt. Fresh wounds, like they'd barely had time to set.

I inhaled sharply, my throat tight. My gaze dropped to the ground—

There were footprints all around me.

1

My footprints?

Messy. Erratic. Like someone had been pacing. Or circling.

They crisscrossed, overlapping, leading in and out of the trees, as if someone kept coming back.

Like someone—or I—hadn't wanted to leave.

A slow, creeping chill settled in my stomach.

I staggered back. The wind whispered through the branches. My pulse pounded. The cold wasn't just outside anymore. It had crept inside me.

Then I heard the softest shift of weight.

Not an animal, the sound was too loud. Something else.

A shadow flickered between the trees.

I wasn't alone.

I became extremely aware of my breathing. I turned, searching the darkness, my eyes burning to focus. Nothing. The wind stirred again, but the air suddenly felt heavier, pressing in on me.

I heard a sharp snap. A branch breaking, close.

Something in my body screamed at me to move.

Run.

My feet moved before my brain could catch up. I ran. Lungs burning, branches slashing my arms. The ground blurred beneath me, my toes stinging against the cold, uneven dirt.

I hadn't even noticed I was barefoot. But the footprints. Weren't they made by shoes?

I didn't stop. I didn't look back.

By the time my house came into view, a sharp, nauseating déjà vu crashed over me.

I had done this before.

The back porch light flickered, a dim, yellow glow against the dark. I fumbled for the door handle with shaking hands, nearly tripping inside.

I slammed the door behind me, gasping, my heart clawing at my ribs.

The kitchen was still. The only sound was my ragged breathing, the rush of blood in my ears.

I stumbled toward the sink, turning the faucet on full blast. Water hissed against my skin as I scrubbed, but the dirt—the dirt wedged deep under my nails—clung stubbornly, like it belonged there.

I barely heard the chair creak behind me.

"You were out there again, weren't you?" His voice was calm, but there was something else. Like he wasn't just asking.

I nearly jumped out of my skin.

I spun.

My brother Eli sat at the kitchen table, arms folded, watching me.

He wasn't surprised.

Didn't look confused.

He was waiting.

A shiver rippled through me, cold in a way that had nothing to do with the night air.

I swallowed hard, my pulse still wild as I stammered something unintelligible.

Eli sighed. He grabbed a dish towel and tossed it at me. "You're shaking." His voice was steady. Like he was trying to calm me down.

"Sit down before you pass out."

I hesitated, my muscles still coiled to run. But my body was too exhausted to fight. I sank into the chair across from him, gripping the towel in my lap.

"You need to tell someone," he said. "The sleepwalking. It's getting worse."

I didn't answer. I couldn't.

Because part of me wasn't sure it was *just* sleepwalking anymore.

A distant hoot echoed through the trees.

I flinched.

And Eli noticed.

His gaze sharpened, concern flickering behind his eyes. "What is it?"

My throat felt like sandpaper. How could I tell him that I wasn't alone out there? That I felt something watching me? That I saw footprints all around me when I woke up. Footprints I wasn't sure—no, didn't *think*—were mine?

That I still felt it now?

I wanted to tell him about the shadow in the woods. About the sinking feeling that made me run.

But I couldn't. Saying it out loud would make it real.

Instead, I shook my head. "Nothing," I whispered.

Eli didn't believe me.

He let the silence stretch between us, his fingers drumming once against the table before he stood. "You should go to bed," he said.

I nodded, but neither of us moved.

Eli took a long breath. Hesitated. Then he turned and disappeared down the hall, his footsteps slow.

I stayed in the kitchen, staring at the window. Outside, the woods loomed. Silent, still.

But something had been there.

I could still feel it.

Watching.

Waiting.

2

OCTOBER 26, 2024, 11 AM - SOPHIA

1 DAY AFTER JULIE WENT MISSING

The bell jingled as I stepped into Grounded Café, the only café in Ordinance, Ohio.

It smelled like a mix of cinnamon and pumpkin spice forced into the air by an overworked diffuser. The warmth was a sharp contrast to the fall chill outside, where pumpkins lined sidewalks littered with fallen leaves.

But the second I walked in, the warmth didn't reach me.

The town buzzed, but not about homecoming, the football team, or who got caught sneaking beer.

No.

Julie Greene was missing.

And for some reason, everyone was looking at me.

Or maybe they weren't.

I could be imagining it.

There was a mix of laughter, conversation, and the hum of the espresso machine. It should have sounded normal. But every now and then, my name cut through, slipping in and out of conversations like a radio station just slightly out of tune. A few did a not-so-subtle double take, whispering behind their hands.

Someone's voice dipped lower, but I only caught the tail end of a sentence.

"...sleepwalking again."

My skin prickled. Were they talking about me?

Heat crept up my neck. I resisted the urge to shrink into myself, to make myself smaller. I hated this. Being looked at. Being the center of something I didn't understand.

I hesitated near the entrance, shifting on my heels. A slow, creeping sensation slithered up my spine.

Mrs. Harrow, who ran the floral shop, stood at the counter with a cup cradled between her hands, her silver hair twisted up in a clip. Her gaze flickered toward me, almost like she was going to acknowledge me, but then nothing. Instead, she turned back to the woman beside her, murmuring something I couldn't hear.

At the window, a group of girls from my school huddled over their phones, fingers darting frantically across their screens. When I caught one of their gazes—Jessica? Jenna?—she looked away so fast it was almost funny.

But the worst part was the older crowd.

Mr. Thompson, who owned the hardware store, sat in the corner with a few retired farmers, their plaid jackets slung over their chairs. They weren't gossiping, not openly. They didn't need to. Their silence was enough.

I forced myself to keep moving, ignoring the weight of their quiet stares. Then, just as I was about to retreat to a corner booth, I caught sight of Mrs. Finch, my chemistry teacher, flipping through the newspaper at the counter.

She glanced up, met my eyes, and just waved.

Like everything was normal.

And it probably was.

Something in my chest unknotted, just a little. I exhaled slowly, grounding myself in the moment, my feet pressing forward at the first sign of acceptance. But it didn't feel like relief. Not really.

Because if one person treating me normally felt this important, what did that say about everyone else?

"Soph!"

Abbie's voice sliced through the tension like a blade. Already at our usual table, she drummed her nails against her coffee cup. Her chipped dark green polish made her fingers look perfect for the season.

Abbie made sweatpants look like high fashion. Today was no different, her long blonde hair was twisted in a sleek knot. She was wearing athletic leggings and a slouchy off the shoulder sweater which accented her golden skin. Her green eyes caught the dim café light like a cat's, sharp and mesmerizing.

I slid into the chair across from her, and she gave me a once over, her eyes narrowing as she slid me a coffee.

"You never even try, and somehow, you still look like you walked out of a magazine," she muttered, stirring her coffee. "It's actually offensive."

I huffed a laugh. "I don't wear makeup."

"Exactly!" She shot me an exasperated look, like I was personally responsible for the injustice.

I smirked, tilting my head. "Look who's talking, Abbie."

"Yeah, but at least I work for it." She popped the lid off her cup and frowned. "Ugh. They burned my caramel latte. *Again*. It's like they hate me."

"Probably."

"Wow, okay, fake friend energy," she scoffed, taking a sip. "Anyway, did you hear about Linworth?"

Of course I had. The whole town had.

The police had taken him in for questioning last night.

"It doesn't mean anything," I said, stirring my coffee, watching the swirl of cream spread into the dark liquid.

Abbie raised an eyebrow. "Doesn't it?" She leaned forward, lowering her voice. "Julie's missing, and the cops bring in Linworth less than twenty-four hours later. You don't think that's suspicious? Connected?"

The words hit me like a stone to the gut.

Julie's missing.

It still didn't feel real. It had only been a day. A single, stretched out, endless day since people started whispering her name like it was already a ghost story.

"You want it to be connected," I murmured.

Abbie shrugged. "I just think it *makes sense.*"

Before I could argue, a shadow passed over the table.

Jay.

His usual easy confidence was gone.

Normally, he moved like someone who had never once been unsure of himself. But today his shoulders were tight, his jaw locked.

A faint bruise bloomed across his right hand. A dull, purplish smear splattered across his knuckles.

I frowned. "What happened to your hand?"

Jay hesitated just a fraction of a second too long.

"Nothing." Then he put his hands under the table, as if that would make it go away.

Liar.

He wasn't just hiding his hands, he was tense all over. His foot tapped against the floor. His shoulders rolled back, then forward, like he couldn't quite get comfortable.

I studied him, waiting for him to meet my gaze, but he didn't. His black hair, which was always a mess, looked like he had just been through a wind tunnel, falling into his face. Beneath the table, I heard the crinkle of a napkin twisting between his fingers, the sound tight and fidgety, like he was trying to strangle a thought before it got out.

"So, they brought Linworth in," Abbie said. "What do you think?"

When Jay didn't answer, Abbie smirked and said, "I *know* he did it."

Jay exhaled sharply. "We don't even know what *it* is."

I kept my eyes on him. "So what do *you* think?"

Something flickered across his face, too quick to catch. "I think people should shut up until they know what the hell they're talking about."

Abbie rolled her eyes. "Defensive much?"

Jay didn't answer.

A strange tension settled between us. He wasn't looking at me, but I could *feel* his attention. Heavy. Calculating. Like he was waiting for me to break the silence.

But before I could, my phone buzzed against the table.

One new message.

Somehow, I knew something was wrong before I even looked.

A shiver worked its way up my arm. I exhaled, slow and deliberate, and flipped my phone over.

> Julie Greene: Why did you leave me?

The words swam in front of my eyes. Julie?

The noise in the café faded into a dull hum. My fingers tightened around the phone, my pulse thrummed in my neck.

I blinked—

The text was gone.

Vanished.

No. That wasn't possible. Was it?

I flicked to my messages. No sign of it.

I stared, stomach hollowing out. I swore I saw it. But the last message in my inbox was from Abbie an hour ago. My fingers gripped my phone like if I held it hard enough, the text would reappear.

It had to be a glitch.

But my skin was ice. It was impossible not to be on edge, because the last call I received was from Julie Greene at 1:47AM on October 25th. The night she went missing. And I had missed it.

"Sophia." Jay's voice was softer than I expected, like he had been saying my name for a while. I blinked, refocusing. His brows knit together, worry threading through his expression. He looked at me like I might disappear right in front of him. I opened my mouth, but no words came. His gaze didn't waver. Abbie was walking back to the table from the counter, I hadn't even realized she left.

"You okay?" he asked quietly before she reached us. I wasn't. And I hated that he could tell.

I swallowed. "It's nothing."

Lie. Now I had lied just like him.

I forced myself to put the phone down, but my hands wouldn't stop shaking.

When Abbie reached us, she brought the latest opinions from the people in the café. All theorizing about Linworth, but I didn't hear a word of it.

The town had already picked its suspect, and decided something horrible had happened to Julie Greene.

But I couldn't shake the feeling they were wrong.

3

─ • ─

OCTOBER 27, 2024, 7 AM - SOPHIA

2 DAYS AFTER JULIE WENT MISSING

Ordinance had woken up early. All 2,000 of us.

Frost coated the lawns, glistening under the pale sun. The air smelled like fresh grass and lingering bonfire smoke. Beneath it, something heavier. Expectation.

Everyone, and I mean everyone, was looking for Julie.

We had classes together, but we weren't close. She was the kind of girl who felt like she belonged. I wasn't. She ran with the cheerleaders, the student council, the newspaper club types. The ones who moved through the halls like they owned them. I was just a face in her periphery, I was the girl who sat near the back in her English class and borrowed her pen once in Chemistry.

Standing in this search party, watching the town close in around itself, I felt like I knew her better in her absence than I ever did in her presence.

The crowd had gathered at the edge of Maple Road... my road. Where the houses eventually stopped and the trees pressed in. Dozens of people stood shoulder to shoulder: parents, classmates, retirees. Even the ones who rarely left their houses had shown up.

Some were here because they cared. Some because they felt obligated. And others, I was sure, just wanted to be part of the story.

One thing stood out, even in the frenzy. Linworth was not here.

Stephen was, though.

He stood near the front beside Newton, nodding like he belonged there. Holding a laminated map. Offering to organize volunteer groups.

He was the only student teachers trusted with the keys to their classrooms. He bugged me though, always a little too polished.

Newton flipped through his clipboard like he wasn't sure how to run something like this. But Stephen? Stephen looked like he already had a plan.

Newton was a stocky man, with short brown hair and a beard peppered with grey. Deep creases bracketed his mouth like he'd spent a lifetime frowning.

"This is a grid search," he said. "Stay in pairs, spread out, and if you find anything, anything, call it in immediately."

I stood near the back, away from the crowd. Away from everyone except for Jay, who had appeared beside me at some point without a word.

"You really trust him to handle this?" I muttered.

Jay let out a humorless chuckle. "Newton couldn't find his own ass with a flashlight and a map."

I huffed a small laugh. "That was weirdly graphic."

Jay smirked. "Yeah, well. I'm a man of vivid imagery."

Across the crowd, Leo stood near his football friends, his jaw set. Our eyes met for just a second, a flicker of something, before he looked away.

But instead of moving on, his gaze slid past me and landed squarely on Jay.

The thing about Leo was he always looked like he wanted to say something. I used to know what that something was, back when we were together. But now? Now it was just silence and long glances that I pretended not to notice.

Something in his expression shifted.

Then, just as quickly, he turned, disappearing into his group like he'd never looked at either of us at all.

Jay nudged me, voice softer than usual. "Ready to go?" I nodded, but neither of us moved right away. His gaze lingered for a second too long, like he wanted to say something but thought better of it. I turned first, ignoring the way my stomach did a little flip.

The deeper we walked into the woods, the quieter it got.

No wind. No birds. Just the sound of our footsteps pressing into damp leaves.

Jay walked beside me, hands shoved into his track hoodie pockets, moving easily over the uneven ground while I tripped over every stick like I'd never walked in my life. He sighed, putting out an arm before I could fall flat on my face.

"You're a menace to yourself, Whitaker." There was laughter in his voice, but something else, too. Something subdued. I swallowed hard and looked away.

Jay was tall and broad shouldered. His eyes—crystal blue, sharp enough to cut through you—stood out starkly against his otherwise dark features. A trail of freckles climbed up his neck, barely visible in the dim light from the overcast sky.

He was objectively handsome. Not that I thought about him like that.

"You ever think about leaving this town?" he asked, pulling me out of my thoughts.

I glanced at him. "What, like forever?"

"Yeah."

I thought about it. "I used to, when I was little. Before."

Jay nodded like he understood. "Before your mom?"

The words landed softly, carefully, but they still knocked the wind out of me a little.

"Yeah," I said. "After she died, it felt like moving wouldn't change anything. Grief follows you, you know?"

Jay didn't say anything right away, just let my words settle between us. "Yeah," he murmured after a second. "I get that." Jay's brother had died unexpectedly two years ago. I was suddenly very aware of my poor choice of words.

"What about you?" I stammered quickly, trying to redirect the conversation.

He hesitated, kicking at a loose rock. "I've moved around a lot." His voice was casual, but something about it felt forced, like he was trying to make it sound like less than it was.

I already knew that much. He'd only been here a year, but unlike other new kids, he didn't carry that awkwardness of someone just passing through.

"That wasn't really an answer. Would you go?"

"If you asked me when I first moved here I would have said yeah, for sure," he admitted. "Since I've never been anywhere more than a few years, it kind of felt bound to happen. But maybe it'd be nice to—" He stopped short, shaking his head. "Never mind."

That caught my attention. "Nice to what?"

Jay glanced at me, then looked away, his hands shoved deeper into his pockets. "Nothing. Just... plant roots somewhere. Staying long enough for it to matter."

Something about the way he said it made my heart sink.

Before I could respond, he nudged me with his elbow, forcing the mood lighter. "Maybe I'll move, start a surf shop," he said. "California. Sand. Sunshine. The whole thing."

I shook my head, laughing. "Right, because last time you got near deep water, Abbie had to practically save your life."

Jay groaned, throwing his head back. "It wasn't that bad."

"Oh, it was that bad," I shot back. "You did some ridiculous flip off the diving board, made the biggest splash I've ever seen, and then completely forgot how to tread water. Abbie had to haul you to the edge before you drowned in what? Five feet?"

He rubbed the back of his neck. "I was fine."

"You were flailing."

"It was a stylish flail."

I snorted. "Why did you even do that?"

He hesitated, a beat too long. Then shrugged. "Dunno. Seemed like a good idea at the time."

His smile stayed, but something flickered behind it. Like he did know. Something tugged at him, but he wasn't letting me see it.

I didn't push it.

"Honestly, I think my real mistake was not committing to the bit," he said. "If I'd stayed under a few seconds longer, Abbie might've given me CPR. Then bam—lifelong debt. She'd have to name her firstborn after me."

I tilted my head. "Wouldn't it be the other way around?"

He laughed, but the sound was just a little too forced. Something sad swirled in his eyes.

"Hey, are you okay?" I asked.

He made a goofy face. "Always."

But the strain in his smile didn't quite go away.

Jay always did this, skating past things that felt too real, too close to something unspoken.

And for some reason, I let him.

The silence that followed felt heavier than before, settling between us as we kept walking.

I thought I saw something at least three times. A flash of red. A shape between the trees. Every time, my breathing stopped. Every time, it was nothing.

But then the air shifted.

Not colder. Heavier.

Like something was watching.

A breath of wind stirred the trees. A branch creaked. The sound was too intentional.

Jay slowed beside me. "Did you hear—"

A voice.

Distant, barely a whisper. My name.

I spun. "Hello?"

Jay stiffened. "What?"

I scanned the trees, my pulse pounding. The sound was already gone, but I had heard it. I knew I had. A girl's voice, stretched thin like a fraying thread.

Like Julie.

My stomach lurched. "Someone just... someone called my name."

Jay's brows furrowed. He glanced around. "I didn't hear anything."

My hands clenched. "No, I—"

The trees seemed to lean in, their skeletal limbs stretching closer, casting jagged shadows that didn't quite match the light.

Jay was still watching me, like he was waiting for me to realize something.

That there had been no voice.

That it was just in my head.

I blew out a breath, forcing myself to turn away. "Forget it. It was probably nothing."

He wasn't looking at me anymore, but I felt it. His attention. My pulse kicked up. I forced my gaze down, but the air between us was full of tension.

My foot caught on something for the hundredth time.

I stumbled, reaching out for balance and catching Jay's arm as my shoe tangled in fabric.

Not just fabric.

A coat.

It was a neon yellow raincoat with a hand-stitched heart next to the pocket.

My mind whipped back to late August, when it rained so hard, they canceled school. I didn't even know that could happen, thought it was only for snow days or freezing cold temperatures. But they had cancelled school, saying the buses couldn't safely take everyone and a bunch of teenagers that just got their licenses shouldn't be driving.

But that only made it worse. Abbie had called everyone to the woods for a squirt gun fight, in the rain. And as ridiculous as it sounded, almost everyone showed up. I remember seeing Julie, laughing as she snuck up on Abbie and squirting her right from behind. Laughing in her neon yellow rain jacket with a heart stitched next to the pocket.

I stared at the coat, willing it to be something else. Something random. But it wasn't. I knew that little stitched heart. I knew who it belonged to. And I knew, Julie wasn't wearing it anymore.

A chill crawled up my spine.

Wait—

I could almost see my house from here.

Was this where I woke up yesterday?

Jay's voice broke through the fog. "Soph."

I turned to him, but before I could speak, Newton's voice called from the trees.

I barely had time to compose myself before he stepped through the brush, his gaze already locked onto me.

14

I couldn't move.

Newton's face hardened.

"What do you have?"

My fingers clenched around the coat. The fabric was cold. Wrong.

Slowly, I lifted it. "I think this is Julie's."

Newton's eyes moved from the coat to my face and lingered too long.

I knew that look. The kind that made me want to shrink. To disappear.

"This is evidence," he said, taking it from me, voice even, but something about the way he gripped it made my stomach tighten.

I let go, but my hands felt empty.

Newton turned it over, about to bag it, then froze.

Inside, something was scrawled in hurried black marker. I couldn't make it out.

Newton's fingers curled tighter around the fabric.

His radio crackled.

"We got something," one of the deputies called.

Newton exhaled, casting one last unreadable glance at me.

"Stay here."

And then he was gone, disappearing into the trees. Coat gripped tightly in his hands. I watched the neon yellow fade into the distance with him.

I let out a breath I hadn't realized I was holding.

Jay, beside me, muttered a curse. "What the hell does it mean that we found her jacket in the woods?"

I shook my head, my pulse hammering. "I don't know."

Before I could say anything else, my phone vibrated in my pocket.

I pulled it out, glancing at the screen.

Another text.

Julie Greene: It wasn't supposed to be you.

The breath caught in my throat. The screen flickered. And just like before—the message was gone.

But I had seen it. I knew I had.

4

— • —

OCTOBER 28, 2024, 8 AM - SOPHIA

3 DAYS AFTER JULIE WENT MISSING

By the time I walked into school the next morning, everyone knew.

Not that I'd done anything wrong, just that my name had slipped even deeper into the conversation. And not just about sleepwalking. But about Julie.

And as if that wasn't bad enough, Jay still hadn't texted me back.

After what we found, I think he's avoiding me.

For a second, I seriously considered turning around and walking home.

It didn't matter that we barely knew each other. I found her coat. I handed it to Newton. That was enough.

And in a town this small, enough was all people needed.

The hallway buzzed with its usual chaos, but today it felt suffocating.

Voices dipped to murmurs as I passed. I caught the tail end of a sentence, something about the woods. Someone else said Linworth's name. Then mine.

I kept my face blank, even as my insides twisted into knots.

It wasn't like people thought I had anything to do with what might have happened to Julie. But my name was in the same sentences as hers now, and that felt dangerous.

I heard another whisper. One that shouldn't have hit so hard.

"What if Julie died, and she was there?"

"She" meaning me.

I turned a corner and passed a cluster of teachers, deep in their own conversation. One of them sighed, frustrated.

"Kids these days. Just up and vanish without a word. Remember Rachel? They run away and don't think twice about who they leave behind."

I spun my locker dial. The metal groaned. I reached to shove my bag in, and my fingers locked up.

16

Tucked between my textbooks was a small, white slip of paper. I thought it was just a schedule or a stray note, until I saw the writing.

Jagged. Bold. Intentional.

I unfolded it slowly.

"You should have stayed asleep."

My fingers tightened around the paper.

Okay.

That was... not great.

A slow pressure coiled in my chest, but I forced my face to stay blank. I wasn't about to give whoever did this the satisfaction of a reaction.

People had been talking about my sleepwalking for weeks. It wasn't a secret anymore. If this had just said something generic like "freak" or "sleepwalker" I would have rolled my eyes and moved on.

But this? This was pointed. Not just gossip. A warning.

I scanned the hallway, my eyes sweeping thoroughly through the crowd.

No one was watching me now. No lingering stares. No guilty faces ducking away at the last second. Just the usual cliques huddled together, talking, laughing, pretending life was normal.

Maybe I'd expected something cinematic.

A masked figure vanishing into the crowd.

A spotlight revealing my stalker.

A villain twirling an invisible mustache.

But no.

Just normal life.

And me, pretending that note hadn't rattled something deep inside me.

I folded the paper and stuffed it in my bag, but the words echoed.

I should have stayed asleep for what?

What did they think I would have seen?

My stomach clenched around something uneasy as a memory tried to claw its way to the surface.

Before I could catch it, a voice behind me cut through.

"Hey. You doing okay?"

I turned. Stephen.

His jet-black hair was combed to perfection. He had piercing blue eyes that should've made him handsome. Except they didn't. There was something off. Too symmetrical. Too smooth. Like an AI-generated version of what a high school golden boy should look like.

He wasn't smirking or whispering like everyone else. Just... watching. Which was still... odd. Because we never talked.

I nodded once, cautious. "Fine."

His gaze swept the hallway, then landed back on me. "You haven't seen Jay, have you?"

I hesitated. "No. Not since we found Julie's jacket. Why?"

Stephen nodded slowly, like that confirmed something for him.

"He'd be hiding now," he said softly. "People don't change."

Then his eyes caught mine with an intensity I couldn't name.

"Ask Jay what happened to his brother sometime. And... be careful."

He turned and walked off before I could say anything.

A crash echoed from down the hall. Billy and Kenny, mid-fight as always. Mr. Calloway stepped out of his classroom to break it up just as Stephen passed by. Their eyes locked for a second. Calloway turned back to the fight with more fire than usual.

Everyone knew Calloway. AP Bio teacher. Ran his class like a dictatorship.

Rumor had it he handed out extra credit for favors, not the academic kind.

But who could trust anything in this town?

Normally, I wouldn't have looked twice.

But something about the fight, the chaos of it, held my attention.

Calloway barked at the brothers, gesturing sharply, stepping between them like it was a performance he'd rehearsed.

And for a second, everything else faded.

The noise dulled. The crowd blurred. Like time skipped.

When I blinked, the hallway was mostly empty—eerily so, like the pandemonium had been scrubbed clean too fast.

And Calloway was no longer watching the boys.

He was watching me.

Not curious.

Not concerned.

Just... watching.

Our eyes locked for a fraction of a second. Then, without a word, he turned and walked back into his classroom.

A tremor slipped down my arm. I told myself it was nothing.

The day dragged, stretching into something long and unbearable.

When the bell for my last class rang, my nerves were frayed.

So, when I stepped into the hallway and saw Newton waiting for me, I wasn't even surprised. His face was a mask, completely blank except for the slight crease between his brows.

He didn't say much.

Just, "Miss Whitaker."

But that was enough to send a fresh ripple of gossip through the halls.

I barely had time to register whatever interaction that was before he turned and started walking.

He expected me to follow.

For some reason I did.

***

Newton led me into the counselor's office for a "talk."

The room was small and cluttered. It felt forgotten, like no one besides the counselor, who was noticeably absent, ever actually used it.

I didn't sit.

Neither did he.

He just stood there and studied me for a long moment, his gaze sharp, weighing.

Then he asked, "Where were you the night Julie disappeared?"

A tight knot formed in my chest.

"I—"

The door behind me opened.

Eli.

His expression was calm, but his eyes locked onto Newton like a challenge.

"Oh, Sophia, there you are," Eli said smoothly, stepping into the room like he didn't just find his sister basically getting interrogated by the police. Like it totally made sense that we'd be here together.

Newton's gaze flicked over him, unimpressed.

"What are you doing here, kid? I'm talking to your sister."

"She was home." Eli cut in, too easily. "I heard you talking when I was walking up."

19

Newton's eyes stayed on me, pinning me to the spot. "That right, Sophia?" he asked, looking straight at me.

Eli didn't miss a beat. "Yep, with me."

Newton pinched the bridge of his nose. "Alright, I didn't realize your name was Sophia."

He and Eli went back and forth for a minute. But that was it. No more questions.

Just as I turned to leave, he said, "You're not just in the conversation with your classmates, Whitaker."

I froze.

Newton's expression didn't change. "People are starting to ask questions."

A slow, heavy weight pressed against my head.

He wasn't just talking about the people in my school.

I walked out, Eli behind me, my mind whirling, trying to decipher Newton's intentions.

I'd just been asked by the head of police for my whereabouts the night Julie went missing. I don't think he believed what Eli told him.

But he let me go.

For now.

Still, the way he said my name...

I knew he'd be back.

5

— • —

OCTOBER 29, 2024, 12 PM - SOPHIA

4 DAYS AFTER JULIE WENT MISSING

I caught my reflection in the window as I walked up to Grounded Café.

The bags under my dark brown eyes were worse than yesterday, bruised looking smudges that no amount of concealer could erase. Not that I owned any. My summer tan was gone, leached from my skin by the creeping chill of October, leaving my complexion a faded, dull olive.

I looked tired.

I blinked... and then I was at the counter.

I didn't remember walking up.

My head became heavy. This wasn't new. The gaps. The missing time. The way my body moved before my brain caught up.

The barista didn't ask for my order. She just said, "The usual." And pulled me back into the present. She started making my vanilla latte, the way she always did. Because I was a regular now. Not just in the casual, stop-by-for-coffee way. No, I was here every day. A month ago, I barely drank coffee.

Now the nights were slipping away. Then the mornings felt like they were dragging me under. And suddenly, I couldn't function without at least four cups before noon.

I should've looked it up by now to find a better fix. Sleep issues. Sleepwalking. Triggers. What it actually means to wake up in places you don't remember falling asleep. But I didn't.

Because if I did, then I'd have to admit something was wrong. And I wasn't ready for that yet.

Instead, I had caffeine.

I watched the barista's light pink hair flip as she spun around to grab the whipped cream. I pulled out my phone to check the time, but my hands felt slow. Sluggish. Like my body hadn't caught up to the day yet. God, I needed that latte.

I had one text.

> Eli: You should head home soon.

No explanation. No context.

I started to frown, then the bell rang.

A deep, hollow chime that rolled through town like a distant echo of something already gone.

One.

Two.

Three.

The café went silent.

For a second, my brain didn't register why.

I was somewhere else. A different time. A different season.

The sharp bite of February air. The whisper of mourning clothes and cold hands.

My mother's funeral.

The bell had rung that day, too.

Not for a ceremony. Not for a town event.

For a death.

I sucked in a breath, and the present slammed back into focus.

A chair scraped back against the floor.

Mr. Thompson, who had been in this town longer than anyone, pushed to his feet. A flake of forgotten oatmeal clinging to his chin as he rubbed a hand over his jaw.

Someone near the window whispered, "Oh my God."

The cheerleaders froze mid-conversation, their laughter dying in their throats. Some reached for their phones, checking for news.

The barista's hands shook. She knocked over a bottle of syrup, coating the ends of her long hair, but no one reacted.

Outside, a police car sped past. Then another. Then another. Lights flashing. No sirens.

I knew before anyone said it.

Julie.

They had found Julie.

The door swung open, and people spilled outside, drawn toward the flashing lights like moths to a flame.

I followed, barely aware of my own movements, stepping into a town that had just turned into a crime scene.

Blue and red lights bounced off shop windows, twisting in warped reflections that most certainly did not belong here.

The cars were heading toward Maple Road.

The woods.

Had they found her in the woods?

The church bell rang again, and someone near me made a choked noise.

Mrs. Evers, who used to babysit Julie, was crying quietly, her hands clasped together like she was praying.

I swallowed, my throat tight, the cold pressing against my skin as I tried to process what was happening.

A voice cut through the chaos. Sharp. Tense.

"Where are they going?"

I turned to see Leo behind me.

His face was pale, his jaw locked tight. His hands curled into fists at his sides, like he was bracing for something.

He looked like he already knew, but he wanted someone to say it out loud. Like he wanted me to say it.

I couldn't.

Maybe the bells were ringing for something else this time?

No. I knew what this meant. My mouth felt wired shut.

A few feet away, Jay stood frozen, hands in his track hoodie pockets like always, his gaze locked on the patrol cars.

His chest rose and fell in measured, controlled breaths.

Like he had been waiting for this.

And then, just beyond him, Newton stepped out of his car.

But he wasn't looking toward the woods.

A flicker of realization hit me.

Newton wasn't rushing toward the search team.

He wasn't talking to another officer.

He was standing still, radio in hand, scanning the crowd.

I watched it happen in slow motion. The way his eyes moved over the gathering mob, skipping past people, skipping past Leo, past Jay, until they landed on me.

A low murmur spread through the crowd.

I caught words in fragments.

"She found the coat."

"She was in the woods."

"Newton questioned her once already."

"She sleepwalks."

That one cut through the rest, sharp and mean. Though I didn't know why I cared anymore.

Newton lifted his radio, muttered something into it, then adjusted his stance, as if he'd just made up his mind about something.

Then he started walking.

Straight towards me.

My breath caught.

I wasn't moving. I hadn't said a single word. I hadn't done anything.

But he was coming anyway.

Leo moved first. His hand firm on my shoulder, not tight, not hurting, but enough to keep me in place.

A few months ago, his touch wouldn't have made me think twice. But by the time summer ended, I had started noticing the way it lingered. A second too long, a little too firm.

The way his questions came slower, more careful, like he was measuring my answers.

"You don't talk to me like you used to."

"Are we okay?"

"Do you even want to be here?"

I had told myself to stick with it, Leo was a good guy. Even if I didn't feel the pull to him. Then the party happened, and I didn't need to pretend anymore.

Now his grip felt cold. His pulse hammering just beneath the surface.

"Don't," he said, voice low enough that only I could hear. "Just. Wait."

Jay didn't move. He just watched.

Newton reached us, his presence casting a shadow over the street.

A new voice rang out. Someone older. Collected.

"She's been acting strange for weeks."

I turned my head sharply.

Mr. Calloway.

He stood near the curb, feigning relaxation, arms loosely crossed, weight shifted slightly onto one foot. But there was something about the way he was looking at me, like he'd been holding something back.

A few heads turned. A murmur of agreement flickered through the crowd.

Newton barely reacted. Like he already knew what Calloway was going to say.

Unease crawled under my skin.

"Strange how?" Newton asked, voice neutral.

Calloway hesitated. Just for a second. But his eyes never left me.

"Restless. Unfocused. Wandering the halls when she doesn't need to be." A slight pause. "Showing up places she shouldn't."

I should've been defensive. I should've been angry.

But my tongue was lead.

Newton's gaze shot back to me.

"Did something happen to Julie?" I asked finally, my voice flat. Hollow.

Everyone simultaneously held their breath.

But Newton didn't nod. Didn't confirm it.

Didn't have to.

My throat tightened, like I had swallowed something jagged.

My hands clenched into fists at my sides, nails digging into my palms, attempting to distract myself. But all I could think about was my mom, then a girl my age whose smile would never be seen again.

I wasn't going to cry.

I wasn't.

But before I could stop it, a single tear slid down my cheek.

Newton's gaze flitted to it. Just for a second.

Then his expression smoothed into something unnervingly blank. Cold.

"Let's go, Whitaker."

6

— • —

OCTOBER 29, 2024, 12:30 PM - SOPHIA

4 DAYS AFTER JULIE WENT MISSING

The ride was silent, except for the occasional crackle of Newton's police radio.

I didn't ask where we were going. Once he headed toward Maple Road, I already knew.

He wasn't taking me to the station. He wasn't arresting me. He was getting me out of there.

What I didn't know was why.

Newton's grip on the wheel was tight. White knuckled. Like he was wrestling with something. His jaw ticked, a sharp, rhythmic clench that didn't stop. And he glanced at me in the rearview mirror pretty much every 10 seconds.

I shifted in my seat uncomfortably. Aware.

The back of a police car wasn't meant for passengers. It was meant for suspects.

I had never been in one before. The door didn't have a handle. The windows were thick, separating me from the front seat. The barrier between us was small but suffocating.

A dull pressure curled in my chest, growing with every passing second. Something was happening. Something big. And I was missing it.

Then the radio flared to life, shattering the silence between us.

"Confirmed. Behind Linworth's house—"

I tensed.

The words had barely registered before another voice cut in.

"Shallow burial. Covered in leaves—"

Newton swore under his breath and turned the volume down, fast.

I stared straight ahead, my pulse pounding in my ears.

Linworth. Burial.

That's where I woke up.

That's where I found Julie's jacket.

The world seemed to tilt.

Julie was buried there.

I had been *right* there.

My hands curled into fists in my lap.

What did that mean?

Did Linworth have something to do with it?

No.

No, that still didn't make sense.

Sure, there were rumors. People talked—said Julie spent too much time in his classroom, that it was weird. But it was just gossip. People loved to twist things, stretch them into stories.

That didn't mean he hurt her. That didn't mean...

But the police thought it meant something.

I huffed, forcing my voice to stay level.

"So, you're already picking a guy?"

Newton didn't answer.

His silence felt louder than anything he could have said.

I looked at him in the rearview mirror this time, studying creases forming between his eyes. He wasn't looking at me, but he knew I was looking at him.

"Do you actually have something?" I pressed, watching for the slightest shift in his expression. "Or is this just another small-town witch hunt?"

His brows furrowed even more, but still, he said nothing.

I let out a laugh of indignation. "That's what I thought."

As we pulled up to my house, I had barely reached for the door handle, then remembered it didn't exist, when Newton finally spoke.

"You should stay inside," he said.

I leaned forward, slowly. Trying to get as close to the glass barrier as possible.

"Excuse me?"

Newton shifted in his seat, rubbing a hand over his jaw before exhaling hard.

Eli was already on the porch, his posture rigid, waiting. I'm sure he heard the bells and saw the police lights flashing a few houses down.

Dad was still out of town, but that didn't matter much. Even when he was here, he wasn't.

Eli was the one who always waited up. The one who kept track of things. The one who acted like a parent, because someone had to.

Our dad had always been a ghost.

Not in the tragic, dead-before-his-time kind of way. Not even in the dramatic, up-and-left-for-someone-new kind of way. Just... absent.

But he never fully disappeared. That was the problem.

He was here just long enough to pay the bills, grab a meal from whatever takeout place he hadn't burned himself out on, and pretend to listen to something we said before his mind wandered somewhere else.

He was here just long enough for us to realize what we weren't getting.

He checked out years ago. After mom died.

Just stopped trying, burying himself in work under the guise of some kind of hero.

At first, it was extra shifts. Local emergencies. Then, disaster relief programs. When the big hurricanes hit the Gulf, he volunteered. When an earthquake leveled a city halfway across the world, he was on the first medical transport out.

And now?

Now, he was in Spain.

A freak meteorological phenomenon. La gota fría, the cold drop, had triggered catastrophic flooding in late October. The worst in decades. Hundreds of people were dead, entire towns submerged. Families were left stranded in the wreckage of their homes. And Dad? He was there, pulling bodies from the water, working trauma rotations, saving people who lost everything.

It was noble. It was important. At least that's what everyone else said...

It didn't change the fact that he had been gone for over a week, and I hadn't heard his voice once.

There had been a text, a short one: "Hope you and Eli are okay. I'll be back when I can."

That was it.

No call. Just another emergency bigger than us.

I didn't remember much from before. I was too young. But Eli did. He was only a year and a half older than me but at that age, 6, it made a difference.

I only knew what I overheard. The occasional slip when Eli got frustrated. It had wrecked him. After mom, Eli needed dad.

And instead of drowning, he used us to stay above water.

He probably told himself he was providing. That we were fine. Now he frequently talked about how we were old enough to figure things out when he was gone. So, he's gone even more.

Eli doesn't argue with him. Not after the last fight.

"Stop pretending like this house doesn't exist." Eli screamed.

"You don't need me here." Dad had said.

"You're right, we don't. But that doesn't mean you get to pretend we're not here."

Dad had just stared at him, eyes glassy in a way that wasn't quite anger. But it wasn't guilt, either.

It was resignation.

Like he already knew Eli was right.

Like he just didn't have it in him to be anything different.

But this was our day to day life with him now.

A week away. A weekend home. Another shift change. Another call to say he had to stay longer.

It was fine. It was routine.

It was bullshit.

Eli picked up the slack. He always had. He filled out school paperwork forging dad's signature, handled the call to the doctor when I got strep in the ninth grade. He was the one who kept the car running, who stocked the medicine cabinet, who made sure there was food in the fridge when Dad "forgot" we existed.

And me?

I let him.

Because the alternative was getting my hopes up.

And I had learned a long time ago that when it came to our dad, hope didn't get you anything but disappointment.

Newton turned off the ignition, then looked at me. For the first time, he met my eyes directly.

"We got a report."

A pause.

"An anonymous call."

A call?

"Said you were being watched."

My stomach dropped.

I had to ask, had to see if that creeping feeling that lingered was all in my head.

I kept my face still. "And you believe that someone is watching me?"

Newton didn't answer right away.

"I believe someone wants us to believe it."

That was almost worse.

I swallowed, my voice coming out in a rasp.

"So, what? You think someone is trying to scare me?"

Newton's grip on the wheel tightened. His voice lowered.

"I think you're in the middle of something you don't understand."

He started scanning the street like he expected someone to be there.

Then, without another word, he stepped out of the car.

I swallowed the irritation curling in my chest as I waited for him to open the back door, a not-so-subtle reminder that I had been a passenger, not a participant, in whatever this was.

Eli started walking down the porch steps, expression blank, but I knew him well enough to catch the signs of tension beneath the calm.

The slight shift of his weight, the way his fingers tapped against his arm like he was counting seconds in his head.

Newton barely spared me a glance as he shut the door behind me, turning to Eli instead.

"I said this to your sister, but it goes for you too," he said, voice edged with warning. "Stay inside."

Eli didn't blink. "I can take care of Sophia. I can take care of both of us."

The words landed solid. No hesitation. No room for argument.

Newton held his gaze for a second longer, then shook his head. Something between annoyance and reluctant approval.

"Whatever you think you're doing, Whitaker, you need to stop. Now." I wasn't sure which of us he was talking to. He took one last glance down the street, then got back in his car.

The second he pulled away, my phone buzzed.

Julie Greene.

I froze.

No. That wasn't possible.

Julie was dead.

My fingers were numb as I swiped open the message.

> Julie Greene: I'm still here.

My heart skipped a beat... or 12.

I stared at the text, barely blinking.

I looked up then back down and this text had not disappeared. It was right here. On my phone.

I had just heard it on the radio. They found her body. Julie was dead.

My hand trembled as I double checked the contact info.

Julie's actual number. The only reason I had it was to share Chemistry notes after she had randomly asked last year.

How?

Eli stepped closer, noticing the shift in my expression.

I swallowed, trying to keep my voice even. "It's not a big deal."

Eli let out a gruff laugh. "You really expect me to buy that?"

I didn't answer.

He stepped closer, voice dropping. "I don't know what's going on, but you need to be careful."

I finally looked at him, irritation flickering behind my exhaustion. "Careful of what?"

He tensed. "Of making yourself a spectacle."

That made me pause.

My fingers curled inside my jacket pocket.

He ran a hand over his face, looking more frustrated than before. "Look, I get it. You don't want to talk to me, fine. But you can't be reckless right now. Showing up in a cop car? Looking like—" He gestured vaguely at me, like that explained everything. "People notice that kind of thing."

Something hot slid through my body.

I crossed my arms, voice sharper than before. "I didn't exactly plan for this, Eli."

"That's not the point."

I looked up, trying to fight the instinct to roll my eyes.

He shook his head, sighing. "I know you don't care what people think, but this isn't the time to drag attention to yourself."

My pulse ticked up even more.

Because he was wrong. But he also wasn't.

Still, the way he said it, made me want to knock his head. Like I was the problem. Just for existing in the middle of this mess. Like I had anything to do with Julie, or any control over what people said.

I grumbled and stepped wide, a little dramatically, around him.

"Good talk."

His hand twitched at his side like he wanted to stop me, but he didn't.

"Whatever," he muttered. "I'm at Ohio State next year. You're on your own."

It hit like a punch. I really was going to be alone next year. And he knew it. I didn't look back as I walked down the hall.

***

I swiped my phone, glued to the message sent from Julie's number. Whoever had her phone wanted me to know it.

I flipped on the living room light. It was too bright. The silence rang in my ears.

I grabbed the remote and flipped through TV show options on Hulu before landing on Family Feud. I wasn't really watching, just letting the noise fill the space.

I stretched my legs, putting the remote down on the coffee table, then it hit me.

That feeling again.

A slow, creeping awareness at the back of my neck.

Like something had just moved behind me.

I turned my head too quickly, heart hammering.

Nothing.

The hallway was empty. The kitchen light still glowed softly from where I'd left it on.

I exhaled slowly, shaking my head. I was being stupid.

But the feeling didn't go away.

I needed a different distraction. I reached for a book on the table, *Lord of the Flies*, and flipped to a random page: *"Ralph wept for the end of innocence."*

I shut it, fast. My fingers pressed too hard into the cover.

My phone was next to me. I didn't need to check it. I already knew the message was there, that it was real, I had confirmed it multiple times by now.

I picked it up anyway.

Scrolled past the headlines. Past Julie's face. Past my call log, with the missed call from the night I now know she died.

The static from the TV buzzed in the background

I told myself I would stop obsessing, that I wouldn't check my phone again.

...I checked it again.

7

— · —

OCTOBER 29, 2024, 1 PM - NEWTON

4 DAYS AFTER JULIE WENT MISSING

I smelled the rain before I saw the body.

Wet earth, thick and unrelenting.

The woods out here had a bad habit of turning into a damn swamp after a storm. The kind of place where water pooled in the dips of the land, dragged loose dirt down with it, and made everything smell like a drowned animal.

Half the houses on Maple Road sat near the flood zone, and every time we had a storm like this, I could count on at least three complaints from angry residents convinced their garden gnomes had been stolen by delinquent teenagers.

Because sure, Mr. Thompson, your ceramic squirrel holding a nut is definitely a hot ticket item on the black market.

Nine times out of ten, I'd find their "stolen" yard junk half buried in mud or floating in the drainage ditch. Not that they'd listen.

If it wasn't missing lawn décor, it was a flooded basement, a backed-up sewer line, a tree branch through a windshield. This town's infrastructure was one bad storm away from falling apart on a good day.

And today? It had given up completely.

The whole morning had been downpour after downpour, hammering the streets, drowning the gutters, turning every low lying patch of land into a waterlogged mess.

Then the flood did something worse. It uncovered a body.

I'd been living off gas station coffee and four hours of sleep for five days now.

Not the good kind of gas station coffee.

The kind that sat too long on the burner, turning into something that resembled sludge, thick, bitter, and burnt. But I drank it anyway because caffeine was the only thing keeping me from crashing into a ditch.

The kind of beverage that only existed at three in the morning, when I was still wearing the same clothes from the day before, because I didn't have time to go home.

My life had turned into one thing: finding Julie Greene.

They say the first 48 hours in a missing persons case are the most important.

After that?

The odds start working against you.

I knew that.

I'd heard it from frantic parents more times than I could count, desperate to get me looking for their kids when they'd only been gone a couple of hours.

But Julie's parents were different, not frantic, just certain. Certain that something had happened.

Julie's mom had locked eyes with me, her gaze burning into my soul as she simply said, "She was taken. Find her." Even then, I had the sick feeling she was right.

So, no. None of those other cases had been like this.

No case had been like this at all.

None of those cases had felt like a hole opening up beneath my feet.

By the time we passed the two day mark, the search had already shifted.

People were still using the right words: Let's bring Julie home. We'll find her soon.

But their faces? Their eyes?

They weren't searching for a missing girl. They were expecting to find a body.

I spent the daylight hours leading search parties, coordinating with the fire department, standing in front of cameras and microphones, giving updates that didn't mean anything.

"We are following all leads."

"We are working with local and state resources."

"We encourage anyone with information to come forward."

The same empty phrases, the same tight-jawed looks from local reporters who were already writing their *What Went Wrong?* pieces in their heads.

I knew what they wanted.

They wanted me to slip.

They wanted a misstep, a mistake, a soundbite to prove I wasn't doing my job.

What they didn't know, what they didn't give a shit about, was that I hadn't been home in five days.

I'd been sleeping in my office chair, eating out of a vending machine, wringing every last drop of manpower out of a department that only had five officers total. And I would keep doing it, until I found out what happened to her.

But we weren't built for this.

We had no homicide division. No specialists. No forensic analysts sitting in a lab.

When we needed a crime scene analyzed, we called Cleveland.

When we needed help, we got put in a queue behind every major crime in the region.

So, when Julie went missing, we prayed we could handle it on our own.

The nights were the worst part.

During the day, I could pretend we were making progress.

At night?

I drove the same streets over and over, checking the same alleys, parking lots, underpasses while dutifully drinking my caffeinated sludge.

I went back to the places she had been last seen.

I stood in front of Julie's house at midnight, watching the light in her bedroom window, the one her parents refused to turn off.

I sat in my car, staring at old case files, fingering the edges of the same missing persons reports from nearby cities... waiting for something, anything, to make sense.

By day three, I had the search party system locked in.

Ten people at a time. Every five hours, combing the area.

The town was divided into grids, and we covered every inch of it.

The park. The benches, the pavilions, the overgrown stretch near the duck pond.

The empty lots behind the strip mall.

The train tracks on the east side, where kids smoke after school.

The cabin at the edge of the reservoir.

The school.

The town square with its 15 total buildings.

The woods. Dense, thick, stretching miles past the reservoir.

Every search ended the same way.

Another grid marked off the map, another shift of people heading home, another dead-end report filed away.

No sign of her.

Until now.

I was halfway to the crime scene when my personal phone rang.

I shouldn't have answered.

Not with my hands still damp from the rain, my brain still tangled in what I was about to walk into.

But I did.

"Newton," I barked.

A pause.

Then, slow. Drawn out. The voice warped, stretched, mechanical.

"Sophia looks so..."

A low exhale, something slithering between syllables.

"Delicious."

My grip tightened on the wheel.

"I hope she enjoys her coffee."

The words landed too clean. Too precise.

They knew.

Where she was. What she was doing.

"She's next."

Click.

The line went dead.

Julie was already gone.

Sophia wasn't.

Whoever this was, they wanted me to know they were watching.

Watching her. I just didn't know why.

I checked the call trace. Burner phone. Pinging off a tower in the town square. Near Grounded café.

I clenched my jaw.

No way in hell was I about to let another teenage girl vanish under my watch.

I immediately called Jenkins. Didn't tell him about the call. Not yet. I needed him focused.

"Lock it down," I said, gripping the wheel.

Jenkins didn't ask why. Didn't need to. That's why I trusted him.

Most of the guys on my team? They were good cops. But they'd never handled anything like this. Not really.

Jenkins was different. Six years at Cleveland PD before he got sick of the city and came back here. Worked homicides, real cases.

If I was going to leave the biggest crime scene this town had ever had in someone else's hands, it was going to be him.

"You got it," he said, his voice clipped. Already moving. Already taking charge.

"Keep everyone out," I added. "I don't care who the hell shows up."

"Not my first day, Newton," he muttered.

I almost smirked. Almost.

By the time I had Sophia locked down at home with Eli, I was thirty minutes behind schedule.

The rain had slowed to a drizzle, but the ground was still swollen with it. Mud slicked across the back roads. Water pooled in the dips of the shoulder.

My windshield wipers dragged sluggishly across the glass.

My mind ran the details.

Julie had been missing for five days.

No sign of forced entry at her house. No ransom, no demand.

The first big rain hit this morning.

Now, suddenly, she turns up.

I cut the wheel, following the flashing blue and red glow bouncing off the trees.

Jenkins was waiting for me at the tape. His face was drawn tight. Still built like the damn running back he used to be—best in town back in the day. Mocha skin, broad shoulders, and the only wrinkles on his face were the kind that came from smirking at idiots.

"You're late," he said.

"You're chatty," I muttered, ducking under the tape.

He fell in step beside me, matching my pace as we moved into the woods.

"Tell me," I said.

Jenkins exhaled through his nose. "High school kid found her. Him and his brother. They were checking a washout near the creek, saw a hand sticking out of the mud."

"You'll wanna see for yourself," Jenkins added.

I moved forward. Felt the shift in the air.

The rain had done a lot of the work.

She was surfacing.

Face down.

Her left hand exposed, fingers curled inward, like she'd tried to grab onto something.

The dirt was dark, slick, disturbed. But not just from the rain.

Someone had already been here. Too many someone's.

Boot prints in different sizes crisscrossed over each other, leading right up to the grave. Deep heel marks, scattered impressions, the kind of careless foot traffic that made forensic evidence worthless.

I squeezed my eyes shut. "Tell me we didn't lose everything."

Jenkins rubbed a hand over his jaw. "Search party panicked. Some of 'em started digging before we got here. Just a little." His voice dropped. "Enough to be a problem."

Fantastic.

My eyes dragged back to her.

The rain had eaten away at the shallow topsoil, pulling loose just enough dirt to show her hand, part of her forearm, the edge of her shoulder. I could see outlines near her arm, where it was clear the search party was digging with their bare hands.

But the rest of her?

Still buried.

Still waiting.

Forensics was going to have a field day with this shit show of a crime scene.

Or, more like, they were going to take one look, swear under their breath, and tell me to go to hell.

I dragged a hand down my face.

And just like that, Julie Greene slipped further away from us.

8

OCTOBER 29, 2024, 2 PM - NEWTON

4 DAYS AFTER JULIE WENT MISSING

Forensics showed up from Cleveland. An hour late.

The rain had stopped. The stink hadn't.

My stomach curled in on itself, tight and hollow, like an empty pit.

It wasn't blood.

It wasn't just mud.

It was the smell of rot.

It clung to the air, seeped into my clothes, crawled into the back of my throat and stayed there.

I forced myself to breathe through my mouth. It was better than smelling it.

Jenkins wasn't reacting.

He stood off to the side, face blank, watching the forensics team work. He'd been quiet.

I realized then, he'd smelled this before.

Julie was found fifty feet in from the tree line behind Linworth's house.

Not deep enough to be hidden.

Not far enough to be strategic.

If someone had really wanted to get rid of her, they would have buried her deeper. Would've dragged her further in.

This was rushed.

Hasty.

The hole was barely deep enough to keep her from being spotted outright.

They hadn't counted on the flood zone.

Hadn't realized the storm was coming.

Hadn't thought about what happens when you bury a body too close to the water table.

Now, she was rising back up.

Pulled loose by the rain, the runoff, the shifting earth.

It almost felt like she had dug her way back out.

Forensics worked fast and efficient. Like this was just another job, another body, another crime scene they'd have wrapped up by dinner.

The first thing they did was set up floodlights, bright against the dark, soaking earth. The overcast sky wasn't giving us much, and the lights cast long, sharp shadows across the uneven ground, making everything feel even more unnatural.

Then, they widened the perimeter, stretching the crime scene tape back further, pushing the onlookers—search party members, deputies, even Jenkins—a few steps away. Too many footprints. Too much disturbance. The search team had done exactly what I told them not to do. Walked straight through a crime scene before it was a crime scene. We'd be lucky if anything useful was left.

A forensic tech, Stensin, crouched low, camera in hand, snapping photos from every angle. He moved clockwise, deliberate, capturing the way her fingers curled inward, the deep grooves in the mud where the rain had started to reclaim her. He didn't hesitate. Didn't react.

Neither did Martinez, who moved behind him, measuring, muttering numbers low under his breath. Depth of burial. Proximity to the tree line. The angles of the imprints. Stensin marked them down in a small notebook, a record of the grave that shouldn't have been here.

Another tech knelt near the disturbed soil, scraping thin layers of mud into evidence bags. He labeled each one carefully, tracking trace elements, decomp seepage, anything that might tell them more than her body already could.

I watched them work, the steady click of the camera, the scribble of pen against paper, the rustling of plastic evidence bags as they picked apart the worst thing this town had ever seen.

And I realized, with a quiet, sinking feeling, that they weren't waiting for me to catch up.

This was routine for them.

I watched them move, unnerved.

I'd worked cases before. Plenty.

But not this.

Not murder.

We didn't just have a murder on our hands. We had our first murder.

And now I was supposed to know what the hell to do next.

When Martinez started clearing the dirt away, the ground gave too easily.

The mud peeled back in thick, wet clumps, coming off her like she'd been cocooned in it.

I held my breath.

Her hair emerged first.

Dark. Matted with filth. Tangled against her cheek.

Then her shoulder, her back, her legs...

One unmoving, sunken shape.

Her skin had gone pale.

The moisture had bloated her slightly, softening the angles of her face.

But it was still Julie.

Even after five days in the ground, she still looked like herself.

And that made my gut wrench.

As Stensin moved in to check her arms, something caught the light.

A thin silver chain.

My curiosity piqued.

I crouched before I even thought about it, pen in hand, using the edge to nudge it open.

Inside was a tiny, grainy photo.

Julie.

And Linworth.

I snapped the locket shut.

Jenkins saw it too.

"That's... well," he muttered.

I didn't answer.

Didn't say what I was thinking.

That it was too convenient.

That Linworth had already been questioned. That he had been vague, hesitant, defensive.

That this... a dead girl. Half buried behind his house, wearing his picture around her wrist. It felt like a damn setup.

And the worst part?

It was working.

Because what the hell else was I supposed to think?

I turned my head slowly, gaze drifting past the trees.

Past the taped off scene.

To the house just beyond it.

And there, standing on the back patio, barely visible through the branches...

Linworth.

Looking guilty as hell.

9

OCTOBER 29, 2024, 3 PM - NEWTON

4 DAYS AFTER JULIE WENT MISSING

"Get him."

Jenkins moved without hesitation.

Linworth didn't run.

Didn't shout. Didn't even blink.

He just stood there, like he'd been expecting this.

I held up the locket between two fingers as we crossed his yard.

He knew.

I let Jenkins take the lead.

"We need to talk," he said.

Linworth exhaled slowly. "Am I under arrest?"

"Not yet."

Linworth's eyes flickered to the locket dangling in my hand.

"Come willingly, or we get a warrant."

His throat bobbed.

I could almost hear the wheels turning in his head, weighing his options.

Finally, he sighed, rubbing a hand down his face.

"Fine."

Jenkins drove. I watched Linworth in the rearview mirror. I wasn't planning to take my eyes off him. Not for a second.

His hands were still, folded neatly in his lap.

But his leg wouldn't stop bouncing.

I leaned my elbow against the door and glanced back at him.

"You look like you wanna say something," I said calmly.

He didn't answer.

Not a single question about why we brought him in. Not a single demand for an explanation.

That just made me more suspicious.

When we got to the interrogation room Linworth sat stiffly, his hands loosely grasping the table, his face resigned.

I pulled out the evidence bag and dropped it onto the table.

The locket clinked against the metal.

"Explain."

His Adam's apple jerked. Breath stalled mid-throat.

"Julie was found today."

No reaction.

"Behind your house."

His fingers twitched.

I pulled the chair out and sat across from him.

"How close were you?"

His voice was tight when he finally answered. "She was my student."

"That all?"

A sharp inhale. Barely controlled.

"Because it sure as hell looks like she was close to you. Close enough to carry your picture around her wrist. Close enough to end up buried in your backyard."

Linworth flinched. A fraction of a movement.

His jaw clenched, and for the first time, he looked pissed.

"What does the locket have to do with me?"

His voice was low. It sounded like he was genuinely asking.

I tilted my head. "You didn't know she had it?"

"I've never seen it before today."

I ripped the heart shaped clasp open revealing the photo inside. "That's your picture. With Julie."

He swallowed hard. His knee bounced again.

"I. Never. Took. That. Picture."

That caught me off guard.

"Say that again?"

His eyes flicked up to mine. Steady.

"I never took that picture. That's not me."

"Linworth, don't be an idiot. That's your face."

"It's my face, but it's not my picture." His voice was calmer now. More controlled.

A cold sliver of doubt cut through me.

He wasn't breaking down or dodging.

I pressed in.

"You're telling me this isn't you?"

His jaw flexed. "I'm telling you I never took that picture."

I stared at him. He stared back.

I didn't believe him.

But I didn't not believe him, either.

"Then how do you explain it?"

His throat bobbed.

For a second, he almost answered. I saw the words forming behind his teeth.

"The Cir,"

Then, he paused.

"Lawyer."

A breath hissed out of my nose.

There it was.

"Say that again?"

His voice was stronger this time. "I want a lawyer."

The tension in the room snapped tight.

I let out a slow breath. "Alright."

Then I stood up.

Put the locket back in the evidence bag.

Walked out.

Jenkins was already shaking his head.

"Forensics just came back." He shoved a file into my hands.

I flipped it open.

No foreign DNA. Possible sedative in her system. No clear defensive wounds or overt signs of a struggle. Small linear skull fracture with mild hemorrhaging, consistent with a fall. But not definitive.

"We don't have crap tying anything to him."

Through the two way mirror, I watched Linworth stare at the table.

He was thinking.

Jenkins sighed. "We gotta let him go."

I knew that.

Didn't mean I had to like it.

"Tell him he's free to leave," I muttered.

Jenkins smirked. "Think this was enough to rattle him?"

I watched Linworth roll his shoulders, try to act normal.

"It better be."

Fifteen minutes later, Linworth stepped out of the station.

Didn't say a word.

I leaned against the front desk and watched him disappear into the dusk.

Jenkins clapped me on the back. "If it's him, we'll get him."

I didn't say anything.

Because I wasn't fully convinced he was the one to get.

10

— ⋄ —

OCTOBER 30, 2024, 9 AM - SOPHIA

5 DAYS AFTER JULIE WENT MISSING

The story had already changed by the tenth time I heard it.

Kenny and Billy weren't just searching the woods. They were deep in the flood zone, chest-high in water, pushing through reeds when they saw it.

Or no, wait. Actually, they were climbing a tree to get a better view when Billy slipped, grabbed onto a branch to stop his fall, and saw something pale in the mud beneath him.

No, no, actually, they had been running from a wild dog, something with glowing eyes and matted fur, and Kenny tripped, fell hard, and landed next to Julie's hand.

That one had been my favorite. If you could call any version a favorite.

People retold the story like it was a grand fictional tale, but everyone knew.

What actually happened was real, and probably a lot more boring.

Kenny and Billy had been part of the search rotation, combing through the woods near Maple Road, more likely for the excuse to skip algebra than any real sense of duty.

All I know for sure is that they dug some of the body up with their bare hands, called the police, then they ran. Bolted straight out of the woods.

Not to the police station.

Not home.

But down the main strip, breathless, pale, and talking over each other.

People saw them. People always saw everything.

Mrs. Harrow at the florist shop caught bits and pieces.

"Julie—the woods—hand"

Mr. Thompson was restocking shelves at the hardware store, letting the fresh air fill his shop with the door propped open when he overheard the tail end of it as they sped past, pale as ghosts.

I only know this because he abandoned his work, crossed the street, and went straight into Grounded without breaking stride.

He didn't even order anything.

Just stood near the counter and said it outright, voice steady, clipped.

"They found Julie Greene buried in the woods."

Abbie was sitting maybe four feet away.

Texted me immediately.

By the time Mrs. Evers showed up, half the town already knew.

And that meant it was her time to act.

Mrs. Evers had been waiting for this moment.

Not in a morbid way.

Not like she wanted it.

But she was the kind of person who always knew what to do when something terrible happened.

She was like mid-thirties, super sweet, always on top of everything — birthdays, anniversaries, even food allergies at the town picnic.

Since she had babysat Julie when she was younger, she had known the Greenes for years, grown close to them.

She walked into the café, got the details in under thirty seconds, and then?

She got to work.

Within an hour, a meal train was set up for Julie's family.

By noon the next day, the vigil was planned.

By three the next day, volunteers had set up a table in front of the gazebo at the center of town square, stacking rows of white candles in glass holders.

Someone made a poster with Julie's face on it, way too big. All pixelated around the edges.

New flyers went up around the already existing "Missing Julie" ones to spread the word: **"OCTOBER 30TH, 8 PM. VIGIL IN TOWN SQUARE: IN MEMORY OF JULIE."**

Even if the whole thing felt wrong, even if the idea of standing in a circle with a bunch of people who barely knew Julie made my stomach turn, I told myself I'd go later.

Because some people were genuinely grieving.

But I wasn't one of them, not really.

I was sad, but I didn't know her.

Not well.

Not in the way that should've made my chest feel tight every time someone said her name. But for some reason, it did. Not a sharp, immediate pain. More like a slow, creeping weight pressing against my chest. Like something pulling at me, asking me to pay attention.

But grief was complicated.

You didn't have to know someone well to feel the shape of their absence.

I know what real loss feels like.

I remembered the way people acted at my mother's funeral—the hushed voices, the sad, knowing looks.

The ones who barely knew her but showed up anyway, saying things like, "she was such a light," like they'd been her best friend.

I remembered sitting in the front row, gripping the edge of my seat so hard my knuckles turned white.

So, I knew the difference.

Between people who actually grieved, and people who just wanted something to do.

I could already hear it.

The way the gossip would start, laced between the well meaning words.

I wanted to go. Because I felt like I should.

Because I wasn't sure what it meant if I didn't.

But I hadn't slept well.

Not that I had been sleeping well before, but last night was worse.

I kept waking up, my body jolting like I'd been mid-fall, feeling my pulse through my neck, in my ears. Looking at the clock every 30 minutes as my body tossed from left to right on repeat.

By the time six PM rolled around, my eyes burned, and my limbs felt like they were filled with wet sand.

I told myself I'd just lay down for a bit.

Not in bed, just on the couch, just for an hour. Enough to feel like a person before I had to go stand under streetlights and pretend to belong there.

I could still hear the TV in the background.

The laugh track from a re-run of *How I Met Your Mother*.

I let it lull me.

Just a little while.

Just a quick nap.

I drifted off.

The cold crept in slow, unnoticed, until it was already in my bones.

I blinked, slow. The world felt slanted, like I was laying on uneven ground.

Then I realized.

I wasn't laying.

I was kneeling, my legs folded beneath me, stiff and half numb from the cold.

Candles flickered in a loose circle around me. Some had already melted down to wax puddles, others were still burning. Their tiny flames swaying with the wind.

Pictures. Flowers. Handwritten notes. A vigil.

Julie's vigil.

And I was in the middle of it.

My breath caught in my throat. I didn't remember coming here. Hadn't I fallen asleep on the couch?

I squeezed my eyes shut, my fingers pressing against my temple like I could force the memories back into place. Nothing.

I wasn't home. I wasn't on the couch.

I was here.

My pulse raced through me.

I scrambled to my feet, legs shaking, but the ground still felt wrong beneath me.

I sucked in a breath, and for the first time, I smelled it. Melted wax, a burnt wick.

I looked down at my hands.

Wax was hardened in small, uneven streaks across my fingertips. Under my nails. Like I'd been holding one of the candles. Like I had lit it myself.

The realization hit me in pieces, too jagged to fit together.

I wasn't just here.

I had been here.

Long enough for the wax to cool on my hands.

Blood drained from my feet.

Then I caught movement.

A few people were walking by me glaring. But as my eyes adjusted to the night, I couldn't quite make out who they were.

Something passed behind me, cutting off the candlelight. Someone murmured my name. I turned too fast, but the figure had already moved on.

I spun, heartbeat slamming into my throat.

A hand clutched my shoulder.

I choked on a scream.

"Jesus, Sophia."

Jay's voice was low and careful.

I yanked back, but he didn't let go immediately. His grip wasn't tight, wasn't painful, but it lingered, just a second too long. Like he wasn't ready to let go.

His fingers finally slipped away, but the air between us stayed tense.

I shifted, shoving my shaking hands into my jacket. Actually... I was wearing Eli's jacket. Was it his? When did I—

No. Focus.

Jay was watching me. Not just looking. Studying. Like he was trying to solve something. Or like he already knew.

His mouth opened then closed.

He tried again. "How long?" He shook his head. "How long have you been here?"

I swallowed. My tongue felt thick in my mouth. "I don't know."

His jaw tightened, gaze shifting to my hands.

I caught myself rubbing them together. Rubbing at the wax. Rubbing until it was one with my skin.

"Stop doing that," he said.

His tone was too sharp, then immediately softened. Like he hadn't meant to snap.

I pressed my hands against my sides.

Jay let out a slow, controlled breath. His shoulders were tight, but his face was a mask of calm. Almost as if he was trying to contain something.

He crouched, swiping his fingers across the dirt. When he stood again, he was holding something.

A photo.

He flipped it over.

It was Julie.

She was smiling wide and frozen in time, but her face was distorted.

Jay's fingers curled around the edges of the picture. Like he didn't want to hold it, but didn't want to let it go, either.

He took a deep breath. Then, finally, he spoke.

"Sophia... this isn't just sleepwalking." He paused. "This is something else."

His voice was calm. But his hands were still shaking.

A strange contradiction. I watched his face, he was trying to look worried, maybe even scared for me, but something didn't quite match.

I pressed my lips together, but the words were already there, tangled in my throat.

"What was I..."

I couldn't finish it.

Jay ran a hand through his hair, pulling at the ends just slightly. He was thinking.

And so was I, trying to rationalize, to make the pieces fit. He was probably just worried. But I was so tired, everything felt strange, like I couldn't quite trust what I was seeing.

His movements were measured as he scanned the square, aware we weren't the only people here.

He looked at me again.

"We need to go." He stretched his arm toward me, hand open. An invitation, not a demand.

But I didn't move.

He didn't push. He just waited.

A gust of wind cut through the clearing, smothering the candlelight beside my feet.

Jay stepped closer, his hand inches from mine now.

I took it.

11

— ◦ —

OCTOBER 31, 2024, 7:30 AM - SOPHIA

6 DAYS AFTER JULIE WENT MISSING

By morning, I had convinced myself last night didn't matter. I wasn't unraveling. I wasn't losing time. I was fine.

Today was going to be normal.

Jay had been there last night.

Other people had passed by, had probably watched me from a distance, but he was the one who didn't walk away.

He was the one who held my hand, who looked me straight in the eye and told me this wasn't just sleepwalking.

The way he said it stuck with me.

Not the words. Just...

I didn't want to go there.

I needed him to believe it was just sleepwalking.

Because if he didn't. If he started watching me too closely, thinking I needed help—

I wasn't sure I could handle it.

I forced myself to focus on something else, twisting the flat iron through a section of my hair, watching as the frizz pressed into submission, turning sleek and dark. One thing under control.

I reached blindly for my baby blue clip.

Nothing.

A frown furled the corner of my lips. I checked the counter. The drawer. The floor.

It had to be somewhere.

I grabbed a different clip instead, ignoring the weird feeling in my head.

Not today. No overthinking.

Today was about answers.

So, I turned to Google and started typing.

Can sleepwalking be triggered by stress?

Can you leave your house while sleepwalking?

Can sleepwalkers light candles?

The last one made me pause.

I wasn't sure why I was asking. It wasn't like I expected an article to confirm I had wandered into Julie's vigil and lit a candle myself.

But I needed something.

And Google delivered.

"Most sleepwalkers stay inside."

"Some can perform complex actions, but it's rare."

So, I guess I wasn't *most* then.

I had left the house.

I had woken up with wax on my fingers.

I clenched my hands in my lap, shifting my focus back to my phone.

Then I found something interesting.

One small study said sleepwalkers can have fragmented memories—hallucinations of past events that feel as real as waking life. Some even return to places they've been before while in that state.

I swallowed hard.

Julie's vigil. The candles. The wax on my hands.

Why would I have gone there?

I was about to close the tab when my phone vibrated. 1 New Message.

> **Julie Greene: L. kept the drafts. He kept everything in the basement. You have to see.**

A cold pulse shot through my chest.

L?

Linworth?

My brain went into overdrive. Linworth ran the newspaper club. Julie had been involved. The drafts. Was that what she meant?

My fingers hovered over the screen, pulse hammering.

Don't disappear.

I exhaled shakily and screenshotted it.

It flickered. A single, jarring blink.

Gone.

Frantic, I scrolled through my texts and deleted messages. Nothing.

I had proof. And then I didn't.

But, I had the screenshot.

I swiped to my recent photos.

It was there.

Relief slashed through me, sharp and fleeting.

I flipped back to my messages.

The text was truly gone.

But the one from yesterday still sat there.

Julie Greene: I'm still here.

I swallowed hard.

Had I imagined the others?

Or worse… what if I hadn't?

My skin prickled. Exhaustion curled into something darker.

I needed to get to school.

My phone buzzed again. I braced myself.

I barely registered the exhale I let out when I saw the name.

Eli.

Eli: Newton's here. He wants to talk to you.

I felt an invisible fist curling tight around my core.

12

—·—

OCTOBER 31, 2024, 8 AM - SOPHIA

6 DAYS AFTER JULIE WENT MISSING

Newton was waiting at the bottom of the stairs.

Eli stood in the entryway, arms folded so tightly it looked like he might snap. He was ready for war.

Newton turned the second he put eyes on me. "We need to talk."

Eli's jaw clenched as our gazes met, his shoulders going even more rigid. He gave a small, stiff shake of his head.

I stepped past him into the living room. Newton followed.

"Sit."

I didn't. "Just tell me what this is about."

"Julie's phone."

My pulse spiked. I kept my expression blank.

"What about it?"

"We found her phone, pulled her call logs," he said, watching me closely. "Last outgoing call was at 1:47 AM the night she disappeared."

My body screamed at me to not react. To stay still, breathe normally, act like I didn't already know.

"And?"

Newton's gaze didn't waver. "It was to you."

I felt Eli go stiff behind me. The room shrunk, walls pressing in.

I had known this was coming. I'd already seen the missed call on my phone. I'd even asked myself why she'd called me. Of all people.

But hearing it from Newton.

That made it real.

I swallowed hard, gripping my arms. Forced my voice to stay neutral. "I don't remember getting a call."

"You don't remember? Or you didn't answer?"

Newton's brows lowered, like he was ready to pick apart my response in real time.

I hesitated. The wrong answer would only make this worse.

"I saw the missed call the next day. I didn't answer, I don't know why she called me."

It wasn't a lie. But it didn't feel like the truth either.

Newton exhaled sharply. He ran a hand over his jaw, frustration bleeding into his expression.

"This isn't a game, Whitaker."

I stiffened.

"You have no idea what's happening behind the scenes. The evidence we're pulling, the people we're looking at." His eyes flickered, just for a second. "You have no idea how easy it is to get caught in something you don't understand. Unless you have something you're not telling me..."

My pulse jumped.

Why wasn't he asking about the texts?

He had Julie's phone. He had her call logs. He had to have checked.

Did he already know?

Or was he baiting me, seeing if I'd offer something he hadn't mentioned first?

Newton was a cop. If he wasn't bringing them up, it was for a reason.

And I couldn't afford to be the one to say it first.

"I'm not hiding anything."

Newton pressed his lips into a line. He clearly didn't believe me.

He reached into his jacket and pulled out a phone.

My eyes widened instinctively.

Julie's.

I could feel every drop of blood pumping through my veins as I braced myself for what came next.

The text messages from Julie. This was it.

He dangled it in the air between us. "If she was reaching out to you that night, I need to know why."

I forced myself to meet his eyes. "I can't tell you something I don't know."

Newton held my gaze for another second, searching for cracks.

Then Eli exploded.

"If she's saying she doesn't know, she doesn't freaking know!"

Newton barely reacted, but I flinched, whipping around to face Eli.

His face was flushed, his eyes blazing, his hands shaking from where he clenched them into fists at his sides.

"Jesus Christ," Eli seethed. "You're standing here grilling her like she's some kind of suspect, but weren't you the one who said you got a call about someone watching her? What the hell happened to that? Or is it easier to harass her than to go after the actual psycho stalking her?"

Newton finally tipped his head. "You done?"

Eli's chest rose and fell hard, fists trembling, like there was so much more he wanted to say, but if he did, he'd combust on the spot.

He didn't say another word.

Newton watched him for one more breath, then looked back at me, tucking the phone back into the plastic bag.

"Stay out of trouble, Whitaker." He didn't say it like a warning. More like an inevitability. "And don't keep anything else from me, it will only make it worse for you."

I watched him leave, my whole body buzzing.

Newton was getting closer.

I wasn't sure what scared me more, that he was asking the right questions... or that I still didn't have any answers.

I leaned against the door, my breath coming too fast. The plastic wrapped ghost of Julie's phone burned in my memory. She had tried to reach me. And I had no idea why.

I fidgeted with the hem of my sleeve.

I felt like I was standing on the edge of something massive, something deep and dark, and if I took one step in the wrong direction, I'd fall straight through the cracks.

I was spiraling, and I knew it.

But how was I supposed to stop when I was sleepwalking into her vigil, and still getting texts from her number, when she was confirmed dead?

I pushed off the door and ran a hand through my hair, fingers trembling as they brushed my scalp. I was already late for school, I needed to pull myself together.

But the second I turned, I saw Eli.

"You need help."

I blinked. "Excuse me?"

He turned, expression tight, like he had been holding this in for a while. "You don't think I notice? You haven't been sleeping. You look like you're about to pass out half the time, and now Newton's sniffing around because Julie called you the night she disappeared... and I heard where you 'woke up' last night."

"I'm trying to get it under control. It's not that bad"

"Get it under control?" Eli snapped. "Newton just walked in here with a freaking evidence bag, and all you did was stand there like you were waiting for something worse to happen."

I swallowed. "That's not fair."

"You want to talk about fair? What happens if Newton starts digging? If you sleepwalk into who knows what... or where? If they find something that makes them think—" he cut himself off, rubbing a hand over his jaw. "We can't keep doing this."

Something in my chest squeezed. "Eli."

"You're going to therapy."

I stared at him. "What?"

"You heard me," he said. "I already looked into it. There's someone close to town, only 25 minutes away. They do sleep disorder stuff. Whatever the hell this is."

I crossed my arms. "You don't get to make that decision for me."

A muscle jumped in his cheek. "Yeah? Well, too bad. Because I already booked the first session. I can't carry the weight of everything for you. I've got my own life. My own problems."

"I'm handling it."

"No. You're ignoring it."

I opened my mouth, but he cut me off.

"You want Newton off your back? You want me to stop acting like I'm waiting for you to disappear next?" He took a step closer. "Then go. One session. Just one. Give me a reason to believe this isn't getting worse."

I didn't continue to argue.

He had made his point, but that didn't mean I was happy about it.

***

The day passed in a blur. I barely made it to the kitchen for dinner, pushing chicken and broccoli around my plate. Barely spoke to Eli. The weight in my chest was getting heavier.

I couldn't just sit here.

59

I stepped onto the porch, the cold air biting my skin as I wrapped my arms around myself, staring down the street.

Newton had practically said it himself. Evidence was stacking up.

Julie had been buried.

She had called me that night.

Someone had texted me from her phone after she was found.

And then Newton had shown up at my house, holding her phone in an evidence bag.

It was all coming together. Just not in the way I needed it to.

I let out a slow breath, watching the frosted air release into the dusk.

There was only one name left in front of me.

Linworth. He had to be "L" from the text.

I looked down the street, past the Halloween decorations scattered through front lawns. A few houses away. That's all.

I started walking.

1 house, 2 houses, 3, 4, 5... 6.

I stopped.

Linworth's house was dark.

I didn't fully decide to break in.

Not at first.

But I knew where the spare key was.

Back when I used to spend time in the backyard, *on purpose*, I saw him use it a few times. Always under the second planter from the left, the one half swallowed by ivy.

That was before the sleepwalking started a few weeks ago. Before I started showing up out there without knowing it.

I never really thought about it before, just one of those things you notice without meaning to. Like how he always had a beer with him around six. Or how he listened to rock music when he was grading papers on his patio.

I wasn't thinking about consequences.

I wasn't thinking about Newton, or the call logs, or Eli forcing me into therapy.

I hesitated, pulse pounding.

I hated that the whispers were getting to me, the ones about Linworth. The ones that sounded too much like the ones about me. I knew how easily rumors twisted, how quickly a town could turn suspicion into fact just because it was easy.

But the texts... the fact that Julie's body was found right here. Where I woke up the night after she died. And now Newton was showing up at my house, already convinced I was tangled up in this somehow.

I had to know.

I crouched, pushing the dying pot of Ivy, fingers closing around the key.

It was cold against my palm.

Slowly, I unlocked the door.

13

OCTOBER 31, 2024, 7:30 PM - SOPHIA

6 DAYS AFTER JULIE WENT MISSING

Linworth didn't live here, not really. The house was too clean. The bookshelves were perfectly spaced, the couch cushions barely used. No throw blankets. No pictures. No personal mess.

I moved forward. The air didn't shift.

Like no one ever breathed in this house. Like there wasn't actually air in here at all.

When I stepped into the kitchen, my pulse skipped.

The basement door was ajar.

The same basement from the texts.

I swallowed hard, pushing the door open the rest of the way. A faint blue glow pulsed from below, casting long shadows against the stairwell. It was strange. Wrong, even. The kind of thing that drew you in.

As if someone wanted you to look at it.

The stairs groaned beneath my weight as I stepped down, my breath shallow, my heartbeat loud in my ears.

As my eyes oriented to the barely lit room, I found the source of the blue glow. A large black floor lamp acted like a spotlight for a desk and a single worn chair.

To the left, a packed bookshelf loomed, books stacked in precarious towers around it. So many books.

I stepped closer, my gaze drifting to the desk. Papers were scattered beneath it, haphazard and forgotten, like they had been dropped in a hurry.

I crouched, reaching for the papers. Old notes, quizzes, essays, things students had written.

I flipped through them quickly, barely paying attention.

Then I stiffened.

Julie's name.

Inscribed on the outside of a leatherbound notebook.

Not just a school notebook.

This looked like a diary.

It was worn, the edges bent, the spine creased like someone had flipped through it a hundred times. My fingers shook as I turned the pages, most of them ripped out. I skipped a few pages in.

August 10th:

I keep telling myself it's nothing. That I'm just imagining things. But sometimes, I think he watches me too closely.

"He" who? Linworth?

A loose slip of paper was tucked into the diary. It looked blank.

I skipped past it and flipped faster.

The handwriting changed, rushed and messy. Like she had written it fast, almost scribbled.

Before I had time to read it, I heard a loud thud.

I jerked back.

Someone was here.

I shoved the diary into my hoodie pocket, snapping the cover shut.

Another sound. Footsteps.

The stairs creaked.

Oh god, someone was coming down the stairs.

My pulse slammed into my throat.

I ducked, fast. Into the closet near the bookshelf, pulling the door shut just as a shadow passed over the basement floor.

The footsteps stopped.

Right at the bottom of the stairs.

I squeezed my eyes shut.

Seconds stretched.

Something dragged on the floor.

I could see the outline of a body moving closer to me from the slit under the door. So close now.

A hand hovered on the knob. I heard a light clink against the brass.

Not opening it.

Just... resting there.

The closet felt wrong, like the walls were pressing in around me. I backed up a half step.

I could hear a breath, low, steady. Right outside.

The air felt too thin, like it had been sucked straight from my lungs.

A soft tap came. Fingertips against the wood. Once. Twice. Almost... thoughtful. Like they were considering opening it.

I clenched my jaw so tight it ached. I could hear my own pulse, fast, ragged, drowning out everything else.

Another shift. A long, slow exhale.

Then, finally. Finally.

The outline retreated.

I waited.

Long enough that my legs started to wobble.

Then I moved. Quickly.

Up the stairs, through the hallway, fingers fumbling for the back doorknob.

I barely had time to shove it open before I burst outside, breath sharp in the cold night air.

I locked the door, then shoved the key back under the ivy pot.

I threw my hands into my hoodie pocket to keep them from shaking, feeling the diary.

I turned onto the sidewalk. My pulse was too fast.

I needed to get home.

I needed to read everything.

I needed to figure out what was in that diary. And why it was in Linworth's basement.

***

I wasn't alone.

A shadow stood at the corner of the street.

Not Linworth.

Not Newton.

Not someone I recognized. Did I?

They didn't move.

Didn't step forward. Didn't step back.

Just stood there.

A streetlamp flickered overhead, the glow stretching long, bending their shape, making it impossible to tell if they were facing me or just waiting.

I turned, quick and sharp. Hands still clenched around the diary.

I'd take the long way home. Cut behind the houses if I had to.

I didn't check to see if they followed.

I didn't look back.

Julie's diary was in my hands.

And I had a feeling it was about to change everything.

14

— • —

OCTOBER 31, 2024, 8:30 PM - SOPHIA

6 DAYS AFTER JULIE WENT MISSING

My room felt hot and suffocating, a contrast to the night outside.

I turned my lights off as if that would conceal me, grabbed a flashlight and crouched over Julie's diary sitting on the edge of my bed. It wasn't until I had locked myself in my room, the curtains drawn tight against the night, that I dared open the battered cover.

My hands shook as I flipped through the pages.

I wasn't sure if it was fear or the unbelievable, crushing weight of my own stupidity.

Because I had broken into Linworth's house. And if I got caught, I wasn't going to be able to say, *oh, my bad, I just needed to see if my dead classmate wrote anything incriminating before I turned myself into the psych ward for sleepwalking into her vigil.*

Newton would love that.

I exhaled slowly, grounding myself in the moment. The pages smelled like old paper and something sour, like they had absorbed pure panic.

The first few pages were normal. Doodles, homework reminders, a checklist of things that didn't matter anymore: find new mascara, ask Mom for an extension on curfew, stop thinking about him.

Then the handwriting got tighter, like she was pressing too hard into the page, like she was trying to shove too much into the space. Looking at the diary now, it wasn't just a few pages torn out. It looked like almost all of them were—aside from the first few notes and that message I read in Linworth's basement, only three entries remained.

***

August 29th

It started out harmless, didn't it?

I mean, he's a teacher. Teachers are supposed to care, supposed to notice when someone's slipping. And he did. At least, I thought he did.

The first time I stayed after class, it wasn't even on purpose. I just needed a minute. Needed someone to ask me how I was and actually mean it. He did. He always did. And maybe that's why it got complicated.

I don't know when it changed. Or how. Maybe it was me... lingering too long after class, making excuses to stop by. Maybe it was him... the way his hand rested on my shoulder a little too often, or how his compliments shifted from my grades to... something else.

"You think differently than other people, Julie."

"You see things others don't."

I liked hearing it. I liked how someone saw me for real. Then I told him I loved him.

I really thought we had a connection. And the worst part? I don't know if I imagined it all.

Because just as suddenly as it started, it ended after that. The warmth in his voice disappeared. The long conversations cut short. The way he used to look at me. Gone.

Then, last week, I tried talking to him again. Not about us. About Stephen.

I stared at the words, the edges of the paper crumpling against my palms.

Why would she need to talk to Linworth about Stephen?

He was the guy who reminded teachers to collect homework. A rule follower. A goody-goody.

I couldn't remember a single time Stephen had ever gotten in trouble. Not even once.

No late assignments. No wrong answers. Nothing.

That was normal. Right?

I turned the page. I saw an unfamiliar symbol etched in the margins next to her entry.

***

September 10th

Linworth pretends to be in control. Like he knows everything. Like he's somehow above it all. But now I know he's lying.

He's afraid too, I can see it.

It's in the way he flinches when I ask the wrong questions. The way his hands shake when he thinks no one's looking. The way he avoids looking me in the eye ever since I brought up Stephen.

And then there's the symbol. I think it's a symbol for a club at school but I'm still investigating.

I see the symbol everywhere now.

On the ring he sometimes plays with that he thinks no one notices.

On their desks, scratched into the wood.

It's not a coincidence. It can't be.

I asked him about it once. Pretended I saw it online. His voice didn't change, but his posture did. He didn't even hesitate.

"It's nothing you need to worry about, Julie."

Like that was supposed to be reassuring.

And Linworth isn't the only one acting strange.

People notice when you notice them. I've felt it... eyes on me when I'm not looking, conversations ending the second I walk by. The silence that stretches just a little too long when I bring up the wrong name.

I used to think it was all in my head. But it's not.

Whatever this is, I need to understand it. And the only way to do that is to get closer.

I blew out a sharp breath. Get closer to what?

The club? Linworth?

I glanced at the symbol again, tracing my thumb over the ink. But I'd never seen it before. Not in hallways, not on any rings or desks, not anywhere. So why had Julie? And whose desks was she referencing?

I turned the page, my fingers cold despite the warmth in my room.

***

September 24th

I shouldn't have brought up his brother.

We were fine.

He stayed late, sat with me like before.

Then I said it. Something about how awful it must've been.

68

He didn't say anything.
Just froze.
Then he punched the wall.
Hard.
Didn't even look at me. Just left.
Stephen says it wasn't an accident.
Says Jay let his brother die.
I didn't believe him.
But now... I don't know.
That look in Jay's eyes... like I knew something I wasn't supposed to.
Almost like I was next.

My throat went dry.
Julie and Jay.
I never saw them talk.
But she wrote, "like before."
Like they'd sat together a lot.
Something pinched in my chest. I didn't know why.
She had been scared of him.
But... wasn't Jay the one who was safe?
The one who was always there for me?
Always there.
There when I woke up at the vigil.
But hiding. Gone after we found her jacket.
The bruises on his hands at the coffee shop.
The way he tucked them under the table when I noticed.
The way he gripped my shoulder just a little too hard when he found me at the vigil.
When his voice was calm and careful, like he was choosing every word.
Julie was scared.
Stephen said he killed his brother.
And now all I could think was...
Was I wrong about him?
Was Jay not the one protecting me, but the one I needed protecting from?
I slammed the diary shut.
A loose slip of paper slid out between the pages.

My heart hammered as I pulled it free.

Like at Linworth's, it was blank. At first.

Then I flipped it over.

Not Julie's handwriting.

Three words in bold, sharp ink:

"You found it."

Then, another line, smaller, sharper:

"Good girl."

My body curled in on itself.

It was like... they'd been waiting for me to do this.

Like they knew I wouldn't be able to resist.

I stared at the letters. Tight, jagged... familiar.

I dug through my backpack and found the note from my locker.

Unfolded it.

Held them side by side.

Same handwriting.

Same ink.

Same underlying message:

"You should have stayed asleep."

"You found it."

"Good girl."

These weren't warnings.

They were commands.

My head spun as one thought looped again and again.

I wasn't the one chasing the truth.

Someone was leading me straight to it.

Who the hell is playing with me?

15

---·---

NOVEMBER 1, 2024, 12 PM - NEWTON

7 DAYS AFTER JULIE WENT MISSING

The station was full of bullshit, and I was done breathing it in.

I'd logged over ten calls about Sophia Whitaker in the last few weeks.

Most came from regulars. Neighbors claiming they saw her walking barefoot down the street in the middle of the night, mumbling to herself. Sleepwalking. Out of it.

But a few were different.

Predatory.

Calls with a warped, mechanical voice. Always blocked.

The first came the day we pulled Julie out of the ground. The voice lingered, watching her, breathing through the static.

Then again, three days ago. Same distortion. Same smirking edge:

"She's outside again. Talking to the dark. You should keep her safe."

It sounded like someone who thought they were untouchable.

Someone watching her like she was prey.

Or, maybe, someone trying a little too hard to make her look like one.

Either way, I wasn't buying it.

Then this morning, I got a call from Mr. Thompson, the hardware store owner, sharp as hell for seventy-five.

Said his neighbor had Ring footage worth seeing.

And he was right.

Sophia, slipping into frame.

Straight to the planter.

Straight inside Linworth's house.

Like she already knew where to look.

I dropped the printed Ring frame on the table in front of her.

She didn't flinch. Just stared.

"So," I said. "You breaking into houses now, or just swapping bedtime stories with Linworth?"

She blinked once. "I didn't break in."

"You expect me to believe you guessed where the key was?"

She didn't answer. Just rubbed her hands against her jeans.

"You didn't even look around. Walked right up, grabbed it, went in. Like you'd done it before."

Still nothing.

I flipped out a second photo—clearer. Her face. No denying it.

I tapped the edge of the photo. "That's Linworth's house, Whitaker. And that's you. Or do I need to get a magnifying glass?"

Sophia's shoulders sank as she said, "I don't remember."

I stared at her. Waited.

I leaned in, my voice sharp. "Yeah, you keep saying that."

Nothing.

"So tell me, Sophia. Was it a break in, or something worse? Because, right now, it looks like you and Linworth were covering for each other."

Her throat moved, a small swallow. But she didn't speak.

I slammed another set of papers onto the table.

Julie's call logs.

The phone had been anonymously dropped off at the station yesterday. It had been wiped clean, so the only records I had were from Verizon. Just timestamps and recipient numbers.

That was it.

"Two calls the night she disappeared. One to you, one to Linworth. Why?"

Her jaw locked. "I don't know why she called me."

When she didn't continue, I carefully placed the evidence bag on the table, displaying Julie's phone.

I'd already shown it to her yesterday, but I knew the effect. I've learned over the years the more physical evidence you show, the quicker people talk. It's self-preservation.

I pushed back from the table, giving Sophia space for the first time. Her left eye was twitching, and she started blinking rapidly.

"You know where I got this?"

Not a word.

I cocked my head.

"Dropped off yesterday. No name. Someone held onto it after Julie died, then just left it on my desk."

I let the evidence bag swing once between my hands. "I find that odd. Don't you?"

I caught it in my left hand, gripped it tight.

"There was one extremely unusual text. It was sent after she died. Dated and timed after we pulled her body from the ground."

Sophia was practically scraping a hole in her jeans now.

"Can you guess who it was sent to?" After a second, I said, "No? I'll give you a hint." I leaned forward just slightly. "They're sitting across from me. So. She calls you the night she disappears, and texts you from the grave."

Her posture was tense, her feet turned toward the door like she was getting ready to make a run for it.

"Start talking, Whitaker."

I waited patiently.

"Can I see the timestamp for the text?" she finally asked.

I pushed it forward and she inspected it closely, eyes crinkling.

She hesitated, but finally she reached into her pocket.

Pulled out her phone.

Unlocked it.

Turned it to me.

"I don't know who sent this," she said softly.

A single message flared to life on the screen.

Julie Greene: I'm still here.

My brows felt like they were touching each other from my scowl. I stared at the screen for a second, then looked at Sophia.

Her expression stayed neutral, but her hands were shaking.

She looked scared. Genuinely scared.

I tapped my teeth together, chewing over what I'd just seen. I hadn't expected her to look so fragile. Or to hand it over so easily.

I'd been half-convinced she was playing me. That the anonymous calls, that warped, mechanical voice was her. Part of some elaborate smokescreen.

But now I wasn't so sure.

If this was an act, it was damn good.

If it wasn't, someone was pulling her strings. Watching her.

Either way, she wasn't leaving town.

"Stay close, Whitaker," I said. "You've got too many eyes on you to disappear now."

I walked out and into the second, and only other, interrogation room.

16

November 1, 2024, 12:45 PM - Newton

7 Days After Julie Went Missing

If Sophia had been stone-cold silence, Eli was fire.

I barely had the door shut before he was already leaning forward in his chair, eyes blazing.

"Did you know your sister was sneaking into houses at night?" I asked, slow.

Eli's arms crossed tight. "Did you know your station is full of idiots?"

I smiled, tight. "Cute."

Then I dropped into the seat across from him, matching his posture.

"Where was she the night Julie died?"

"With me," he said, voice flat. "Like I told you a few days ago. At home."

Too clean.

I watched him. Let it get uncomfortable.

"You really expect me to believe that?"

Eli shrugged.

"Let's go with that." I kept my tone easy, casual.

"Here's something you might find interesting. There was a lot of activity on Julie's phone the night she died." I let the air hang between us. "Including to you."

Eli held his composure, but I saw the scrunch in his eyebrows ever so slightly.

I stretched my arms, reaching as far out as possible, then stretched my legs, like I had all the time in the world.

"And what's probably the most interesting part," I lured, "are the texts she sent to you."

Eli didn't move a single muscle.

I pressed my pointer finger into the page in front of me. "The thing is, I looked through all of Julie's call and text logs. Spent a good amount of time looking them over in fact. And one thing struck me. She never texted you before October. Not a single text before then."

75

I didn't mention the rest. Didn't tell him that Julie's text activity exploded the week before she died—five times more messages than usual. Didn't mention that she had reached out to over 40 different people that week. Like she was looking for something, or someone.

I'd already dropped enough bait. Eli was looking at me directly now, not breaking eye contact for a second.

I shrugged, matching his earlier movement. "So, I guess my question is... why?"

Eli let out a small sigh, shaking his head. "Man, I knew you were gonna get hung up on that."

I raised a brow. "That so?"

"Yeah, because I thought it was weird too. Julie and I didn't talk. Ever. But out of nowhere she texts me saying she needs to ask me something."

I stayed silent. Letting him keep talking, waiting for the slightest voice inflection, a misplaced word.

"She told me she saw Sophia outside one night. Late. Said she looked... off. Asked me if she sleepwalked." His hands curled into fists on the table. Not defensive. Protective. "Said it freaked her out."

I shifted forward. "And what did you tell her?"

Eli shook his head again. "That yeah it happens sometimes, just started recently. That Sophia's been through a lot and doesn't need people digging into it." His voice was steady, but I caught the edge of something sharp.

"I told her to leave my sister alone." I studied the lines of his face. His posture. Measured his tone. There was no hesitation, no stumbling.

"And why do you think she suddenly cared about that?" I asked.

Eli scratched his jaw. "I don't know. Maybe she saw something she didn't understand. Or she just wanted to stir stuff up. Julie liked attention."

I let that sit, then cocked a brow. "Let's say I believe you. Let's say Julie was just looking for gossip, or she saw something that spooked her. Why text you? Why not talk to Sophia directly?"

Eli's jaw stiffened. His voice was flat. "Because she didn't need to deal with it."

I narrowed my eyes. "And you made sure of that?"

Eli leaned forward, matching my stance now. "You got a little sister, Sheriff?"

I didn't answer.

Eli's lip twitched. "Then you wouldn't get it."

He was right about one thing. I didn't get it. Not yet.

But I would.

I watched Eli walk out, then sat in the stillness for a long time.

I'd brought Linworth in earlier that morning. Thought I could get ahead of the spin. Instead, he'd given me a name.

Calloway.

The way he said it stuck with me. Calm on the outside, but his fingers were twitching under the table like he was trying to smother something. Like he knew he was handing me a match but didn't want to watch what burned.

"She was looking in the wrong places," he'd said. "She thought she had it figured out. She didn't."

And then, quietly, "If you want answers... talk to Calloway."

It wasn't a suggestion. It was a handoff.

Something about it didn't sit right.

Linworth looked scared. Not guilty. Not grieving. Scared.

And that's not how you react unless the answers you're holding onto aren't yours to give.

Then there was Sophia. Her statement still sat open on my desk. Cold black ink on white paper.

"I don't remember."

She'd said it over and over. In the interview. When I questioned her about Julie calling. A damn refrain.

I didn't buy it. But then again, maybe she wasn't lying. Maybe someone didn't want her to remember.

Hell, maybe Eli didn't want her to either.

He was too defensive. Too protective...

The way he'd watched me during the interview, like I was circling something fragile and he was ready to strike.

When they left the station, he walked beside her like a shield. Not guiding. Guarding.

I'd seen that kind of protection before. It usually meant someone had something to hide.

***

I found myself back at the case boxes.

Julie's personal effects were in the third one. I flipped through the inventory: phone, photos, bracelet, jacket.

The jacket.

My hand landed on it before my brain caught up. Neon yellow. A stitched heart on the pocket.

The one Sophia found in the woods.

I turned it over, ran my fingers along the lining. And there it was.

I almost missed it the first time. Faded black ink at the bottom of the inside zipper.

Jagged letters. Pressed hard into the fabric.

"Ask her if she remembers."

I stared at it, unmoving.

My eyes dropped again to her statement: *I don't remember.*

Something tightened in my gut.

This wasn't coincidence. This was choreography.

Whoever left this message, knew she'd find it. Knew I'd be looking. Hell, maybe they knew I wouldn't take her word for it.

And now Linworth had thrown out Calloway's name like it was his last card to play.

Which meant I was done waiting.

Calloway was next.

And Sophia Whitaker?

If she really didn't remember, someone damn well wanted it that way.

17

November 4, 2024, 8 AM - Sophia

10 Days After Julie Went Missing

The first thing I noticed was the sideways glances.

Not outright staring. No, this was worse. The kind where people pretend not to look at you. Where they talk just loud enough for you to hear.

"That's her."

"You know, the one the cops took in."

"Freak was sleepwalking at the vigil too."

"Sophia was sneaking out of Linworth's house. What do you think she was doing?"

I kept walking.

Didn't stop. Didn't slow down.

Even when I felt their eyes follow me.

Even when I caught the glow of a phone screen, someone taking a picture.

My locker was the only place I could breathe.

Or at least, it should have been.

My left hand gripped my backpack like a lifeline while I twisted the dial with my right, yanking it open.

A crumpled ball of paper tumbled to the floor.

I stared at it for a second. Didn't want to touch it. Not after the last time I found a note in my locker.

But my fingers moved anyway. Slow. Hesitant.

The paper unfolded in jerky motions.

One word. Big. Black. Sharpie.

MURDERER.

It was not the same handwriting as the first note. This was neat, with perfect lines like someone had taken time with every stroke.

I didn't breathe.

Didn't move.

Didn't feel the ground under my feet.

I stuffed it deep into my bag and slammed the locker shut.

I just need to keep moving.

The shove came from behind.

Not hard. Just enough to make me stumble.

Low, mean laughter followed.

"Watch it, freak."

My jaw ached from clenching too hard. I swallowed down the tight, hot feeling in my throat and kept walking.

"So... did you do it?"

Heat flushed through my face as I turned toward the voice.

Jessica Carmichael stood a few lockers down, smirking.

The hallway was quiet.

People were watching. Waiting for me to react.

I swallowed. "What?"

Jessica tilted her head in fake curiosity. The kind that cut.

"Julie," she said, voice sickly sweet. "Did you kill her?"

The words slammed into me.

I stared at her. At the smirk on her lips, the light in her eyes like this was fun.

A few people snickered. Someone whispered something I couldn't hear.

I turned away from her.

"Yeah, that's what I thought," Jessica snarled.

That hit harder than the shove.

And suddenly I wasn't in the hallway anymore. My mind went back to Abbie's bonfire. It was late August, and the air was thick with smoke.

I had been sitting on an oversized Yeti cooler, balancing a half-empty water bottle on my knee, already halfway to leaving.

Then I saw them.

Jessica standing too close. Leo not moving away. The flicker of firelight. The way she whispered something into his ear. The way he didn't pull back.

The kiss.

Not long, not dramatic. It was quick and easy. Like it didn't mean anything. Like I hadn't been pulling away for months already. Like he knew it was over. But he had still done it.

I had walked away before he could see me, before he could stop me.

By the next morning, we were done.

And now, of course it was Jessica taunting me. Sneering like she had been waiting for this moment.

I forced myself back to the present.

Because what really bothered me was that no one stopped her.

No one defended me.

No one was on my side.

I saw Leo out of the corner of my eye.

I heard him before he fully caught up. His footsteps were quick, urgent. "Sophia, are you okay?"

"Fine."

The word left too quick. Like if I didn't get it out fast enough, my voice might crack.

He took a half step in front of me. "Just. Wait. Can we talk?"

My eyes burned into him as I shot back. "We don't need to."

His hand dropped. Just like that. Like I'd cut the last thread between us.

"Soph," his eyes flicked to the floor, jaw tightening before he looked back up. Like he was trying to find the right words but kept coming up empty.

"It wasn't about her. It never was."

I stiffened. He still didn't get it.

"I know," I said. And I did.

But that didn't mean it mattered anymore.

I could see the longing in his eyes. That quiet hope. Like he wanted me to say something, anything, to make this hurt less.

But it wasn't about us.

There was no "us." Not anymore.

And Jessica? She had made sure of that. She had it out for me now, and the worst part? He still didn't see it.

I turned and walked away.

Heading towards my English class.

When I turned the corner I saw Jay.

Leaning against the lockers, head tilted like he'd been waiting.

No side stepping in front of me. Just... there.

His face unreadable. But his eyes. Sharp.

He didn't ask anything. Just fell into step beside me.

We walked. People whispered.

I didn't look. Jay didn't either.

When I glanced over, he pulled an extra hoodie from his bag and shoved it into my hands.

"I'm not cold," I said, confused.

Jay shrugged. "You look like you need something."

I glanced at my arms, goosebumps everywhere.

I didn't argue. Just pulled it on.

The fabric smelled like campfire and detergent.

We kept walking.

But everything felt different.

He was still beside me. Still stepping into the storm for me.

Still the person who showed up.

But Stephen's voice was in my head.

"People don't change. Ask Jay what happened to his brother sometime."

And then Julie's diary.

"I shouldn't have brought up his brother... he didn't even look at me. Just left. Punched the wall."

"Stephen says it wasn't an accident. Says Jay let him die."

I swallowed hard.

Jay had always been quiet. Steady.

But maybe I'd mistaken silence for softness.

I opened my mouth.

Wanted to ask:

Why haven't you told me more?

What happened to your brother?

Why did Julie seem scared of you?

But the words stuck.

Because Jay's hand brushed mine, and the touch was lightning.

Brief. Electric. Dangerous.

And I didn't know what scared me more...

That I still wanted him close.

Or that maybe Julie had been right to be afraid.

Someone behind us whispered just loud enough to hear:

"Bet she's sleeping just fine, knowing she got away with it."

Jay's arm wrapped around my shoulder.

Pulled me with him.

Like he wasn't letting me go.

Like he wasn't letting them win.

And I couldn't tell if that made me feel safe, or trapped.

Because as we moved through the hallway, their eyes followed us.

Not us...

Me.

Because as much as I was starting to question Jay...

The town had already judged me. I was the one questioned by the cops.

It didn't matter what I said.

Didn't matter what the truth was.

Julie was gone.

And now?

They thought I had something to do with it.

18

— • —

NOVEMBER 4, 2024, 3:30 PM - SOPHIA

10 DAYS AFTER JULIE WENT MISSING

Dr. Olivia Patel didn't do the therapy head tilt I was expecting.

She didn't stare at me like I was a puzzle she was already halfway to solving. She didn't lean forward, clasping her hands in that slow, deliberate way therapists do in movies. She had on a black turtleneck tucked into a black pleated maxi skirt. All black, for some reason it made me think about a funeral, death, about my mom.

After what happened at school and with everything else, I decided to suck it up and go to the appointment Eli had scheduled for me.

Dr. Patel just sat, legs crossed, pen tapping idly against her notepad, watching.

Not like she was waiting to diagnose me.

Like she was waiting for me to stop wasting her time.

"You don't want to be here."

Her voice was smooth. Even. No judgment, just an observation.

I shrugged. "I didn't say that."

"You didn't have to." She glanced at her notes, then back at me. "Your brother did a lot of the talking when he set this up. He seems concerned."

"He worries too much," I said automatically.

She cocked her head slightly, but still not in the therapy way. More like a scientist observing a particularly stubborn test subject.

"I hear that a lot," she said.

Silence.

I shrugged, shifting in my seat. "So, fun fact. Turns out if you get hauled into the police station for questioning, your Yelp reviews as a human being tank overnight. Or I guess... tank even more."

Dr. Patel's lips tugged upward, just slightly then returned to a professional line. "Tell me more about that."

"Everyone has been talking about me since I started…"

I couldn't say sleepwalking. Just couldn't. I didn't need another person thinking I was a freak.

"Started what?" She probed.

I bit my lip. I focused on the faint rain sounds from the noise maker in the corner and didn't say anything.

"So," she said after a while, "Let's go back to this—what you phrased as *Yelp-tanking*. That sounds tough on you. How are you feeling more specifically?"

I huffed a laugh, shaking my head. "Like I should start wearing a 'Not a Murderer' t-shirt to school."

She gave me a look. The kind that said try again.

I sighed, leaning back. "I don't know. I knew people talked. I just didn't think I'd be the town's next great conspiracy theory."

"Do you feel unsafe?"

I thought about the notes in my locker. The whispers. Jessica Carmichael's voice, slick with cruelty, like asking if I killed Julie was just gossip.

And I thought about Jay.

How he didn't ask, just walked beside me.

How he handed me his hoodie like it was a shield.

But shields can hide things, too.

I swallowed. "No," I said finally. "Not exactly."

Dr. Patel nodded slowly and perceptively, like she understood everything I wasn't saying.

I let my gaze wander around the office, warm-toned walls, a bookshelf lined with academic titles, a small potted plant on the window ledge that looked fake, but expensive.

Dr. Patel didn't break the quiet. She just let it stretch, waiting me out.

I exhaled, crossing my arms. "I sleepwalk sometimes. It's not that big of a deal." I admitted surprising myself.

"Define sometimes."

I hesitated. "A couple of times over the last month. I think."

Dr. Patel raised an eyebrow. "Think?"

"Look, it's not like I keep a spreadsheet. It's not even that bad. I just wake up somewhere else. The floor, the hallway…"

"The woods?" she asked.

My vision tunneled, the edges of the world shrinking down to a pinpoint.

Dr. Patel caught the shift in my expression. "Eli mentioned you've woken up outside before."

I shrugged again, but it was stiff now. "A couple of times."

Her expression stayed neutral, but her voice softened just slightly.

"Sophia, from what I've heard from your brother, this is a more advanced case of sleep-walking," she said. "Waking up outside, especially repeatedly, isn't typical. It's something we should take seriously."

Something about the way she said it made my throat feel tight.

What the hell did Eli tell this lady?

"Tell me about your stress levels," she continued, flipping a page in her notebook. "Are you experiencing any unusual paranoia? Gaps in memory?"

"No," I said too quickly.

She didn't react, just tapped her pen against her knee, considering me. "Have you tried tracking your episodes? Writing down any patterns?"

I shook my head.

"Let's start there." She slid a small, leather notebook across the table. "Write down everything. When you sleepwalk. What you remember before you go to sleep. Any trig-gers. Even if it feels insignificant, log it."

I took the notebook, but it felt heavier than it should. I didn't particularly like writing, so I wasn't really sure if I should be going along with this. But given how her and Eli have already been talking I'm not so sure I want it getting back to him that I'm refusing something.

I went through another 30 minutes of intake questions before she added, "One last thing."

"If the sleepwalking persists, there are methods we can use to access those missing pieces. Cognitive exercises. Guided work." She paused. "Hypnosis."

I huffed out a short laugh. "You mean, 'look into my eyes, you're getting very sleepy' hypnosis?"

Yeah... hard pass on that woo-woo stuff.

Dr. Patel's lips quirked, but her gaze stayed sharp. "Not quite. It's a relaxation tech-nique to help you recall things your conscious mind might not pick up. But that's for later. If it comes to that."

It won't, I told myself.

She didn't push any further. Instead, she gave a small nod. "Let's see what your logs tell us."

***

Back at home I made it six hours before breaking.

The rational part of me, the part that still believed I had some amount of control over myself, knew Dr. Patel was probably right. Stress, subconscious anxiety, lack of sleep. That's what made people sleepwalk, right?

So, I did what any rational person would do.

I went down a Reddit rabbit hole.

At first, it was fine. Funny even. People talking about waking up in weird places in their houses. Some guy who kept rearranging his fridge in his sleep. A girl who sleep-shopped on Amazon and ended up with twenty identical pink bathrobes.

I could live with that.

Then the stories started feeling more real.

A guy whose mom called him at 4 AM, saying she was calling him back, because he'd just spent ten minutes talking to her in gibberish.

A girl who woke up with blood on her sweater, no clue where it came from.

Someone who woke up digging.

My shoulders tensed, and I forced myself to unclench my jaw.

I scrolled faster. Past the paranoia, past the I think I hurt someone in my sleep posts, until I found a title that actually felt relatable.

There were over 15 comments. People were sharing similar stories, some even worse. I backed out to the main r/sleepwalkingstories page and clicked on a post from someone else looking for an explanation for it.

My fingers felt completely numb.

I threw my phone on my bed.

Nope.

I inhaled sharply, pressing my palms against my temples. This was stupid. None of this had anything to do with me.

These weren't my stories. Most of that's probably made up anyway right?

I exhaled hard. Enough.

I wasn't going to sleepwalk tonight.

I couldn't.

My hands fidgeted, but how could I make sure of that? Before my mind could fully catch up to what I was doing I shoved my desk against the door. Stacked my chair on top of it. Threw my backpack into the pile for good measure.

I tried to pull my door open to test how strong my barrier was, it didn't budge.

If I moved in my sleep now, I'd know.

That was the plan, anyway.

Tonight, I was going to put on my most comfortable clothes, set the rain sounds on my phone, and zonk out. No weird feelings, no waking up out of place.

I yanked open my dresser drawer and grabbed the biggest sweater I could find, the Red Hot Chili Peppers one Eli gave me last time Dad went on the road, like he just knew I'd need it. I pushed aside a folded pair of leggings to grab my fleece Lulu Lemon joggers, then I opened my top drawer already knowing exactly what I was looking for.

My white lace underwear.

My favorite pair.

I didn't know why I wanted them specifically. Maybe because they were comfortable, maybe because I'd worn them a hundred times before and never had to think about it.

But when I reached for them, they weren't there.

I frowned, sifting through the stack. Cotton. Satin. The pair I never wore because the waistband was weird.

No lace.

I stopped.

That didn't make sense.

I always put them right here.

I dug deeper, flipping through every piece. Then I went back through again, slower this time, like I'd somehow missed them the first time.

Nothing.

A weird feeling crept up my spine.

I turned, checking the laundry basket. I probably hadn't washed them yet.

I couldn't find them.

Were they still in the hamper?

Not there.

The uneasiness settled deeper.

They were probably in the dryer.

I mean, they had to be somewhere.

I just wasn't looking in the right place.

Right?

I exhaled, shaking it off. I was always losing socks and t-shirts, mostly courtesy of Abbie "borrowing" them and never returning them.

This was just one more thing.

I crawled under my covers, put on the rain sounds, and forced my body to sink into the mattress.

My muscles still felt coiled, alert. But exhaustion pressed in, my eyelids fluttered closed.

Then something felt wrong.

***

A chill ghosted across my skin.

I shifted, reaching for the blanket.

Wet.

My fingers fumbled against nothing. Just air.

My brows knit together. I reached again, further this time. Still no blanket.

I blinked, trying to shake off the heavy pull of sleep. My body felt sluggish, like I was swimming through syrup.

Something damp grazed my arm.

Rough. Gritty. Coarse.

What was that?

My fingers brushed over the surface again, slow, searching. The texture was sharp against my skin, not wood. Not carpet. Something else.

Sandpaper? No not quite.

My eyes cracked open. Just a sliver.

Black. Grey. Dusty. Grit.

My chest seized. Roof shingles.

No, no, no!

I sucked in a breath, but the air didn't feel right. A gust of wind cut through me, sharp as a blade.

I wasn't in my bed.

I wasn't even inside.

The realization hit all at once.

Too high up. Too much space. Too far down.

The ground wasn't where it should be.

I was on the roof.

A scream ripped from my throat before I could stop it. It tore through the night, raw and desperate, before I slammed my hands over my mouth. Too late.

Lights flicked on inside.

A shadow moved in the window at the end of the house.

Eli shoved it open, peered out.

His face turned white.

"Sophia!"

He disappeared. I heard pushing at my door then it abruptly stopped.

Panic surged in my throat. My hands shook violently, fingers curling into... wait. Not my hoodie. A tank top. Had I changed?

I slowly backed up against my house, as far from the roofline as I could.

There was movement to my left.

The attic window swung open.

Eli climbed out onto the roof.

I was still frozen. Still trapped in a body that wasn't mine.

His steps were slow. Controlled. Like I was a wild animal he was afraid to spook.

"Soph, you have to move."

His voice was calm, almost comforting.

I couldn't breathe. My legs were numb.

Then his hand wrapped around my shoulder. Solid, warm, real.

"Come on." His grip tightened.

"I've got you."

I let him pull me toward the window. Toward safety.

But just before we climbed inside, something shifted.

I caught movement from the corner of my eye.

A figure, standing across the street, half-shrouded by the shadows of the neighbor's hedge.

Still.

Watching.

Tall. Broad shouldered. Hood up on an Ordinance High track hoodie.

Jay.

It had to be.

My breath caught. I opened my mouth, but the words snagged in my throat.

What was he doing here? Why wasn't he moving? Saying anything?

"Sophia," Eli said, tugging gently. "We have to go."

I turned back toward the window, still dazed.

When I looked again—

The figure was gone.

Just the empty street, quiet and still, like no one had been there at all.

The second I was inside, the barricade caught his attention.

He exhaled sharply, pushing the coffee-dark strands of hair out of his face. His eyes flicked to the desk. The chair. The backpack. It was pushed forward slightly in his attempt to get in when he heard me.

He looked at me.

"Sophia."

I didn't say anything.

I couldn't.

Because my hands were still shaking. His phone lit up beside me and I glanced down and caught the time: 2:36 AM.

I didn't know how long I had been out there, or how I got there.

19

NOVEMBER 5, 2024, 7:30 AM - SOPHIA

11 DAYS AFTER JULIE WENT MISSING

Eli was already in the kitchen when I came downstairs. Leaning against the counter, shoulders tense, like he'd been there waiting. He looked like he hadn't slept either, hair uncombed, dark circles under his brown eyes, jaw set like he was holding something in.

He had our father's olive skin, same as mine. But where I looked tired, he somehow still looked like the guy half the girls at school whispered about. It made me cringe. His face wasn't his fault, but I still resented it.

"You slept?" he asked. It wasn't really a question. More like a test.

I hesitated too long.

His brows lifted slightly. "How are you... feeling?"

I grabbed a water bottle from the fridge. Twisted the cap off, focusing too hard on the seal breaking. "I'm fine."

Eli didn't react right away. Just studied me, his expression unreadable. Then he exhaled, shaking his head.

"You're not even gonna bring it up?"

I took a sip of water. "Bring what up?"

His jaw tightened. "You know what."

I did.

I just didn't know how to talk about it.

What was I supposed to say?

Sorry for waking up on the literal roof?

Sorry for screaming loud enough to send you into full-blown big brother panic mode?

Sorry for making you climb out of a third-story window to pull me back inside?

Because I wasn't sure which part was worse.

The fact that I had no memory of climbing onto the roof.

93

Or the fact that I'd barricaded my door, to prevent something just like that, and it hadn't mattered.

"I don't know what you want me to say," I muttered.

Eli let out a sharp, humorless laugh. "I want you to talk to me. I want to know if you even remember what happened."

I swallowed hard. "I remember enough."

His jaw ticked. "Enough?" he asked exasperated.

I could feel his stare, heavy with all the things he wasn't saying.

"This isn't just sleepwalking, Soph." His voice was quieter now. Not angry. Just tired. "This is something else."

I hated that everyone kept saying that. I forced a shrug. "Dr. Patel says stress can make it worse."

He scoffed. "Stress?" He gestured toward the window. "Stress made you sleepwalk onto the roof?"

I didn't answer.

For a second, neither of us spoke. Then Eli sighed, rubbing a hand over his face. "Did she say anything useful?"

I hesitated, "She gave me homework."

That caught his attention. "What kind of homework?"

"Tracking my sleepwalking." I shifted my weight, watching his face. "Writing down when it happens, what I remember, how I felt before and after."

Eli exhaled slowly. Some of the tension in his shoulders loosened. Not a lot. Just enough.

"And you're actually gonna do it?"

I shrugged, casual. "I wouldn't have told you if I wasn't going to do it, would I?"

He didn't look convinced.

I wasn't either.

But it was enough to make him let it go. For now.

"Good," he muttered. Then, quieter, "Just... don't scare me like that again."

Like I had a choice.

My phone buzzed in my pocket, the vibration rattling against my thigh.

I almost ignored it. I had been ignoring basically every call and text...

But then I saw the name on the screen.

Dad.

I stared at it for a second. He never called. Not unless it was something important. Not unless he had to.

I hesitated, then swiped to answer.

"Hey, kid," he said. His voice was rough, worn down, like he hadn't slept in days. I could hear something in the background, static, distant voices. "I've got a minute."

A minute.

Right.

I swallowed. "Where are you?"

"Still in Spain." He let out a breath. "The flooding's worse than we thought. Whole towns are gone. They're finding more bodies every day."

Bodies.

I gripped the phone tighter. He wasn't saying it to make a point. It was his reality.

"I need to stay longer," he continued, like he was just adding another task to his schedule. "They need all the hands they can get."

Of course they did.

Of course he did.

Something bitter burned in my throat. I sat up straighter. Now or never.

"Dad, things are bad here too." My voice came out smaller than I wanted.

A pause. "Bad how?"

I clenched my jaw. "People think I had something to do with Julie's death."

A longer pause.

My fingers curled. "Someone called me a murderer in the middle of the hallway at school."

"Jesus," he sighed, long and heavy. "Sophia..."

"I got pulled into the station for questioning." I cut in. I felt the early pang of tears well behind my eyes. "Me and Eli."

His silence stretched.

Like he didn't know what to say. I knew he was trying to find a way to downplay it.

Finally, he exhaled. "Honey... hundreds of people are dying here."

The words slammed into me.

The line in the sand. The reminder.

His emergencies will always be bigger.

What happens to me will never be enough.

My grip on the phone tightened. Something inside me curled up, small and brittle.

I forced a breath in. Forced my voice steady.

"Yeah." A pause. Colder than I meant. "I figured you'd say something like that."

"Honey I—"

"No, it's fine," I cut him off. "You should go."

He hesitated, but I knew how this ended.

How it always ended.

"I'll be back when I can," he said finally. "Take care of yourself, okay?"

Then the line went dead.

I stared at the phone in my hands, my heart pounding too fast.

Take care of yourself.

Right.

Because no one else was going to.

I shut my bedroom door behind me. Locked it.

Then I just... stood there.

My hands were still shaking. After waking up on the roof, being accused of murder, my dad's voice still echoing in my ear.

And Jay.

Watching it.

Or... it was Jay wasn't it?

I pressed my palms into my eyes. Breathed in. Out. Then grabbed the notebook from my nightstand, the one Dr. Patel gave me. The one I'd been avoiding like it might bite.

I flipped to a blank page. Wrote:

November 5th

"I woke up on the edge of my roof."

The words stared back at me and I continued writing.

"And I think I'm scared of Jay."

The moment the words left the pen, I felt a sharp, involuntary squeeze in my chest.

No.

I gripped the pen harder and dragged it across the sentence. Once, twice, again. Heavy, angry lines that tore slightly into the page.

Ink bled on my fingers. Letters vanished.

Now it was just a black mess, jagged and frantic.

My pulse thundered.

Why did I write that?

Why did it feel true?

I slammed the notebook shut.

Then opened it again.

Flipped to a clean page. One that didn't feel like it might swallow me.

I couldn't go there yet.

Not about me.

Not about Jay.

But Julie?

Julie, I could face.

***

I reached under my mattress where I had carefully tucked away Julie's diary. I skimmed past the parts I already remembered. The way she talked about Linworth, how she had fallen for him, she had tried to talk to him about Stephen.

Then there was that symbol. I studied it. It was an oval with an x etched into the center and a word that looked like some foreign language at the top wrapping around the oval: "ordo".

It was written into the margins of the entry from September 10th, about a month before she disappeared.

"I think it's a club at school, but I'm still investigating."

"It's on Linworth's ring... He pretends it doesn't mean anything, but it does. It has to."

"The way he avoids looking me in the eye ever since I brought up Stephen."

But Stephen's not the story. Not really. He's just the town brainiac. Linworth... he was the one with Julie's diary pages in his basement. And that symbol? That's my way in.

I yanked my old yearbook off the shelf, flipping through the pages too fast at first, the glossy paper slipping under my fingers. The weight felt different, like it held something I wasn't meant to find.

If this symbol was something real, something connected to the school, to them, I could find it here.

I wasn't expecting much. Maybe a club logo on a T-shirt. Something small.

I flipped past the student pages and didn't see anything, then started to gloss over the faculty photos.

Administration then teachers, sorted by subject. A.P. first. Other general faculty after.

I barely skimmed the first few, mind already moving ahead. The page crinkled slightly under my fingers as I stopped at the A.P. section.

And there they were.

Freshman year.

Mr. Linworth. A.P. Literature. Mr. Calloway. A.P. Biology.

Side by side. Smiling.

Calloway's hand rested on Linworth's shoulder, casual but firm. Like they were close. Like they were aligned.

My fingers hovered over the picture. I grabbed my other yearbook and flipped to the A.P. page.

Sophomore year.

A few inches between them now.

Linworth's expression had changed.

The easy, comfortable smile? Gone.

His lips pressed thin, his eyes sharper, like he had been forced to stand there but wanted to be anywhere else.

Calloway, meanwhile, looked exactly the same.

Something about it nagged at me.

I stared harder. Looking.

Oh...

The ring.

Linworth had one freshman year.

Calloway had one, too.

Same insignia. Same symbol.

But sophomore year—

Linworth wasn't wearing his anymore.

My stomach tightened.

Julie had written about the insignia. She had seen it on Linworth's ring, even his desk. But she hadn't mentioned Calloway. Had she not noticed? Or had she just been focused on Linworth?

What had changed between Linworth and Calloway, or was the difference in the picture just a coincidence?

I dropped the yearbook onto my bed and grabbed my laptop.

Searched "ordo"—it was Latin for Order.

My stomach clenched.

Order... yikes.

Sounded like something out of a conspiracy movie teaser. Overblown. Fake.

Except... it wasn't. Julie had written about it. Linworth wore the ring with the insignia. So did Calloway.

And something had changed between them. I shifted focus and searched again.

"Linworth + Calloway"—Nothing

"Linworth + Calloway Ordinance High"—General staff pages

"Conflict Ordinance High"

I clicked on a local article.

"A faculty restructuring at Ordinance High led to internal investigations into staff practices. While the administration has not disclosed specifics, an unnamed teacher was removed from extracurricular responsibilities following an internal ethics review. No formal charges were filed."

My mind buzzed.

It didn't say who.

But it was from last year.

Right when they stopped looking friendly in the yearbook.

I scrolled back up, rereading.

"Removed from extracurricular responsibilities."

For what?

There was nothing about police involvement. No scandal.

Just something quiet. Buried.

I clicked on related articles.

Nothing.

If there had been something bigger, they'd shut it down fast.

But something wasn't right.

Not with the teachers. Not with any of it.

20

—·—

NOVEMBER 11, 2024, 4 PM - SOPHIA

17 DAYS AFTER JULIE WENT MISSING

Dr. Patel studied me with that too-calm, too-perceptive gaze, her pen tapping lightly against her notepad. The office was quiet. The kind that made your thoughts louder, stretching the space between words like she was waiting for me to fill it.

I wasn't going to.

I slouched a little further in the chair, one leg bouncing as I pretended to be fascinated by the tiny crack in her ceiling.

"You're jittery today," she noted.

"New personality trait," I muttered.

She smirked like she knew I was full of it. "How was the tracking exercise?"

I swallowed. My fingers tightened around the journal in my lap. "It was..." Horrifying? Something I avoided looking at? "...fine."

I sighed, passing the journal over.

Dr. Patel didn't read it aloud. Just scanned the page, her eyes slowing as she reached the bottom.

She tilted her head.

"You scratched something out."

I froze.

She didn't press, just waited.

I looked away. "It was nothing."

She turned the page so I could see. Ink ripped, smeared, dug into the paper like I'd wanted to erase more than just the words.

"It doesn't look like nothing."

I swallowed hard.

"I wrote that I was scared of Jay," I admitted.

Her expression didn't change. "Are you?"

I hesitated, "No... I don't know. I don't think so."

She didn't blink. "But you thought it enough to write it. Enough to black it out after."

My fingers curled into my sleeve.

"He's always there," I said quietly. "That night I woke up on the roof. He was in the yard. Just... standing there. Watching. I thought it was him, at least."

Her brow furrowed. "You're not sure?"

"It's hard to know for sure it was so dark. But he was wearing a track hoodie and Jay is..." My voice dropped and I shook my head. "He was there when I sleepwalked into the vigil, that I know for sure. Just happened to find me."

I paused, the pieces starting to rearrange themselves.

"And he was close with Julie before she died. Closer than I realized. And when she brought up his brother..." I swallowed. "Julie said he punched the wall. Just. Froze, then snapped."

Dr. Patel watched me carefully.

Something in my chest pulled tight.

"What if I'm not scared of him for no reason?" I said. "I'm... scared that I can't remember how I got onto the roof."

She didn't speak right away, but she didn't look surprised either.

Just steady. Calm. Present.

"Then let's try to figure it out." She paused, "Would you be open to trying a different approach today?"

I tensed. That vague phrasing.

I knew what she was about to suggest before she even said it.

"We could try a guided relaxation technique," she continued. "Nothing deep, just a light exploration. We stay in control the entire time."

My palms started sweating.

Hypnosis.

Just thinking the word sent a pulse of anxiety up my spine. I'd seen enough bad TV to know that this wasn't some mind-control thing, but still, what if I found something I couldn't unsee?

I hesitated. "What if what I remember isn't good?"

She gave a small, knowing smile. "Then we'll face it together."

Face it.

I exhaled through my nose. I didn't even know if I could look at it. Whatever "it" was.

Her voice softened. "You're not alone in this, Sophia."

That shouldn't have made my throat tighten.

I gripped the arms of the chair. If I said no, I was admitting that I was scared. Not just to her, but to myself. If I said yes...

My knee bounced. I forced it still.

"You'd be in control?" I asked.

"The entire time."

I swallowed.

It was the way she didn't press too hard but still saw right through me.

And the way she never softened her words just to make me comfortable.

She didn't tiptoe. Didn't give me that cautious, worried look like Eli.

She asked. She listened.

And then she let me decide.

No one else did that.

That's why I trusted her.

Or maybe it was because, for the first time, I had someone to talk to about this, really talk, without fear of what came next.

No judgment. No whispers behind my back. No sideways glances in the hallway.

Just her.

I looked at her, and I nodded.

Dr. Patel's expression didn't change, but something in her eyes shifted. Approval, maybe.

She gave me one last moment to back out. Then she spoke.

"Alright," she said. "Let's begin."

***

At first, it felt like nothing.

Dr. Patel guided me through slow breathing, her voice steady, even. I let my muscles loosen, my mind slip into the easy rhythm of inhale, exhale.

My thoughts drifted, weightless, slipping through the cracks of the present.

Not physically. But in that strange, dreamlike way, where your consciousness starts sliding somewhere else, into something older.

Suddenly I heard whipping through the trees.

I was running.

Bare feet slamming against wet leaves. Cold air slicing through my lungs. The wind howling through the forest.

I couldn't see where I was going, but I knew, I had to keep moving.

I didn't know what I was running from.

My head whipped around.

A voice. Faint. Distant. A name.

"Sophia!"

My stomach clenched.

"Wake up!"

Branches cracked. Too loud. Too close.

I turned, hands grabbed my wrist. Hard. Yanking.

And just before the world snapped back into focus—

A flash

Dark wood. A door hanging off its hinges. The smell of damp rot and something metallic. A place I knew but couldn't place. A place that made my skin crawl.

The memory fractured, blurred into something half-seen, half-felt.

The smell of earth. Water. A sensation. Something slipping from my grasp.

My head tingled.

A whisper. Right at my ear.

I couldn't make out the words. But the feeling—

I knew that voice.

Something ancient in me froze.

It was familiar—too familiar. My stomach dropped. Not fear.

Recognition. I ripped myself out.

***

I inhaled too sharply, sitting up fast.

Dr. Patel was already watching me, calm but ready.

I pressed the heels of my palms into my eyes. I was shaking, and my lungs felt tight.

"Your breathing is fast," she noted gently. "Can you try to slow it down? Breathe in for 4 seconds, hold for 4 seconds, out for 4 seconds."

I forced my lungs to comply, even though my heart wouldn't.

She waited. Let me come back to the present before speaking again.

"You stopped yourself."

I let my hands drop. "It cut out."

Dr. Patel didn't look convinced. "Did it? Or was it something too hard to look at?"

My fingers curled against my leg.

Her voice softened, more curious now.

"Sophia," she said carefully, "a moment ago, you spoke while you were under."

Did I?

I hadn't realized.

Dr. Patel studied me. Not judgmental. Just watching.

"You said, 'why are you calling for me?'"

A slow, sinking feeling pressed against my ribs.

"You said it like you were answering someone," she continued. "Like you heard someone calling your name."

My throat went dry.

Dr. Patel gave me a moment, then gently asked, "Did you recognize it?"

I didn't answer right away.

She angled her head slightly. "That pause you just did." She pointed between us, keeping her tone light but perceptive. "That's your mind hesitating. That's why I think there's more there. I don't think you forgot. I think you stopped yourself."

She slid my journal back across the desk.

"For this week, let's try something different," she said. "I want you to write more. Not just what happened, but how you feel. What your body remembers. The textures, the sounds, the details you try to brush off. Anytime you start to remember something. I think your mind is trying to protect you, but we have to teach it that it's safe to remember."

Safe.

That word felt like a joke.

But I didn't argue.

I grabbed the journal and stood, my legs shaky but steady enough.

"You did well today, Sophia."

I nodded vaguely, gripping the journal tight.

I knew what she meant. I'd gotten close.

But close wasn't enough.

I had heard my name.

Soft but sharp. Like a warning.

And I knew the voice.

I just didn't know what I was more afraid of. Who it belonged to.

Or why they sounded so desperate.

21

— • —

NOVEMBER 12, 2024, 2 PM - SOPHIA

18 DAYS AFTER JULIE WENT MISSING

Twenty-five minutes. Gone.

I blinked.

The bell was ringing. Students were already zipping their bags, pushing back their chairs, standing up to leave.

I had no memory of class even starting.

My notebook sat open in front of me, my own handwriting filling the margins, over and over:

Ordo.

Ordo.

Ordo.

Some letters were clean, some jagged, like I'd been pressing too hard into the page. Like I had been writing it the entire time.

I snapped the notebook shut and shoved it into my bag, heart slamming into my chest.

I couldn't be losing time again.

Not now.

Not with everything else.

This was not sustainable. I needed to—

My phone buzzed.

Two messages from Jay.

Jay: Hey... is everything okay? It feels like you've been dodging me this week.

Jay: I just want to know if you're okay. I heard you woke up on your roof last week.

I stared at them. And the 11 texts before them from the last few days.

How else would he know about the roof? Unless he was the one watching me.

The hallway was buzzing when I stepped out of class.

Lately, the whispers were getting worse.

First about Linworth.

He had been out for days and no one fully knew why.

I caught pieces of conversation as I moved through the crowd.

"...He didn't even show up for the morning staff meeting."

"...think they searched his place again?"

"...no way he's coming back."

I kept walking, tuned it out as I had been learning to do.

Then I heard Kenny and Billy.

"You hear about Jay and Stephen? Got into it last week. Supposedly bad."

"Stephen had a busted lip. Jay missed practice the next day. Coach was pissed."

"They said it was about some girl."

My skin prickled.

Some girl.

Julie? Me?

Then my name drifted into the mix.

"Do you think Sophia and Linworth both did it?"

"...you know the cops took her in."

"I can't believe she's still coming to school..."

I wanted to curl up into a ball of nothingness and disappear. But more than that, I wanted to defend myself.

But I knew disappearing was impossible and being defensive would make it worse.

So, I kept walking. One step, then the next.

That's when I heard Jessica. "I saw her outside my house like weeks ago. She is such a freak. Like just... standing there. The way a serial killer would."

Someone nearby inhaled sharply. A few heads turned. A shift in the atmosphere, like they *wanted* to believe it.

Samantha, a girl from my English class, said in a hushed voice, "You're kidding."

"Nope. And she looked like... dangerous. Totally out of her mind." Jessica laughed.

"She probably would say she doesn't remember doing it but, I think she does." Jessica added in fake horror.

A hand landed on my back twirling me around.

"Okay, *nope*. You, come with me."

I barely caught myself before slamming into a locker.

"Jesus, Abbie!" I gasped.

She ignored me, standing there with her arms crossed, looking like she had just decided my entire fate.

"Dude," she said, tilting her head, green eyes sharp with evaluation. "You look like you just saw a ghost. And I'm saying that as someone who knows your whole aesthetic is '*girl who haunts her own house.*'"

A startled laugh escaped before I could stop it. "Thanks?"

She nodded. "I mean, no offense. If I ever get murdered, I am summoning you as my creepy Victorian spirit guide."

"Good to know?"

"But until then." She pointed two fingers at me like she was casting a spell. "We are fixing *whatever* this is."

I frowned. "Abbie, I swear to—"

"Shut up, Whitaker." She grinned, all teeth. "We're buying so much sugar."

***

The convenience store greeted me with its usual charm, and Abbie had already bulldozed through half the candy aisle.

We'd been friends since elementary school, but Abbie was popular now. I kept waiting for her to realize she didn't need me anymore, especially with everything going on.

She waved a bag of Sour Patch Kids at me. "If you don't eat something horribly processed in the next ten minutes, I'm going to start getting concerned."

I grabbed a Kit Kat, arching a brow. "This better be life-changing."

"It will be. And also—" She grabbed a neon bottle of soda, shoving it into my hands. "Drink this."

I squinted at it. "It looks like radioactive waste."

She shrugged. "Tastes like liquid happiness."

I cracked it open, took a sip.

Immediately choked. "Oh my god. *What is this?!*"

Abbie took a long gulp of hers, totally unfazed. "Energy drink, I think? Maybe antifreeze. Who cares?"

"You *should* care!" I wheezed. "I think my esophagus is melting!"

"See!" She threw her arms out "That's a sign that it's working."

I huffed a laugh, shaking my head as I reached for a bag of Peanut M&Ms.

My fingers brushed against someone else's.

I pulled back, muttering a quick 'sorry' but when I glanced up—

I froze.

Mr. Calloway.

He didn't acknowledge me. Didn't even look in my direction. Just picked up his bag of candy, added it to his basket, and kept moving down the aisle like I wasn't even standing there.

But my eyes caught on something else.

The silver ring on his hand.

An oval-shaped insignia. An "X" carved into the center. Ordo etched right above it.

I knew that symbol.

I had seen it before, sketched in the margins of Julie's diary and in Calloway and Linworth's yearbook pictures. Even though I'd seen it in pictures and read about it... something about seeing Calloway now in real life, wearing the ring, made my throat go dry.

This wasn't just Julie's mystery anymore. This morning, I had written it. Over and over.

Ordo... the word had filled my notebook like a warning I didn't remember writing.

The symbol on Calloway's ring became an eye staring right at me. Seeping its deep, watchful glare into my skin, my soul.

A sharp chill crawled up my spine.

Julie thought it was a club. Was it? If it was and Calloway was wearing it now...

Did that mean it was active? I hadn't ever heard of it, not once. Which was, well, weird.

Linworth had worn the same ring.

And then, he stopped.

At least that's what it looked like from the yearbook photos. Freshman year, they stood side by side. By sophomore year, there was space between them.

Had something gone wrong?

I swallowed hard, my fingers tightening around the bag of M&Ms.

Julie had been looking into this. She thought it mattered.

What if she was right?

"Whitaker, what the hell are you looking at?"

Abbie waved a Kit Kat in front of my face, snapping me back to reality.

I blinked. Calloway was already at the register, chatting with Stephen, like it was any other afternoon.

Like it was nothing.

Like I hadn't seen something mysterious at all. But my instincts were telling me Julie was onto something.

"Nothing," I muttered, grabbing my candy and heading for the checkout.

Stephen rang us up without saying much, but he didn't stop staring at me. It felt too direct, too aware. His lip was fully busted open, just like I heard at school.

Abbie turned up the radio way too loud as she pulled out of the parking lot playing 'Shake it Off' by Taylor Swift, which is the epitome of what I needed to do right now.

I took another sip of my toxic neon liquid and winced. "This better not actually kill me."

"That would be an embarrassing obituary." She tossed a Twizzler at me. "Like: *local girl tragically murdered by off-brand Mountain Dew, warning all local teens to start drinking off-brand Coca Cola instead.*"

I snorted, shoving the Twizzler in my mouth. "Could be worse."

She pointed dramatically. "It *could* be worse! And that's exactly why we are here, consuming unsafe levels of sugar and caffeine. Because you, my friend, are spiraling."

I rolled my eyes. "I'm not spiraling."

"You *are* spiraling."

"I'm fine."

"Whitaker. You've been sleepwalking outside." She waved a Butterfinger at me like it was evidence. "And you haven't even blinked at a Snickers bar in three weeks."

I sighed, rubbing my temple. "I eat normal food, Abbie."

"Do you? Do you?!"

"Yes?"

She turned her most judgmental stare on me. "Name one normal thing you've eaten in the last forty-eight hours."

I opened my mouth. Paused.

She gasped. "You can't! Oh my god, I knew it! You're actually a ghost. You died last month, and no one told you!"

"You're ridiculous," I groaned.

"Don't worry, babe, I'll still be your best friend when you fully cross over. But first—candy."

I shook my head, but I was smiling now.

***

One horror movie marathon later, I had eaten so much sugar that I could practically feel it replacing my bloodstream.

We tried to act tough through the first *Saw* movie. But by the second, we were clutching each other on the couch.

And by the third?

I was texting Eli to make sure he was still alive, and Abbie was demanding a detailed account of how secure the locks were in my house.

"You know what we should do?" she said, popping another Sour Patch Kid into her mouth. "Buy a taser."

"Oh, for sure."

"And maybe a crossbow."

I nodded solemnly. "I'd feel safest if I had access to a medieval weapon at all times."

"Right? Just imagine walking to your car with a full-on crossbow strapped to your back. No one would even look at you weird."

I exhaled a laugh, stretching out on the couch. For the first time all day, I felt almost normal.

Even after Abbie insisted I stay over, I declined. I hadn't slept over since my sleepwalking started... and besides, I liked the walk home at night. My house was just a few minutes away.

I stuffed my hands into my pockets, letting the cold air clear my head.

For a few blocks, it worked.

Then I passed by Julie's house, noticing a light on in the back side window. My heart sank a little. I bet that's her room.

I'm not sure why, but I feel like I've been there.

I shook my whole body, forcing myself to count each step in sets of 8 as a distraction.

After a few minutes I was starting to shake the knot in my chest but when I reached my street, the feeling hit me again.

Like someone was watching.

I slowed slightly, scanning the darkened windows, the shadowed porches, the empty driveways. Nothing out of place.

And yet—my skin prickled.

I swallowed hard, shaking it off.

Probably just the *Saw* movies messing with me.

Probably.

Then my stomach full-on plummeted as my eyes landed on the black car parked across the street.

Newton.

He was just sitting there.

Not getting out. Not making a move.

I kept walking but my eyes stayed fixed on the car.

Newton had already questioned me. Already asked about the phone call. Already made it clear he was suspicious.

So, what was he doing here now?

And since he was here, why wasn't he coming to talk to me?

22

—·—

18 DAYS AFTER JULIE WENT MISSING

I didn't expect anyone to be in the kitchen.

The door had barely clicked shut behind me when I saw them. Eli leaned against the counter like it was any normal night while Jay was perched on one of the barstools like he belonged there.

Like nothing had changed.

But everything had.

My feet stopped. Just stopped.

Jay looked up at the sound. His eyes locked on mine, steady, unreadable. My chest tightened like something was pulling it inward. He wasn't supposed to be here. Not anymore.

"Hey," Eli said casually. "Jay swung by. Figured you two might want to talk."

Talk.

My mouth went dry. Eli didn't know. He had no idea how twisted things had gotten in my head. How I'd spent the last week dissecting every memory I had of Jay. Splitting them open, trying to figure out what he was hiding. Trying to figure out if I ever really knew him at all.

Jay shifted in his seat.

He was wearing a plain black hoodie, soft at the edges, sleeves pushed up to the elbows. The fabric clung just enough to show his forearms, stronger than I remembered. Defined. Not big, but lean. Like every line meant something. My pulse stuttered, unsteady.

What was that?

It startled me. How suddenly aware I was of him. Of his body. Of the air between us. When had that started?

113

He was my friend. For over a year now. Just Jay. Easy to be around. The kind of guy I used to lean on without thinking.

But now...

Now the way he was looking at me—quiet and searching—it made my throat close. It made me feel like the ground might shift beneath me.

Something in my chest fluttered.

I didn't know if it was attraction or fear or both. I wasn't sure I could tell the difference anymore.

Maybe that was the most dangerous part.

Did he know I saw him that night?

That I thought it was him, standing in the dark?

Was it even him?

Why did it feel like the air was shifting?

Eli had no clue. He just gave us a lazy smile and pushed off the counter.

"I'll give you guys space," he said, already heading for the stairs. "Try not to make it weird."

Too late.

Jay stood slowly. And now that he was standing, I could feel the full weight of him. Not physically—emotionally. Like he took up more space than anyone else ever could.

"Want to go upstairs?" he asked.

His voice was gentle.

I nodded, because I didn't know what else to do.

As I turned, I could feel him behind me. Not too close. Just enough. Quiet. Steady. Like gravity. My skin prickled.

I stepped into my room first. Jay followed.

Then the door clicked shut behind us.

I turned.

He was right there.

Not touching me. But close. Inches away.

Jay leaned back slightly to give me room. His jaw was tight, that little muscle ticking. His hair was messier than usual, like he'd been dragging his hands through it. There were bruises on his knuckles, faint but fresh.

It was his eyes that made my chest ache. Usually crystal blue, they looked like a storm now. Dark, unreadable, but... open. Wounded. Like he was bracing for something and trying not to flinch.

And even now, even with everything, I felt that pull.

It was so stupid. So helpless. My brain screamed that he might not be safe. That I didn't know who he really was.

But my body didn't care.

My heart didn't either.

"Soph," he said gently. "What's going on?"

I crossed my arms. Part protection. Part anchor. Mostly just to keep from unraveling.

"Were you watching me?"

His brows pulled. "What?"

"The night I woke up on the roof," I said, louder now. "Were you there?"

Jay shook his head. "No. Of course not."

"Don't lie to me."

"I'm not."

My heart was in my throat.

"Then how did you know? That I woke up there?"

He looked down. "Someone said something. At school. I... I wanted to check on you."

I didn't answer. I couldn't.

Because what if he was telling the truth?

And what if he wasn't?

My voice shook. "What happened to your brother, Jay?"

His eyes darted down. "You know what happened."

"I know that he died." I stepped back once, he flinched like I'd slapped him. "I'm asking what happened."

He didn't speak.

I waited. The silence stretched.

"Stephen said—"

"Stephen is a psychopath," Jay snapped. "He manipulates people. He twists things."

"Don't turn this on someone else," I said, my voice sharper than I expected. "I'm not asking what Stephen thinks. I'm asking you."

His hands curled into fists at his sides. Then, slowly, he unclenched them and dragged in a breath. It looked painful.

"I didn't mean for it to happen," he said finally. "It wasn't. It wasn't what..." His voice cracked.

"Jay." I took another breath. "If you don't tell me, then I'm left with what other people say—" I faltered. "I just need to understand."

Jay turned away, hand dragging down his face like he was scraping off something he couldn't stand to wear anymore. Then he looked back at me, and his face was different. Not guarded. Just raw. Like something cracked open, and he couldn't shut it.

"I was fifteen," he said. "He took me to my first high school party."

He paused, glancing up toward the ceiling like he was searching for the right thread to pull.

"There was a bonfire. Out past the quarry. Kind of hidden, tucked behind the woods. People were drinking, joking around. I hadn't even had a sip before that night—was trying to play it cool."

He swallowed hard. His fingers twitched at his sides.

"It started dumb. Just me and Joel acting like idiots. We were arm wrestling. Talking trash. He dared me to jump over the fire. So I did. Burned my jeans. Everyone laughed."

There was a flicker of something, bittersweet and hollow, on his lips.

"Then I said... I said, 'Bet you won't cannonball into the quarry.'" He winced. "Not serious. Just mouthing off. Stupid."

I didn't move. Just listened. Held still like the moment might shatter if I breathed too loud.

"But he looked at me," Jay went on, "and then he grinned. Took off running. Toward the high edge. Not from the part we'd jumped earlier that summer. This was higher. And steeper."

His voice dipped.

"I yelled. Tried to stop him. Grabbed his arm. Told him to quit being a showoff, that I didn't mean it. But he just laughed. Shoved me back. Said something like, 'Watch this.' And then..."

Jay blinked. Once. Twice.

"He jumped."

Silence swallowed the room.

"I thought he was messing with me," he said. "He always did that. I waited to see his head come back up. But it didn't. Just... waves. The sound of people laughing behind me."

Jay's voice thinned to a whisper.

"I still thought he was joking. But I didn't see him. Not even a ripple. Just black water."

He shook his head, fast. Like he wanted it out.

"I dove in. And the second I hit that water, it was ice. It stole everything. My breath, my balance. I scraped my arm on a rock, but I didn't feel it. Just kept going under, again and again, screaming his name. But I couldn't see anything."

His voice was almost a whisper.

"I stayed in until the squad came. Twenty-five minutes. They dragged me out. Said I was lucky I didn't drown too. Joel..." His voice broke. "They found him right after. Said it was his neck. He never had a chance."

"I killed him, Sophia." His eyes met mine. Shiny. Broken. "I dared him. I watched him run. I didn't stop it."

I wanted to say something, anything, but nothing fit.

"Even when I was questioned I never told anyone the full thing," he said. "People say I was brave. That I tried to save him. But I wasn't brave. I was just a dumb kid with a big mouth and a brother who thought he was invincible."

Jay stared at the floor again. His next words were barely audible.

"I swear I still see him sometimes."

He finally looked back at me, like he was bracing for impact.

But I didn't move.

Because I knew that look. That weight. That quiet ache that only people carrying ghosts understood.

Jay was haunted.

Just like me.

We stood there.

The silence felt dense. Like something alive between us.

Jay had just told me the worst night of his life, and he had told only me.

I couldn't stop thinking about the way his voice had broken. The way he'd looked when he said he killed his brother. Not like he wanted sympathy. Like he thought he didn't deserve any.

The weight of what he gave me didn't fit in words. It barely fit in silence.

I stepped closer.

My hand moved before I even knew what I was doing. Reaching for him, needing to feel something solid. My fingers grazed his.

He didn't pull away.

His hand shifted, brushing mine back, tentative, warm. Like he didn't trust it. Like he didn't trust himself.

He looked up at me.

And there was something different in his eyes. Exposed.

I wasn't just looking at Jay anymore. I was looking at every piece of him he'd tried to bury.

The boy who jumped in after his brother.

The boy who'd carried that weight alone ever since.

I swallowed hard.

We were inches apart now, standing in this fragile quiet where everything felt like too much. My pulse raced for a dozen reasons I couldn't name.

And for a breath of a second, I thought...

He might kiss me.

Part of me wanted him to.

But a louder part, the part that was still scared, still sorting the truth, froze.

I stepped back.

Not far. Just enough.

"I can't," I said, the words catching in my throat. "Not right now."

Jay nodded. Like he already knew.

"I get it," he said.

But there was something in the way he said it that made my chest ache.

Because even though he got it, even though he wasn't pushing me, he still looked like he was waiting for the moment I'd change my mind. Like part of him didn't believe he deserved anything better than being left standing there.

"I'm glad you told me," I said. Quiet. Honest.

His eyes met mine, and in them, I saw it.

That same thing I felt.

23

NOVEMBER 13, 2024, 2:30 PM - SOPHIA

19 DAYS AFTER JULIE WENT MISSING

The next time I saw Newton, he was in Calloway's classroom.

I slowed as I passed. The door was cracked open just enough for me to catch their voices.

"*...ethics reviews...*"

What were they talking about?

I couldn't make out anything else, it was just too quiet. So I slipped a little bit closer to the door.

That's when I heard Newton again.

"When was the last time you had to defend your job?"

A pause.

"It wasn't criminal," Calloway said. "It wasn't misconduct."

My breath caught. My hand hovered near the doorframe.

"Rachel Caldwell. She was one of your students, right?" Newton said.

Another pause, longer this time. I leaned in.

"She hasn't been back since she ran. You remember her now?"

Calloway's voice came soft, almost amused. "I remember her."

That was when his gaze slid past Newton, straight to me.

It didn't happen right away. It was slow. Like he was already expecting to see me there.

I stiffened.

"Can I help you, Miss Whitaker?"

His voice was polite. But there was something in his gaze. A weight, a warning.

I wasn't supposed to be here.

And he wanted me to know it.

I kept walking as my heart skittered but I kept my expression blank. I even forced my pace to stay steady.

But I knew, I'd made a mistake.

Because Calloway wasn't the only one watching.

I turned the corner and nearly collided with Stephen.

Wait.

I had turned the corner.

Hadn't I?

Just for a flicker of a second, I could've sworn I'd already passed this spot. That I had already stepped into the hallway. Hadn't I just seen this locker with the smiley face magnet? These posters?

My stomach twisted. No. That didn't make sense.

But for half a second, it was like time had looped back on itself.

And then Stephen was there, too close, like he had been waiting for me to run into him.

His lips curled slightly, a smirk that didn't reach his eyes.

After what I'd read about him in Julie's diary, I felt a wave of unease every time I saw him, though it might be misplaced.

His jet-black hair was spiked up with too much gel. He was wearing grey chinos and a plaid button-down shirt. He looked more like a teacher than a student.

"Careful," he murmured, voice low enough for only me to hear. "You never know who's watching."

His eyes darted past me, toward Calloway's room, then back. He was putting something together. I could see it.

Stephen just smiled. Not his usual smirk, something tighter. Like he knew something I didn't.

"You're really bad at blending in, you know," he added, tone almost amused.

I didn't react. Just pushed past him, my pulse thudding too fast.

When I walked a few lockers away I looked back. He was still staring at me.

The rest of the day passed in a blur. By the time the last bell rang, I already knew what I was going to do.

I just wasn't sure I should do it.

Calloway's classroom was empty. I lingered outside for a second, listening, knowing this was my last chance to back out.

I didn't.

I chewed on the inside of my cheek.

Newton was closing in.

If he figured things out first, I'd be stuck playing catch-up.

And Calloway. Calloway was part of this.

The insignia on his ring. The ethics review I overheard. The way he never quite looked surprised to see me.

I needed to know what he was hiding.

The hallway was empty. Now was the time.

I twisted the door handle, and it was locked.

Of course, it was.

That's my sign to walk away.

I should turn around and forget I ever thought about this.

But... I can't.

I reached into my hair, fishing out a bobby pin, twisting the end between my fingers.

I could do this.

I'd done it before.

Once.

I smirked thinking back to Eli's room break in. His secret candy stash under the bed. I had been so pissed when he stole my last Snickers bar, so I spent an hour watching YouTube tutorials, learning how to break in and steal something from him.

That had been easy.

This?

This was different.

Maybe I was getting too bold.

I crouched, sliding the pin into the lock. Slow. Steady. The mechanism inside was stiffer than I expected.

Come on.

I twisted the pin, feeling for resistance. Nothing. I adjusted my grip, teeth grinding.

Click.

The lock gave. My stomach flipped.

I slipped inside and eased the door shut behind me.

I tugged at the desk drawers. Locked. All of them.

Seriously? Who locks every single drawer?

I moved to the filing cabinets near the back. Also locked.

Fine.

I bent the pin again and got to work. One by one, I popped them open.

The first drawer was useless—just a bunch of graded quizzes.

The next was a binder full of lesson plans.

In the bottom drawer there was nothing at all.

Disappointment flooded through me.

Maybe I was being too desperate to find something. Too sure about Calloway.

I heard a noise.

I froze.

In the hallway?

I couldn't tell.

I felt each hair on my arm stand at attention as I dropped to the floor, pressing myself as far under the desk as possible.

The footsteps grew louder.

But faded away.

I held my breath. Counting in my head.

By the time I got to 30 I exhaled and looked up.

There was a faint carving.

At first, I thought it was just scratches, a jagged indent in the wood, nearly invisible in this lighting.

But when I leaned my head, when I ran my fingers over the rough edges, there was the oval with the X through the center.

My eyes widened.

The symbol. The one from Julie's journal.

I turned toward the door to leave.

Paused.

I knew if I didn't leave, the next set of footsteps could actually walk in.

But my fingers were already reaching for the last drawer. I couldn't help myself.

The only one I hadn't opened yet.

It would just take a second.

The insignia had to mean something. Something was in there.

I bent the pin again, slotting it into the lock, hands moist from nerves.

The lock turned.

Slowly I pulled it open.

Just more files, more useless school forms.

I dug through to the bottom of the stack.

There was an odd-looking page. It was yellowed at the edges which stood out in the contrasting white documents. The ink faded just enough to tell me it had been printed years ago.

Formation of The Circle Charter—Ordinance High, 2014.

I scanned the rest.

Faculty sponsors:

- Mr. Calloway (A.P. Biology)

- Mr. Linworth (A.P. Literature)

- Two other names I didn't know.

At the bottom: a stamped insignia. Oval with an X through the center.

I traced the date. 2014.

A decade ago.

Before I ever set foot in this school.

Before Julie disappeared.

This wasn't some rumored club. This was sanctioned. Real.

Calloway had been part of it. From the beginning. So had Linworth.

Why had no one ever mentioned this?

Why did Julie think Linworth was afraid of it?

It looked normal. But it couldn't be. Not with this level of secrecy.

Something was buried in this.

I pulled out my phone and snapped a photo under the dull glow of Calloway's lamp.

I turned to put the paper back, then paused.

Something white was stuck to the bottom of the drawer.

I peeled it loose. The tape ripped some of the color off, but it was still clear enough.

A Polaroid.

Of me.

At Julie's vigil.

My mouth was open, mid-sentence— like I was talking to someone just out of frame.

I was holding a candle burned so low the flame nearly touched my skin.

But there was no one else in the photo.

Just me—with too much space around me.

And it had been hidden underneath The Circle's charter.

A hollowness filled my stomach.

Why would Calloway have this?

Was he taking photos of me? Watching?

A shadow stretched across the floor underneath the door.

I stuffed the photo back in the drawer. I stepped back, my shoe barely making a sound on the floor.

Someone was standing in the doorway.

My pulse hammered so hard I could feel it in my throat.

I couldn't make out the face, not yet, but the silhouette was tall, unmoving, blocking my only way out.

For a second, neither of us moved.

I held my breath.

"Turn around," a voice ordered, low and firm.

My heart stopped.

Shit.

24

NOVEMBER 13, 2024, 4:30 PM - NEWTON

19 DAYS AFTER JULIE WENT MISSING

I saw her break into Linworth's house.

I saw her sneak out.

And now?

She was at it again.

Sophia Whitaker had a hell of a habit for being exactly where she shouldn't be.

This time, it was Calloway's classroom.

I caught sight of her through the narrow glass window as I passed. She wasn't just hanging around. She was searching for something. Her back was turned, shoulders stiff, head dipped toward Calloway's desk, her phone screen glowing in the dim light.

I had seen that look before.

I pushed open the door.

She didn't flinch. Didn't jump.

I shut the door behind me, hard. The knob rattled slightly.

"Really?" I said flatly. "I thought we just had this talk."

Sophia had her arms crossed behind her back, looking like she was concealing something. But her face was calm.

She was assessing.

"You following me?" she asked, tilting her head.

I smiled without humor. "If I was, you wouldn't have made it this far." I nodded toward her phone. "Let me guess. You were just 'borrowing' school property?"

She crossed her arms. "I'm not stealing anything."

"No? Just standing alone in a teacher's office after school for the scenery?"

She studied me like she was trying to calculate my next move. Her fingers tightened around her phone.

"You think I don't know how this works?" she murmured.

"I give you something," she continued, voice calm, controlled. "And in return, you keep treating me like I'm guilty."

"Whitaker—"

"Just admit it," she pressed. "I could show you proof I didn't have anything to do with Julie, and you'd still be looking at me like I had something to hide."

My jaw tensed.

Because she wasn't wrong.

She exhaled sharply, then, finally, set the phone on Calloway's desk and pushed it forward.

"Look for yourself."

I glanced down.

It looked like a school document.

"Formation of 'The Circle' Charter – Ordinance High, 2014."

A strange symbol.

A list of faculty sponsors: Calloway, Linworth, Hubert, and Toya.

Hubert and Toya had both skipped town at the same time a few years ago.

I kept my face neutral, but my mind was already moving ahead of me.

My jaw tightened as I read the bottom.

"Funded by the Department of Community & Education Resources."

There was no Department of Community & Education Resources.

I'd looked into every single publicly available board, committee, and funding source tied to this school when I pulled Calloway's ethics review.

But that didn't mean it never existed. It could have been defunct. Rebranded. Merged into something else.

I did another quick search as a sanity check. Nothing.

One thing was for sure, this wasn't something Calloway wanted anyone to find.

Which meant Sophia wasn't supposed to see it.

And neither was I.

I smiled thinking back to Calloway's smug evasions.

I studied Sophia's face, watching closely.

There was no way she knew what she had.

But I did.

I pulled out my phone and tapped it three times. "Send it to me."

She hesitated. "And then what?"

I raised a brow. "Then I handle it, Whitaker. Like I should've been doing before you decided to play detective."

Her expression hardened. I wrote my number down on the back of a gas station receipt and handed it to her.

She took it, but scoffed. "You're not handling it. You're questioning me while the whole town turns against me."

I tensed.

She continued, voice sharp. "Ever since you pulled me in, they think I did something. And I'm not just going to sit back and let that happen."

Her words hit me in a way I wasn't expecting.

People accused me of a lot over my time as Sheriff. Mostly garbage lies.

But this? It wasn't.

Because she wasn't wrong. Ever since I pulled her in, the town had turned.

And I hadn't done a damn thing to stop it.

I could feel the weight of that choice in the silence. The part I didn't want to acknowledge.

The truth is, she wasn't some grieving best friend.

She wasn't some helpless victim.

She was in this. I just didn't know how deep.

And yeah, I still believed she was holding something back. But did I believe Sophia Whitaker murdered Julie Greene?

I didn't know.

And that was the problem.

Because the town wasn't unsure.

They had already made up their minds.

And I had let them.

She wasn't just pissed.

She was backed into a corner.

And people who feel trapped?

They do desperate things.

My eyes locked on hers.

Then I looked back at the document on her phone.

I had a lot of dead ends in this case. But this wasn't one of them. This was an actual lead.

"Just send me the picture, Sophia." I said, tapping my foot as she huffed a breath squinting at the receipt.

"You've got horrible handwriting," she said as my phone dinged with her incoming message.

I gestured toward the door. "Go home, Whitaker."

She didn't move right away. But after a moment, she left.

I unlocked my phone and traced my finger over the picture on my screen, reading the charter again.

Faculty-sponsored. Formal. And completely absent from any record I'd seen.

I'd reviewed programming logs and activity listings when I opened Calloway's ethics file. Nothing about The Circle. Nothing about the Department of Community & Education Resources.

This should've come up.

Unless I missed it.

Or it was buried.

I'd been here before.

Rachel Caldwell. Eighteen. Talked about leaving town. Wanted out. She wasn't like Julie, didn't have a perfect life, a perfect family. She just wanted something different.

And then she was gone.

Her friends hesitated when I asked if she could have run away. Then they said yes. Because Rachel had changed. Because she talked about leaving. And then she did.

No forced entry. No missing money. No suspicious texts or calls. Just a note.

"I need to leave. I can't stay here. It's not anyone's fault. I just have to go."

Clean. Concise.

Her parents fought it. Pushed me to dig deeper. But legally? She was an adult. And everything pointed to her leaving willingly.

So, I let it go.

Because all the facts said she ran. Because I had nothing to prove otherwise. Because following the rules, doing it right, meant I couldn't chase something that wasn't there.

And now?

Her parents still looked at me like I was supposed to bring her home. Like if I'd just looked a little harder, I could've found her before she was gone for good.

Maybe they were right.

Maybe I should have looked harder.

Maybe if I had, Rachel Caldwell wouldn't be a ghost in her own town.

I pulled out my phone and called Jenkins.

"Yeah?"

"I need you to pull everything on Ordinance High," I said. "Full financial records for all club and program funding. Discretionary, external, enrichment. Anything tied to The Circle. From 2014 to now."

He paused. "All of it?"

"Everything. Especially anything under the name Department of Community & Education Resources, or anything that looks like it was routed through a front."

"That's... vague. What's this tied to?"

"A club," I said. "Faculty-run. Funded. And now it doesn't exist."

Another pause. "You think it's fake?"

"I think if it isn't, it's been buried. And I don't like either option."

He let out a slow breath. "I'll start pulling."

"Do it quietly. And fast."

"You know this kind of thing takes time."

"How much?"

He paused. I could almost hear him flipping through timelines in his head. "Could be two weeks."

"Two weeks?" My jaw clenched. "The state can process a speeding ticket in three hours, but this takes half a damn month?"

Jenkins sighed again. "You want it fast, or do you want it to actually count for something when this blows up?"

I exhaled sharply.

This was going to be a long game.

And the long game's a problem when there's already a body in the ground.

Calloway wasn't just a name on a page—he was part of something designed to be forgotten.

And now I wanted to know why.

25

- · -

NOVEMBER 14, 2024, 2:30 PM - NEWTON

20 DAYS AFTER JULIE WENT MISSING

I didn't have proof yet, not without the records Jenkins was pulling, but everything kept pointing back to Calloway.

His was the first name on The Circle charter. A supposedly funded group. Now wiped from every record I could find.

And the kicker?

He'd already survived one school ethics complaint. It just disappeared in a week. No investigation. No follow-up.

Just a polished denial. A glowing letter from the superintendent, and silence.

The kind of clean that means someone's cleaning for you.

Right on schedule, Calloway walked out of school and slid into his blue Mustang.

I followed just far enough behind.

Calloway pulled into the hardware store, his turn signal blinking lazily before he eased into a parking space.

Mr. Thompson gave him an easy nod. A few casual words. Effortless, like muscle memory. Years of trust will do that. He was the well-liked teacher, after all. The good guy. Everyone said so.

I parked two spaces away, leaning back slightly.

Through the front window, I could see Calloway browsing, lingering long enough for it to look normal.

He hesitated near the end of an aisle, fingers tapping lightly on a shelf before picking something up. It was subtle, but enough to make me take note.

He slipped down an aisle and out of view.

I drummed my fingers on the wheel.

A few minutes later, he reappeared at the counter, laughing at something Mr. Thompson said. The sound carried faintly through the door when he pushed it open. Relaxed. Friendly. Like any other customer.

He waved on his way out, two bags in hand.

I watched him walk to his car.

I ran my tongue over my teeth.

It all looked normal. But the way he lingered just a little too long, like he was hitting his marks instead of moving through his day? He was hiding something.

His next stop was Carmichael's Grocery, a family-run staple that had been in town for nearly fifty years. The produce section always smelled faintly of oranges, and their daughter Jessica usually handled the cash register when she wasn't in school.

That girl had a sugar-coated mean streak. She'd smile at you while scanning your groceries, then turn around and start a rumor before you even made it to the parking lot.

Calloway wasn't in there long. A few minutes, tops. He walked out carrying a single brown paper bag, tucked neatly under his arm.

As he reached his car, I saw Mrs. Evers struggling to load groceries into her trunk. One of her cans, which looked like soup, slipped free, hit the pavement, and started to roll.

Calloway chased it down without hesitation. Bent to grab it before it could slip under a nearby car, then walked it back to her with an easy smile.

Mrs. Evers beamed, patted his arm like he was one of her best friends, and said something that made him chuckle.

He waved it off like it was nothing.

I flexed my fingers once, slow. Rolled my shoulders like that would shake off the way my instincts were kicking up.

I followed Calloway to the edge of town.

The strip mall was mostly closed down, only a few places still open. A pawn shop, a vape shop, a Dollar Tree. The rest was just boarded-up windows, peeling siding, and a parking lot held together by hope and faded yellow paint.

Calloway pulled in, but instead of parking out front, he drove around back.

I frowned.

Not outright suspicious. But not normal, either.

I pulled into a spot near the strip mall entrance.

I got out, moving casually, cutting through the nearly empty lot until I reached the side of the vape shop. The brick was warm from the sun earlier, but the temperature had dropped.

I leaned against the wall, far enough around the corner that I could see Calloway's Mustang without being obvious.

He wasn't moving.

He was sitting there.

Waiting.

A minute passed.

Then another.

My interest started to wane, until a second car pulled in.

A glossy black Audi A4. It had sharp lines and an aggressive grille, the kind of car that looked more at home outside a country club than a half-dead strip mall.

I recognized it.

The Burns family.

It was Stephen's car.

He was the most frequent volunteer outside of Julie's parents for the search parties. Knew how to make people like him.

I'd seen Stephen work a room before. When I pulled security at school events, he was the type who'd float between groups, chatting up teachers like they were his peers, shaking hands with the adults, always knowing exactly when to laugh.

The kind of kid people liked because he made them feel important.

And now?

Stephen walked straight over, handed Calloway a plain white envelope. Not thick, but stretched at the seams, like it had been filled with something barely able to fit inside.

Calloway took it like he already knew what was in it.

Then Stephen pulled something else from his coat pocket, a flash drive.

Held it between two fingers.

Didn't give it up right away.

He said something else. Slower this time.

Calloway waited.

Then nodded.

Only then did Stephen pass it over.

Calloway slipped both into his bag.

Something was... wrong. Calloway didn't just respect Stephen. He deferred to him.

And that—that didn't make any damn sense.

Stephen? He didn't look like a kid in over his head.

He looked like someone used to being listened to.

The exchange didn't look like it was for the first time.

It was coordination.

Planned. Rehearsed.

Whatever this was though—Calloway, Stephen, quiet exchanges behind strip malls—it wasn't about Julie.

So why had Linworth sent me here?

Because he panicked? Because he was stalling? Or because he wanted me looking in the wrong direction?

He said Julie was looking into something, and that I should talk to Calloway.

I had. And yeah, Calloway looked dirty. But more in the money-laundering way, not the murder kind.

Julie didn't fit the scene.

So was this ever about her?

Or did Linworth just need me far enough away not to see what he was hiding?

26

—‧—

NOVEMBER 14, 2024, 6 PM - NEWTON

20 DAYS AFTER JULIE WENT MISSING

Linworth hadn't been seen in town for days.

But his lights were still on. He wasn't gone—just hiding.

I parked two houses down, killed the engine, and walked up the drive.

I knocked.

No answer.

Knocked again, harder.

He didn't come.

I banged my fist against the door one more time. Louder. Enough to make sure he knew I wasn't leaving.

There was shuffling inside.

Then, finally, the lock clicked.

Linworth cracked the door open an inch. He looked terrible—thin, hollow-eyed. His face pale, like he hadn't seen sunlight in days, hair slicked with grease. He was wearing plaid pajama bottoms and a plain white T-shirt that had a coffee stain in the middle.

"Where did you park?" His voice was low. Shaky.

I arched a brow, watching his reaction. "Down the street?"

He exhaled, tension easing just slightly, but not enough.

His fingers pressed into the doorframe, tense. He swallowed hard, then let his eyes dart past me, scanning the street with a nervous flick.

Like he was expecting someone.

"Go away."

I pushed the door open before he could shut it. Stepped inside like I belonged there.

Linworth stumbled back, caught off guard. "You can't just—"

"I can," I said flatly, shutting the door behind me. "And I will."

134

The place reeked of must and stale air. Linworth hadn't been outside in a while, didn't seem like he had showered either.

He stood stiffly in the dim light, fingers digging into his sleeves like he was trying to hold himself together.

He kept glancing at the window.

Every few seconds, his fingers twitched toward the curtain, pulling it back barely enough to peer outside.

He didn't just look scared. He looked trapped.

"I already told you everything," he muttered.

"No," I said. "You didn't."

I took a slow step forward, lowering my voice just enough to make the walls close in.

"I know about The Circle."

A muscle twitched in his cheek, his breath slowing slightly.

I pulled my phone from my pocket. Tapped the screen once. Pulled up the photo of the charter.

"Your name's on it."

His fingers curled against his sleeves, gripping the fabric tightly. "It... it was just a mentorship program," he stammered.

"Right," I said. "Because mentorship programs have fake funding and laundered money."

His weight shifted, his eyes darting away. I didn't need anything more.

I didn't know for sure if money was moving. Not yet. But I wanted to see if he did.

I pressed on.

"You were in it. So was Calloway."

His face gave him away before his mouth could.

Calloway was dirty, but I still didn't see how that related to Julie. And I knew he knew more.

I narrowed my eyes. "How is Julie tied to this?"

Linworth's fingers twitched at his sleeves. "I don't—"

I stepped closer. Just enough to let the pressure settle.

"You don't what?" I asked. "You don't know? Or you don't want to say?"

Silence.

Linworth's jaw locked. He wasn't going to talk.

Fine.

I changed tactics.

I sighed, shaking my head. "You know what I think? I think you sent me to Calloway hoping I'd waste my time. Hoping I'd chase something that had nothing to do with Julie."

His posture stiffened.

I leaned in slightly.

"But here's the thing, Linworth. Julie was found buried behind YOUR house."

His chest rose in a quick, uneven jerk.

"Why did Julie keep showing up at your office?" I asked loudly.

He froze.

"You think I don't know? People saw her, Linworth. She was asking you something. Over and over again. YOU told me she was asking questions. And now she's dead."

He scrunched his entire face.

"I—I told her to stop."

"Stop what?"

He shook his head, shoulders curling inward. "I c-can't... I shouldn't".

"What was she asking you, Linworth?"

A long, dragging moment of hesitation.

Then, his voice dropped, barely above a whisper.

"She was in The Circle."

He swallowed hard.

I stiffened.

That hadn't been what I was expecting.

Julie wasn't just looking into The Circle.

She was part of it.

I let the facts settle. Turn them over in my head.

A mentorship program.

That's what he called it.

But mentorship programs don't make you look scared shitless.

I narrowed my eyes. "You're telling me Julie joined a school mentorship club... and that somehow got her killed?"

Linworth's fingers twitched. He wouldn't look at me.

He didn't need to.

I stepped in closer, my face only a few inches away from his. "No. That's not it."

I pressed harder.

"What did she find, Linworth?"

"I don't know." The words tumbled out too fast. Too evasive.

Bullshit.

I leaned in even closer. "You're lying."

Linworth's hands clenched. For the first time since I walked in, I saw something flitter behind his eyes that wasn't fear. Guilt.

Julie found something. And whatever it was, whatever it meant, she never got the chance to tell anyone.

I pressed one last time.

"Did she confront Calloway?"

Linworth's entire body went rigid.

He opened his mouth.

Just as fast, he shut it again.

His breathing picked up, sharp and uneven. He shook his head. "I can't—I can't do this."

I didn't move. Didn't blink.

"What did Calloway do to her?"

Linworth turned away from me.

I changed angles, stepping in front of him again.

"What about Stephen?"

Linworth's breathing stopped.

Just for a second.

Then he inhaled sharp, resembling someone that had just touched a live wire.

His entire body stiffened, like I'd just said the kind of name that gets you hexed in a fantasy novel.

I stepped in closer. "What does Stephen have to do with this?"

Linworth's face was pale, blanched.

And then, he panicked.

His hand shot out, gripping my arm, his fingers ice cold.

"You have to leave."

"Linworth—"

"Now."

I didn't move.

His grip tightened. His voice dropped to a whisper, shaking.

"You sh-shouldn't have c-come here."

I stared at him as he tried to drag me to the door.

And then, he looked right at me and said quietly, "I can't help you."

I stepped back, pulling my arm free.

Linworth turned away, hands bracing against the wall, his breathing coming out in rapid bursts.

I watched him for another beat.

Then I walked out.

I didn't need him to say anything else.

Stephen.

Linworth wasn't scared of Calloway. He was scared of Stephen.

But why?

27

─ • ─

NOVEMBER 15, 2024, 7 PM - SOPHIA

21 DAYS AFTER JULIE WENT MISSING

The whole town had shown up for the football game.

The scoreboard glowed against the night, casting flashes of red across the bleachers. But tonight wasn't just about school spirit, it was about distraction. Something to fill the space. Something that wasn't Julie Greene.

Or me.

Abbie shoved a hot pretzel into my hands like it was some kind of life-saving device.

"Here. Eat. Let the carbs do their job."

I sighed, peeling a piece off. "This isn't a hostage situation, you know."

I knew what she was doing. The incident with Jessica had spread all over school. I had heard it retold, felt the stares. Abbie had too. Principal Tinson even called me into her office to "talk."

But none of it compared to what was stuck in my head now...

A photo of me at Julie's vigil.

That I didn't remember being taken.

Mid-sentence, talking to someone I couldn't see.

In Calloway's desk.

I hadn't told anyone. Not even Abbie.

Instead, I let her pull me toward the bleachers and into her world of normalcy.

"Sure it is," she said breezily, looping her arm through mine and steering me toward the bleachers. "I saw you lurking in the halls today, looking like you were solving a murder, which is your usual vibe, but it's practically holiday season, Sophia. We are doing something normal for once."

Her tone was light, but there was something sharper underneath.

She was worried.

Not just about the school's reaction to me. Not just about Jessica.

She had known something was up with me for a while. And Abbie, for all her jokes and sugar-fueled energy, was good at knowing when to push and when to back off.

Tonight, she was pushing.

And maybe... maybe I needed that.

Abbie stretched her legs out, tilting her head toward the field. "You seen Jay?"

"No," I said too fast. I reached for my pretzel, tearing off a chunk I didn't want to eat.

She shot me a knowing look. "You two have been thick as thieves for months, and now it's like you're allergic to each other."

I stared ahead. "We're not—"

"Uh-huh." She popped a piece of candy into her mouth. "You're not avoiding him. He's not avoiding you. You're just... accidentally never in the same place at the same time?"

I chewed slowly. Said nothing.

Abbie leaned back, squinting into the stadium lights. "It's weird," she said. "Like, you two were always close. But now it feels like... more. When did that happen?"

I didn't answer.

Because I didn't know how to explain it. How to explain *him*.

Jay had never tried to be anything. He just was. There in the silence, in the wreckage, in the places where I didn't know how to ask for help.

He didn't reach in with promises. He just stood beside me when it mattered.

Offered me his hoodie when the whispers got cruel.

Led me home when I woke up disoriented at a vigil.

Caught me before I hit the ground.

But after his brother... after what he told me in my room.

I saw it. The full shape of his grief. And it was bigger than anything I'd ever carried.

He wasn't just haunted.

He was living inside the aftermath.

And somehow, he let me see it.

And now... now every time I think of him, it's different.

The almost kiss.

His fingers brushing mine.

The way he looked at me like I was the only one who understood it all, like I might be the one person who didn't turn away.

I kind of did turn away though...

But... I don't want to turn away.

God, I don't want to.

Because we see each other in ways no one else can.

The broken parts. The buried weight.

His pain makes mine feel less lonely.

But I can't be the one to drag him down deeper.

He's barely surfacing.

And if I reach for him now, when I'm getting *you're a murderer* notes shoved into my locker...

I don't know if either of us would come back up.

Abbie watched me, waiting. She didn't push, but I could feel the question in her silence.

"Well," she sighed, finishing off her candy, "whatever it is, you should probably figure it out."

Before I could respond, Leo appeared in front of us with a look on his face that said he was ready to fight. His gaze flitted over me, then landed on Abbie. "Hey, I need a second with her."

Abbie hesitated, her eyes darting between us. I barely had time to brace myself before she patted my knee and stood. "Fine. But if you make her spiral, I'm launching you off the bleachers." She walked off toward the concession stand.

I forced a breath, facing him. "What's going on, Leo?"

He fidgeted, "I wanted to bring this up when I saw you at school... but... with every-thing..."

His eyes studied me. "I just don't know what's going on with you."

I tensed. "What's that supposed to mean?"

Leo let out a sharp breath, like he couldn't believe I was playing dumb. "You've been wrapped up in something since Julie went missing. And now you and Stephen are hanging out?"

Stephen?

I frowned. "I don't know what you're talking about."

"Yeah?" Leo's voice was tense, almost... jealous. "Because I've seen you two, Sophia. At night."

Heat filled my veins. First off, he has no right to comment on anything or anyone in my life anymore. But more importantly—what?!

Before I could respond, another voice cut in smoothly.

"You wound me, Leo."

141

Stephen emerged out of nowhere.

He moved into my peripheral vision with practiced ease, his smirk set just right. "You make it sound like something illicit."

I stared at him. His presence here didn't make sense. I barely knew him, and yet, he had jumped into this conversation without missing a beat.

Like he was ready for it.

Leo narrowed his eyes. "I don't trust you."

Stephen placed a hand on his chest in mock offense. "What did I do?"

I hated how he said it. Like it was a game. Like we were playing parts in a script only he knew.

Leo sneered. "You always show up where you're not wanted."

Stephen shrugged. "And yet, here I am."

Jay appeared at my side, like he had been waiting for the moment to intervene. His expression was calm, but his posture was anything but relaxed.

"Let's go," he muttered, voice steady and low.

Leo scoffed but didn't stop me as I followed Jay down the bleachers, weaving through the crowd.

Abbie caught my eye at the bottom, giving me a little wave, like she knew we needed space. She turned toward the concession stand, slipping seamlessly into another conversation.

Jay didn't speak as we walked toward the parking lot. The air between us felt stretched too thin, like something was going to snap.

I broke first. "Jay. What's going on?"

He exhaled sharply but didn't stop walking. "Leo's an ass, but he's right about one thing. You shouldn't be around Stephen."

Something about the way he said it made my pulse pick up.

"I'm not ever around Stephen. And why do people keep saying that?"

"Why did you ask if I was watching you? That night on the roof."

I hesitated. "Because I saw someone. In the yard. Wearing a track hoodie. It looked like you."

Jay went still. His brow furrowed, not in confusion. "I think it was Stephen."

My stomach dropped. "What?"

"I don't even know where to start... we went to middle school together," he said. "Different town. Different school. But I knew him before I came here."

"Okay? You've never told me that before," I said.

Jay's jaw tightened and his tone dropped low. "Because I didn't want you near him in any way. And I figured, if I didn't say anything, maybe, maybe I wouldn't have to think about it."

"Think about what?"

His fists curled and he closed his eyes like he was transporting himself back somewhere, visualizing something. "There was a girl at school, she was super quiet. We were thirteen. And Stephen, he cornered her. Pushed her down. Tried to..."

I felt nausea creeping up.

Jay's voice was sharp, forced, his eyes open now. "I walked in, saw it, and I lost it. It didn't get too far before I intervened. We fought."

I inhaled sharply still trying to process what he was saying. "And?"

"And he spun it," Jay said bitterly. "Turned the whole thing around. Played the victim. Said it was a misunderstanding, that I was the one with anger issues." His laugh was humorless. "I got suspended and he walked."

I was quiet, waiting for him to continue.

"He moved here freshman year, the next school year after that happened. Like his parents were trying to run from it." A pause. "I moved here sophomore year, after my brother..." His voice dropped lower. "And we never talked about it."

The weight of his words settled over me.

"I thought maybe he was different now," Jay admitted, shaking his head. "I mean at first, I was suspicious of him, but he's in all of the A.P. classes, helped people with their homework. He seemed to be a different person, responsible even. And I wanted to believe that, I *needed* to believe that. I needed to move on after everything."

The silence stretched between us, unrelenting.

Jay hesitated. Then, finally, his eyes met mine.

"He said something sick about you. In the locker room."

My breathing slowed.

"What did he say?"

Jay looked away, but his fists curled tight.

"Jay."

He huffed sharply. "He said he should've 'started with you'. That Julie was... second choice."

The words slammed into me like a punch. I rocked back, my breath shallow.

Julie?

He said it like a mistake. Like she was a consolation prize. And I was the one that got away. Only I didn't get away, did I? Not really. He's still here. Still waiting for whatever twisted thing he thinks is owed to him

The nausea curled sharp in my stomach, my hands going clammy. I swallowed, but it didn't help. I could barely hear past the rush of blood in my ears.

Jay fought for me.

And I hadn't even known.

I should have felt grateful.

But all I felt was cold.

Because Stephen hadn't just said Julie's name.

He said mine. Like a claim.

A door he still planned to walk through.

Like he thought... god.

What had he done to Julie?

A slow, twisting panic unfurled in my chest, an aching, suffocating dread that threatened to swallow me whole.

Jay saw the shift in my expression. "I'm sorry. I shouldn't have told you here... now."

The nausea in my stomach coiled tighter, and suddenly, I wasn't looking at Jay anymore.

I was looking at myself.

At the way Stephen looked at me.

At the vigil. The wax on my hands. The missing time. The call and texts from Julie.

I wasn't just standing at the edge of something dark—I was already tipping forward, gravity making the choice for me.

And Jay?

Jay had known.

He had known how bad Stephen was.

And he hadn't told me.

I turned on him. "You shouldn't have told me now."

He flinched. "I—"

"Not after the fact. Not after a fight. We've been close for a year, Jay. And you let me walk blind into something you already knew was dangerous."

His jaw tensed. "That's not fair."

"Not fair?" I shot back, my voice rising.

Jay looked like he was trying to keep his voice even. "Sophia, I—"

I shook my head. "This isn't middle school. Stephen isn't some schoolyard bully. You think a locker room fight is going to fix this?"

He looked at me like he wanted to say something. But then his shoulders stiffened, and he looked away.

"Forget it," I muttered, stepping back.

"Forget what?"

I swallowed hard. "This conversation."

Jay let out a dull laugh. "Of course you'd say that."

I stilled. "What's that supposed to mean?"

He looked at me, something guarded in his expression. "You don't let anyone in Sophia. You flinch when anyone gets too close, even me."

I clenched my fists. "How could I let you in when I can't even trust you? When you're keeping so much from me?"

I threw my head back. "I thought I could handle this. But I can't, not when you're one more person I can't count on."

I turned away, my pulse slamming in my ears.

I didn't stop walking. Not even when I heard him curse under his breath, not even when something in my chest screamed at me to turn back.

28

— • —

NOVEMBER 18, 2024, 3 PM - NEWTON

24 DAYS AFTER JULIE WENT MISSING

I parked in the back lot at Ordinance High, killing the engine. It was mostly empty now, save for a handful of lingering cars and a couple of late buses idling near the gym.

I wasn't here to start an interrogation. Not yet. I was here to listen. And find out more about Stephen Burns.

So, I kept it casual. No notebook. More smiling. Just moving slow, observing.

Still, people noticed.

Near the vending machines, two kids stopped talking when I passed. Further down the hall, a group of cheerleaders lowered their voices, glancing at me before shutting their lockers and darting away dramatically. A few gave me quick nods, polite but wary.

They weren't just cautious.

They were guarded.

You didn't get people to talk by making them uncomfortable. You got them to talk by making them forget they weren't supposed to.

I spotted Mrs. Finch first, outside her classroom, flipping through a stack of papers. Red pen tapping against the edge.

"Sheriff," she greeted, barely looking up as if she was in a hurry.

"Mrs. Finch," I said. "How's everything going?"

She adjusted her glasses, tucking the stack of papers under her arm. "We're managing."

No one said fine anymore.

"Got a second?"

She smoothed a hand through her hair, her gaze sharpening as if resetting herself. When her eyes met mine again, she was ready. "Of course."

I stepped inside her classroom, letting the door click shut behind me.

"I wanted to ask about Stephen Burns," I said, keeping my tone easy.

That got zero reaction.

"What's your experience with him?" I prompted.

"Stephen?" she said, nodding. "Oh, he's wonderful. Truly one of the most dedicated students I've had. Brilliant kid. Well-prepared. Takes initiative. A natural leader. Honestly," she continued, shaking her head with a soft laugh, "I always say if we had a hundred more Stephens, this school would run itself."

Not if all my students were like him.

Not if the school was full of bright kids like Stephen.

If we had more of him.

Like he wasn't a student. Like he was a system that worked.

I tipped my head slightly. "Yeah? What's he like outside of class?"

Her smile tightened. Just a little.

"Oh, well, I mean, he's involved in so much. Always has something on his plate. Student council, debate club, he does a lot."

"Right, but who's he close with?"

A pause.

Not long. But it was there.

Her fingers moved over the stack of papers against her arm.

"Oh, I'm sure he has plenty of friends," she said lightly.

She didn't offer any names.

I thanked her and left.

***

I walked outside to see if I could catch any of the football players after practice. Leo was behind the bleachers, leaning against the metal, one foot braced against the frame.

"You seen Stephen around much?" I asked as I approached him.

His fingers tensed against the bleacher bar.

"Why?"

I shrugged. "Just trying to get a read on him."

A scoff. "Yeah, good luck with that."

I raised a brow. "Not a fan?"

Leo finally looked at me. Not quite defensive, not quite interested, somewhere in between. "He's a weirdo."

147

"How so?"

He let out a short, humorless laugh. "You ever talk to the guy? He says all the right things, acts all polite, but... I don't know. Feels fake. Like he's playing a part."

"That bother you?"

Leo shifted his weight, gripping the bleachers a little tighter. A second passed.

Then he said, "Sophia won't listen."

I stayed quiet. Let him keep going.

"She acts like he's just some guy," he muttered. "Like there's nothing to worry about."

His fingers drummed loudly against the metal now.

"I've seen them," he added, like he hadn't meant to say it out loud.

"Where?"

"Near the reservoir. Late."

He still wasn't looking at me, but his shoulders were tense now, his grip on the bar overly firm.

"She shut me out a long time ago," he muttered. "Beats me what the hell they're doing out there."

It was quiet for a minute.

"Jay fought him, you know."

I tilted my head. "Stephen?"

Leo finally looked at me, something bitter in his expression. "Yeah. A couple weeks ago, then again a few days ago. Finally, one thing I agree with Jay on."

I didn't react. "What was it over?"

Leo's mouth pressed into a hard line. "I don't know about the first time, but Stephen said some creepy shit about Sophia recently. Jay lost it."

There it was.

Jealousy. Frustration. And something else. Something unsettled.

I let it sit between us.

"What did Stephen say?"

Leo looked like he had more to say, but instead, he pushed off the bleachers, shaking his head.

"Ask him yourself."

I watched him walk off.

That was enough.

For now.

Jay was running around the track. When I approached, he was stretching. He saw me coming and straightened immediately.

Like he'd been expecting me to talk to him.

"Detective," he greeted, guarded.

I nodded at him. "Good meet yesterday?"

He hesitated. "Yeah. Killed it in the relay."

"Nice," I said. Then, casually, "You ever run with Stephen?"

Jay's expression shut down.

"Nah," he said. "He's not on the team."

"But you've had run-ins."

Jay didn't answer. Just rolled his shoulders, stretching again.

"What happened to your hand?" I asked, gesturing to the prominent bruise on his knuckles.

"Not sure," he said.

"Word on the street is you fought with Stephen."

He flexed his fingers but waited for me to say more, like he was trying to see how much I'd heard.

"What was it about?" I asked.

Jay shook his head. "Nothing."

I waited. Just let the silence build, get uncomfortable.

He threw his head back after a while and said, "He said some crap about Sophia."

His voice was sharp.

"What kind of crap?"

Jay let out a slow breath. "You ever see a guy smile when he knows he can get away with anything?"

I didn't answer.

"That's Stephen," Jay seethed.

I nodded slowly.

That wasn't just resentment.

That was history.

Jay wasn't afraid of Stephen.

But he hated him.

And hate like that?

It didn't come from nothing.

I needed to talk to Stephen directly.

I pulled out of the school lot and headed toward Kensington Court. Stephen's house was near the reservoir, not far from where Leo had seen him with Sophia.

The road curved along the water, the trees thinning just enough for the surface to catch the last stretch of daylight. The reservoir was still.

I kept one hand on the wheel, the other drumming against my thigh.

What the hell had they been doing out here?

Leo didn't know. Or didn't want to say.

But Sophia was meeting Stephen in the middle of the night. Near the water.

That didn't sit right.

I passed a narrow gravel turnout that overlooked the water. It was where kids parked late at night to get away from town eyes. The kind of place you could meet someone and not be seen.

So, did Stephen and Sophia not want to be seen?

There was a car parked there.

Nothing unusual.

Except—

The brake lights beamed once. A tap. Someone adjusting their foot.

I slowed slightly, let my eyes sweep the vehicle as I passed.

Dark interior. Tints too heavy to see inside.

No movement.

I made the last turn onto Kensington Court, checking the rearview mirror.

The car was gone.

***

The Burns house sat at the end of a quiet, well-manicured cul-de-sac where the town's wealthiest families kept their lives polished to a high shine.

Not the kind of obscene wealth you saw in gated communities a few towns over, but for Ordinance, this was the closest thing to a country club neighborhood.

Every house looked like it had been plucked from a high-end real estate catalog—lawns sculpted, hedges trimmed with geometric precision. The sprinklers alone probably used more water a day than a family in a developing country got in a week.

The air smelled fresher here.

Cut grass. Gardenia.

With something else underneath.

Citrus? Maybe.

Or just wealth, bleach, and effort.

Stephen's house fit the scene.

A classic colonial. Big, but not ostentatious. It exuded old money without the vulgarity of announcing it.

It was wrapped in crisp white siding. A jet-black door was framed by cedar pillars, perfectly centered beneath a second-floor balcony. The porch light glowed just right, warm but calculated. Not too bright, not too dim. It sent the message, "Welcome, but only if you belong here."

A BMW SUV sat in the driveway next to a sleek black Audi—Stephen's car. Both spotless.

I parked on the street and made my way up the stone-lined path, stepping around the sparkling pebbles like they might shatter. The bell rang with a soft, refined chime, I could tell that it probably cost twice as much as a regular doorbell because it was "tasteful."

Mrs. Burns answered, and she matched the house.

Her blonde bob framed high cheekbones. A pearl bracelet dangled just loose enough to look effortless. Expensive floral perfume clung to her. Light, but made to linger.

Her smile was practiced.

"Sheriff Newton," she greeted, smooth as glass. Not warm. Just... appropriate.

"Mrs. Burns," I said, keeping my voice light. "Just a routine follow-up regarding some school matters."

Her smile didn't slip, but something shifted behind her eyes. A split-second calculation.

"Oh?" she said smoothly. "Stephen's always been such a diligent student. I can't imagine there's much to follow up on."

"Nothing serious," I said. "Just checking in on some extracurriculars. Who's involved, what kind of structure it has. You know how it is. One thing comes up, and sometimes we have to look a little deeper."

Another pause.

She was good. The kind of woman who could steer a conversation without making it look like she was steering it.

"Of course," she said, stepping aside. "We're happy to help in any way we can. Stephen's father is here as well. Let me get him."

A perfect answer. A safe answer.

Which meant she wasn't going to give me anything for free.

I stepped inside.

The floors gleamed under soft lighting, waxed to a level that suggested obsessive maintenance.

I followed Mrs. Burns into the kitchen which stretched open like a magazine spread. White quartz countertops. Glass-front cabinets. A bowl of lemons at the center of the island, arranged too neatly to have just been tossed there.

It wasn't only clean.

It looked performed.

A tall, broad-shouldered man stepped up from a barstool at the island.

Stephen's father.

He had salt-and-pepper hair, a sharp jawline, and sleeves rolled up just enough to seem casual, but neatly folded.

A man who owned the room before he walked into it.

He extended a firm, deliberate handshake. Meant to test the other person.

"Sheriff," he greeted, cautious but smooth.

I took his hand.

"Mr. Burns," I said. "Appreciate your time. Just following up on some things at the school," I said, keeping my tone even. "Routine."

He didn't react right away. Didn't nod. Didn't shift. Just let the words sit there, waiting to see if I'd add something else.

A measured pause.

Then, finally, he nodded.

"Didn't realize there was anything that needed following up on."

I gave a small smile. "Neither did I. But here we are."

His hand rested on his wife's shoulder.

"What can we help you with?"

"Well, I was hoping to talk with Stephen too if that's alright."

"He's studying," Mrs. Burns said quickly.

Her husband shook his head, a small, dismissive gesture.

"If this will speed things along, I'll get Stephen," he said, already turning toward the stairs.

Stephen appeared a moment later, moving like someone who had already rehearsed this conversation.

Same sharp features as his father. Same effortless composure.

His fitted polo looked tailored, his khakis pressed, his hair styled with an attention to detail most seventeen-year-olds wouldn't bother with.

His expression was calm, interested.

Polite.

Like he had nothing to worry about.

"Sheriff Newton," he greeted, extending his hand. Same handshake. Same performance.

I took it, let it linger a second too long.

"Stephen," I said. "Hope I'm not interrupting anything."

"Not at all," Stephen said easily. "What can I do for you?"

Not a moment of hesitation. Nothing thrown off balance.

I gestured toward the sitting room. Stephen moved first, unhurried. His father remained by the staircase, arms crossed, watching. His mother followed, posture straight but not rigid, her presence subtle, but... there.

We sat.

Stephen folded his hands neatly in his lap, his expression set in polite curiosity. His mother perched on the edge of a chair nearby.

"So," I started, keeping my tone light, "just doing a little follow-up on some school-related matters. Checking in with a few students."

Stephen nodded. "Of course."

No questions.

No concern.

I reclined back slightly. "You involved in a lot at school?"

He gave me a smile that belonged in yearbooks and Ivy League brochures. "I try to be," he said. "I think it's important to stay engaged with the community."

"Student Council?"

"President."

"Debate team?"

"Captain."

"National Honor Society?"

"Of course."

Everything. Just like Mrs. Finch had said. Every prestigious club. Every leadership position. Always in control.

"I heard you were part of The Circle, too."

Not even a blink.

"Oh?" he said, politely. "What's that?"

I watched him closely. "A mentorship program."

Stephen inclined his head slightly. "That sounds nice," he said, like I'd just told him about a club he might be interested in joining.

Not a single crack.

I changed the subject.

"Julie Greene. Did you know her?"

A flash of something crossed his face.

"I didn't know her that well," Stephen said.

I let the words settle.

He held my gaze, still perfectly composed.

"That so?"

"Yes."

No elaboration.

I nodded, slow. Neither of us spoke for a few long moments.

Then, casually, "What about Sophia Whitaker?"

And there it was.

The amusement. That twinkle of something behind his eyes, like he knew a joke I didn't.

His smile stretched just a little wider.

"I see her around," he said, voice easy.

His mother's posture shifted, small, subtle, but noticeable.

I caught it.

"Leo said he's seen you with her," I said. "Late. Near the reservoir."

Stephen didn't react.

"Did he?" he asked unbothered.

The answer was nothing. But the way he said it?

That was something.

I pressed. "Yeah. Late at night. Seems like an odd time for a study session."

This time, he hesitated.

Like he was deciding how to play it.

And then, just as smoothly as before, he exhaled a soft chuckle.

"You ask a lot of questions, Sheriff."

A beat.

Too long.

"That's my job," I said.

Stephen nodded, like he understood something I didn't.

And for the first time since I walked in, I had the distinct feeling that I wasn't the only one doing the questioning.

I stood.

Stephen stood too, at the exact same time.

"Well, I appreciate your time," I said.

His mother's smile was back, voice light. "Of course."

His father hadn't moved from the staircase. Still watching.

I stepped outside. My instinct told me to turn back, just once.

I didn't.

Instead, I kept walking.

I'd questioned a lot of people over the years, liars, criminals, men who had something to lose.

Stephen wasn't like them.

He was... something else.

29

— • —

NOVEMBER 19, 2024, 3 PM - SOPHIA

25 DAYS AFTER JULIE WENT MISSING

I hated the empty pit in my chest every time I thought about walking away from Jay.

The way his jaw had gone tight. His shoulders tense, like I had actually hurt him.

But I had walked away. I had turned my back, left him standing in the parking lot, watching me go. And now we hadn't talked in three days. Three days.

And it sucked.

I sighed, pressing my forehead against my locker, stopping to grab my books before going home. I wasn't doing this. I wasn't thinking about him.

Except, I was.

I was thinking about his expression when I threw his words back at him. The frustration in his voice. The way he didn't chase after me.

I hated replaying it.

I missed him.

And worse, I wanted him.

"Rough night?"

The voice made my skin crawl before I even turned.

Stephen.

He was leaning lazily against the lockers, that same practiced smirk pulling at his mouth. He had this way of standing overly still that put me more on edge.

I straightened, forcing my body to stay relaxed even though my mind was screaming at me to run after what Jay told me. "What do you want?"

His eyes snapped to me, like he was glad I had asked.

"You left the game early on Friday."

I frowned. "So?"

Stephen angled his head, like I had said something interesting. "I thought you and Jay were close."

I just stood there. My feet felt cemented to the ground.

Why was he bringing up Jay?

I said nothing, but he grinned like I had answered anyway.

"Funny how he always steps in for you."

My pulse spiked.

I wasn't sure if he was referencing the game or what went down in the locker room.

Either way, I didn't like it.

His smirk stayed, but something in his eyes flitted. Something sharp.

"Didn't realize you needed someone to fight your battles, Whitaker."

The words slid under my skin.

Like he thought he knew me. Like he didn't like the idea of someone else standing at my side.

My fingers curled against my palms, forcing my expression to stay flat. "You have a point, or are you just standing there looking creepy for fun?"

His teeth flashed now in a full smile, as if I had proven something to him.

Then, just before he walked away, he leaned in slightly. Not close enough to touch, but close enough to feel.

"You talk in your sleep, you know," he murmured.

My heart stopped. A full-body freeze.

The hallway tilted.

I heard my own breathing sharp and uneven.

He couldn't have said that. Could he?

How would he know?

A chill slithered down my spine, my nails digging into my palms as I forced myself to move. To shake off the feeling that Stephen's voice was still wrapping around me, squeezing too tight.

I walked fast, all the way home.

And the whole time, my fingers itched toward my phone. Toward one name.

Jay.

I wanted to tell him everything.

But what I really needed to tell him was I'm sorry.

I typed and deleted at least ten different texts, each one feeling more useless than the last. This conversation couldn't happen over the phone.

I was going to his house. Tonight.

But when I rounded the corner, I stopped.

Jay was already there.

Leaning against my porch railing, head bowed, fingers picking at his sleeve like he was working through something he couldn't quite put into words.

Something about seeing him just standing there, shoulders tense, brows drawn, made my breath catch in my throat.

I hesitated at the top step, fingers tightening around my bag.

This was the part where I should say something.

Hadn't I just spent the entire walk home thinking about what to say? But now, staring at him, I had nothing.

Jay had tried to protect me from Stephen. He had always tried to protect me. And I had pushed him away. Brushed him off like he was overstepping or lying to me when, deep down, I had known he wasn't.

And now, looking at him, *really* looking at him, I felt it settle low in my stomach.

Regret.

Because Jay had never asked me for anything. Not space, not gratitude, not even a second glance.

And I had spent so long pretending I didn't feel this. That he wasn't something real, something impossible to ignore.

I was done pretending.

My pulse pounded, a different kind of weight pressing against my ribs now.

I swallowed hard and stepped forward, willing my lips to move.

"Jay,"

"No."

His voice was rough.

"You don't get to walk away again, Whitaker."

I let out a shaky breath. "I didn't—"

"You did."

His voice was sharp, raw.

"You ran because it was easier than dealing with this."

I opened my mouth to argue. But I couldn't.

Because Jay was right.

And he knew it.

"Just tell me."

His voice had dropped—softer now, but still sharp. His fingers curled slightly at his sides. His throat bobbed with a hard swallow.

"If you don't want this. If you don't want me. I need you to say it."

I froze.

Not just because he was asking if I wanted him.

But because, in true Jay fashion, he was putting me first.

Giving me an out.

A clean break.

He was standing right here, ready to walk away if that's what I needed. Making it clear I was something worth waiting for, but not someone he'd force into staying.

I didn't want the out. I never had.

I had tried to convince myself this was nothing... then that it was too much. That if I let him in, if I let myself have this, I'd just drag him down with me.

Jay was steady. Solid. A weight that could hold me in place when everything else was shifting beneath me.

But he deserved better.

Someone who wasn't drowning.

Someone who wasn't unraveling at the seams.

That's what I told myself.

But Jay?

He had been there through all of it. Through the whispers. The sleepwalking. The fights. Stephen.

And he was still here.

He wasn't looking for an escape.

He was asking me to choose.

My pulse pounded, my breath coming fast and tight, I couldn't quite get enough air.

I stepped forward. Then again.

Jay didn't move.

His body was tense, his hands curled into fists at his sides, but his eyes. God, his eyes. Dark and heavy with something he hadn't let himself touch.

Waiting.

And suddenly, it wasn't about dragging him down.

Because looking at him now, I could see it.

There was no stopping it. Stopping us.

Because for once, I wasn't running.

I was reaching.

"I want this."

That was all it took.

Jay exhaled sharply, a sound somewhere between relief and surrender. And then I felt it snap.

The space between us.

He moved.

His thumb brushed my cheek, before his mouth crashed into mine.

Heat and electricity flooded my body as I felt a sharp inhale against my lips.

His other hand found my waist, fingers tightening like he needed to feel every inch of me, needed proof that this wasn't slipping through his fingers. He kissed me and I felt everything we'd been holding back for months pretending we didn't want this.

When we finally broke apart, my pulse was a mess, my hands still fisted in his sweatshirt. I needed to anchor myself. Jay was staring at me, breathless.

His eyes moved over my face, his thumb tracing absently along my jaw.

He huffed a quiet laugh, shaking his head. "God, you make everything harder than it has to be."

I smirked, still breathless. "And here I thought you liked me for my effortless optimism and bubbly nature."

His laugh was short, disbelieving. But I saw it, the way something in him let go.

His grip tightened on my waist. "You think I don't like you?" His voice was teasing, but there was something under it. Something thick. Something real.

I met his gaze, my pulse still hammering. "I think you haven't actually told me."

His throat bobbed. His gaze skipped away for just a second.

"You're everything," he said, barely audible.

I don't think he'd meant to say it out loud, but now that it was here—there was no taking it back.

The words hit low, deep, spreading through me like fire.

He shook his head once.

"I don't," he rubbed the back of his neck. "I don't know how to do this. I don't know how to want something like this and not be afraid of losing it."

My throat tightened. I swallowed, my voice softer now. "Me either."

His gaze snapped back to mine. Sharp. Searching.

"I don't know what this is supposed to look like," I admitted. "I just know I don't want to pretend it doesn't exist."

His breath came out unsteady.

A pause.

Then he nodded, once. Like a silent agreement. Like a promise.

His hand slid down my arm to my hand, his fingers locking between mine. Relaxed, but enough.

Enough to feel the pulse between us.

Enough to know I wasn't pulling away.

My fingers curled tighter around his.

The space between us felt thinner than ever, like it could collapse at any second.

And for the first time, it didn't feel terrifying.

It felt inevitable.

We talked about everything after that, legs tangled on the porch swing, his hoodie zipped halfway up my body like armor.

The air cooled. The sky shifted.

Hours passed without either of us checking the time.

Then, my phone vibrated.

Jay's shoulders tensed as the phone buzzed again. "Now what?" His eyes bounced from my face to the street, scanning our surroundings suddenly aware. A figure moved in the distance, so fast I almost wasn't sure I'd seen anyone at all.

I pulled my phone out, expecting another text.

But it wasn't.

It was a call.

No caller ID.

My thumb hovered over the screen. A weird pressure built in my ears.

Jay noticed my hesitation. "Who is it?"

I didn't answer. Just swallowed hard and pressed accept and put it on speaker.

For a second, there was silence.

Then a voice came through. Distorted. Mechanical. Warped like it was coming through a machine.

"It's time for you to remember. Check your locker."

A cold chill snaked down my spine.

Click.

The line went dead.

30

NOVEMBER 19, 2024, 6 PM - SOPHIA

25 DAYS AFTER JULIE WENT MISSING

"We're going."

Jay didn't wait for me to say anything. He guided me into his truck and threw it into drive. The tires screeched against the pavement as we tore down Maple Road.

My pulse pounded in my ears. I stared at my phone like the words were still there, hanging in the air.

That voice. That warped, distorted voice.

Who the hell had called me?

Jay's jaw was tight as he gripped the wheel. "You good?"

No. I wasn't good. Not even close.

I swallowed hard. "Just drive."

Jay obliged but put a hand on my thigh. "Soph, you're shaking the whole car."

I looked down and my legs were bouncing so hard the seat belt was clinking.

"I talked to Stephen..." I said as he turned off my street.

"You what? Did you hear anything I told you at the game?" His voice was worried, frustrated.

"It wasn't like that. I ran into him at school, and he said," the seat belt clinking grew louder, "He said I... talk in my sleep."

Jay's fingers were strangling the steering wheel. The engine roared as he pressed the gas pedal harder.

We reached the school in minutes, barely slowing before Jay killed the engine and pushed open his door.

"Come on," he said.

I followed, my legs feeling unsteady as we cut through to the side of the building. The parking lot was empty. The main doors were locked.

Jay led me around the back, toward the gym entrance. He grabbed the handle of a side door and pulled. It opened without resistance.

"Track guys use it after school," he murmured, holding it open. "Coach doesn't care."

I stepped inside.

The hall was silent.

Dark, except for the faint emergency lights humming overhead.

Something was wrong.

I could feel it.

Jay's footsteps echoed beside me as we moved through the hall, past empty classrooms and bulletin boards overstuffed with flyers. I could see the edge of Julie's memorial announcement underneath the chaos. My locker was just around the corner.

The second I saw it, my ribcage locked around my lungs like a vice, squeezing with every inhale.

It was wide open.

No, *ripped* open.

My locker door hung off the hinges, the metal twisted at the edges like someone had pried it apart.

Jay swore under his breath.

I barely heard him. My feet moved forward on their own, pulse hammering as I peered inside.

Pictures. Of me.

Scattered on the bottom of my locker.

I picked one up, my fingers trembling.

Me.

Walking in the street.

Me.

Kneeling in the woods.

Distant. Unaware. Completely exposed.

Some of the photos were grainy, far away. Like someone had taken them while hiding or in a rush.

Others looked more controlled or like they were taken right next to me.

There was a single picture of Julie—taken from outside her house, looking in through her window. On the back of the photo one word was scrawled: Almost.

My breaths were shallow, as if I was sipping air through a straw. Who had taken these pictures?

Then I saw the pages underneath.

More of Julie's diary pages.

The first thing that stood out was the ink. Smudged, hurried, frantic. The second was the blacked-out sections, huge chunks of words scribbled over so violently the paper was almost torn through. Each page was ripped, hurriedly, at the seam.

But what I could read made my breath go thin.

***

October 15th

I woke up last night and she was there.

_____

I don't know how long she had been standing outside, but when I looked out my window, she was watching.

I thought maybe I was imagining it. That the shadows were playing tricks on me.

_____

_____

But then _____ like someone caught doing something wrong.

She tilted her head. I knew she was waiting.

_____

_____

I didn't turn _____ my light. I didn't move.

I just stayed perfectly still, holding my breath, hoping she would go away.

But she didn't.

Sophia just stood there wi_____.

Watching.

***

October 17th

I told _____ today that I was done. That I didn't want any part of this anymore.

_____ *told me it wasn't my choice.*
_____ *said Sophia*
wouldn't let me go that easy.

    I laughed. I thought it was a joke.

    Then _____ looked at me. And they didn't laugh back.

_____
_____
_____ *ever again.*

***

October 18th

    I tried to ignore her today.

    I saw her in the hallway. She _____ felt her behind me. I felt her.

    I don't know how to explain it. I can always tell when she's close.

    It's like a weight pressing against the back of my skull. A crawling under my skin.

    I didn't look at her. I kept my head down, focused on my locker, but I knew she was there.

    And then she whispered my name.

    So quiet.

    Right behind me.

_____
_____
_____ *like always.*

    But she wasn't looking at me.

    Sophia was smiling.

***

October 19th

    I can't believe _____

_____
_____
_____

I don't know what she's done.

I don't know what she might do.

I just know that when I wake up at night, I can't tell if Sophia's really there.

And I think that's worse.

***

My vision swam.

I flipped to the last page, hands trembling.

At the bottom, scrawled in the same familiar handwriting as the note in my locker weeks ago—

"We are the same."

A sound crawled up my throat. My skin burned.

Jay said something I didn't register.

My name. MY name, was all over Julie's diary pages, but it wasn't mine.

It felt wrong.

Like I was reading about a stranger.

"Sophia wouldn't let me go that easy."

My breath caught. My fingers were numb, but I could feel Jay's hand on my arm.

"I don't know what she's done. I don't know what she might do."

I didn't do anything.

...Did I?

Julie had been scared of me.

Scared of what I might do.

Scared of what I already did.

My pulse slammed against my ribs.

"What if—" My voice came out hoarse. "She was right?"

What if I did something to her, I wanted to say.

No. No, I wouldn't. I couldn't. But the nights. God, the nights. The gaps. The mornings were off, like waking up mid-step, like I'd been somewhere before I even opened my eyes. And I had woken up *exactly* where she was buried. Julie wrote it. She felt it. She'd seen me.

Jay's grip tightened. "Soph, listen to me. You didn't do anything. Julie was obviously confused. Look at the way she was writing."

"You don't know that. She was... scared of me."

I looked down at Julie's words again.

The pages blurred.

What if she was right about me?

What if I wasn't Sophia at all?

What if I was capable of something... bad?

What if I was the thing she thought I was?

31

—•—

NOVEMBER 19, 2024, 6:30 PM - SOPHIA

25 DAYS AFTER JULIE WENT MISSING

"This is from Stephen."

I gripped the note, stretching it out in front of Jay while he read it out loud: **"We are the same."**

The words felt heavier spoken. Like hearing them made them more real. Jay tensed.

I exhaled shakily. "I've seen this handwriting before. I've gotten other notes like this. And after what he just said at school today, I know it's him."

His expression darkened. He ran a hand down his face.

CRACK.

Jay's fist slammed into the locker beside him.

I jumped. "Jay!"

His jaw clenched. His breathing was sharp, like he was trying to pull himself back. His knuckles pressed into the dented metal, shoulders rising and falling with controlled force. As if he knew losing it wouldn't help, but he was close.

Then, something in his eyes shifted.

A thought. A realization.

His fingers uncurled. His breathing steadied. And when he turned to face me again, his voice was quieter, but somehow more dangerous.

"We need to check his locker."

I blinked. "What?"

"If it is him, we're not gonna wait around for him to make the next move. We break in." He looked like he wanted to say more.

I hesitated, glancing back down at the message. The words blurred together, but the meaning stayed sharp.

A shiver ran through me.

Jay was right.

We needed to make the next move.

We moved quickly, keeping close to the lockers as we reached the second row. I was vividly aware of every sound around us.

When we stopped in front of Stephen's locker, my pulse kicked up.

It looked like every other locker.

But it wasn't.

My fingers hovered over the lock. "I don't know the combination."

Jay glanced down the hallway before looking back at me. "Start with something obvious."

I nodded.

Something simple. Logical. The kind of thing someone might use if they didn't want to forget.

2... 4... 6.

Click.

Nothing.

I wiped my sweaty palms on my jeans then tried a dozen more obvious combinations.

"Try his birthday," Jay muttered.

"How would I know his birthday?" I asked exasperated.

"I know it. September first," he said quietly.

I gave him a questioning look.

"In seventh grade, my science teacher brought in treats for everyone's birthday. I remember because she made Cinnamon rolls for his."

I shook my head not even trying to process that, my fingers twisting the dial.

9... 0... 1.

Nothing.

0... 9... 1.

Again, it didn't budge.

A faint sound echoed down the hall.

I froze.

Jay tensed beside me, glancing over his shoulder. "Hurry up."

"I'm trying," I whispered.

I stared at the lock, my pulse racing, my mind scrambling.

Then Jay spoke again, voice low. "What if it's Julie's birthday? What if he... what if this is him proving something?"

I swallowed hard. "Proving what?"

Jay's fingers curled into fists. "That he had her in his sights long before any of us knew. The way he talked in the locker room—it was like he was admitting he'd done something to her."

The pit in my stomach deepened, a gnawing hollowness that wouldn't go away.

I spun the dial. I know her birthday from the local news—August 21st.

8... 2... 1.

Click.

Nothing.

Frustration was setting in.

Jay's hand pressed against my back, grounding me. "It's okay, just think. Something he'd be obsessed with."

The words hit me.

Something he'd be obsessed with.

A cold dread uncoiled in my stomach.

Jay saw my face. "What?"

I thought about the notes, the way he said I talk in my sleep, my locker...

I swallowed hard. "I'm trying mine."

He blinked. "Your birthday?"

I spun the dial.

6... 0... 8.

Click.

The lock snapped open. The tiny sound might as well have been a gunshot. I jerked my hand back like I'd been burned.

Jay took a step back, hands flexing, then clenching so tight his knuckles popped.

His nostrils flared. A sharp inhale. No exhale.

"He used your birthday," Jay said, voice low, rough. Not a question.

I just... stared.

His fingers twitched against his jeans. Then, slowly, deliberately, his shoulders rolled back.

Without another word he reached out and yanked the locker open.

At first, it looked like nothing.

Crumpled papers. An empty soda can. A few random notebooks stacked haphazardly. Jay pushed them aside.

Then I saw a shoebox.

Sitting neatly in the back of the top locker shelf, begging to be opened.

Like he knew I would come looking.

Jay leaned in beside me. "That's weird," he cut himself off. "We need to open it."

I couldn't move.

I didn't want to touch it.

Jay didn't wait. He reached in and tugged the lid off.

More photos.

And not just a few like at my locker.

It was a collection of me.

Stacks of them, crammed inside the box, bundled together with twine. Like he'd been storing. Sorting.

I threw an arm over my stomach as if it could keep it from plummeting.

Jay swore violently. He grabbed a stack, flipping through them. His breathing ragged.

Me.

In the woods.

Me.

Walking home.

Me.

At the vigil. The same shot from Calloway's desk.

All with handwritten dates, some of them were from more than a month ago.

Some were from this week.

I took a staggered step back.

The last one I saw was of me in the woods. Julie's house looming in the background. The handwritten date in the corner was the day she went missing.

Jay and I looked at each other. I stammered trying to form even one intelligible word.

"This isn't," My voice cracked. "He's been watching me."

Jay stepped closer to me as if he could shield me from what was happening.

At the very bottom of the box, beneath the stacks, there was a single, unfolded piece of paper.

Jay grabbed it first. His fingers tightened.

I stared at his face, at the way the muscles in his throat twitched.

"What?" My voice was barely a whisper.

He turned the paper toward me.

Same handwriting as the notes I'd found before.

It said one thing.

"I see you."

A violent shiver ripped through me as Jay tore the note in half.

I flinched.

"This is Stephen. This is the same psychotic Stephen from years ago. I'm not letting him do this. I'm going to *kill* him," Jay's voice was terrifyingly calm.

I couldn't breathe.

Stephen knew something.

He'd been watching me.

And now, he wanted me to know it too.

A door creaked open at the end of the hall.

Jay moved fast. He grabbed the box, shoved the lid on, then locked eyes with me.

"We have to get out of here."

32

— · —

NOVEMBER 19, 2024, 7 PM - SOPHIA

25 DAYS AFTER JULIE WENT MISSING

I broke the silence first. My voice was hoarse. "We should go to the police."

Jay was still gripping the wheel, his knuckles pale from the pressure. The box sat between us like a loaded gun, its weight pressing into the space, into the air.

"We can't."

"Jay, we have proof. Pictures of me. Hundreds of them. I'll explain the ones of me in the woods. We can't just walk away from this."

Jay turned toward me, his face shadowed in the dim glow of the dashboard. His expression was grim.

"Sophia, you don't know him like I do. If there's even the slightest crack in the story, he'll find it and twist his way out. Just like he did in middle school."

He paused, "And... have you really looked at the pictures?"

I hesitated. "What?"

He rolled his shoulder, then reached for the box and flipped the lid off, rifling through the stacks of photos while keeping his eyes trained on the road. He pulled out a handful and tossed them into my lap.

I looked at them through new eyes.

And my blood ran cold.

They weren't just pictures of me.

They were pictures of Julie.

Some of them were casual. Me walking behind her at school, standing in line behind her at lunch, my gaze sliding toward the cheerleaders... toward her.

But the others—

My stomach twisted as I flipped through them one by one.

I was in Julie's backyard.

I was standing beneath her bedroom window looking in.

The pictures were taken from behind, I was motionless, my head tipped up, staring.

The timestamps written in the corner burned into my brain. Some had dates, others just had times.

2:14 AM

3:07 AM

3:41 AM

4:02 AM

Me. Just standing there in the middle of the night. Watching her.

Oh my God.

The air rushed out of my lungs.

This wasn't right. This wasn't real.

I wasn't following Julie.

Was I?

My hands started shaking. "Jay, I don't remember being in half of these places. I don't remember ever being in her yard."

He was quiet, his hand twitching like he wanted to reach for mine but didn't.

"That's what I'm trying to say... this looks bad," he said as he pulled into my driveway.

"No shit," I whispered.

He didn't move. Just stared at the box like it might rearrange itself into something that made sense. His fingers tapped once against the lid before he shoved it shut.

"These photos—these diary pages—" His voice was careful, but something in his jaw twitched. "They make it look like you were following her."

"But you weren't," he said with growing certainty.

"How do you know?"

His gaze snapped up, locking onto mine without hesitation.

"Because I was with you," he said as he brushed his fingers against mine.

The words hit somewhere deep. Not dramatic, just raw and true.

I felt a pang of tears well behind my eyes.

"Half these days, we were together," he said. "We walked to class. We sat at lunch."

I blinked fast, suddenly aware of the way his voice softened. Not because he was scared. Because he didn't want me to be.

"And the rest?" I asked.

"You were sleepwalking. You weren't stalking Julie, Sophia."

A pause.

"You weren't."

He didn't say I *believe* you. He didn't say I think.

He said you weren't. Like it was a fact.

"Then why does it look like I was?" My voice barely made it past my lips.

Jay's knee bounced once. Then he stilled himself.

"Because Stephen wants it to."

That landed heavy and sharp.

"Other facts, other names are blacked out in the diary pages," Jay continued. "You know whose isn't?"

I swallowed hard.

"Mine."

His jaw ticked. "Yeah."

The air between us thinned. I couldn't look away from him.

My name was all over those pages. My name. Not Stephen's.

I exhaled shakily, gripping the seat beneath me. "So, this is a setup?"

Something shifted in Jay's expression, a choice.

He looked out the window when he spoke again, voice quieter but no less certain.

"We need to figure out what Stephen wants."

I watched him. My pulse was erratic, as if it didn't know whose side it was on.

Then Jay looked at me. Not the box. Not the road. Me.

With no dramatics, no performative anger, he made a quiet, unwavering promise. "I'm not letting him get to you, Sophia. I won't."

I stared at him, my throat tight.

For a second, I wanted to cry. Not from fear, but because someone was finally standing between me and the fire.

33

— • —

NOVEMBER 19, 2024, 11:30 PM - SOPHIA

25 DAYS AFTER JULIE WENT MISSING

Hours had passed since Jay dropped me off.

Now it was late, almost midnight.

I had texted him.

Called twice.

No answer.

He was probably asleep. He'd done enough tonight. Held it together when I couldn't, stayed calm when the world cracked open.

He deserved sleep.

But I couldn't sit still. I couldn't shut my mind off. I kept pacing. Back-and-forth, back-and-forth, my room feeling smaller with every pass.

Jay is right, we need to figure out what Stephen wants.

But sitting here, waiting, wasn't getting me any closer to that.

My fingers curled around my keys.

If I didn't move now, I'd lose my nerve. I knew it.

Plus, what if he had copies of the pictures? He could be going to the police right now.

I had thought through every possible place to find Stephen and how to confront him. I needed somewhere public, but private at the same time. Somewhere people wouldn't pay attention. Somewhere I could talk to him without feeling trapped.

Then I remembered.

I had seen Stephen working the evening shift at the convenience store on Third Street when Abbie and I had gone out for snacks.

It struck me as odd when I saw him there. He was smart. His parents were loaded. He didn't need a job. Especially not one there.

A place with flickering fluorescent lights, shelves half-stocked with expired chips. A place where no one really lingered.

But maybe that was the point.

Maybe he wanted an excuse to be somewhere else at night. A place where no one would question him being there, yet no one would truly see him, either.

By the time I pulled into the parking lot, my hands left a sweaty mess on the steering wheel.

I didn't know what I was going to say.

I just knew I needed to hear him say something.

I shoved open the door and stepped inside.

The store was open.

But no one was here.

I took a few steps, scanning the aisles. Empty. No cashier. No movement.

Something felt off.

I turned back, gripping the handle.

A hand pressed the door shut.

Not rough. Just there.

Cold fingers brushed my wrist, just for a second, before pulling away.

"Going somewhere?"

Stephen.

I went still. My pulse spiked.

He stood just behind me, too close. His dark eyes blank, pupils swallowing the brown of his irises.

"Why are you here?" he asked, amused.

I forced my breathing to stay steady. "We need to talk."

His gaze moved over me, then past me, like he was checking to see if anyone was around.

I stood my ground. "You left those notes for me."

Stephen sighed and slowly shook his head, like I was being dramatic. "You don't want to do this, Sophia."

I stepped closer. "Why? Because you don't want me to know the truth?"

His eyes sharpened, lips curving into something that wasn't quite a smirk. Something that almost looked like anticipation. "I think, deep down, you already do. You just don't want to see it yet."

I felt my pulse hammering. "I know you set me up."

"Set you up?"

I gritted my teeth. "The photos. The diary pages. You want people to think I was watching Julie. You want me to doubt myself."

Stephen sighed. "Sophia, if I wanted you to doubt yourself, I wouldn't have to try very hard."

A cold shiver ran through me.

I squared my shoulders. "Why? Why go through all this?"

Stephen didn't answer right away. Instead, he took a slow step forward, closing the space between us.

"You think Julie was the victim here?" he asked.

"What are you talking about?"

Stephen studied me, like he was waiting to see how much I could handle.

"She played games," he said finally. "She liked to pretend she was in control. Just like you."

A slow, cold dread unfurled inside me. "You're lying."

His smirk didn't waver. "You say that a lot."

Then, softer, "But you've started to remember, haven't you?"

A sharp pulse of nausea made its way up my throat.

"I don't know what you're talking about."

Stephen bobbled his head side to side, like I had just said something he didn't think was true. "That's the thing about memories. They don't come back all at once. They creep in, little by little."

He took another step closer. His face filled with darkness and... desire?

Then his expression evened, and his eyes locked with mine.

The deepest part of me was pushing my legs to move, to leave.

I turned on my heel, but he moved faster.

His hand shot out, brushing against my fingers before curling around them, just enough pressure to make me stop.

I flinched.

"I've done everything for you," he said, voice almost tender. "And you still don't see it."

He paused, his lips curled slightly. "One day you will."

He dropped my hand, then I bolted out of the store, my footsteps slamming against the pavement.

I didn't stop running until I was in my car, doors locked, hands shaking on the wheel.

I drove home in a daze. Every red light, every turn, every breath felt distant, like I was watching myself move, but I wasn't really there.

Stephen's words looped in my head.

I barely remembered getting inside. Kicking off my Nikes.

My room was dark, the only light coming from the streetlamp outside. I didn't turn anything on.

I didn't want to see myself in the mirror.

I changed into oversized sweatpants, moving on autopilot. Crawled under the covers. Pulled the blankets up to my chin, tucking them beneath my toes like a cocoon.

My limbs felt heavy. My eyes burned.

Sleep tugged at the edges of my mind, but I fought it.

I didn't want to sleep.

Not after tonight.

Not after him.

But I wasn't strong enough to stay awake.

The last thing I remembered before my eyes slipped shut—

The unmistakable feeling that I wasn't alone.

34

— • —

NOVEMBER 20, 2024, 4 AM - SOPHIA

26 DAYS AFTER JULIE WENT MISSING

My head throbbed. A dull, relentless ache, pulsing in sync with my heartbeat.

The world was sideways.

Or maybe I was.

My fingers flexed, scraping against something rough and jagged.

I blinked sluggishly, the world slow to take shape. A sharp yellow glow burned into my retinas, the streetlamp overhead humming like a wasp.

I was outside.

Again.

In the middle of the road.

For a moment, I couldn't breathe. My chest felt tight, as if all of my muscles had coiled like cobras around my lungs. The street stretched endlessly in both directions, eerily quiet. The occasional flicker of a distant porchlight was the only sign of life.

A breeze whispered past, chilling my arms.

I was in my sweatpants and a pajama top.

Oh God.

My skin buzzed as I sat up, the pavement biting into my palms. A wave of dizziness crashed through my body. I pressed my fingers to my temple, and froze.

My hands were smeared with something dark. Sticky. Almost like the consistency of chocolate syrup.

But it wasn't chocolate. This was warm... red.

Blood.

A panicked noise tore from my throat as I scrambled to my feet, my knees nearly giving out beneath me. I held my hands out in the streetlight, the faint shine of crimson glistening underneath.

Was it mine?

I frantically searched my body. Head, arms, legs, stomach then head again, running my fingers across my forehead, scalp, cheeks. No cuts. I caught my blurred reflection in the lamp post. I looked terrifying. Blood was smeared across my face.

It clung to my fingers too, thick and tacky. I bent down to scape my hands against the pavement but the feeling made my stomach lurch, fresh... warm. My hands twitched, muscle memory grasping for something I couldn't name. Something soft. Something alive.

A low rumble cut through the silence.

I jumped up and turned, my pulse spiking, just as headlights tore through the dark. A horn blared, sharp and violent.

I stumbled back, throwing up my arms just as the car screeched to a halt inches from where I had been standing.

The driver yelled something, but the words barely reached me over the blood roaring in my ears. I staggered to the curb, my legs trembling, barely managing to stay upright.

The car idled for a moment, then sped off, its red taillights disappearing into the void.

I was shaking.

I had been somewhere before this. I could feel it.

The cold, the weight in my legs, it wasn't just from sleepwalking. My body ached like I'd been somewhere I wasn't supposed to be, then ran for my life.

A voice emerged from the darkness.

Low and amused.

"Tough night?"

The words slid down my spine like ice.

I knew that voice.

I turned slowly, every cell in my body buzzing on high alert.

Stephen stood under the next streetlamp, ankles crossed, watching me like he'd been there for hours.

The harsh glow warped his face, sharp angles cast in deep shadows, making him look hollow, not fully human. Though I didn't look fully human right now either.

He took a slow step forward. "You look lost."

I swallowed hard. I wouldn't let him see my fear.

"What are you doing here?" My voice was hoarse.

He cocked his head, studying me like I was an unknown organism. "I could ask you the same thing. But I think we both know... you don't have an answer."

I shivered. Because he was right.

He moved closer, closing the gap between us in seconds. "That blood on your hands?" he mused. "Feels different, doesn't it?"

I took a step back. "Stay away from me."

Stephen's smirk widened. "I've seen you like this before," he said, tapping a finger against his chin. "Lost. Confused... violent. I wonder if it was still breathing."

The air rushed out of my lungs.

"What are you talking about?" I demanded, but I think I already knew.

"You were there that night." His voice was soft. Certain.

"With Julie."

I clenched my jaw so hard it hurt. Then I tried to even my breath, release the tension.

"You're lying," I whispered.

Stephen took another step, his voice turning almost gentle. "Am I? I've seen you. At Julie's house. Standing in the kitchen, holding that knife like it was the most natural thing in the world."

I shook my head. "No."

"You don't even remember, do you?"

The pavement changed under me.

I clenched my fists. "Shut up."

Stephen chuckled. "That's the thing about you, Sophia. You're asleep half the time, but it doesn't make you any less dangerous."

"I didn't hurt anyone," I choked out.

His gaze locked onto mine.

"Did you not?" he asked casually, as if asking something mundane.

A sharp spike of fear shot through me.

He leaned in, his voice barely a whisper. "I'm the only one who sees you for what you really are. The cracks. The darkness. The beauty. I've seen it all."

I staggered back. "No, you don't know me."

Stephen didn't blink.

"I saw Julie for who she really was, too. Perfect, pretty Julie." His lips curled. "But you? You're raw. Real."

I felt sick.

He angled his head, something almost fond in his gaze. "And I'm not going anywhere, Sophia. I'm the only one who can protect you."

My voice broke. "From what?"

Stephen's eyes gleamed.

"From yourself."

I stood there, frozen. My face, my hands, still stained with blood. Thoughts spiraling.

Stephen turned away, his relaxed figure melting into the dark.

As if he knew I wouldn't follow.

As if he didn't need to look back.

As if he'd already won.

35

— • —

NOVEMBER 20, 2024, 8 AM - SOPHIA

26 DAYS AFTER JULIE WENT MISSING

I wasn't going to talk to Jay.

Not today.

Not after last night.

I winced, not from pain, but from the kind of exhaustion that sinks bone-deep.

The morning rush of students swarmed around me. Voices overlapping, lockers slamming, but it all felt distant. Too loud. Like I was moving through a tunnel.

Three coffees deep, and all I had to show for it was a pounding heart and a jittery thrum in my ears. I was running on fumes. But it wasn't just exhaustion, something in my body still felt off. My hands felt like they weren't actually attached to me, my skin overly clean. Like the blood was supposed to still be there.

Stephen was somewhere in this hallway. I could sense it.

The thought twisted in my stomach, nausea curling like last night hadn't ended.

And if I saw Jay, I wouldn't be able to lie. Not about the sleepwalking. Not about Stephen. Not about the way his voice still sat in my head repeating over and over.

Last night had already gone too far before Stephen. The photos in the lockers, the diary pages, the implications. Jay saw the look in my eyes when I started to doubt myself, and when I realized someone had been watching me.

But if he looked at me today, he'd see something worse.

Because this morning, I left the house different.

I needed to make it to first period before he saw me, before he asked how I was… because I would crumble. I wasn't fine. Not even close.

I missed who I used to be.

The version who didn't flinch at every sound.

The one who could sleep through the night without waking up somewhere else tangled in panic.

The one who didn't wonder what she was capable of in the dark.

I wanted to tell Jay. God, I wanted to.

But if I did, there'd be no pretending I was okay.

Maybe part of me still hoped I could fix this quietly, alone, without dragging him any deeper into my mess.

But hope was starting to rot at the edges.

And underneath it, a darker truth was settling in:

What if this was it?

What if I never got back to who I was before?

What if I'd done something so horrible, I didn't even deserve to?

"Oh my God."

The words cut through my thoughts, sharp, almost panicked.

I barely had time to process them before Abbie grabbed my arm, yanking me to a stop.

Her eyes were wide, darting between me and something over my shoulder.

"What happened to your locker?!"

I went still.

For a split second, I didn't understand what she was talking about. Then, my eyes moved further down the hall and my heart rate tripled.

My locker.

The door was barely hanging on.

The entire metal frame was bent outward, jagged at the edges where it had been ripped open. It looked worse in the daylight, standing out stark against the neat rows of undisturbed lockers beside it.

Crap.

I had been so focused on everything inside that I had barely processed what had been done to it. The second Jay and I had seen the photos, the diary pages, everything had turned into a blur. We hadn't thought. We'd just grabbed everything, broken into Stephen's locker, and got the hell out of there.

But we had left behind the evidence that someone had broken in.

And now, everyone could see it.

I forced a casual shrug. "I-I don't know."

Abbie gaped at me. "You don't know? Sophia, WHAT! Someone completely destroyed it!"

I glanced around. People were staring.

Of course they were.

My fingers curled around my bag strap.

Don't react. Don't give them anything else to talk about.

Before I could respond, a voice cut through the hallway.

"Miss Whitaker."

I jumped.

I turned to see Principal Tinson standing near the lockers, her expression tight.

Oh, God.

She motioned toward her office. "Come with me."

Abbie shot me a look, half *are you in trouble?* and half *do you need me to cause a distraction so you can run?*

I just shook my head. "It's fine."

It wasn't.

But I still followed.

Ms. Tinson's office should have felt comforting.

The walls were painted a warm olive, a deliberate choice, something meant to put people at ease. Framed photos of her two little kids, Sally and Tommy, smiled down from the shelves, frozen in time, all baby teeth and sticky hands. Their crayon masterpieces were pinned beside her neatly framed college degrees, their jagged lines and uneven coloring standing out against the sterile perfection of her credentials.

A small lamp cast a soft glow over the desk, and the faint scent of vanilla lingered in the air. It was personal. Inviting.

But it didn't make me feel comfortable.

If anything, it made me feel more out of place. Like I was sitting in someone else's perfect life while mine unraveled around me.

The door clicked shut behind me, and I sat awkwardly across from her desk, wringing my hands together.

She just studied me.

Finally, she folded her hands. "Sophia, I wanted to check in on you."

I blinked. "Check in?"

"I know things have been... difficult lately. And with everything people have been saying, I just want to make sure you feel safe here at school."

My pulse spiked.

I kept my expression neutral, forcing a small nod. "I'm fine."

Ms. Tinson didn't look convinced.

"Your locker was broken into," she said carefully. "We've been reviewing the security footage, but—" she hesitated just slightly—"the cameras outside your locker didn't pick up anything. The footage from last night is missing."

The footage was missing.

I barely heard the rest of what Ms. Tinson said after that.

Relief hit first, almost dizzying. No footage meant no evidence, the pictures, the diary pages, the proof Stephen planted to make me look like I was stalking Julie, scaring her... and worse.

But the relief didn't last.

Because footage doesn't just go missing.

Someone made it disappear.

And that... that was worse.

Ms. Tinson's voice cut back in. "I was hoping you might be able to provide some insight."

I forced my face into something neutral.

"I have no idea who would do this," I said smoothly.

Lie.

She studied me again. "Are you sure?"

"I—yeah, I mean—it was probably just some stupid prank. It's not a big deal."

The words tasted wrong even as I said them.

Ms. Tinson didn't break eye contact. "A prank."

I nodded quickly, shifting in my seat. "Yeah. Just someone playing around."

A long silence stretched between us.

Then she sighed, leaning forward slightly. "Sophia, I know people talk. And I know sometimes they don't always say kind things. But if something is going on, you can tell me."

I forced a smile. "I really am fine."

She didn't look convinced.

But she didn't push, either.

Instead, she just nodded. "Alright. If you change your mind, my door is always open."

I barely muttered a thanks before slipping out of the office.

I had no idea how much she knew.

But the way she looked at me, waiting for me to say something, sent a chill down my spine.

36

NOVEMBER 20, 2024, 4 PM - SOPHIA

26 DAYS AFTER JULIE WENT MISSING

The drive to Dr. Patel's office was a blur. I barely registered the stoplights, the turns. Just the low hum of the engine and the dull throb behind my eyes.

But the second I stepped inside, something shifted. Not relief, just a sharp, artificial awareness, like my body had hit emergency reserves. The exhaustion was still there, deeply set, but my nerves buzzed, stretched thin and wired tight. It wasn't energy. It was desperation, just enough to hold it together a little longer.

As soon as I sat down it all came spilling out. The sleepwalking. The locker door barely hanging on its hinges at school. I didn't give anything up, just listed the shitstorm like rattling off a grocery list. Like if I said it fast enough, it wouldn't be real.

Dr. Patel collected herself before she spoke. "You said you had another episode, tell me what happened."

I hesitated, my gaze dropping to the floor. The words felt like stones in my throat, too heavy to say all at once.

"I woke up," I said finally, my voice barely audible. "In the middle of the street. I don't remember how I got there."

Dr. Patel nodded, her expression calm, inviting me to continue.

"There was blood," I admitted, the words tumbling out in a rush. "On my hands. I don't know where it came from. I don't know what I did."

My chest tightened as the images slammed into me.

The asphalt biting into my knees.

The harsh glow of the streetlamp, turning my skin sickly yellow and red.

The blood.

Dripping between my fingers.

Sticking into my face... I couldn't even tell her about my face.

And Stephen. His voice. His distorted features.

Dr. Patel's pen moved now, jotting down notes. "That's a lot to process. Let's take it one step at a time. What part feels the heaviest to talk about right now?"

I swallowed hard. I could've said the blood. Or waking up in the street. But that wasn't it.

My throat tightened. "That I don't remember... and that Stephen does," I said, tears falling now.

Dr. Patel leaned forward slightly, her voice soothing but steady. "Sophia, it's clear these episodes are taking a toll on you. But what Stephen says doesn't define you. What you feel right now, this fear, it's not who you are. It's your mind trying to protect itself."

I nodded, though her words felt distant, like they were coming from underwater. "I need to know," I said finally. "I need to know what happened that night."

She studied me carefully. "Then let's find out," she said. "I want to try another hypnosis session, something to help you access your memories of that night."

I hesitated. What if I admitted to something horrible? What if I never remembered, but Stephen did? He already knew too much.

I couldn't keep avoiding this.

"I'll try it," I finally said.

Dr. Patel dimmed the lights, and the room shifted into soft, muted shadows, as if the air itself had thickened. The faint hum of the white noise machine became more pronounced, and I could feel my heart beating in time with its low rhythm. I reclined on the couch, adjusting my body stiffly until my hands rested flat on my stomach. The leather beneath me was cool against my back, grounding me even as my mind began to swim.

"Close your eyes," she said softly, her voice steady and measured. "Take a deep breath in... and out. In... and out. Let your body relax, let your mind drift. We're going to go back to that night, Sophia. Back to the street. Back to the moment you woke up. I'll be with you the entire time."

My eyes fluttered closed, and I followed her instructions automatically, as if my body were no longer mine. My chest rose and fell in slow, deliberate movements. In. Out. In. Out. My arms, rigid moments ago, felt like they were sinking into the couch, boneless and heavy.

I focused on her voice, it was rhythmic, hypnotic, pulling me deeper with every word. The tension that coiled in my body unwound slowly, like someone had turned a dial in my head and released it.

The night came into focus, but not all at once.

First, the cold.

Then the silence.

Then the feeling that I wasn't supposed to be there.

Something pulled me forward.

Not my own will.

Like I was being led.

Then, the whimper. It pierced the silence, faint but sharp, making something deep in my chest clench.

My feet moved toward it before I could stop them.

A golden retriever came into view.

Chest heaving. Fur dark with blood. Its eyes flitted open.

It wasn't dead. But it was close.

And then Stephen stepped into my vision.

His hands were in his pockets at first, casual. Then he crouched down, slowly.

A knife gleamed in his palm.

The dog let out a strangled whine, its body twitching.

I should have run to the dog. Should have screamed.

I wanted to.

Every inch of me screamed to move, to stop this.

But I didn't.

Stephen's voice was low. Patient. Certain. "Touch it."

I tried to shake my head, to step back, something.

But my body didn't belong to me.

His head tilted, his smile calm. "Sophia." The pull tightened.

"Touch it."

I obeyed.

My hand moved, betraying every part of me that fought it, pressing against something slick, warm.

The dog flinched beneath my palm.

My mind screamed.

But I didn't pull away.

I couldn't.

So, I did the only thing I could.

I poured every ounce of warmth I had into my touch.

I willed the dog to feel something other than pain.

I pushed against whatever force was controlling me, trying, begging, to make this something else.

Stephen exhaled, pleased. Like I had proven something to him.

Like I had proven something about myself.

But he didn't know what was in my head.

That I hadn't just obeyed.

That I had fought.

"See?"

I didn't know what he wanted me to see.

I only knew that I had done what he asked.

That I had listened.

But not in the way he thought.

My eyes snapped open, and the dim light of the floor lamp filled my vision. My chest rose and fell rapidly, my heart pounding as though I'd run a marathon.

Dr. Patel was sitting beside me, her expression calm but watchful.

"You're back," she said gently. "What did you see?"

I swallowed hard, my throat dry. "I was walking," I said, my voice hoarse. "I found a dog. It was hurt. Bleeding. I... I think I tried to help it."

Dr. Patel nodded slowly. "That's good, Sophia. That's important. You were helping, not harming."

I hesitated. That wasn't true.

I had touched it.

Because Stephen told me to.

Dr. Patel kept watching me. "Do you remember anything else?"

I closed my eyes, and there was nothing. Then, like a glitch in my memory, something surfaced from after I woke up that night.

Stephen's hands. The way they had been shoved into his jacket pockets at first, casual, loose. Then how he had pulled one out, tilted his wrist just slightly as he spoke. A flash of silver.

I sucked in a breath.

A ring.

Not just any ring. The insignia.

The same one Calloway and Linworth wore.

Stephen, Calloway, and Linworth were connected.

One way or another, I was going to find out why.

***

When I got home, I saw a text from Eli.

> Eli: Working late. Grab food if you need it.

Which meant no dinner.

Lately, he'd been... off. Less present. Like he was always one step out the door, even when he was in the room. I kept telling myself he was just busy, but deep down, I wondered if I was the reason. Maybe I'd just been too much. I was literally drawing attention from half the town, and the sleepwalking was out of control.

He'd set me up with Dr. Patel, and somehow, it had only gotten worse.

It felt like he'd been avoiding me.

And honestly? I couldn't blame him.

I dropped my car keys onto the counter and instinctively went for the freezer, already knowing what I wanted. My favorite comfort food.

And also, the best food of all time.

Ice cream.

I yanked open the drawer, pulling out the carton of cookie dough and peeling off the lid. Rock solid.

I sighed, grabbing a spoon and running it under hot water, letting the metal heat up before pressing it into the ice cream.

Success.

I scooped out a huge wad of cookie dough, dropping it into my bowl. I went back and forth between the sink and the carton, warming the spoon, digging more out.

By the time I turned off the faucet, my bowl was borderline excessive.

I leaned against the counter, smiling down at the deliciousness in front of me, bowl in one hand, spoon in the other. Something simple. Something normal.

The sugar spiked my dopamine immediately as I shoveled my first bite into my mouth.

But my neck prickled.

That feeling.

Again.

My stomach dropped mid-bite.

192

I froze, spoon in my mouth, suddenly hyper-aware of the quiet pressing in around me. I looked out.

The kitchen windows were dark, the backyard an empty stretch of blackness.

The hallway was still.

Nothing was wrong.

Except everything was.

Not here. Not in this moment. But in all of it.

My heart wasn't racing because of the dark.

It was racing because last night was messed up.

Because Stephen was in my head.

Because I had touched blood-warm fur and let him smirk like he had won.

Because I wasn't in control.

But I could be.

I swallowed, slowly setting the spoon down. My eyes darted back toward the window.

Still nothing. But that wasn't the problem.

Stephen was the problem. Calloway was the problem. Linworth was the problem.

And tomorrow, I was going to get answers.

I was done feeling helpless.

37

NOVEMBER 21, 2024, 12 PM - NEWTON

27 DAYS AFTER JULIE WENT MISSING

The school's financial transactions had finally come through.

One week. Shorter than what Jenkins had predicted, but still too damn long.

I was sick of the runaround. The deflection. The Circle, the money, the people. Julie Greene.

No real answers. Just more questions.

So, when Jenkins called me over to his desk, I was half a second from grabbing him by the collar and shaking him out of anticipation.

I dropped into the chair across from him, eyes already on his monitor.

"Tell me this was worth the wait."

Jenkins kept scrolling through the files. "Depends on what you were expecting."

Not the answer I wanted.

Jenkins clicked through years of financial records. Page after page of state-funded grants, scholarships, and operational expenses.

The school had received steady funding for eight years.

From organizations like The Department of Education & Community Resources, The Circle Birmingham Chapter, and The Future Leaders Initiative.

The money was big. Hundreds of thousands in total.

I leaned in. "Pull up that one."

Jenkins opened it, expanding the details for "The Future Leaders Initiative," a $2,000 deposit from October 2021.

I scanned the document. Everything about it looked official. Proper state formatting, approved disbursement forms, signatures.

Except, I'd never heard of it.

"That organization exist?" I asked.

Jenkins didn't answer right away. He ran a quick search, his fingers clicking over the keyboard.

Nothing.

I frowned. "Try The Circle Birmingham."

Jenkins did, but got the same result.

I sat back, my jaw tightening.

I tried searching myself. Dug through old state budget reports, education oversight documents, nonprofit records.

No mentions. Of any of the organizations. No restructuring announcements. Not even a footnote.

My gut twisted.

This wasn't government money shifting hands. This was money that never existed in the first place.

They had been funneling money through the school.

Which meant someone had set up an entire operation just to keep it hidden.

And I had no idea why.

I watched as Jenkins scrolled further down the transactions.

"That's weird," Jenkins said.

The neat, official-looking state grants stopped. Starting October 10th two years ago, it was nothing like what we saw before.

Instead, the funding turned into a long string of letters and numbers where a bank name or vendor should have been.

I leaned forward, tapping the screen. "What happened here?"

Jenkins shook his head. "That's when the external funding stopped." He scrolled through the rest of the records quickly, "This is all anonymous from that point forward."

Jenkins combed through the recent records, slower this time. Then he stopped scrolling and looked at me.

I scrunched my face. "The hell is this Jenkins?"

Jenkins puffed out his lips. "No clue. Doesn't match any routing number, transaction ID, or anything else in the system. Could be an internal reference code, but... it's out of place."

Jenkins stared back at the screen for a second too long. His fingers hovered over the keyboard, hesitating. Then, almost unconsciously, he glanced over his shoulder. When he looked back at me, his usual nonchalance was gone.

"I don't like this," he muttered. "Whoever did this knew what they were doing."

"Can you trace it?"

Jenkins clicked around, doing things I legitimately didn't understand then shook his head. "This is above my head."

I let my gaze linger on the screen. Something about it didn't sit right.

I leaned in, stomach twisting. If this wasn't something Jenkins could figure out, what the hell was it? A shell account? A fake routing number? A message disguised as a transaction?

Jenkins tapped at his keyboard again, but nothing new came up.

"It's just numbers," he said. "Doesn't link to a bank, doesn't follow any known formatting."

Which meant someone made it up.

I swallowed hard. This isn't just fraud. This was something else. Something worse.

"Flag it," I said, shifting to get up. "We'll dig later."

"Hold on, there's one more thing" Jenkins said opening a second folder on his desktop.

"Something else came through with the transactions. Old personnel documentation, faculty onboarding stuff. It's all buried in the district files, should've been archived, but someone kept it live."

He clicked open a document labeled *Calloway, D.—Onboarding Packet.*

"Why are we looking at this?" I asked.

"Because of this," Jenkins said, scrolling down to the attached recommendation letters. There were three.

One from a former superintendent in Chicago. One from a now-defunct education nonprofit. And one from The Future Leaders Initiative, which appeared in The Circle transactions.

My pulse jumped.

I scanned the letterhead. Same stylized symbol with the Latin word for *order*. Included were phrases about "discipline," "order," and "legacy."

And the dates? 2014. Months before The Circle's first known transaction.

"You're telling me he was sent here with this kind of backing?" I asked.

Jenkins nodded. "Calloway didn't land in Ordinance. He was placed. And if this was a system for whatever they were funneling—"

"Then he wasn't just in on it. He helped build it." I finished.

I stared at the letters, unease crawling up my spine.

One of the letters ended with the line:

"Mr. Calloway has demonstrated exceptional ability to implement discreet and sustainable leadership pipelines, particularly in emerging communities."

"Who the hell writes a letter like that for a high school hire?" Jenkin asked, eyes squinting.

It wasn't just a recommendation.

It was a mission briefing.

I leaned back in my chair, rubbing my jaw.

Julie was in The Circle. Linworth had said so.

She was asking Calloway questions. Linworth had said that, too.

And now she was dead.

Had she seen money passing around?

Had she started asking the wrong people?

Was Calloway that wrong person?

I clicked the pen in my hand, scanning the screen again.

Then my mind went back to Stephen.

Stephen, who had looked me in the eye and acted like he didn't know what The Circle was.

Stephen, who had handed Calloway an envelope in a near-empty parking lot.

I still didn't know how deep he was in.

He was too young to be there when the government money was flowing in. So, he wasn't the one who built the system.

But the money trail had shifted two years ago.

And Stephen was at Ordinance High when it did.

Was he just following orders?

No. He didn't look like a pawn in that parking lot.

He looked like the one in charge. Like he was giving the orders... and Calloway was taking them.

I clicked the pen again. Too hard this time. The tip cracked against the desk.

Calloway and Stephen were at the center of this.

They knew something.

Or everything.

One of them was going to talk.

And if they didn't?

I'd make them.

38

— · —

NOVEMBER 21, 2024, 2:30 PM - NEWTON

27 DAYS AFTER JULIE WENT MISSING

Stephen Burns didn't flinch easily.

That much was obvious.

He'd smiled through every question at his house. Looked me straight in the eye and lied without hesitation.

So I didn't waste my energy going back there.

I found him alone in the library at Ordinance High. No parents. No audience. Just him.

I pulled out the chair across from him and sat down.

Stephen didn't even blink.

"Detective Newton," he greeted, closing his notebook at a measured pace.

Polite. Unbothered. Controlled.

Cut the crap.

"You ever wonder where all that money comes from?" I asked, voice light.

A blink. Slow, considering. Not thrown off, watching me now.

"Money?" he repeated, confused, as if I'd just asked him why the sky was green.

"The Circle," I said. "Fake organizations funneling money in."

Stephen didn't answer immediately. "Funneling money? Into what exactly?"

"Cut the shit, Stephen. I know what you're up to."

"Well... it sure does sound serious, Sheriff. But if it's true, if I was involved in something like funneling money... why would you be questioning me? Wouldn't you already have your answer?"

I let the silence sit.

Then, innocently, "Is this one of those times where you have a hunch, but you're not quite sure how to prove it?"

I watched him. Didn't react.

"Calloway's mixed up in this," I said. "And I saw you with him. Strip mall parking lot. Looked like a drop to me."

Stephen leaned back slightly. A fraction.

"A drop?" he repeated, like he was running the word through a filter in his head before deciding what to do with it.

"You passed him an envelope."

"If you say so," Stephen replied smoothly—neither confirming nor denying.

I let my eyes drop to his wrist.

A small, almost imperceptible bruise. Like something had pressed against his skin too long.

His hand shifted slightly, covering it.

I filed that away.

"So what was in it?" I asked.

Stephen lifted a brow.

"I don't know," he said lightly. "You seem very sure of what you saw. Why don't you tell me?"

I didn't answer. I just let my eyes flick back to the wrist he covered.

Stephen caught it.

He moved his hand, slowly. Then smirked at me, like it had never been a concern.

But it was a correction. A subtle one.

I didn't smile back.

"Julie was in The Circle," I said instead. My voice even.

"That's what Linworth said," I added. "And she was looking into something."

Stephen's lips pressed together just slightly.

Then, he exhaled like he was indulging a child who didn't quite understand the rules of the game.

"Was she? The Circle... that's the mentorship program you mentioned?"

That mock curiosity was back.

My teeth pressed together so hard my molars ached, but I didn't unclench. Didn't let the frustration show. That's what Stephen wanted. To see me crack first.

"She started asking the wrong questions. And now she's dead."

"So tragic what happened to her," he said, so overly dramatic it was insulting.

Like this was fun for him.

Fine.

"I've been hearing some things about you, Stephen. About Sophia."

His smirk shifted into a full smile. Brighter, sharper.

"I did tell you I see Sophia around," he said easily.

I narrowed my eyes.

"Word is, you've said some disturbing things about her."

"Disturbing?" Stephen repeated, clasping his hands like the idea was ridiculous.

"That's a strong word. Who told you that?"

"Jay Parker, for one."

Stephen shook his head at that. "Ah. That explains it."

"Jay has a temper, doesn't he?" Stephen mused, as if we were discussing an annoying trait of a mutual friend.

"I think he broke his hand on your face."

Stephen touched his jaw absently.

"It doesn't feel broken. But thank you for looking out for my safety."

His lip quirked on one side.

"He has a temper," he repeated. "I'm not sure what control I have over that."

I raised my brows slightly. "Fighting's a bad look for a golden boy like you. Don't you think?"

"Good thing I didn't start it, then."

"But you said something that made him punch you in the face."

Stephen paused for the second time.

"Sheriff Newton," Stephen said, slowly dragging his fingers over the edge of his notebook. "I know you're trying to piece something together, but I think you might be reaching." He paused, the slightest crease forming between his brows. Like he was genuinely puzzled. Like he almost felt bad for me.

His mouth just barely curled at the corner. "But I'm sure you've got a theory. You always do."

"I'm more interested in what you have to say. What are you doing with Sophia, Stephen?" I asked.

Stephen's composure faltered for a fraction of a second.

"You should ask her that."

He was good. But I was better.

"It's cute, the way you try to deflect," I said.

Stephen leaned forward just slightly, like I had finally, finally caught his interest.

"Tell me, Sheriff," he said, casually, "do you think you're good at your job?"

I smiled now.

"Because from where I'm sitting, it looks like you've been circling the same questions for weeks now. And I haven't done anything." He lifted his hand in a Scout's Honor gesture. Mocking.

"You've got theories. But not much else," he said.

He tapped his chin before continuing, "So what do you do when the facts don't add up?"

A pause.

"Do you change the theory?" His eyes glinted. "Or do you just start changing the facts?"

"Sheriff Newton."

I turned to see Mrs. Burns.

Her smile was still polished, practiced. The kind meant to disarm. But her eyes, those had sharpened, cutting straight through the space between us.

"I hope you're not upsetting my son. He's about to compete in debate club."

Not I hope my son isn't in trouble. Not I hope this is a misunderstanding.

She wasn't questioning. She was redirecting.

I didn't answer.

Stephen didn't look at her. Didn't acknowledge her at all.

He just watched me. Steady. Patient.

But I caught something in the way he moved.

That slight shift in his posture.

The quiet victory in the way his shoulders relaxed, in the way he sat just a little taller in his chair.

Because he knew it.

And I knew it.

The second I looked like the problem, he'd already won.

I didn't look back when I left.

Didn't let myself.

I made it to my car, yanked the door open.

Then my phone buzzed.

I pulled it out, thumb hovering over the screen before I unlocked it.

A text from an unknown number.

"Always a pleasure, Sheriff. You do ask interesting questions."

My grip tightened.

The slow burn of anger settled in my chest, curling, expanding.

Stephen.

Of course it was Stephen.

I ran a hand down my face.

I could hear his voice in my head, perfectly amused, perfectly untouchable.

Like he was waiting to see what I'd do next.

I inhaled slowly, trying to suppress the pressure building behind my eyes. My thumb hovered over the screen.

Should I delete it? Respond?

No. He wanted a reaction.

I locked the phone, exhaled through my teeth. I was going to get that kid...

I slammed my hand against the steering wheel.

By that afternoon, my office phone rang.

The principal at Ordinance High.

"Sheriff Newton, I was wondering if you could come in for a conversation."

I already knew what this was.

And I already wanted to break something.

When I stepped into Principal Tinson's office, Stephen was waiting.

His parents flanked him. His mother, composed as ever, legs crossed at the ankle, hands folded neatly in her lap. His father sat stiff, scrolling on his phone, jaw set like he had better things to be doing.

And Stephen?

Stephen sat there like he owned the place. Relaxed.

Mrs. Burns was already speaking before I even sat down.

"Sheriff Newton, I have to say, I'm concerned."

Principal Tinson hadn't even finished adjusting her chair.

Mrs. Burns was the picture of poised disappointment. "It seems my son has been the focus of quite a bit of attention lately. And frankly?" She adjusted her head. "It's starting to feel personal. A little... obsessive."

Stephen didn't speak. Didn't need to. His mother was already clearing the board for him.

Principal Tinson exhaled, rubbing her forehead. "Sheriff, I understand you have a job to do, but..." Her eyes ticked over Stephen, who, for the first time, lowered his gaze. Just enough.

Like he was playing the reluctant victim. Not eager. Not enjoying this, just deeply, deeply concerned.

Stephen sighed softly. "I respect Sheriff Newton, I really do." His voice was so measured, it was comical. "But lately... he's been watching me. Following me. It's making me uncomfortable... I don't feel safe."

It was a performance.

A damn good one.

I felt like I should clap for him honestly.

I wasn't going to push back.

Not here.

Not without proof.

Not now.

I was not going to make myself look exactly like the thing he was trying to paint me as.

39

— • —

November 21, 2024, 6:30 PM - Sophia

27 Days After Julie Went Missing

The sun was lower now, my eyes adjusting to the changing light as I approached Linworth's house.

He lived so close I could see his front porch from mine if I craned my neck. Close enough that I could walk there—here—before my mind had time to formulate an actual plan.

I hesitated at the base of his porch, staring up at the dark windows.

I shouldn't be here.

But I couldn't just let this go. I knew Linworth had information. And as much as I hate to admit it, out of him, Calloway and Stephen, he's the one I'm not scared of.

I took the steps two at a time and knocked, loud.

A long pause.

Then, slow footsteps.

The door creaked open just enough for me to see Linworth's face drawn and pale. Eyes shifting past me like he was checking for someone.

He already looked guilty, and like a complete mess. His face, which was typically clean-shaven, was now peppered with brown and white. He also had purple rings under his eyes.

"Sophia," he said, voice tight. "Go home."

I pushed my foot in to hold the door open as he tried to push it shut.

I ignored his words and stepped forward until my shoe was fully wedged in.

"You used to wear the ring every day, the one from The Circle," I said.

I didn't wait. I went for it. "But you're not the only one who wears it."

Linworth's body tensed.

I reached into my pocket and pulled out a folded scrap of notebook paper, slowly opening it so he could see.

The insignia.

The symbol I'd seen on Stephen's and Calloway's rings.

Linworth's breath hitched. His eyes darted to the drawing, then back to me. For a second, just a flicker, something crossed his face.

Recognition. Then alarm.

Like I had just shown him something I wasn't supposed to know.

Then, just as quickly, regret.

"I-I don't know what that is," he stammered.

Liar.

"You wore the ring in the yearbook photo," I said. "Faculty spread. Two years ago."

His jaw clenched. His fingers twitched at his sides.

"I stopped wearing that ring last year," he admitted. But even as he said it, something passed over his face, like he knew he'd just made a mistake.

"But you wore it," I pressed.

He exhaled sharply, shaking his head. "It wasn't—" He stopped, running a hand over his face. "It was for a club. A stupid, overblown club."

For the first time, a hint of something close to hope stirred in me. However reluctant, he wasn't denying it. Finally, someone was saying the club existed beyond on just a piece of paper.

"Julie didn't think so," I said quietly.

"She wrote about it," I continued. "She wrote about you. And she was scared."

A long pause.

"She came to you, didn't she?" I pressed. "She told you she was scared of Stephen."

His hands curled at his sides.

"No she didn't..." he started.

"Don't lie. I read her diary."

His face blanched, "Julie... Julie thought she saw things other people didn't."

"And?"

His nostrils flared slightly. "And I told her she was reading too much into it. That Stephen was just trying to get in her head." His voice flattened. "That she should lay low."

I waited for him to continue, but he didn't.

"You told her to back off?"

I could practically hear Linworth's teeth cracking.

205

"I told her it wasn't her fight," he admitted finally. His voice was quieter now. "That if she stayed quiet, she stayed safe."

I looked him dead in the eye. "And now she's dead."

He looked away.

"So who's setting you up?" I asked, voice sharp. "If it's not you that did something to her, then who?"

His fingers tapped against his arm, restless.

"I think you already know," he said barely above a whisper.

His grip tightened on the doorframe.

For a second, I thought he might shove me and shut it.

But his fingers just flexed.

Like he was at war with himself.

Like he wanted to tell me to leave.

He sighed hard and yanked the door open.

"Inside. Now."

The door shut behind me quickly.

Linworth didn't turn on the lights.

His house was dim, the air slightly stale, like no one had opened a window in too long, like he'd been holed up in here.

The last time I was here, it had felt colder, emptier. Now, I noticed things I hadn't before. A jacket draped over the back of a chair. A framed photo, slightly askew on the bookshelf. A coffee mug with rings staining the table beneath it.

The place looked worse than I remembered. He'd stopped keeping up with it. Dust settled in the corners. The sink was stacked with dishes that hadn't been washed. A bag of chips was left open on his coffee table, ants lining up along the opening to feast on crumbs.

But it wasn't the house that unnerved me now. It was the anticipation of this conversation.

"I shouldn't be talking to you," he muttered, running a hand through his stubble.

"But you will," I said, defiantly.

He let out a nervous chuckle, shaking his head. "You don't get it, do you?"

"Then explain it to me." I threw the paper down onto the table, the insignia stark against the white. "What does this mean? What is The Circle?"

His face looked tired, so tired. Like he had absolutely no fight left in him.

And it was clear he knew exactly what it meant.

206

"It was a club," he repeated a little reluctantly. "An old charter that Calloway brought to Ordinance about ten years ago. Sold it as a way to create leadership opportunities, a network for students with potential, all that polished, school-approved crap. And he got it sanctioned by the school board... I've been a part of over 20 school clubs, and they never go through that level of official approval."

He looked around the room cautiously as he spoke, as if someone else might hear him.

"And *you* got involved?" I asked.

He let out a bitter, humorless laugh. "At first? Yeah. Calloway sold me on it. Said we could build it together, be principals in a few years if we played it right, made the right connections."

He looked past me, like he was remembering a version of his life he didn't quite recognize. "For me, it was little things. Tutoring gigs for rich families a few towns over. Meetings with a couple of district admins who suddenly had time to talk about my 'future in leadership.' Perks, I guess. But nothing flashy. But Calloway? He started showing up in tailored clothes, driving a new car. Stuff that didn't line up with a teacher's salary, or his lifestyle when he first showed up in town. But I didn't ask."

He rubbed his face with one hand, as if trying to wipe the memory away. "For a while, it was what I expected. Overachievers with too much ambition playing secret society. Thinking we were in on something special. But then..."

His voice dropped. "Then someone new got involved."

"And that changed things?"

Linworth exhaled sharply. "You have no idea."

"Was it Stephen?" I asked.

Linworth's gaze darkened.

"Was it?" I pressed.

"He's... a problem." Linworth said.

My stomach turned.

"And Julie knew Stephen was a problem?"

Linworth hesitated.

And that was the answer.

"She tried to talk to you about him," I repeated. "And you ignored her."

His expression cracked even further. His face completely sagged.

"She came to me a couple of times," he said. "Said Stephen had been following her. That he was... obsessed."

My heart pounded. "And you told her to what? Act like nothing was wrong?"

Linworth flinched, like I had slapped him.

I didn't back down.

"She's dead, Linworth." My voice sharpened. "And Stephen is still here."

His breath shuddered.

His fingers twitched, an anxious, useless motion, as he picked at the tiny roots of his beard.

Like if he could just scrape away his mistakes, he might be able to pull himself back together.

He squeezed his eyes shut, but his lips kept moving, like he was whispering something to himself.

The first audible thing I could make out, "She asked me for help... and I shut her down."

His voice cracked.

"I can't fix that," he said. "But I can stop you from making the same mistake."

"How?"

Linworth's fingers curled around the edge of the table, tension creeping into his grip. For a moment, I thought he wouldn't answer. That he would retreat back into this shell of himself.

But, finally, "I can't give you the answers you want."

Frustration flared in my chest. "Why not?"

He stared past me like he was measuring every word before he spoke it. "Because it can't come from me."

"That's not good enough." My voice was sharper than I meant it to be, but I didn't care. "Stephen is messing with me now. Julie is dead. I need to know why."

Linworth's face was a war between fear and guilt. "If you want real answers... you need to look in the right place."

"Where?"

His eyes lifted to mine, pausing, weighing. "The cabin," he said.

"The one near the reservoir?"

Linworth shook his head. "Not the one you probably know. There is another one, past the ridge, deep enough into the trees that most people don't even know it's there. About a half mile in from the gravel lot."

I did know it. There *was* an old cabin back there. One I had only seen once, years ago when I was young enough to still wander the woods with Eli. It had looked dilapidated even then.

"What's there?" I asked, frowning.

Linworth pressed his fingers into his eyes like he was trying to will this entire situation away.

"You will find... at least some answers there."

The *way* he said it.

Like he wished he didn't have to.

Like he knew exactly what I'd find.

I didn't press any further, didn't linger. I turned toward the door.

But Linworth's voice stopped me cold.

"Sophia."

I glanced back.

His face had changed. The exhaustion was still there, but something else had crept in. Something sharper.

Terror.

"Julie thought she could handle this too," he said.

I swallowed hard.

His voice dropped lower.

"*She was wrong.*"

40

— • —

NOVEMBER 21, 2024, 8 PM - SOPHIA

27 DAYS AFTER JULIE WENT MISSING

If there's an award for worst places to be at night, the route to this cabin would win by a landslide.

"Good decisions are overrated anyway," I muttered to myself, tripping on a branch as I pulled out my phone. I looked down, swiping for my flashlight and sighed as the battery symbol shifted to red. "Here lies Sophia Whitaker," I continued, "killed by questionable phone charging choices."

A text popped up as I toggled the screen:

> Jay (7:02 PM): Hey, missed you today and yesterday. Wanna hang out?

> Jay (7:45 PM): You good?

> Jay (8:02 PM): Getting kinda worried. Just text me back, okay?

I stared at the messages, guilt curling tight in my chest. I wanted to talk to him. More than anything. But I couldn't.

Not yet.

My thumbs hovered before I finally typed back.

> Sorry I disappeared. I just need a few days to deal with some stuff. Talk soon?

I watched three dots appear. Disappear. Appear again.

Jay didn't send anything back.

He was the only person lately who made me feel even remotely happy, like there was still some version of me that wasn't completely unraveling.

And here I was, pushing him away.

But I couldn't drag him deeper into this... when I don't even know what I've done.

Especially when I was out here chasing half-baked clues from Linworth after sleep-walking with Stephen and now wandering around the woods like I was starring in some low-budget horror movie.

Linworth had given me just enough to follow while being as vague as possible.

I stumbled my way through the forest, counting my steps as I stretched deeper and deeper.

When I finally glimpsed the cabin, flashes of memory flitted at the edge of my awareness.

A cold floor.

A voice—mine? Whispering something I couldn't understand.

Something sharp.

The cabin had been sitting in the back of my mind like a splinter I couldn't pull out. Looking at it now, I knew this is what was surfacing when I was under hypnosis. A flash of something half-buried.

That was just yesterday, but it feels like so much has changed.

I was done waiting for the next awful thing to happen. Now, I was doing something.

Still, as I walked up the creaking stairs, unease settled deep.

This place had been waiting for me.

And I hated how certain I was of that.

The door creaked as I pushed it open, the sound loud enough to make me freeze momentarily. My flashlight beam swept across the room, illuminating broken furniture and shattered glass.

"Definitely haunted," I whispered, stepping inside. My voice sounded too loud in the empty space, so I shut up and focused on not tripping over the debris. My foot caught on something anyway, a chair leg? A demon's claw? Who could say.

I hesitated just past the threshold, my fingers tightening around the strap of my bag. The floorboards groaned under my weight, protesting each step as if they hadn't been walked on in years.

Maybe I would have believed that. That no one had been here for years.

Except there were footprints all around.

Not just one set.

Some crisp, clearly recent. Others half-faded, like ghosts pressing into the dirty floor. Some from shoes, others from bare feet.

Dust floated in the beam of my flashlight, the air shifting only where I moved. A single moth fluttered near the sink, wings batting against the grimy windowpane, trapped in its own cycle of escape.

I shivered and forced my feet forward.

A wooden chair sat tipped over near the door, its legs half-splintered, as if someone had thrown it or stomped it into the floor. But the couch cushions, pristine, untouched, didn't belong. It looked new, like someone had just put it there.

The coffee table in front of it was barely holding together, one side warped from years of moisture creeping into the wood.

There were so many places to search. I wasn't even sure where to start... or what I was looking for.

I moved to the nearest wall, running my fingers over a bookshelf packed tight with old textbooks and paperbacks too warped to be readable. I pulled one free and flipped through the pages, only to find them fusing together, brittle and curling at the edges.

A noise, small and quick, skittered across the floor.

I jumped, my whole body tensing, as the book slipped from my hands.

A cockroach darted across the floorboards and disappeared into the gap beneath the sink.

I swallowed hard and wiped my hands against my jeans. Keep it together, Sophia.

There was too much here, too many things to dig through. If Linworth wasn't leading me into some kind of trap, if this place actually held something, I needed to focus.

The table was covered in old receipts, stray wrappers, and water-stained papers curled at the edges. I nudged through them carefully, my fingers brushing over a rusted lighter, the kind you had to flip open. When I picked it up, my thumb dragged against something faintly engraved on the side.

The insignia.

A restless energy buzzed under my skin.

I set it down and turned toward the desk in the corner.

Outside of the oddly perfect couch, this was the only thing in the cabin that didn't look like it had been completely damaged from time. There were scratches on the surface, fresh enough that they hadn't rounded like everything else. The top drawer had a rusted lock hanging loose, barely holding it shut.

I tugged it open.

Inside there were a mess of papers.

Not organized in any way I could tell. Shoved in haphazardly, like someone had been in a rush.

I pulled them free. Some were receipts, old schedules, notes that didn't make sense. But beneath them—

I pulled out a stack of loose-leaf pages, bundled together with twine.

My breath locked up.

They were torn from a notebook. Julie's diary.

I didn't even need to read the first word, I knew from the handwriting.

The edges were frayed, some of the ink smudged. Some pages were missing whole corners, but the words, the ones that weren't too damaged, were still legible. And... Stephen's name was everywhere.

I flipped through quickly, my fingers trembling, skimming for anything that stood out. There were at least a dozen pages. Too many to read here. My heart pounded as I forced myself to focus, I couldn't move until I read at least some of the entries, my feet like weights, pushing into the rotten wood.

***

October 2nd

I tried to talk to Linworth again today. I thought maybe... since he'd been in it longer... he'd know how to leave. How to back out before things got worse.

I joined The Circle for him.

But ever since I found out, he won't even look at me.

His hands are always shaking. Not just a little. Trembling, barely holding himself together.

I asked him if he regrets it.

His jaw just tightened. He stared at the desk, fixated on a deep scratch in the wood like it was the only thing keeping him grounded. Like if he focused hard enough, maybe I'd disappear.

He said it didn't matter if he did.

That's when I knew.

He wasn't going to help me.

And whatever I'd uncovered... he already knew about it.

He chose to live inside it. Like it was safer to be part of the machine than to fight it.
No one leaves.

***

October 4th

I told Stephen I wanted out.

He smiled like he'd been expecting it.

"Everyone panics at first," he said. "But you'll understand soon. This is bigger than you. Bigger than any of us."

He said The Circle was about structure. Discipline. That we were chosen to lead because "the rest of them don't know what they need."

I told him it felt wrong.

He said something about right and wrong just being words. That control was all that mattered.

Then he looked at me and said, "You're lucky I see your potential. Most people don't ask the right questions."

It didn't feel like luck.

It felt like a warning.

***

October 7th

I'll never be the same.

I don't even know what I am anymore. What he's made me.

I keep thinking about my yard. How the grass felt wet. Cold. How the sky was empty of stars, and the wind didn't move. Like the whole world was holding its breath.

How Stephen whispered things in my ear like it was a promise, like it was inevitable.

Like it was already decided.

I told him no.

He laughed.

I didn't scream.

Not until after.

214

And even then, no one heard me.

I'm not going to tell anyone.

Not because I don't want to.

But because I know what he's capable of.

And it's not just him.

Sure, Stephen's in charge now.

But The Circle listens to him. They protect him.

They made it clear, if I said a word about any of this, I'd be gone.

That's how they worked.

***

October 9th

I think Stephen has found someone new.

Sophia Whitaker.

He says her name like it belongs to him. Like he's already decided something for her, and she just doesn't know it yet.

I don't like the way he talks about her.

Like she's an idea, not a person.

I think he's making her do things.

And I think she doesn't even know.

Today in the hallway, she walked past me. Her eyes were distant, like she wasn't fully there.

Like I was looking at the first version of myself. Before I understood what he was capable of.

I'm scared for her.

And I'm scared of her.

And I don't know which is wor

***

The ink trailed off.

A break in the line.

Like she had been interrupted.

Or like she never got the chance to finish.

The pages felt heavier now.

Julie had seen what was coming for her, and for me. But no one listened. Or maybe they were too scared to stop it.

I shoved the pages into my bag.

I could read the rest later, I needed to get out of here.

I stepped outside, shutting the door behind me.

And the second it clicked shut, something moved inside.

Just a shift. A creak.

Like the cabin was breathing.

I walked faster.

And I swore to myself that I would never come back here again.

41

— ⋅ —

NOVEMBER 22, 2024, 4 PM - SOPHIA

28 DAYS AFTER JULIE WENT MISSING

Detention was a waste of time.

Forty-five minutes of watching the clock tick toward the twelve mark.

Tick. Tick. Tick.

Like it was counting down to something eons away.

I had been late to school too many times this month. Too many mornings spent trying to piece together where I had been.

Now I was stuck in a half-lit classroom with a teacher who barely acknowledged me and a handful of my classmates who were either sleeping or whispering to each other like I wasn't there.

When the teacher's phone alarm went off signaling the end of detention, I should've felt relief.

But I didn't.

It was already dusk, the sky a deep, endless gray. The school parking lot stretched out in front of me, empty except for a few scattered cars. Mine sat beneath the flickering streetlamp, pulsing off and on.

I shoved my hands deeper in my jacket pockets.

There was a prickling down my spine, then the hair on my arms stood on end. The wind kicked up, rattling loose leaves across the pavement, the cold pressing against the back of my neck.

I told myself I was being paranoid.

I was *always* paranoid now.

Julie's diary pages were burned into my brain.

Every word.

Every warning.

"I think Stephen has found someone new. Sophia Whitaker."

I swallowed hard, trying to shake it off.

Julie had been scared—for me. Of me.

I was starting to understand why.

I reached for my car door.

"You've been busy."

My whole body went rigid.

The voice was too close.

I turned slowly and saw Stephen.

He stepped away from the truck parked beside mine, hands in his back pockets, head cocked in amusement. Like we were picking up where we left off.

A slow smile crept across his face. "I was wondering when we'd finally talk again."

I didn't move.

Didn't breathe.

But my pulse was already hammering.

I thought about the pages. About Julie's words.

I could tell him I knew.

But that would give him something.

And I wasn't ready for what came after.

"I know what you did to the dog," I said instead.

Stephen stilled for just a moment, then grinned.

"Good." His voice wasn't surprised. It was pleased. "And?"

The word slithered down my neck.

My grip tightened around my keys. "And?" I echoed.

"And what did you do?"

The breath stalled in my throat.

The way he said it, like there was something to answer.

My nails pressed into my palm. "I tried to help it."

Stephen let out a slow exhale, like that answer wasn't true. "Is that what you did?"

My skin felt too tight. "I didn't hurt it."

Stephen's smile widened. "You didn't pull away either."

My stomach twisted.

His eyes lit up like Christmas lights. "You're remembering. Finally."

"I know what YOU did to that dog." My voice was sharp now. "And I know what you are."

Stephen took a step forward, measured. "Do you?"

"I'm not like you," I said, remembering the note he left for me.

His gaze flashed with something unreadable. Then he hummed. "You keep saying that."

I put my hand behind my back and weaved my car key between my fingers like a dagger. "Because it's true."

Stephen groaned, almost theatrically. "Maybe you should be focusing less on what I did, and more on what you did."

I stiffened.

"I didn't do anything."

He tilted his head. "No?"

He paused, "What *do* you remember about Julie?"

Something crashed through me.

A spike of nausea, a flash—blurry, fragmented.

Julie's face. Yelling my name. A wrist yanked back. Something sharp.

My vision blurred.

I sucked in a breath.

No.

No, that wasn't real.

I didn't do anything to Julie.

I couldn't have.

He did.

My heart was pounding so loud I barely heard him when he spoke next.

"Just like you didn't touch the dog, right?"

My stomach lurched.

I shoved him.

Hard.

He barely stumbled.

And then, he laughed.

A slow, quiet, thrilled kind of laugh.

I ripped my car door open, but he was faster.

His fingers barely brushed my neck.

Not grabbing—just feeling.

Like he was memorizing the way my pulse was slamming beneath my skin.

I pushed back.

"You're running again," he said, voice teasing. "Why do you always run when you start to see the truth?"

His eyes were shining now, like he was watching something unfold in real time.

"It's okay," he whispered. "You'll remember soon enough."

He leaned in, slow.

I went completely still.

He inhaled, like he was breathing me in.

His nose brushed just over my hairline. "You smell like adrenaline."

I thrust my key into his side and yanked the door open.

Stephen whooped and fell into a full-body, giddy, high-on-victory laugh as I scrambled into my seat.

"See?" he called after me. "You're just like me."

I slammed the door shut and locked it so fast my hands shook.

Stephen didn't move.

He just stood there, still laughing.

Waving at me as I peeled out of the parking lot, breath coming in gasps, my vision blurred.

The lines in the road were hazy.

I didn't stop driving.

Didn't stop shaking.

Didn't stop hearing his voice in my head.

I needed help.

I had to drown him out.

I had to hear someone else say something, anything, real.

I hit the call button before I could think.

Dr. Patel picked up.

42

November 22, 2024, 5 PM - Sophia

28 Days After Julie Went Missing

My hands were still shaking as I sat on Dr. Patel's couch, fingers digging into the worn fabric of my jeans. The office felt smaller than usual. The air thick with the weight of what I wasn't saying yet.

Dr. Patel watched me, pen poised over her notebook, waiting. I'd called this emergency session, but now that I was here, I didn't know where to start.

"Tell me what's on your mind, Sophia." Her voice was calm, steady. Expectant.

I swallowed hard, my fingers twisting in my lap. "The night Julie was killed." The words barely came out. "I don't remember it. Not where I was. Not what I was doing. Nothing. It's like my brain just... skipped it."

Dr. Patel inclined her head slightly. "Has it always felt that way?"

"Yes," I admitted. "It's been eating at me for weeks. Every time I think I'm close to remembering, it just... vanishes."

"And how does that make you feel?"

I let out a bitter laugh. "Like I'm losing my mind." My voice was sharper than I intended. "Everyone keeps asking me questions. Newton. Eli. Jay... Stephen."

His name came out lower, almost involuntary. Dr. Patel noticed.

"Sophia," she said gently, "do you remember the last hypnosis session? When you woke up with blood on your hands the night before and thought you'd done something terrible. But when we looked closer, we found the truth."

I froze. I did remember. But I hadn't told her everything.

"You weren't hurting anyone," she continued. "You were helping. But fear convinced you of the worst. This could be the same thing."

Did I not hurt it?

I wanted to believe her. But the truth was, I had done something wrong that night. I had touched the dog when Stephen told me to. And what if there were other things I'd done that he had told me to do...

"Then why can't I remember?" My throat tightened. "Why does it feel like there's this... fog in my head, blocking everything out?"

She studied me carefully. "Remember what we've talked about. Your mind may be protecting you from something it wasn't ready to face. That doesn't mean you did anything wrong."

But what if I did?

Dr. Patel hesitated. "Last time, hypnosis helped you find the truth when fear convinced you otherwise. If you're ready, we can try again."

Hypnosis had given me one piece of the puzzle. One night. One moment. It had shown me the dog. Stephen's voice. The control he had over me.

But this was different.

This was the night Julie *died*.

I had no idea what I'd find.

But what choice did I have?

I couldn't keep losing that night to the gaps in my memory. Even if I didn't get everything, I had to get something.

My pulse thudded. I took a deep breath.

"Okay," I said finally.

The lights dimmed, and the room shifted into a cocoon of shadows and stillness. I laid back on the couch, my body stiff and unyielding. Dr. Patel's voice was steady, drawing me into her rhythm.

"Close your eyes," she said softly. "Take a deep breath in... and out. In... and out. Let your body relax, let your mind drift."

I followed her instructions, my breaths shallow at first but gradually deepening, just like last time. The tension in my limbs melted away, replaced by a strange, floating sensation.

"We're going back, Sophia," she said. "Back to the night Julie died. Back to where your memory is blurred. You're safe. You're in control. Let your mind take you where it needs to go."

The air around me seemed to shift, growing colder and heavier. My heartbeat slowed, each thud echoing in my ears like a distant drum. Images came alive in my mind, fragmented, like pieces of a broken mirror.

Then came the pull.

The first thing I saw was Julie's house, glowing faintly under the pale light of the moon. I was standing outside, my bare feet sinking into the damp grass. The air was thick with the scent of pine and earth, but something else too.

I didn't remember walking here. I didn't remember why I was here.

The scene shifted. I was still in the backyard, hidden in the shadows of the tree line.

My gaze snapped toward the house. Not because I chose to. Like something had turned my head for me.

Then I saw him.

Stephen.

He was standing near the back door, his figure blending into the darkness. Waiting.

He called my name.

My body moved. My feet stepped forward. One, then another. But I didn't tell them to.

The memory blurred again.

I was inside Julie's house now, the cool tile pressing against my toes. The light over the kitchen sink dimly illuminated the space, the faint hum of the refrigerator the only sound.

And then my hand curled around something.

Cold and hard.

I looked down.

A knife.

The blade caught the faint light, gleaming like liquid silver.

Why was I holding a knife?

A whisper brushed against my ear. No, inside my head.

It was a memory. Stephen's voice, "Hold it."

My breath stilled.

A noise came from the living room, a soft creak shifting under weight.

I moved toward it.

Not my choice.

But my body obeyed.

The knife was heavy in my hand.

Each step was slow. Mechanical.

My breath came in shallow gasps, my fingers locked around the hilt, unable to let go.

"Sophia?"

Julie's voice cut through the fog, sharp and panicked.

I stopped. The knife dangled loosely in my grip.

Her face was pale, her eyes wide with fear as she stared at me.

I opened my mouth, tried to speak.

Tried to tell her I didn't know why I was here.

But no sound came out.

The memory fractured again, splintering.

Stephen's voice echoed somewhere in the distance.

"She doesn't even know what she's doing, does she?"

Not talking to me. To her.

Julie gasped. He grabbed her. I think she tried to run.

Then, blackness.

I was outside again.

The cool night air bit at my skin.

A house loomed behind me.

My feet kept moving, carrying me into the trees.

A violent jolt tore through me.

No, wait.

Go back.

What happened with Julie?

The blade was gone now. My hands were empty.

I looked down and saw Julie's body in the dirt.

The trees loomed overhead, dark and endless, swallowing the sky.

She was sprawled out, her eyes wide open, unblinking, staring at... nothing.

I couldn't move.

I couldn't breathe.

I was standing near her.

But I wasn't alone.

Something shifted in the memory, a presence just at the edge of my awareness. But my mind refused to focus on it. Like I was blocking it out.

I caught a glimpse of my hands, dirt was under my nails.

Had I been digging?

My fingers twitched. I felt it, the weight of something heavy. The feeling of pushing. Of covering.

I staggered back.

Did I put her here?

224

Was I trying to bury her?

I didn't know.

A sound pierced through the fog, a voice? A name? Something just beyond my reach. But the harder I grasped for it, the more it slipped away.

Julie's lifeless face burned into my vision.

I had been here.

I had seen her like this.

I had done something.

A sound ripped out of me, raw and jagged, like something had just cracked open inside my chest.

My eyes flew open.

I was in Dr. Patel's office. The walls tilted. My stomach lurched.

I barely made it, grabbing the trash can just as everything inside me wrenched itself free. Vomit hit the plastic hard, acid burning up my throat as my body shook violently.

Dr. Patel's voice was somewhere behind me, but it was muffled.

Like I was underwater.

Like I was still there.

Still in the woods.

Still staring down at Julie.

Her body lifeless.

Her eyes open.

Unblinking.

I couldn't stay here. I had to get out of this office.

Someone was with me in the woods.

It had to be Stephen. What had he made me do?

I staggered to my feet, still clutching the trash can, my breath uneven.

I stumbled out of the office, feet barely finding the floor beneath me. My hands were shaking so badly the trash can tilted, bile splattering onto my sleeve, onto the hallway floor.

I didn't stop.

Didn't look back.

Because if I stayed in that room, if I stayed in this nightmare one more second—

I was never getting out.

I can't live like this.

I need to get out.

I need the truth.

Not reassurance. Not comfort.

Someone who wouldn't hold my hand, wouldn't tell me it was okay.

Someone who would rip this apart, piece by piece, until there was nothing left to hide.

Until I finally knew what I had done...

43

NOVEMBER 22, 2024, 10:30 PM - SOPHIA

28 DAYS AFTER JULIE WENT MISSING

The need for answers clawed at my skin.

I couldn't stay in the dark anymore.

The room was spinning. Whether from the leftover nausea or the memory slamming against the walls of my skull, I didn't know. I woke up still clutching the trash can. I must've passed out from sheer exhaustion.

I grabbed my phone. Newton's direct number was in my contacts from when I'd sent him The Circle document in Calloway's office.

My thumb hovered over the call button.

I'd already taken pictures of everything. Captured every detail, even the ones that made me look bad. The ones that made me look guilty.

Because maybe I was guilty.

But I wasn't hiding anything anymore. That was the point.

I sucked in a sharp breath and hit the green phone icon before I could talk myself out of it.

Newton answered, his voice rough with exhaustion. "Tell me why I'm answering the phone at 10:30, Sophia?"

I swallowed, forcing my voice steady, even as my pulse ricocheted inside me.

"I... I need to meet you."

A long beat of silence.

Then sounding exasperated, "That so?"

I nodded, then realized he couldn't see me. "Yes. It's important. I—" I hesitated, inhaling sharply. "I found something."

This time, the silence was heavier.

Then Newton's voice grew lower, edged with something I couldn't place.

"Found what?"

"Evidence. It's about me. About Julie. About Stephen."

That shut him up.

The pause on the other end of the line stretched.

When he finally spoke, his voice was different. More careful.

"Let's meet at the station."

"No, I'm not going back there. That's what made everyone think I had something to do with Julie. We need to meet somewhere else."

As if that really mattered after what I was about to tell him...

Newton made an audible sound of annoyance. "Where then?"

"There's a diner. Thirty minutes out. Off the highway. 24-hour place. I don't want to do this in town."

I could hear him thinking.

Weighing it.

"Thirty minutes."

Not a question.

I swallowed. "Okay."

I gave him the diner name then the line went dead.

The pressure in my chest didn't disappear, but it shifted. I'd done it. I had put it in motion. Newton didn't have the pages yet, or my story, but he would.

I turned toward my closet, reaching for a jacket—

And then I noticed something.

The door.

It was slightly open.

I stopped.

Stared.

Had I left it open?

No.

I never did that.

I always closed it. Some holdover paranoia from childhood horror movies still made me close closet doors religiously. Just in case.

My pulse ticked up, the air around me suddenly too still.

Slowly, I moved toward the closet, like I was expecting one of the monsters to jump out.

My breath shallowed.

I pushed the door all the way open. Stepped back.

Nothing.

Just my clothes. My shoes. The same things that had always been there.

But the creeping feeling in my stomach settled deep.

I grabbed my denim jacket then shut the door. All the way.

And for the first time, I wondered...

Had someone been in my house?

My heart slammed against my ribs as I turned.

Jay.

Perched on the roof outside my window like it was any other night. But it wasn't.

His hood was up. Hands in his pockets. Eyes locked on mine through the glass.

I opened the window. "Jay..."

He didn't move.

"I dropped you off three days ago," he said, voice low. "After we found out a known psychopath had photos of you in a shoebox. And you shut me out."

"I told you I needed a few days," I said quietly.

"I know what you said. But do you really think I could just... sit with that? With everything we found? With everything that's happened? And not hear from you?"

I looked down. My throat burned. "I didn't know what else to do."

He climbed through the window. Slower than usual, like he didn't know if he was still allowed.

I sat on the edge of my bed. Julie's diary pages were spilling from my bag.

Jay's eyes landed on the pages. "Is that—"

"Julie's," I said. "What's left of it."

He sat next to me. Not touching. Just close enough that I could feel him.

"I didn't mean to shut you out," I said. "Things just... got worse."

Jay didn't say anything. Just waited.

"I woke up in the road that night," I said. "After the lockers. After you dropped me off."

His face changed—barely, but I saw it.

"Stephen was there," I whispered. "I don't know what happened. I don't remember how I got there, but he made me do things... and since then I've been seeing—Julie, in the woods, dead—and I think maybe I—"

My voice caught. I shook my head. "I can't do this, Jay. I can't bring you into it."

He stepped forward. "Soph—"

229

"No." I backed away. "You don't get it. I think I might've helped him. Or watched her die. Or—I don't even know. I can't remember. And if I really did something, I don't want you anywhere near it."

"I'm not near it," he said. "I'm already in it. Don't you get that?"

I looked away. "I'm meeting with Newton tonight."

Jay stared at me. "You're what?" He ran a hand through his hair. "You were just gonna go alone?"

"I don't have a choice."

He stepped closer. "Then I'm going with you."

"Jay—"

"Stop. Just stop." His voice cracked. "You don't get to decide this. Not for me. Not after everything. You think I can just turn it off? Walk away? After you finally let me in?"

"I'm trying to protect you."

"From you?"

He let out a short, bitter laugh. "You think I don't see you right now? You're scared out of your mind, and acting like pushing me away is some kind of strength."

"I'm trying to survive," I said. "Trying to make sure we both do."

He stepped in, close now. "And I'm trying to stay. And you won't let me."

That hit harder than I wanted it to.

"I don't need protecting from this," he said, quieter now. "I just need you not to run."

I didn't answer. Couldn't.

He looked at me like he was daring me to argue.

"I'm in this, Sophia. Whatever it is. There's no walking back from it. Not for me."

I swallowed hard. Everything in me shaking.

"I don't know what's going to happen," I said.

Jay didn't even blink. "Then we'll find out. Together."

44

— • —

NOVEMBER 22, 2024, 10:50 PM - SOPHIA

28 DAYS AFTER JULIE WENT MISSING

We didn't speak as we left. But this silence wasn't heavy. It held.

Somewhere between my front door and the edge of town, with headlights cutting through the dark, I started talking. There was no clean way to explain it. So I didn't try. I just told him everything.

When the neon diner sign came into view, my stomach turned.

The C in *COFFEE* was burnt out—leaving only *'OFFEE'* in blinking red.

Felt about right.

Jay parked the truck, engine idling. I stared at the light bleeding onto the pavement, heart hammering.

"This is it," I whispered. "The part where I hand myself over."

Jay reached for my hand. Held it like it was the only steady thing left in the world.

"You don't have to do this," he said, eyes burning. "There's still time. We could go. Right now. Drive until the map runs out."

"Jay…"

"I'm serious," he said, but it came out rough. "We could disappear. I don't even care where we go. If you said the word…"

My throat tightened. "That's not the answer."

"I don't care," he said, leaning closer. "I'd still do it."

He kissed the inside of my wrist. Gentle. Devastating.

"I'd run for you, Sophia. I'd go anywhere for you."

My chest cracked open, because I believed him.

And I couldn't let him.

Part of me wanted to say yes. To let him take me anywhere and forget all of this. But the other part, the part buried under weeks of fear, knew I'd never outrun it.

"I have to go," I whispered.

He nodded, but his hand lifted toward me before falling uselessly to his side.

"I'll be right here," he said. "No matter what happens. I'll be right here when you get out. Or—if you need to run—I'll be ready."

I looked at him one last time.

Not a boy. Not a crush. Not even just a friend.

But someone who saw me. And stayed anyway.

"I know," I said, as I opened the door.

The cold air hit me.

But I didn't look back.

Because if I did, I wouldn't be able to go.

Inside, the air was thick with fryer grease. The floors had that familiar stickiness that made you question if anything was clean. A lone waitress refilled napkin dispensers while an old guy nursed his coffee at the counter, staring straight ahead.

I had picked this place for a reason. Neutral ground, on the way to Dr. Patel's office. It was in the middle of nowhere. Somewhere no one could listen too closely.

I spotted Newton before he spotted me, sitting in a booth at the back, one arm draped over the back of the seat, the other hand wrapped around a steaming mug. He wasn't in uniform, but he still looked like a cop with his stiff posture. The kind of presence that made people look away rather than at him.

I hesitated. Just for a second.

Newton hadn't seen me yet.

This was the last moment I could walk out. Just turn around and disappear.

But I didn't.

Because it didn't matter.

This was happening, whether I was ready or not.

Newton's gaze snapped up.

I was out of time.

I walked over, slid into the seat across from him, and pulled my bag into my lap. My fingers curled around the strap, grounding myself in something solid.

"Appreciate the drive," Newton said sarcastically. "Next time, let's meet on a mountaintop. Really maximize the convenience."

I ignored him, pulling out the first folder and sliding it across the table. "Look at the pictures first."

Newton frowned but didn't argue. He flipped the folder open, then stopped.

The first photo was me, standing in the woods. Outside Julie's house the night she died.

Handwritten timestamp: October 25th 2:47 AM. The night she went missing.

His expression darkened. His entire body went still.

He flipped to the next one. Another angle. Then another.

3:07 AM 4 days before she went missing.

3:41 AM 7 days before she went missing.

4:02 AM 8 days before she went missing.

Each one of me. Standing beneath Julie's window. Just... watching.

Newton exhaled, controlled. Then he set the photos down and folded his hands over them.

"What the hell, Whitaker."

And I told him everything.

The sleepwalking. The break-in at Linworth's. The diary pages that Stephen planted, making it look like I was stalking Julie. The notes left behind. The locker break-in. The additional page with "I see you" scribbled on it.

And the cabin.

Where I found the final pages. The ones about Stephen.

Where Julie wrote that she was never the same after what he did to her.

Where she wrote about The Circle.

Where Stephen's obsession with her shifted—to me.

Newton listened.

His fingers twitched against the tabletop, his eyes locked onto me with an intensity that made my skin feel too tight. His jaw worked like he was biting something back.

"Alright," he said finally. "Now let me see these diary pages."

I slid him the second folder.

I watched as he read. This time, his reaction wasn't instant. It built. There were subtle shifts—his brows drawing together, a sharp inhale, the way his fingers clenched slightly around the edges of the pages on and off.

I could tell when he hit the passage about Stephen.

The one where Julie wrote what he did to her.

Newton swore.

Louder this time.

His entire demeanor changed. The tension in his shoulders wasn't about me anymore.

He flipped another page. Then another.

When he finally straightened, I felt something exuding from him.

Newton shut the folder. He didn't speak. Didn't look at me, either. Just pressed his thumb against the edge of the table, staring at the pages like he could burn them with sheer will.

He drummed his fingers once against the tabletop.

"I need to see the cabin," he said.

I nodded. "I can take you."

Newton finally looked at me. His expression gave nothing away, but I could feel it—the measuring. The weighing. Like he was lining everything up in his head, stacking it against what he already knew.

He pulled a few bills from his wallet, tossed them onto the table, and stood.

"Let's go."

I hesitated. "So, you believe me?"

Newton looked at me, his eyes tired. Frustrated. Like the entire case was shifting under him, and he wasn't sure if that made things better or worse.

"I think Stephen's dangerous." His voice was careful, measured. "And I think you've been in the middle of this a lot longer than you realize."

A breath I didn't know I was holding shuddered out of me.

But Newton wasn't done.

His gaze sharpened. "I also think you're still not telling me everything."

My stomach twisted.

Because he was right. I hadn't told him what I'd remembered at Dr. Patel's... I knew I needed to.

I followed him out into the cold and into the police car.

The door shut with a hollow *thunk*.

Across the lot, Jay stood frozen beside his truck, hands clenched at his sides, eyes locked on mine through the glass.

He didn't move.

Just watched me disappear behind the red and blue lights.

And I watched him, until the car pulled away—

He was gone.

45

— · —

NOVEMBER 22, 2024, 11:45 PM - SOPHIA

28 DAYS AFTER JULIE WENT MISSING

Dread pooled in the back of my mind as we reached the reservoir.

Newton's grip flexed on the wheel. "You remember the path once we get there?"

How could I forget? I'd tripped, crashed, and nearly gotten eaten alive by the trees the first time. All in my relentless quest to reach a building that belonged in a horror movie.

"Obviously," I muttered.

Newton scoffed. "Okay then."

Going to the cabin tonight with Newton wasn't what I expected when I made the call to talk to him, but maybe that was a good thing. Doing anything at all was better than sitting in my own head. Newton was here. We were chasing the truth. That was enough. For now.

And maybe it was the adrenaline, or the fact that I wasn't hiding anymore—but something in me felt... steadier. Bolder. Like for the first time, I was steering the car instead of being dragged behind it.

When we got closer, I pointed toward the gravel inlet. "Pull off here. We need to walk the rest of the way."

I heard the tires crunch as Newton slowed and killed the engine.

Branches groaned overhead as the wind ripped through the trees. Dry leaves scratched against each other, whispering in constant movement. An owl let out a low, haunting cry somewhere in the darkness.

Newton grabbed a flashlight the size of my forearm from the back seat, flicking it on with an authoritative click. The sharp beam sliced through the dark like a blade.

I swallowed hard. "It's this way."

Newton followed, close but not crowding.

The ground was a minefield, just like I remembered. Uneven dirt, snaking roots, fallen branches hiding beneath the leaf cover. The moment I took a step, something cracked under my foot.

Loud.

Newton sighed. "You have no stealth, do you?"

"Oh, I'm sorry, did I miss all my Navy SEAL training? My bad."

Another step. Another crack.

Newton shot me a look. Exasperated.

I gritted my teeth and kept moving. "Do you want me to show you where this is or—"

Then, a rock.

A traitorous, evil rock.

I didn't see it until my foot caught the edge, my ankle twisting, my balance vanishing beneath me.

I barely got out a muffled "*Oh, crap—*" before Newton grabbed a fistful of my jacket, yanking me up like a freaking toddler about to fall on its face.

Not graceful. Not heroic. Just... lifted like a helpless, walking disaster.

Heat burned up my neck.

I straightened immediately, brushing myself off like it hadn't happened. "I had that under control."

Newton didn't even look at me. "Sure."

I scowled harder.

"You okay?" he asked after a second.

Not mocking. Checking.

I nodded, ignoring the mortifying wave of embarrassment.

We kept walking.

There was a rustling.

Not nearby.

Ahead.

I turned sharply, eyes scanning the trees.

Newton's hand drifted near his belt. He heard it too.

Probably an animal, I told myself. A deer. A squirrel. I ran through every cute woodland creature I could possibly think of.

We kept moving.

Then, a sharp snap.

Newton's flashlight shot toward the sound. Nothing was there.

My pulse ticked up.

The wind rattled the branches above us again. A sharp, hollow groan.

The cabin loomed ahead. Its edges swallowed by the thick, unlit woods around it.

Newton pushed the door open, and the air changed.

Not just the temperature.

Something felt wrong.

Newton stepped inside first, his flashlight cutting a sharp line through the dark, sweeping over warped floorboards, peeling wallpaper, and the rotted remains of furniture that hadn't moved in years.

Except, it had.

Everything was still where I last saw it.

But the room felt occupied.

I shivered involuntarily, arms crossing tight against the chill that crept up my spine.

Newton's eyes scanned everything. Not rushed. But methodical. Like he was analyzing a crime scene.

I hovered near the threshold, refusing to move deeper in.

The last time I was here, I had been alone.

Now, standing next to Newton, something about it felt more real.

The beam of his flashlight landed on me, sharp and unforgiving. I squinted.

"Whitaker, don't touch anything."

I rolled my eyes. "Who led who here?"

Newton didn't react, just turned back toward the room. "Just... don't."

The whole place looked just like I remembered—straight from *The Amityville Horror*.

Everything except the couch.

Still pristine. Still the only clean thing in this entire nightmare of a place.

I stepped toward it, feeling the presence of Newton's flashlight tracking me.

Then I sat down.

The moment I did, something lurched inside me.

Not a memory.

Just something wrong.

A sensation, crawling up the back of my neck. My stomach twisted. My whole body buzzed with something I couldn't name.

I shot up fast. My knee slammed into the coffee table, sending a crumpled beer can rolling onto the floor.

Newton turned sharply. "What?"

I shook my head. "I—I don't know."

His flashlight hovered. Watching me.

I stepped back, throat dry.

I shouldn't have sat there.

I didn't know why exactly. But I knew it with every nerve in my body.

Newton didn't push. But he didn't stop watching me, either.

A skittering noise scraped across the floor, sharp and sudden.

I jumped again.

Newton sighed. "Relax. Just a mouse." He shook his head. "Kids..."

I shot him a glare. Not the time, Sherlock.

Newton moved toward the desk.

"What the hell?" his voice had a hard edge.

I turned. He was crouched, his flashlight angled downward. The bottom drawer of the desk was partially open, just enough to reveal the contents.

Something glinted in the light.

I stepped closer.

Syringes.

Dozens of them. Some empty. Some half-filled with an almost colorless liquid.

"What is that?" I asked, my voice tight.

Newton didn't respond. He grabbed a plastic evidence bag from his satchel and slid one of the syringes inside.

The expression on his face gave me a sinking feeling.

He didn't look surprised. Just disgusted.

Like he'd seen this kind of thing before and knew exactly what it was.

I forced myself to look away, my heartbeat pounding in my ears.

He rifled through the rest of the drawers, scanning old papers, receipts, useless junk, nothing else like the syringes.

There was a soft creak.

Behind the bookshelf.

Something was here.

I barely had time to react before a shadow launched toward the door.

The screen slammed shut.

"FREEZE!" Newton's voice roared through the cabin, bouncing off the walls.

His flashlight whipped around, his gun already raised.

I turned, pulse spiking.

A shadow was running.

Tall. Lean.

They tore through the trees, their silhouette vanishing into the dark.

Newton bolted after them, flashlight bouncing wildly.

I didn't think. I just ran.

The cold bit into my skin, branches whipped against my arms, sharp and cutting. The ground was twisting beneath my feet.

I tripped. Caught myself. Kept running.

But they were so much faster.

Newton's light bounced ahead, disappearing between the trees.

Within seconds, I lost sight of him completely.

I lost sight of everything.

I stopped.

Cold air burned in my lungs.

I reached for my pocket, but my fingers closed around nothing.

I probably left my phone in the car.

Crap.

I turned, but there was nothing to adjust to. Just solid black, stretching in every direction.

No flashlight.

No Newton.

No path.

Just darkness.

The realization hit like a gut punch.

I was alone.

The woods weren't silent. They were deafening.

A branch creaked somewhere above me.

Leaves hissed as the wind curled through them.

A low, distant howl echoed across the trees.

I turned slowly, trying to orient myself.

Okay, I could do this. Just think, Sophia.

The road ran north to south. I knew that.

Moss. That's north, right? I felt for it—

It was on all sides.

That wasn't how it was supposed to work.

I tried to picture the road, the reservoir. But the dark swallowed it all.

I pressed a hand against my chest, trying to force down the panic clawing its way up.

Newton would find me. He had a flashlight. He'd come back.

I just had to wait.

I swallowed.

A whisper of air moved against my leg.

I froze.

The wind? No. The wind didn't breathe.

Something moving.

I turned sharply, staring into nothing.

A twig snapped.

This time behind me.

My breath locked in my throat.

I didn't move.

I couldn't.

Something was out there.

My heartbeat pounded even louder in my ears.

I crouched down, fumbling blindly until my hands found the rough bark of another tree.

I pressed my back against it. Tried to listen.

The wind rattled through the branches.

I heard a shift.

Not far.

I clenched my teeth, forcing my breath to stay steady. I wasn't actually alone. Newton had to be out here somewhere.

I pressed a hand to my ribs, trying to slow my breathing. "Newton?" I whispered, barely audible.

All I heard was the groan of trees shifting in the wind.

I hesitated, pulse hammering, then tried again, louder. "Newton!"

My own voice sounded pathetic and panicked against the vast emptiness of the woods. The second his name left my mouth, I regretted it.

What am I doing? That was dumb. How desperate am I?

Someone else is out here too. They could hear me.

I clenched my jaw. *Stupid.*

I forced myself to move, my arms stretched out in front of me to feel my way around. One step. Then another. Leaves crunched too loud beneath my feet.

I heard a sound that wasn't mine.

A sharp rustle.

The air lodged in my throat like a stone. Not the wind. Not an animal.

Footsteps.

Someone was coming.

Closer.

I braced myself ducking down, every muscle locking up. My fingers scrambled at my sides, grasping blindly until I found a stick.

Not much, not a real weapon. But something.

I tightened my grip around it, knuckles white. My heart slammed against my ribs, beating so hard it drowned out everything else.

Then another step.

Faster.

A sprint.

Coming straight for me.

I sucked in a sharp breath, legs frozen, stick clenched uselessly in my hands.

A blinding beam flooded my vision, erasing everything in a flash of white.

It was Newton.

I let out a shaky breath and slumped forward.

A few tears slipped before I could stop them.

I swiped at them fast, maybe he wouldn't notice.

He noticed.

But he didn't say anything.

Didn't move towards me.

Didn't tell me it was fine.

Because it wasn't. I could still feel the adrenaline shooting through me.

I swallowed hard, my throat dry. "Who was that? Where did you go?"

Newton didn't answer.

Just stared past me into the trees, jaw so tight I thought he might break a tooth.

Finally, he exhaled sharply and pulled out keys. "We're going back to the station."

No explanation. No elaboration.

Just clipped, furious restraint.

Like he wasn't just pissed at whoever ran.

He was pissed at himself for losing them.

46

— · —

NOVEMBER 23, 2024, 1 AM - NEWTON

29 DAYS AFTER JULIE WENT MISSING

I slammed the door to the interview room behind me, not bothering to check if Sophia flinched.

She didn't.

She was too busy staring at her hands, fingers curled tight against her palms like she expected to see something there. Like she was trying to piece herself back together in real-time.

I didn't have time for whatever storm was unraveling in her head.

The rush hadn't worn off. My limbs still buzzed, fingers stiff from the cold, shoulder barking from where I hit the ground. I hadn't gone down easy. Neither did he.

Stephen was fast. Worse, he was smart.

The second I tackled him, he twisted like a damn escape artist. Slipped out before I could lock him down. I landed one good hit. I had him. Right there. Half a second more. If I hadn't turned—

But she called my name.

I ran a hand down my face.

Damn it, it wasn't her fault. She didn't know.

But something in me shifted when I heard her.

Like the wrong kind of déjà vu.

A feeling I didn't have time to name.

And now he was gone.

All I had was the flash drive.

I bagged it the second I saw it hit the ground. Small, silver, barely a blip in the dirt. Must've slipped from his jacket when I took him down. Maybe he didn't notice—or couldn't risk going back. Either way, it was mine now.

I turned.

She was still in the chair.

"Stay here," I said. My voice came out sharper than I meant. "Don't move."

She looked up, face tight. "I'm not under arrest?"

"No, but you're the only person in this town who keeps ending up in the middle of the same damn mess, and until I figure out why, you're not going anywhere."

That should've gotten a reaction. A protest. A glare. Something.

But she just nodded once, accepting.

I turned on my heel and pulled out my phone as I walked. The station was dead this time of night, just me, Sophia, and Jenkins once he got here.

And a hell of a lot of questions that needed answering.

The phone barely rang before he picked up.

"Christ, Newton. It's one in the morning."

I was already sitting at Jenkins' desk, waiting. I reached into my pocket, pulling out the evidence bag, letting the flash drive catch in the light.

"We have a problem."

There was a pause. A rustling of sheets. Then Jenkins' voice, more alert this time. "That kind of problem?"

I hesitated, my eyes bouncing to the evidence bag on my desk, the flash drive, the diary pages, the pictures spread out like something fragile and dangerous all at once.

"Worse."

Jenkins stayed quiet. Then came a sigh and the slow creak of bedsprings.

"Shit. Be there in ten."

I hung up.

The pleather chair groaned under my weight as I dropped into it, dragging a hand down my face. My jaw ached from how tightly I'd been clenching it, but I couldn't bring myself to relax.

I flipped through Julie's diary pages again, scanning words I'd already read, trying to make sense of them.

Linworth was looking less and less suspicious by the minute. She hadn't been investigating him, she'd been obsessed with him. Every line confirmed it. She joined The Circle just to be closer to him, convinced they were meant to be.

And then there was the strangest part, the entry where she described how they were going to end up together. How it was inevitable. How she had already photoshopped a picture of them side by side to put into her locket. Until the day it became real.

By the time Jenkins walked through the door, I'd all but worn a hole through the pages with my stare. He looked rough. His hoodie was pulled on over whatever he'd slept in, hair flattened on one side. But his brown eyes were sharp beneath the bleariness. He knew this wasn't nothing.

"What now?" His voice was gruff, but not annoyed. He was past that. This was concern.

I just gestured to the chair across from me. "Sit down."

Jenkins frowned but obeyed, sinking into the chair. His eyes jittered toward the evidence bag in my hands.

He blinked, leaning forward a little.

"Is that... a flash drive? Who even uses those?"

I bounced my leg. "Stephen Burns. Haven't looked yet."

Jenkins raised an eyebrow. "Wait—Stephen gave you that?"

I shook my head. "Dropped it while running."

He scrubbed a hand over his face as an unspoken understanding settled between us.

I'd already told him everything about my latest encounters with Stephen.

"Shit."

I ignored the tension crawling up my spine.

We weren't just pulling at threads anymore.

I turned the flash drive over in my hands, the plastic cool against my fingers. I wasn't sure what was on it. But after reading those diary pages, seeing the way Sophia looked when she handed them to me...

I knew it wasn't good.

I inserted it and the screen roared to life, three folders appearing on the monitor.

CODE.

TRANSACTIONS.

ARCHIVE.

I frowned, my fingers hesitating over the touchpad. I clicked the first folder.

It contained a single document.

The Circle – Chapter 13 Operational Code *(Document last modified: 5 months ago)*

Jenkins let out a low whistle. "Operational code? Like a handbook?"

I clicked it open.

The screen filled with four sections, and my gut tensed.

THE CIRCLE – OPERATIONAL CODE

"They falter. We act. Peace endures."

SECTION 1: PURPOSE

- The Circle exists to uphold peace through structure, selecting those fit to lead and guiding those who are not.

- We do not seek control for its own sake. We preserve the stability others threaten to undo.

- Where chaos begins, The Circle intervenes.

SECTION 2: MEMBERSHIP DOCTRINE

- The Circle is above all.

- The existence of The Circle is never discussed. In external contexts, it may be referred to as a mentorship program or innovation incubator.

- Operational and financial details are restricted to approved internal sessions.

- Do not ask where it comes from. Accept it. Use it.

- Failure is not tolerated. Expulsion is permanent, and not without consequence.

SECTION 3: RECRUITMENT

- Selection is based on two primary criteria.

    a. Promise – Intelligence, persuasion, ambition. Leaders in the making.

b. Control – Influenceable, eager to belong, easily molded.

- Chapter leadership determines the ideal balance. Too many Promising members breeds disruption. Too many Controlled weakens the structure.

- Induction is non-negotiable. Once chosen, candidates proceed or are quietly redirected.

SECTION 4: LOYALTY & DISCIPLINE

- Loyalty is not earned. It is assumed. There are no second chances.

- Structure is safety. Discipline is mercy. Control is peace.

- The outside world believes in freedom. We believe in function.

- To betray The Circle is not rebellion. It is to misunderstand your place.

- There is no neutrality. You are either a hand of the structure, or in its way.

FINAL NOTE:

- You are either at the top, or you are beneath it. There is no in between.

Jenkins exhaled through his teeth. "Loyalty is everything? This sounds like a cult."

"I knew The Circle was off, but I didn't realize it was so... structured. I don't know how far this goes," I said.

Jenkins shook his head. "What do you think the Expulsion consequence means?"

Julie's diary flashed through my head.

My hands curled into fists. "I think it means you don't leave."

Jenkins stilled beside me.

I clicked out of the folder and into the one titled **TRANSACTIONS**.

A black window popped up. **ACCESS RESTRICTED.**

Jenkins grabbed the mouse and tried again. The folder blinked open—but the files inside were incomprehensible. Strings of characters, randomized symbols.

"That's encryption," Jenkins said

"Can you break it?"

"Not here." His face scrunched, already reaching for his phone. "I'll send it to Cleveland PD's cyber unit. If anyone can pull this apart, it's them."

"How long?"

"Hard to say. Could be days. Could be never."

That wasn't an answer I liked.

"Whoever set this up knew exactly what they were doing," Jenkins muttered. "This isn't just basic file protection. This is next-level. Someone wanted this locked down."

I leaned back. The money. The secrecy. The way the funds completely shifted two years ago.

The Circle had buried their tracks.

We weren't going to get very far with a document of operational code alone.

There was one last thing to check.

I navigated to the **ARCHIVE** folder.

Twelve video files. No labels. Just dates.

I hovered over the most recent one.

Two weeks ago.

***

November 7th, 2024

Grainy, black-and-white footage.

A bedroom.

Sophia's.

My muscles felt strung too tight, like a wire about to snap.

She was asleep.

Curled under the sheets, face relaxed.

The door opened.

A shadow moved into the room.

Stephen.

Jenkins muttered a low, steady stream of curses.

Stephen stood there. Watching her.

Then he stepped closer.

His lips moved, but I couldn't make it out.

Sophia stirred.

Then she sat up.

Her eyes were open.

But she wasn't awake.

Jenkins tensed, "What's happening?"

Stephen whispered again.

Sophia nodded.

Then, audible this time, Stephen purred, "You're such a good girl."

Jenkins turned to me. "Newton, what the hell are we looking at?"

I clenched my jaw.

This wasn't just manipulation.

Stephen had control over her.

***

October 17th, 2024

The timestamp was about a month ago.

Julie.

Jenkins stiffened beside me. "This is before she—"

I didn't answer.

Julie was standing in her bedroom.

She wasn't moving right.

She swayed slightly, fingers pressing into the fabric of her shirt. Like she was trying to keep herself grounded.

Her pupils were too large.

Her movements too sluggish.

Jenkins exhaled sharply. "She's drugged."

Julie turned slightly. The camera tilted with her.

She reached out, grasping at her dresser like she was looking for something.

Someone moved behind her.

Julie's voice came, soft, distant.

"What... what's happening?"

We heard the bedroom door shut out of sight.

The screen cut.

Jenkins swore. "If that's what I think it is I swear I'm going to get that kid."

I couldn't respond, I thought back to her diary pages... then clicked on one of the earlier videos.

***

October 8th, 2024

The timestamp read 3:12 AM.

It was dim, the screen filling with the inside of a cabin. The cabin I was just in.

Stephen and Sophia were there.

I sat forward. She was sitting on the couch, barefoot, wearing a hoodie that looked oversized on her small frame with an "Ordinance Student Council" logo printed largely on the front.

I remember digging into the school's club records, including the student council, I don't remember Sophia being in it.

Her posture was slack. Not asleep, not fully, but not awake either.

Sleepwalking.

Stephen stood directly in front of her. Way too damn close.

I forced my eyes to stay on the screen.

He knelt in front of Sophia, staring at her.

Not like she was some random girl.

Not like she was someone he was messing with.

Like she was... his.

His hand lifted and he tucked a strand of hair behind her ear.

Sophia didn't so much as flinch. I ground my teeth.

His fingers ghosted over her wrist, soft and careful.

He lifted her hand to his cheek, closed his eyes like he was savoring it. Like she was something precious.

I felt something spasm in my chest.

This looked like something I couldn't fully place. Devotion?

For a long time, they stayed like that.

Then there was a small drop of her hand as her fingers twitched. Tiny, barely noticeable.

Her breathing began to change, gradually sharper.

She was waking up.

All at once, she jerked back. Her shoulders tense and posture stiffening.

I saw the exact moment she became aware.

Not just of the room, but of Stephen.

Her hand yanked back from his grip, fear in her eyes now.

"What—" she started.

Stephen just smiled like he was waiting for this, then he moved fast, pulling something out of the bottom desk drawer.

Before she could register what was going on, he pricked her neck with a syringe, practiced.

She struggled for a few moments, then slumped.

The tension in my head was unbearable. I watched him catch her head as it fell. Then he stared at her for a moment, like he was checking his work. Making sure she was fully under.

With little effort he scooped her into his arms, like he had done this a hundred times before. He carried her out of the frame.

I could hear Jenkins breathing beside me. "What has he done to these girls? What happens when the video cuts out?"

He sounded as haunted as I felt. I clicked one of the earlier videos.

***

September 10th, 2023

The image was shaky. Like the camera was being held.

It was focused on Rachel.

She was sitting in a car. Passenger seat.

Her hands twisted together in her lap.

A male voice spoke from behind the camera. Low. Almost soothing.

Stephen, I could tell from the sound.

Rachel shook her head.

"No. I—I don't want to—"

The camera jostled.

Stephen said something too quiet to hear.

Rachel's breath stuttered.

251

Her hand lifted.

Pressed against her chest.

Her pupils were huge.

Something in my gut twisted.

She looked dazed. Like she had been awake for days.

Her entire body tensed.

She turned her head away slowly then back toward the camera.

And she smiled.

The kind of smile that was forced.

Like she knew something was wrong.

And she was trying to hide it.

The screen cut.

Then flickered back on.

The camera was on the ground in the parking lot, angled up toward the car. The door was wide open, there was blood splattered on the lens.

Rachel wasn't in the car anymore.

Jenkins stared. "That was—"

I slammed my hand against the desk, making the monitor rattle.

This footage was from the same month she went missing.

Was it the same day?

I couldn't remember.

My pulse pounded hard enough to shake my vision. My entire body locked up, my fingers digging into the desk.

How the hell had this been under me the whole time?

How many times had I told myself we had done everything we could? That we had exhausted every lead? That everything pointed to her running away? That we didn't miss anything?

Something snapped inside of me, as a scream of tension welled up in my chest.

My fingers curled so tight my knuckles cracked. My breath sawed through my chest, slow and forced.

I pressed my palms against the desk, grounding myself. One breath. Two. Three.

Then my vision tunneled.

The next thing I knew, my hands were under the desk, and I was flipping the whole thing over. The crash echoed through the station like a gunshot.

Jenkins shot up. "Newton!"

But I wasn't listening.

I had failed her.

I had failed all of them.

I squeezed my eyes shut. Control it.

I let out a slow, steady breath.

Then I stopped, and I stared at the screen now on the floor.

There were still eight more videos.

The air in the station was suffocating.

I rocked back on my heels, sighing with resignation. "We have enough."

Jenkins ran a hand through his hair, eyes locked on the screen. "But, do we?"

I knew he was right.

There were hints, suggestions. But nothing concrete. Outside of drugging Sophia.

And Stephen?

He was still out there.

Jenkins shook his head. "What the hell do we do now?"

I couldn't watch another video tonight, and I didn't need to.

I could feel the determination setting in.

We find Stephen.

I'd spent over a week thinking I was nailing him down.

But the truth was, Stephen had never been hiding.

He was the predator.

This stops, now.

No more waiting. No more reacting. I got the ADA on the phone and prepped the affidavit.

I was done playing by Stephen's rules.

Now, he plays by mine.

And I was going to make damn sure no one else ended up on the other side of his camera.

47

— • —

NOVEMBER 23, 2024, 2 AM - NEWTON

29 DAYS AFTER JULIE WENT MISSING

The girl in the interrogation room wasn't the same one I'd put in there earlier.

This one was smaller.

Quieter.

She sat with her elbows on the table. She wasn't looking at me. Or Jenkins. Still just staring at her hands like she was waiting for them to stop shaking.

I didn't sit right away. Just stood in the doorway, studying her.

She looked exhausted.

Not just tired. Depleted. Like she had been running for miles and suddenly realized she wasn't getting anywhere.

Jenkins shifted beside me, rubbing a hand over his jaw. We weren't sure how to do this, at least not with her. This wasn't the same girl I'd dragged into this room before. She wasn't a suspect.

She was a victim.

I stepped forward, pulled out a chair, and sat. Didn't say anything at first, just let the quiet settle.

Jenkins sat too, but only for a minute. Long enough to make it clear he wasn't the guy for this. He glanced at me. I nodded, and he stood again.

"I'll go put some coffee on," he muttered. His voice was gruff, but I caught the way his eyes bounced to Sophia before he left, indecision.

He knew she wasn't the enemy.

When the door clicked shut behind him, I leaned forward, clasping my hands together on the table.

Sophia still hadn't looked up.

"Tell me what you remember."

Her shoulders tensed. She let out a short breath.

"I told you everything I remember," she said, her voice flat. "That's why I came to you, so you could be the one helping me fill in the gaps. To tell me what I've done, what Stephen did... to me, to Julie."

I studied her. There was no fight in her voice. No sarcasm. Just resignation.

I knew exactly what she meant, what the diary pages had been hinting at all along. That Julie had been afraid of her. And honestly? On paper, it didn't look good for Sophia.

I didn't piece it all together until after the diner. After she told me everything—and the videos backed it up and even more. Stephen had manipulated her. Drugged her. Set her up. But it wasn't until I looked again at the notes she'd given me, the ones she found in her locker... that it hit me. The handwriting. It matched the timestamps on the photos—Stephen's handwriting. He'd written them. Framed her, even in the details.

"You want me to tell you that you killed Julie?"

I waited.

She swallowed. Shook her head once, voice coming out in a rasp. "No."

"So, what do you want me to say?"

She finally lifted her head. Her eyes were wet, red-rimmed—but contained. Like she had been holding back tears for so long they stopped trying to escape.

"I want you to tell me I didn't."

The room felt smaller.

She exhaled shakily, then rubbed her eyes with the back of her hands and looked away. "But you can't do that, can you?"

I studied her for a long time.

Then I shook my head slowly. "No."

I still didn't know what happened to Julie, not fully.

Something in Sophia's expression cracked.

"But I can tell you that Stephen was manipulating you. And I can tell you that I believe you."

She blinked.

I kept going. "We just came into some footage, Sophia. We know what he was doing to you. To Julie." I paused. "To Rachel."

That name hit her hard.

She inhaled sharply, lips parting like she was about to say something, but nothing came.

Her fingers gripped the fabric of her jeans.

I lowered my voice. "Whatever he made you believe about yourself? That's exactly what he wanted."

Her body became stiff.

She twitched, almost flinched, like something had just hit her.

And then she whispered, "I remember something."

I froze.

She didn't look at me. Just starred, glassy-eyed and unfocused.

"I was in the cabin," she murmured. "It was dark. Someone was... touching me."

I sat still.

"Someone was behind me," she continued. "Close."

My fingers curled into fists.

"Who?" I asked.

She blinked. Her voice dropped to a whisper. "Good girl. You're just like me."

The moment the words left her mouth, her entire body jerked.

The words weren't hers. They were his.

She wasn't just remembering. She was reliving.

She gasped as a shudder ripped through her.

"Stop—no—don't—"

I moved fast.

Her chair scraped against the floor as she shoved back from the table. Her arms folded over her stomach like she was about to be sick.

Her breathing was wrong, too fast.

Her fingers dug into her scalp. Knuckles white.

This was a panic attack.

I was already on my feet when she went down.

I *barely* caught her before she hit the floor.

She collapsed into me.

Deep, gut-wrenching sobs tore out of her. Ugly. Painful.

Her entire body shook. I could feel her pulse racing against me.

I hesitated, but only for a second. Then I held onto her.

I didn't say anything, and I didn't let go.

She didn't fight me. Didn't tell me to back off.

For once, she wasn't alone.

And as she fell apart in my arms, I realized, maybe, I was the only one left to catch her.

48

— ◆ —

NOVEMBER 23, 2024, 8 AM - NEWTON

29 DAYS AFTER JULIE WENT MISSING

Stephen's father filled the frame as the door cracked open. No welcome, just a stare.

"Officers." The word was clipped, measured. His gaze skipped to Jenkins, then back to me. "What's this about?"

I kept my voice steady. "Mr. Burns, we have a search warrant and an arrest warrant for Stephen Burns. Is he home?"

His expression barely changed. A slow blink. A slight shift of weight, like he was deciding how to play this.

"What is this?" Mrs. Burns called from inside.

She appeared a moment later, dishrag in hand, smoothing it over her palm like she was wiping away something unseen.

Her gaze swept over us, a glimmer of recognition settling into instant control.

"Officers," she greeted, voice smooth. "There must be a mistake."

"It's not a mistake, ma'am."

She exhaled, her shoulders squaring like she was about to step into a negotiation. "Well. It is." She was trying to maintain a polite tone, but there was an edge beneath it.

Mr. Burns finally spoke, sharp and to the point. "What's the charge?"

"Murder," I said. Mrs. Burns stepped forward slightly, just enough to shift the conversation back into her control.

"Murder? That is outrageous. You've been harassing my son for over a week," she said, voice coated in carefully restrained indignation. "Now you're here with accusations? No." Her brows raised slightly, like she was just getting started.

I let her words settle before replying.

"This isn't harassment, Mrs. Burns," I said evenly. "Your son is a suspect in an active investigation."

She was strangling the dishrag now.

Jenkins cleared his throat. "We're here to search his room."

That did it.

"Absolutely not." She seethed. She turned to her husband, as if waiting for him to shut this down.

Mr. Burns' jaw ticked. "If you have a warrant, let's see it."

I held up the document, unfolding it neatly. He barely glanced at it before looking back at me.

"What's the real reason you're here, Sheriff?" Mrs. Burns asked. Her voice turned calculated. She angled her head. "You have something against my son, this is personal, we both know it."

There it was again.

I kept my face neutral, but Jenkins' patience thinned next to me. "Ma'am, step aside." Jenkins said.

She shook her head slightly, as if she were already preparing for the damage control. "No. You are fixating on my son because you can't seem to find the answers you're looking for."

She turned to Mr. Burns. "And now they want to search our home? Arrest our son?"

Mr. Burns hissed, silent fury in every inch. He didn't yell. He was a businessman. And businessmen cut through the noise.

"You have a warrant," he said finally. "Get on with it." He shot Mrs. Burns a look I couldn't place.

Her nostrils flared slightly, but she stepped aside.

I met her gaze as I crossed the threshold.

We made our way up the staircase, our boots heavy on the perfectly polished wooden steps.

I could hear Mrs. Burns voice coming from the hallway just below us.

"...Yes, I understand that," she said, voice clipped, the kind of tone reserved for negotiations she expected to win. "But I want this handled immediately. This is harassment."

A pause. A controlled inhale.

"No, I don't care what they think they have. My son is not—"

She stopped.

Her voice faded as we walked into Stephen's room.

Jenkins gave me a look.

I gave him one right back.

She wasn't fighting this.

She was getting ahead of it.

***

Stephen's room was exactly what you'd expect from a high schooler with control issues. The bed was neatly made, the desk meticulously organized, and the shelves were lined with trophies and framed photos of Stephen in various stages of academic glory. It was the kind of room that screamed, *'Look how perfect I am'*—but the perfection was skin-deep. I could feel the rot underneath it.

"Start on the desk," I said to Jenkins. "I'll take the bed."

I crouched down, running my hands along the underside of the mattress and the bedframe finding nothing unusual.

Jenkins was the first to reach the dresser, pulling open the top drawer. Inside, everything was folded too neatly, clothes untouched, like they'd been placed there for show. At the very top was the student council hoodie matching what Sophia was wearing on the video footage from the cabin. Jenkins pushed it aside.

Then his hand paused. He reached in and pulled something from the back.

A picture.

It was of Sophia.

I stopped moving. She was standing outside Julie's house. Distant, just beyond the tree line.

She looked asleep.

A familiar blurred figure stood beside her, a hand barely visible on her arm.

Stephen.

Sophia had the mechanical stance, the emptiness in her eyes. The same as the footage.

Jenkins swore under his breath, already moving toward the closet. He yanked open the doors. Shoes lined up with military precision, jackets hung on stiff wooden hangers. It looked too normal.

"What's this?" He asked, pulling out a metal box.

He opened it, and the first thing I saw was a tangled lock of deep red hair, bound with twine.

The exact same shade of red as Rachel Caldwell's hair.

Jenkins stilled beside me. He didn't react the way I did. But I felt it. The way the air shifted. The way he clenched his fists for just a second before letting them go loose at his sides.

Because we both knew what this meant.

I knelt beside him now and forced my eyes to move. To scan lower.

Jenkins picked up a small bundle, wrapped in a piece of yellowed cloth, almost delicate, like some fucked-up gift. I reached forward as he opened it, my fingers hovering just above the contents.

There were... teeth.

My heart drummed.

Jenkins swore under his breath and grabbed my arm. Then he looked me right in the eyes, "We won't know for sure until..." he stopped himself.

I couldn't look away. Some still had roots. I started counting. Why was I counting? Twenty. There were at least twenty teeth.

A sick, rotten horror spread through me. The kind of cold that settles deep into your soul. The kind that doesn't leave.

I had to make myself continue to breathe.

I knew this case. I had meticulously gone back through it before coming here. After the flash drive. After seeing her face on that damn screen. Her innocent face, the red hair that matched the hair in this box perfectly, her forced smile.

I grabbed the next item.

A Polaroid.

The edges were bent, as if they had been handled too many times. The image inside was sharp.

It was Rachel.

In a car.

Passenger seat.

Her pupils were blown wide, red hair partially covering her cheeks as if trying to conceal herself behind it. Her mouth was pressed into a tight, unreadable line.

But the worst part?

She was staring directly at the camera.

Not at Stephen. Not at anything else.

Just at us.

Jenkins' hands dropped to his sides, sounding like dead weights hitting the floor. "She's wearing the same shirt. That's the same night as the flash drive footage." His voice was low. "The same damn night."

After looking over everything again, I knew what the flash drive timestamp meant.

She had vanished that day.

And I let her go.

Not the night she vanished—after.

I told myself she ran. Let the easy answer win.

I stopped looking.

And now here she was. In pieces. In photos. In trophies.

I hadn't just *failed* her. I had buried the truth with her.

The Polaroid image was slightly angled, a movement caught in the reflection of the car window. A distorted face. Stephen's.

I pushed myself to keep looking through the box, taking the lead now.

Underneath it was a picture of Julie.

She was standing inside her house.

It was taken from the hallway just outside her bedroom.

Brushing her hair in the mirror, completely unaware she was being watched. And in the corner of the reflection, Stephen holding the camera.

My fists clenched.

There was no timestamp. No way to pin down when this was taken.

Jenkins swallowed hard. "Stephen was there. In her house."

Not like we really needed the confirmation. We knew it was him in the flash drive video even though we hadn't seen his face. This just solidified it.

I reached the bottom of the box, my fingers hesitating over a thin sheet of cardboard.

It wasn't part of the container.

It had been added.

Like a barrier, a wall between two collections.

My stomach twisted as I lifted it.

Underneath, the makeshift compartment was tidy and meticulously arranged.

There were two items and a photo that made my blood turn to ice.

White lace.

Delicate. Soft. Perfectly folded.

A pair of panties.

A tiny red rose was stitched into the front, the thread slightly frayed but still intact.

Like they had been handled.

Kept.

Cherished.

And a baby blue hair clip. Nothing special, the kind you could buy in a five-pack at any drugstore.

But it wasn't new.

A few strands of dark brown hair were still caught between the teeth.

A common hair color, but it looked deeply familiar.

I squeezed my eyes shut, feeling my heartbeat race through my bones.

I knew whose it was.

The back of the polaroid was face up, so I read the note scrawled on it in Stephen's jagged handwriting: "Perfect"

Then, I was sure.

I didn't want to, but I flipped the photo.

Sophia laid asleep in her bed.

She was wearing a pink T-shirt. Her face was soft, peaceful. Completely innocent.

And Stephen's hand was on her face.

Fingertips barely grazing her cheek.

I felt something ugly come alive in my gut.

Jenkins took a sharp breath then went rigid. "What the f—"

I barely heard him.

Because my hands were still moving to the very bottom of the box contents.

To a thin notebook.

The black and white checkers in the binding were creased, worn from use. The edges frayed, pages curling from the pressure of being flipped too many times.

Jenkins stared at the contents. Then the notebook. Then me.

I reached for it.

These weren't diary entries or notes, they were... logs.

Scattered dates. Scribbled names.

I scanned the first few pages, stopping only when I saw one of the girls.

"Rachel was too volatile. The structure didn't hold."

"Julie learned faster. Fear works better than shame."

"Sophia is different. She listens in her sleep."

This wasn't just a murder.

This was something else.

262

I flipped further.

"Sophia belongs to me. She just doesn't know it yet."

I stopped on the second to last page, where the writing became even more jagged, pressing into the paper. It was titled, like a thought-out plan.

SOPHIA'S FINAL PLAN
— FULL INTEGRATION —

'Phase 1 – Acceptance' was crossed out, rewritten, crossed out again.

- ~~Start small. Letters? A note in her locker?~~

- She doesn't see it yet. She isn't ready. She needs guidance.

  - *She needs me to guide her.*

'Phase 2 – Ownership' was underlined, circled, emphasized.

- ~~Sleep training = already successful. She listens. She follows.~~

- Condition her deeper. Whispers are enough for now. Soon, she will obey while awake, too.

  - *She's already responding.*

'Phase 3 – Isolation'

- Distance her from distractions. From Eli. From Jay. From Abbie.

- She still reaches for them when she's afraid. That can't happen.

'Phase 4 – Submission' was barely legible, scrawled over itself, rewritten multiple times.

- ~~Dark room? Sensory deprivation?~~ Not enough.

- ~~She will learn to love it.~~ She will learn to love me.

'Phase 5 – Full Integration' was written in larger, more frantic strokes.

- ~~Doesn't matter if she's afraid. Fear is part of love.~~ She is not afraid of me.

- She is afraid of herself, and I am the only one who can help her.

  - *I will make her see.*

"This kid is a damn psycho." Jenkins said shakily.

I didn't speak.

At the very back of the notebook, the final page caught my eye.

It was blank except for one word: *Soon.*

My hands curled around the notebook so tightly my knuckles went white.

I had spent the last month chasing the wrong thing.

Stephen Burns was the monster.

He had gotten to both Rachel and Julie.

And Sophia wasn't just a plan anymore.

She was the next victim.

Jenkins was pacing now, muttering. "We've got him, Newton. This is it."

But I wasn't so sure.

The evidence was damning.

But it still didn't put Stephen at the scene of Julie's murder.

Rachel's death? That was another story.

The hair. The teeth. The photo and video timestamped the night she disappeared. This was more than enough to tie him to her.

"Let's bag everything," I said finally, my voice hollow. "And call it in to Cleveland. We need a team out here."

Jenkins nodded, but his expression darkened as he glanced at the door. "And Stephen? What if he doesn't come home?"

My focus was on the notebook in my hands.

I couldn't stop looking at that last word: Soon.

My hands were steady, but the ground was shifting. We were behind.

I pulled out my phone and dialed the station.

"Get a unit to Sophia Whitaker's house. Now!"

49

— • —

November 23, 2024, 11 AM - Sophia

29 Days After Julie Went Missing

I felt like I was sinking, like gravity had doubled overnight and no one bothered to tell me.

Every noise in Dr. Patel's office felt louder than it should be, the receptionist clicking her pen, the hum of the lights overhead, the distant murmur of someone talking down the hall. My own heartbeat.

I stared at the motivational poster across from me: You Can Climb Any Mountain.

What if the mountain is inside your own head? What if the climb isn't the problem, it's what's waiting at the top?

I curled my fingers into my sleeve, my nails digging into the fabric as the door creaked open. The memory I had at the police station replayed like a scratch on a record, stuck, looping over and over, me and Stephen. Him... touching me... commanding me.

Newton had organized the few officers we had in town to take rotating shifts stationed outside of my house. One had followed me here. It should have been reassuring, but instead, it only made me more paranoid. I still didn't know exactly what he had seen on those videos, but from what I was starting to remember, I could make an educated guess.

And now, sitting in this office, something else settled over me, the shame of completely breaking down in front of Dr. Patel yesterday.

I hadn't wanted to come back here.

Not to this office. Not to Dr. Patel's watchful gaze. Not to the memory of me spiraling, vomiting into a trash can before running out like a grade A disaster.

But I had picked up one of her calls this morning, and now I was here.

And I couldn't decide if that meant I was getting stronger...

Or just desperate.

When I'd gotten home last night, the sky still bruised and barely holding the dark, Jay had been waiting for me.

He was sitting on the couch in my living room with his head bowed, like he'd been up all night and was fighting off sleep. Eli had fallen asleep on the loveseat and woke up when I came in. Eli's eyes softened in that rare way he reserved for me when things got bad. Neither of them asked questions. Not right away.

Jay had just stood, stepped toward me, and said quietly, "You think I'd let you go through this alone? Not a chance."

And somehow, those words cracked me wide open.

I told them everything. What happened at the diner, what Newton found, the memories.

And they listened, really listened. Like they weren't afraid of what they heard. Like they were going to carry it, too.

Eli had nodded once, his voice tight but steady. "Okay. We're going to game plan together."

So now, when I sat in this chair, surrounded by too-white walls and fake motivational posters, I wasn't just spiraling.

I was held.

I didn't know what the next session would bring.

But I knew this: Jay and Eli were waiting.

And this time, when I walked back out into the world, I wouldn't be alone.

"Sophia."

Dr. Patel's voice was steady like always. Still, it took me by surprise. I tried to hide the heat rushing to my face as we locked eyes.

I forced myself to stand, but my legs felt wrong, like they might crack beneath me at any second.

The door shut behind me. A dull click. A lock sliding into place.

I swallowed hard and sank into the chair across from her.

She watched me, her quiet patience unsettling in a way that made my skin itch.

"I was worried about you," she said. "I called. Several times yesterday. I'm glad you answered today."

I toyed with the hem of my sleeve. I already knew she had. My phone had been a graveyard of missed calls and voicemails I couldn't bring myself to open.

"When I couldn't reach you," she continued carefully, "I checked in with Eli. I didn't break confidentiality," she assured me, her tone even. "I only let him know I was concerned. That you left suddenly, and I hadn't heard from you."

Dr. Patel let the silence settle for a moment before she spoke again. "You don't have to carry this alone. How have you been holding up?"

I let out a brittle laugh. "Oh, you know. Spiraling anxiety, fragmented memories, and the creeping fear that I might have been a pawn in someone else's game. Maybe even worse."

Dr. Patel remained neutral.

But I caught the slight arching of her brow. The way her gaze sharpened like she was reassessing everything she thought she knew about me.

"That's a lot to carry," she said finally.

I expected her to push. To bring up hypnosis. To pry open my memories like a locked box.

Instead, she just folded her hands over her notepad.

The silence between us tried to feel comfortable, but it wasn't.

I waited for the catch. Dug my hands into the leather couch to brace myself.

"Why don't we start smaller this time?" she finally said. "Something gentler. We don't have to address this all at once."

Something in my chest eased, just barely.

No hypnosis. No forcing. Just. Slower.

I let out a breath I didn't realize I was holding.

Maybe I could do that. Maybe.

She nodded, like she expected this reaction. "Tell me more about what's been happening."

I hesitated, my throat like sandpaper. "I keep having... flashes." The word felt too small, too weak. "Like pieces of something I should remember, but they're all wrong. And Stephen..."

His name felt poisonous in my mouth.

"He said things," I forced out. "Stuff that makes me wonder if he—" I couldn't get it out without stopping, focusing on making my pulse calm. "If he was controlling me somehow."

Something broke in my voice at the end. I couldn't tell her what else I remembered.

Dr. Patel leaned forward slightly, waiting to see if I'd continue before speaking.

"What kinds of things did he say?"

"To keep walking... that I was a... good girl."

Dr. Patel's expression didn't change. But I swore I saw a spark of empathy in her eyes.

"Sophia, let's take a step back," she said. "Away from Stephen. I know we've talked a lot about Julie, I would like for you to establish a baseline for yourself there. Before Julie's disappearance, what do you remember about your interactions with her?"

I exhaled slowly. I knew what she was trying to do, make this less scary to talk about. But the walls still felt too close.

"Not much," I admitted. "I mean I saw her in school of course. But starting in October it's just... fragments. The woods. Her voice." I swallowed. "Then nothing."

Dr. Patel's brow furrowed slightly. "Memories tied to trauma can be difficult to access. Have your sleepwalking episodes gotten worse?"

I laughed. A sharp, hollow sound.

"Oh, you mean the part where I wake up in random places with no idea how I got there? Yeah. That's still happening."

She studied me.

"There are two things I'd like to try," she said carefully. "The first is a new medication. It's a low-dose sedative designed to stabilize your sleep cycle and suppress episodes."

Something tightened in my chest. "Medication?"

Her voice remained unshakable. "Not something you'd take every night. Just as needed. It won't fix everything, but it should help you regain some control."

Control.

The word hit harder than I expected.

Like I'd been craving it without even realizing.

I swallowed. "And the second thing?"

She set her notebook aside. "A visualization exercise. It's a technique you can practice on your own, much gentler than in office hypnosis. Think of it as creating a safe space in your mind where you can explore memories without fear or judgment."

I raised an eyebrow. "So... mind palace, but make it therapy?"

Dr. Patel's lips twitched slightly. "Something like that."

I hesitated. "And this will help me remember?"

She didn't lie to me. She never did.

"It might," she said. "But more importantly, it can help you process what you do remember at your own speed."

I bit my lip. The idea of medication felt like admitting defeat.

The visualization exercise? *A shot in the dark.*

But what other choice did I have?

There was a clock ticking inside me. I didn't know what it was counting down to, but I knew, if I didn't figure this out soon, I wasn't going to like what happened when time ran out.

I let out a slow breath.

"Fine," I said. "I–I'll try."

Dr. Patel told me to lie down and her voice guided me as I closed my eyes.

**

"Picture a place where you feel safe," she said. "Somewhere you can explore without fear."

Safe.

I almost laughed.

What did that even mean anymore?

Every place I had ever felt safe was tainted. Rotting at the edges. My own home, my own bed...

But I forced myself to imagine something.

A field. Open sky. The colors muted, like a dream just out of reach.

"Let's start with someone who makes you feel grounded," she said. "Someone who reminds you of who you are."

The tension in my arms eased. "Jay."

Dr. Patel nodded. "Good. Let's focus on him."

"Now imagine a door," Dr. Patel continued. "This door leads to the part of your mind where your memories are stored, memories of Jay. When you're ready, open it."

A door materialized in my mind.

I opened it.

Jay's stupid lopsided grin. The way he threw fries at me during lunch, just to get a reaction. The warmth of his jacket draped over my shoulders in the back of his car after a long night. The way he always showed up.

A faint smile ghosted over my lips.

"Stay there for a moment," Dr. Patel said. "Stay with that feeling."

For the first time in a long time, my chest loosened, I could breathe.

Dr. Patel's voice shifted, still gentle, but careful. "If you're ready... try to think about Julie."

The warmth flickered.

"Not the night she disappeared," she added. "Before that. October. You mentioned things got blurry then."

The knot in my chest was starting to form again.

I almost pulled away. Almost told her no.

But instead, I thought about Julie.

The last moments before everything blurred.

The back of her head in English class, strands of blonde hair tucked behind her ear. Mr. Linworth's voice drifting through the room, steady and measured, reading from *Romeo and Juliet*.

I could still hear the scratch of my pencil against my notebook, feel the dull weight of routine settling over me.

My mind skipped over to lunch, the cafeteria.

Julie sitting a few tables down, the soft hum of voices surrounding us. Jay beside me, laughing, as Abbie told us a story about how she got sassy with the barista at Grounded. The warmth of that moment, fleeting but real.

A snapshot of before.

"Now," Dr. Patel said, her voice gentle. Anchoring.

"Imagine a door."

I shifted in the chair.

"This door leads to the part of your mind where your memories are stored of Julie."

The image formed in my mind, solid.

"When you're ready... open it."

I hesitated.

But I pushed.

The hinges groaned. The door creaked as it swung open.

Chaos.

Sharp, disjointed images.

The woods.

Julie.

Her face pale, streaked with tears, her voice raw and splintered.

She was yelling. Terrified.

And then I saw myself.

A chill shot down my spine.

I was standing at the edge of the clearing. Stiff. Wrong.

Like I wasn't really there.

Like I wasn't me.

"Julie," I whispered.

Dr. Patel's voice grounded me. "What's happening?"

"She was arguing with someone," I said. My fingers dug into my own arms. "But I wasn't... I wasn't myself."

The shadowy figure turned toward Julie, their movements predatory.

I couldn't see their face.

Dr. Patel's voice was firm now. "Sophia, close the door."

Julie screamed. A sound like a rock, a crunch.

"Sophia."

My name.

A plea.

I reached for her. Or, I thought I did. My limbs felt slow, disconnected, like I wasn't inside them at all.

Something wasn't right.

The figure in the clearing, the shadowy shape beside Julie, moved.

And I knew.

I knew I had to see their face.

I forced my mind to sharpen, to focus. I was so close.

Just a little more.

The memory rippled, shifting like water disturbed by a stone. The figure turned.

No. No, I need to see—

The weight of reality slammed into me like a tidal wave.

My breath hitched. My body lurched forward.

Dr. Patel's voice was suddenly too loud. Too real.

"Sophia! Close the door!"

I gasped, my eyes snapping open.

The room shoved into focus, the too-bright lights, the too-sterile air pressing against me. My chest heaved.

Dr. Patel's voice was steady. "You're safe."

What a lie.

"I was there," I whispered, my voice hoarse. "But I don't know what happened."

Dr. Patel held my gaze. Not immediately reassuring. Not dismissing, either.

A beat.

Something about her posture shifted, like she was choosing her words carefully.

272

Finally, she took a deep breath.

"Sophia," she said cautiously, "your mind isn't ready to process this."

She paused.

"We need to take this slower. Much slower."

Without another word, Dr. Patel reached into her drawer, scribbled something on a small slip of paper and slid it across the table.

I stared at it.

"We'll get there," she said softly, but her eyes held steel. "Not all at once. But step by step. And you won't be doing it alone."

I pocketed the slip of paper. It was a prescription for the medication she mentioned earlier. Its weight was heavier than it should have been.

When I stepped outside, the air hit me like a slap.

It didn't clear my head.

It only sharpened the dread.

Because deep down, I knew, I wasn't just remembering something.

I was about to live it all over again.

50

— · —

NOVEMBER 24, 2024, 7 PM - NEWTON

30 DAYS AFTER JULIE WENT MISSING

I hadn't slept.

Neither had Jenkins.

Cleveland PD was involved, their cyber unit combing the flash drive and tracking Stephen's movements. But it wasn't enough. Not yet.

We still had more to watch.

I opened the copied flash drive folder on my desktop—**ARCHIVE** stared back like a dare. Twelve videos.

We had only seen four.

And that was already enough to keep me awake at night.

I clicked the next one.

***

September 3rd, 2023

Stephen sat at a desk, poised, confident.

The camera was set up deliberately, like he was filming a job interview.

"This is for consideration into The Circle."

"I've studied your values: Control. Order. Discipline. Not as constraints, but as structure. As power."

He shared his screen.

"This model outlines a private transaction ecosystem. An internal economy, based on anonymized crypto exchanges. Cold wallets. No traceable ledgers. All internal."

He flipped through tabs:

Prototype dashboards. Token-based reward structures.

Digital tiers. *Roles*. Influence tracking.

"We build loyalty by measuring it. Controlling it."

"This system doesn't replace structure. It enhances it."

He leaned closer to the lens, like delivering a final thesis.

"People want freedom. But they need control. That's where we come in."

"I can build what you believe in."

I clenched my teeth.

Jenkins muttered under his breath, "He studied them. Like a playbook."

He had.

And maybe that's what made him dangerous.

He wasn't just mimicking The Circle, he saw it for what it was.

A machine built to reward control.

And he used it to justify the darkest parts of himself.

I clicked over to The Circle's financials Jenkins pulled a few weeks ago.

The first anonymous crypto transfer into The Circle's discretionary tech fund was October 3rd, 2023.

Exactly one month later.

They'd watched this.

And said yes.

***

August 2nd, 2023

Calloway sat stiffly in a chair in a dimly lit office. His hands folded on his lap. Across from him, a man whose face was obscured by shadow slid an envelope across the desk.

Cash.

Calloway exhaled sharply, running a hand over his face before picking up the envelope and tucking it into his drawer.

"I don't want details," he muttered. "Just the deposit."

"And the oversight?" the man asked.

Calloway's jaw clenched. "Not my problem."

I shook my head. I knew it from the start.

"He's dirty," Jenkins said, "you were right Newton."

Calloway had never been the mastermind. But this? This was willful ignorance. He was paid to look the other way, and that's exactly what he did.

I clicked on the next file.

***

August 30th, 2024

Linworth and Julie.

It was from the start of the school year, her junior year. She looked bright-eyed. Almost bashful.

He leaned in, smiling at something she said. She laughed, and he brushed her hair behind her ear. It looked like a moment, sweet, quiet.

But he was a teacher and she was a student, a child.

It was a secret.

And it was being filmed.

Stephen's reflection hovered in the glass, camera steady.

He wasn't shocked.

Wasn't intervening.

He was documenting.

"Damnit," I muttered, pushing back from the desk.

No wonder Linworth had been unraveling.

Maybe he hadn't killed her. But he stripped her of her innocence.

And he knew it.

The next video blared to life on the screen.

***

October 10th, 2024

A sleek conference room was filled with men in suits. Not just from Ordinance.

This was bigger.

A thin man stood at the head of the table, tapping his ring, The Circle's ring, against a tablet.

"We need her gone," he said. "She's deviated from the structure. Discipline matters."

"Fine," someone replied. "The board will initiate redirection this week."

A pause.

Long enough to feel loaded.

Then Stephen's voice, low, assured. "She won't talk."

He waited a beat.

"She understands the order now."

Jenkins flinched beside me.

I did too.

This was recorded the day after Julie wrote that she'd never be the same.

Was this conversation about her?

Either way it was clear this wasn't just an organization. It was doctrine.

A system designed to absorb the worst of them.

And Stephen—

He made Julie the proof that it worked.

Not just proof.

A test run.

Julie was never a person to him. She was a tool.

And The Circle didn't care what he did to her, as long as it worked.

He gave them a crypto plan.

He proved he could control silence.

That was all they wanted: results.

The how never mattered.

I clicked into the next video, then the next.

Each one showed a different kind of power—The Circle's reach, Stephen's control.

Clips of administrators dismissing complaints.

A student being initiated, blindfolded, kneeling, repeating words like *discipline, structure, obedience*.

Calloway, seated silently while Stephen outlined a "re-education plan" for a troublemaker.

Even Linworth, pale and trembling, accepting a sealed envelope. His expression already broken.

Stephen had been collecting these moments.

Not just for sport.

For leverage.

For proof of loyalty.

For insurance.

Mementos of corruption.

Documentation of obedience.

A portfolio of influence.

Jenkins let out a low whistle. "Subtle."

I snorted. "Yeah. Just your average high school club."

He didn't laugh. Just stood there, hands clenched against the desk like it might start floating if he let go.

I felt the tension rising behind my eyes. Static, sharp.

We almost stopped there.

Almost.

But one video remained.

The final file.

***

October 29th, 2024

This was recent, less than a month ago.

The screen flickered, revealing Sophia's bedroom.

She was asleep.

Curled beneath the sheets, breathing slow and steady. The moonlight cast a pale glow across her face. She looked untouched and safe.

Until the door opened revealing Stephen.

He moved silently, like he belonged there, pausing at her dresser and opening the top drawer.

My stomach turned.

He reached in, fingers rifling until they found something. He pulled it out slowly, delicately, almost reverently.

A pair of white lace underwear.

He brought them to his face. Breathed in, then tucked them into his pocket.

My whole body went cold. We'd found underwear just like this in his box.

Then, as if nothing had happened, he walked to her bed. Stood over her and watched.

She didn't stir.

His hand lifted, brushing against her cheek.

He was talking. Not loud enough to hear every word, but his tone was unmistakable. Possessive. Loving.

Stephen leaned in closer, his fingers slipping through Sophia's hair.

"*Perfect*," he murmured.

My stomach turned. Not because of what he did, but because she never flinched. She didn't even know. That's what he took from her.

I had seen this before.

My hand instinctively shuffled through the evidence piled on my desk, something pulling me toward it—

The polaroid.

A rotting sensation settled in my gut.

I stared at it, at the picture I had held in my hands just yesterday. It was the same shot.

The same angle. The same pink t-shirt.

That night. That was this night.

I felt a stone form in my stomach.

I turned the polaroid over, rereading the back. Seeing it with new eyes.

Stephen's sadistic handwriting: "Perfect"

The laptop snapped shut with a clap so sharp it made my teeth clench.

He'd been escalating. Testing how far the system would bend before it broke.

And Sophia, she was going to be the next milestone.

Not for control. Not for power. For pleasure.

Stephen was on the run now.

Sophia was here in town.

Suarez was stationed outside her house right now.

So why the hell did I still feel uneasy?

I shut my eyes, squeezing them tight before jarring them back open. I had seen men like Calloway before—weak, greedy, willing to look the other way.

But Stephen... he didn't look away. He wanted to watch, to touch.

He didn't just follow the system. He used it to sharpen the worst parts of himself.

The Circle handed him structure. He turned it into shelter.

"Calloway's predictable. The Circle makes sense. But Stephen?"

I clenched my jaw.

"He calls it love. But really, he wants ownership. Total control. And when that slips—"

I pointed at the polaroid.

"*They pay for it.*"

51

―・―

NOVEMBER 24, 2024, 8 PM - NEWTON

30 DAYS AFTER JULIE WENT MISSING

I fired off a quick text to Suarez—*be on high alert*—then turned to Jenkins.

Adrenaline was keeping us upright. Cleveland PD was pulling every resource they had. The Circle's funding was being tracked across multiple states, bank accounts flagged, storage facilities raided. But none of that mattered right now.

Not when Stephen was still out there.

The briefing room was chaos. Screens flashed with surveillance feeds, ATM transactions, and traffic camera footage. Detectives from Cleveland were coordinating on burner phones, trying to predict his next move.

Jenkins rubbed his face. "We've got movement on his accounts. Stephen pulled two grand in cash. No card use since."

Survival mode. No digital trail. No way to track him clean.

"He's got a new car." One of the cyber detectives looked up from his laptop. "Fake plates. He bought it off a private seller two days ago."

Jenkins swore. "So, he's prepped for this."

The cyber tech nodded grimly. "Everything's pointing to him having left town. But we're checking traffic cameras in case he's circling back."

I barely heard them.

Because my phone buzzed, an unknown number displayed on screen.

I answered, my grip tightening.

"You're too late, Sheriff," said a warped mechanical voice. There was a pause. A breath. Like he was savoring this. "She's already mine."

I was moving before my brain caught up.

Jenkins saw my face go white. "What?"

I shoved my phone into my pocket, already yanking my keys. *"Stephen's at Sophia's!"*

Jenkins didn't hesitate.

"Shit, we need back up!" he yelled.

Sirens ripped through the night. Suarez wasn't answering. Seven calls. Nothing.

The roads were empty this late, but the houses, they weren't. Porch lights flipped on as we flew down the street. Neighbors stepped out, drawn by the sound of two squad cars barreling toward Sophia's house.

Dispatch screamed in my ear about leads from other states. A storage facility outside Cincinnati. A dead-end rental property in Pennsylvania. Cleveland PD was covering every lead that made sense—but this?

This wasn't logical.

This was obsession.

And I should have seen it sooner.

Should have known he wouldn't run, not when she was still here.

Should have stationed more than one guy outside her house.

Should have been there myself.

The road leading to Sophia's neighborhood curved. Just as we rounded the bend—

A wrecked sedan blocked part of the street.

Jenkins barely braked in time, tires shrieking as we skidded to a halt.

My pulse slammed against my ribs. "What the hell—"

Jenkins leaned forward. "Let me guess. Just some random wreck with no plates blocking the path to the girl he's obsessed with?"

My head snapped toward the houses. All dark. All quiet.

Dispatch crackled in.

"Neighbor called in, saw a strange car parked outside Sophia Whitaker's house about 10 minutes ago. Blue Toyota."

Jenkins floored it.

The tires screamed against the pavement.

CRACK.

The side mirror collided with the abandoned sedan, snapping clean off. That didn't matter. *Nothing* mattered except the house in the middle of Maple Road.

Sophia's house.

As we pulled closer, I could see there were no lights, no movement, no sign of life.

A pit formed in my stomach.

I saw Suarez slumped over his steering wheel as we came to a stop.

Jenkins threw his door open. "What did he do to him?!"

I gritted my teeth. My fingers strangling the door handle as I swung it open.

We weren't too late.

We couldn't be.

52

---·---

November 24, 2024, 8 PM - Sophia

30 Days After Julie Went Missing

The second I heard the floorboard creak, I knew.

I wasn't alone.

The thought hit like ice water dumped over my skin—sharp and unforgiving. But I forced it down.

Don't panic. Not yet.

It was so quiet. Eli was at work. The TV was off. My phone was on the bed next to me. The only sound was my own heartbeat, a slow, thudding pulse in my ears.

I sat frozen for three long seconds.

Then, a shadow passed under the gap in my bedroom door.

Oh God. No.

A cold wave of nausea curled in my gut. My mind raced, running through every possible explanation. Maybe Eli came home early? Maybe I imagined it? Maybe—

Another step. Closer this time.

I grabbed my phone, my fingers shaking as I opened my contacts. Jay. Call Jay. He was the only one who—

The door burst open.

Stephen stood smiling.

I didn't have time to scream.

I launched off the bed, shoving past him as hard as I could, but his grip was iron, his arms clamping around my waist like a vice. I wrenched myself away, nails digging into his skin, but it didn't matter.

He was stronger. Faster. Prepared.

I was barefoot and off balance, he wasn't.

His arm hooked back around my waist, the force slamming my spine into his chest. My muscles were taut with strained effort. I kicked out wildly, twisting, clawing, trying to break free.

His breath was hot against my ear.

"You're making this harder than it needs to be, Soph."

Within a millisecond I felt rage. Then terror. Then full-blown panic.

I slammed my heel down onto his foot as hard as I could. He grunted in pain, his grip loosening just enough. I ripped forward, fingernails tearing at his arms, scrambling to get away.

I felt a sharp sting that made my body stiffen.

The sensation spread fast, a burning cold seeping into my veins. My vision blurred at the edges. My heartbeat slowed, a sick, syrupy sensation crawling under my skin.

No. No. No.

My knees buckled.

I hit the floor.

"Shhh." His voice was soft, almost tender.

I tried to move but I couldn't. My arms wouldn't work. Like I was trapped inside my body, screaming behind glass.

"I'm still here," the words slithered from his lips curling around me like smoke.

I tried to cry out. My throat wouldn't cooperate.

"I've always been here, Sophia."

Oh my god.

I'm still here. Julie's phone. *The text.*

I mustered up every ounce of control I had left. "Wha—"

That's all I could get out, drool sliding out of the side of my mouth.

"You still thought the texts were from her?" he laughed.

"Oh, Sophia, it's always been me." His grin widened. "I left that one—just for you. So, when you remembered, you would know I would be with you. Spoofing a number is easy. Deleting the rest remotely? Even easier."

The drug dragged me under, an unbearable heaviness pressing down on my limbs. My fingers twitched uselessly against the hardwood.

Stephen crouched beside me, his touch gentle, brushing damp hair from my forehead.

"See? That's better."

The world tilted.

Dark spots danced in my vision. My eyelids fluttered, my body betraying me, my mind screaming at itself to stay awake.

His arms slid under me, lifting me easily. My head lolled against his shoulder.

"We're finally going to be together, Soph."

I wanted to thrash, to fight, to tear his freaking eyes out, but my body was nothing. Just dead weight.

A door creaked. Cool night air brushed against my skin.

I was being carried out the back door.

Through the yard.

Out of sight.

I fought to hold on to consciousness. My vision blurred. I could still make out shapes and colors. Green grass, brown trees. Then—

Light.

Too bright.

A muffled voice.

A gun.

Newton.

The last thing I saw was him.

53

— • —

NOVEMBER 24, 2024, 9:30 PM - SOPHIA

30 DAYS AFTER JULIE WENT MISSING

I woke up gasping.

Cold.

Heavy.

Trapped.

My limbs wouldn't move fast enough. My vision wouldn't clear. The air smelled wrong, too sterile. A room with soft light, unfamiliar shadows stretching across the walls.

No!

My pulse roared in my ears, breath coming too fast. I swung out blindly, body twisting, trying to orient myself—

A hand caught my arm.

I jerked back, my breath snapping in my throat.

"Whoa! Soph, it's me."

Jay's voice tore through the panic like a blade. I froze. And in that single breath, everything shifted.

The hum of the TV, low and steady.

The soft glow of the bedside lamp painting familiar corners in golden light.

The scent of "Laundry Day" from the Bath & Body Works diffuser.

The weight of a blanket tucked around me.

My room.

I was home.

Not in a basement. Or in a trunk. Not wherever the hell I thought I was going to wake up.

Jay didn't let go right away. His hand was still wrapped around mine, like he was scared if he let go, I'd disappear again.

My muscles still trembled, the fear refusing to let go, like it was a part of me now.

I felt him shift closer. Felt him trying to hide it, but his voice cracked anyway. "You were freaking out in your sleep," he said, voice tight. "I didn't know if I should wake you."

I didn't answer. I didn't trust myself not to cry.

Something glinted on the TV, a shot of flashing police lights, a dark figure being shoved into the back of a cruiser.

The edges of my vision went dark.

It was Stephen.

The news ticker scrolled beneath it:

BREAKING: TWO DEAD GIRLS TIED TO LOCAL TEEN SUSPECT – POLICE INVESTIGATION EXPANDS INTO TEACHER SCANDAL

Two dead girls.

Julie. Rachel.

I couldn't breathe.

Jay's voice came from far away, muffled. "They're saying Stephen was tied to teachers skimming money, too. Calloway's getting investigated."

I barely heard him. I was staring at the TV.

The camera panned over my house.

The familiar rope of dread wrapped around my neck.

Even though my name wasn't mentioned, I knew.

Anyone who knew me would know this was my house.

A shaky exhale pulled from my lungs.

From the corner of my eye, Eli moved. I hadn't realized he was there.

I turned to look at him.

He was standing just behind Jay now, arms crossed, jaw locked so tight it looked painful. His chest rose and fell too fast, his hands clenched into fists.

Not like Jay, who was shaken.

Eli looked furious.

Like something was coming apart inside of him.

And he wasn't looking at Stephen on the TV anymore.

He was looking at me.

For a split second, my stomach twisted, he wasn't acting right.

Eli never looked at me like that.

The moment our eyes met, he turned away.

"I need to step out," he muttered. He was already moving, grabbing his coat, heading for the door.

Jay didn't react much, just let out a tired sigh, rubbing his hands on his neck. "Yeah, man, I get it. I'll be here with Sophia."

The door clicked shut behind him.

Jay looked at me then. "I'm sorry. I'm sorry I wasn't there. I shouldn't have left your house after you got back from the station."

He dropped his hand from his neck, his voice low.

"Just... tell me what you need."

I didn't move.

I should have felt relieved. Stephen was caught. I was safe.

But something felt wrong.

I dragged my sluggish body into a sitting position, every limb heavy with leftover fog. My muscles protested as I swung my legs over the edge of the bed, feet sinking into the carpet like I was underwater.

Jay hovered near the edge of the bed, eyes flicking to me like he wasn't sure whether to come closer or back away.

"Do you want to go downstairs and eat something?" he asked, voice careful. "Or I could bring something up to you?"

I shook my head slowly, still trying to get my bearings. "Can I meet you downstairs? I... need a minute."

"Yeah. Of course." He turned toward the door, then stopped, hand on the knob, back half-turned.

"Hey..." he said, voice dropping. "Just so you know... the paramedics said you were okay. Breathing normal, all that. Newton stayed till they cleared you. Eli... he kinda fought to keep you here. Thought it'd be better if you woke up at home."

He glanced down, "We just... we were trying to do the right thing."

I nodded, even though I wasn't entirely sure what the right thing was. "Thanks for telling me," I said. "I'm... glad I'm home."

Jay looked at me like he wanted to say more, like something unsaid was wedged behind his teeth, but instead he just held my gaze. His eyes were glassy, unguarded. The raw emotion there made me want to look away.

He left without another word. The door clicked softly shut behind him.

The sound felt too final. Like it sealed me inside.

My eyes snapped to my bag.

The prescription from Dr. Patel was there, I had picked it up on my way back from her office, but I hadn't touched it. Not yet.

I had a feeling I was going to need it tonight.

I ripped open the bag, crinkling violently in my grip. The pill bottle was cool in my palm, its plastic smooth against the sweat on my fingers. I didn't bother reading the instructions. I already knew what it was supposed to do.

I shook one pill into my hand.

Tiny. Almost insignificant.

But it felt enormous.

A weight I couldn't put down.

I turned it over between my fingers. The edges pressing into my skin.

It was supposed to help. To quiet the noise. To give me control.

But what if it didn't work?

Or... what if it worked too well?

What if it shut down the wrong things? The memories I needed, the pieces I was barely holding together.

I thought about the nights I'd woken up in strange places, my skin cold and damp, my heart pounding like it was trying to escape.

I thought about Stephen.

His voice. His hands in my hair. The way he whispered like I belonged to him.

And then I thought about Eli.

The way he just looked at me.

Like I was breaking him down.

I needed to pull myself together, for him.

With a deep breath that felt like a gasp, I tipped my head back and swallowed the pill.

It went down easily.

But the lump in my throat stayed.

I went downstairs and ate the mac and cheese Jay made for me, the warmth of it settled in my stomach as I watched him blow up an air mattress in the living room.

He told me he lied to his mom, said he was crashing at a guy from his track team's place tonight to finish a project for school.

I didn't question it. Didn't even ask if he was sure.

I was just thankful he was here.

When the mattress was finally full, I climbed on and let Jay pull me against him, his arm wrapping around me like it was second nature. His heartbeat was steady beneath my cheek, a quiet, rhythmic anchor.

I closed my eyes.

And for the first time in almost 2 months—

I didn't wake up gasping.

Didn't wake up in a cold sweat.

Didn't wake up at all.

Just sleep.

Deep, uninterrupted.

And mercifully quiet.

54

— · —

NOVEMBER 24, 2024, 9:30 PM - NEWTON

30 DAYS AFTER JULIE WENT MISSING

Stephen sat cuffed to the table, wrists resting lightly against the metal like we were gearing up for a game he had already won.

I had proof.

The forensics team had confirmed it just hours ago. The teeth found in his room were Rachel's.

There was no walking away from this. No clever word games, no legal loopholes, not even Mommy and Daddy's money, though Stephen's mom was certainly trying. She'd stormed into the station a few minutes ago, shrieking threats until we warned her she'd be detained if she kept it up.

We were on borrowed time before his lawyer showed, but for now, Stephen seemed open to talking. And I wasn't about to waste it.

He should've been scared shitless.

But he wasn't.

He wasn't pacing. Wasn't panicking.

Not because he was brave. Because he believed someone would make this disappear.

I planted my hands on the table, letting him feel the weight of me.

"You're done."

Stephen tipped his head, that lazy, deliberate smirk curling at his mouth.

"Am I?"

Not today.

I slid the first photo across the table.

Rachel.

His eyes dropped to it.

I tapped the picture. "Tell me about September 10th of last year."

His fingers drummed once on the table. A calculated beat.

"I don't know what you could be referencing, Sheriff."

I clenched my jaw. "Rachel."

His sigh was almost theatrical. "So tragic."

I wanted to break his face.

Jenkins stood behind me. Silent. Letting me work.

"You were the last person seen with her," I said. "We have a video to prove that."

Stephen feigned shock. "You sound so sure about that."

I leaned in, closer than I should have.

"Tell me what you did to her."

Stephen shrugged. "I didn't do anything to her. She made choices. We all do."

Something cold slithered through me.

"That's not an answer."

He tilted his head, watching me. Measuring.

"Maybe it is."

Psychopath.

I kept my voice even. "Where is she?"

Stephen's smirk widened just slightly. "Why do you ask as if I would know?"

I didn't blink. "Because I know she didn't run, I know you killed her."

He paused and sighed, stretching his fingers, like he was almost bored.

"What makes you so sure?"

I wasn't going to give him what he wanted.

I wasn't going to tell him we had her teeth.

I wasn't going to tell him forensics already confirmed they were Rachel's.

Instead, I pushed.

"Because I know you." My voice was calm. Certain. "And you don't let things go."

The air between us thickened.

"Tell me where she is."

Stephen inhaled deeply, dragging it out like he was savoring something. He smiled. "I suppose if she is dead and if you haven't found her by now, you're looking in the wrong place."

My pulse ticked.

Jenkins shifted slightly behind me, but I didn't react.

Stephen's smirk widened even more.

"Keep digging, Sheriff. I know you'll figure it out." He winked.

The muscles in my face were so tight I thought my head might explode.

I slid the next photo across the table.

This time, his smirk faded.

Not completely. But there was something else in his eyes now.

Something interested.

"Tell me what you did to Julie," I said.

Stephen stared at the photo.

Then his smile returned, slower this time.

Like he was enjoying something I hadn't caught onto yet.

Jenkins spoke first. "Cut the shit, Burns. We have you on footage inside her room."

He angled his head, voice dropping to something almost intimate.

"Do you ever wonder why she was so scared?"

I forced my face to stay neutral.

"What?"

Stephen's smile didn't waver.

But it wasn't the same as before.

This one was sharper.

More certain.

I hated it.

"Are you sure she was afraid of *me*?"

I heard Jenkins move abruptly beside me.

But I wasn't breathing at all.

I had seen fear before. I had seen Julie's fear in the video.

She had been terrified.

Of Stephen.

But also...

Jenkins shifted beside me. "What the hell does that mean?"

Stephen wasn't looking at him.

His eyes were still on me.

I forced my voice to stay even. "You're full of shit."

His smirk twitched.

Like he knew exactly what I was thinking.

Exactly where that doubt was hitting.

He leaned in, his voice barely above a whisper.

"We're not so different, she and I."

I wasn't sure if he was fucking with me.

Or if it was working.

I wasn't sure about anything.

I forced myself to step back.

He wanted me to react.

I turned and walked toward the door.

Stephen leaned back in his chair, watching me walk away.

That plastered smirk never leaving his face. Jenkins followed me out, silent.

He let out a sharp breath as the door clicked shut. "He is a damn psycho. We're going to get him to talk."

I didn't answer.

Because for the millionth time since this whole case started—

I wasn't so sure who exactly killed Julie Greene.

The entry door burst open, rattling the frame.

Julie's mom, Margo, stormed in. Her breath ragged, her eyes wild with something beyond grief. Her hands were shaking, white-knuckled as she clutched a stack of Julie's diary pages, some of them bent and smeared with tears.

"Did you know?!" she shrieked, her voice cracking.

The entire station fell silent.

All eyes turned to her, to us.

She shoved the pages at me, her hands trembling so hard that one slipped free, fluttering to the floor.

Jenkins snatched it up before it could slide under the desk.

He didn't need to read it. We had already seen the diary pages.

Sophia had given them to me herself.

But no one else here had.

And as Margo started reading them aloud, the station shifted.

"They said Sophia wouldn't let me go that easy."

"I don't know how long she had been standing outside, but when I looked out my window, she was watching."

"I don't know how to explain it. I can always tell when she's close. It's like a weight pressing against the back of my skull."

Unease swept through the room.

I could *feel* the tension turning, like a pressure drop before a storm.

A few officers exchanged uneasy looks.

Maurice, who had been an officer here for over 10 years, took a slow step back, like he didn't want to be anywhere near this.

Jenkins' jaw clenched. "Jesus…"

Margo choked on a sob, her body folding in on itself. She grabbed another page, her voice turning raw.

"She was scared! She was terrified of her!"

Her hands crumpled the paper against her chest like she could force the truth out with her fingers.

"What did she do?" Her words hit like a hammer.

Her knees buckled. She collapsed into the lobby chair.

She was sobbing. Broken. Clutching the diary pages like they were the last pieces of her daughter left in the world.

The atmosphere was suffocating, thick with spoken and unspoken words.

"What the hell do we do?" Jenkins whispered in my ear.

I didn't know.

Because Stephen had planted the doubt.

And now, Margo had just ripped it open for everyone to see.

55

NOVEMBER 25, 2024, 9 AM - SOPHIA

31 DAYS AFTER JULIE WENT MISSING

The air mattress shifted beneath me, the cheap plastic groaning under my weight. So much of the air had depleted during the night that I felt my tailbone hitting the floor. I blinked against the dull morning light, my body aching like I had spent the night curled inside a fist.

The room smelled like sleep, stale air, and the faint scent of Jay. The hum of the TV played softly in the background, a news anchor's voice droning on about something distant. We all made a pact that we weren't going to school today.

Eli was on the sectional, his back to me and Jay, one arm thrown over his face like he could block out the world.

Jay was still next to me, his arm draped loosely over his stomach, his chest rising and falling in steady, even breaths. His face was slack with exhaustion, the sharp edges of his usual expressions softened in sleep.

His hand was close to mine. Not quite touching, but close enough that if I moved even a little, our fingers would brush.

I swallowed and shifted on my right side.

The air mattress dipped slightly between us, and for a second, I let myself stay there, feeling the quiet weight of him, the warmth radiating from where our shoulders almost met.

Then Jay stirred, his brow twitching before his eyes fluttered open. He blinked at me, bleary and unfocused, his voice still rough with sleep.

"You good?"

I nodded, but my chest felt too tight.

His gaze searched mine, and for a second, I thought he might say something else. But then he stretched one arm over his head, letting his fingers briefly brush my wrist before he let his hand drop between us.

Not an accident.

Not quite on purpose either.

"Morning sucks," he muttered, voice dry.

Despite everything, the corner of my mouth twitched. "Yeah."

I turned toward the window, and whatever warmth had settled between us vanished.

Because that's when I heard them.

Many, many muffled voices.

I sat up fast, the air mattress wobbling underneath me. I braced myself with my palms, my breath stifling in my throat.

Jay tensed beside me. "Who—?"

I didn't answer. I was already moving, shoving myself off the mattress, crossing the room to the window.

I reached for the blinds.

Paused.

Breathed.

Then I pulled them open.

I should have expected it.

I really, really should have.

But seeing them—seeing the cameras, the news vans, the reporters lined up outside my house like they were waiting for a freaking press conference—it still knocked the air from my lungs.

Jay was beside me in an instant. His entire body went rigid. "What the hell?"

Eli was slower to sit up. But when he did, I saw it. The slight shake in his hands as he ran them over his face. The tension in his shoulders, tight and locked.

He didn't have to ask what was happening. He already knew.

I tried to swallow but my throat was so dry nothing went down. The reporters were talking, gesturing, their cameras pointed directly at my house.

The weight of it settled deep. They were here for me.

I wasn't in the background anymore. Wasn't a name whispered in passing. I wasn't just a rumor. I wasn't just being confronted by Jessica in the hall.

I was the story, the headline.

Jay let out a slow breath. "Okay. We're gonna fix this." He got up and walked straight to the door, "*Do you have no soul,* this family has been through—" he stopped abruptly, taking a sharp right and walking all the way out of my view onto the driveway.

My body moved on instinct. Before I knew it, I was next to Jay, staring at it.

My veins turned to sludge before I even fully registered the word.

"MURDERER."

Spray-painted across the garage in dripping, perfect-lined, deep red.

Like fresh blood smeared over white.

The word stared back at me.

Like whoever did it wanted me to feel it.

And I did.

I felt Jay stiff beside me, his tone furious. "I'll get rid of it."

Eli appeared next to me, so still I wasn't even sure he was breathing.

I turned to him, my pulse hammering in my ears. My throat felt tight. Say something. Please.

But he just stared.

His eyes locked on the word. His jaw clenched so tight his muscles twitched.

But... he didn't look shocked.

Like he had seen this coming.

Like he had been waiting for it.

His shoulders dropped—suddenly but slightly. Not quite relief. But something close to it. Like the worst thing had already happened, was past us.

I should have gone inside, away from all of the people and commotion.

I should have shut the blinds, locked the door, disappeared.

But I didn't.

My feet fused to the ground, my body betraying me, I wanted to move, but nothing happened.

I just stood there.

Fingers numb.

I had been standing there for at least 30 seconds with no one noticing—until the shift hit. I felt it. The moment someone saw me.

A ripple went through the crowd.

The cameras snapped up. Microphones lifted. The low murmur of voices swelled, surging toward me like a wave.

I felt their eyes.

"Sophia!"

My name sounded loud and recognizable.

Jessica.

Just like that I snapped out of whatever weird trance was holding me there. I ran.

I barely heard Jay slam the door behind us. "Freaking vultures," he said.

I felt sick. My hands were shaking. My breath was too fast, too shallow.

I don't know why I reached for my phone, why I tried to reassure myself this was just limited to my house and no one else saw it.

But I had to check.

I didn't even have to search on TikTok. The algorithm knew what I wanted before I did. A video stared back at me from my For You page, my name in bold white letters across the screen. Jessica had stitched someone else's post, layering her own theory on top.

> *"NEW THEORY: What if Sophia did it?*
> *People said she was sleepwalking that night. How do we know she didn't do it?*
> *Maybe Stephen was covering for her.*
> *That whole family is messed up.*
> *Her dad isn't around for a reason."*

The comments were worse. Some joked. Some... *didn't*.

My vision swam.

I wasn't going to cry. Not for them.

I kept scrolling until I hit a comment that was liked 2,453 times:

"Why isn't she in jail yet? If it was a guy, they'd already have him in cuffs."

I turned off my phone.

The damage was done.

I knew how this worked. I had seen it happen before, to myself already. And to other people with even more exaggerated stories.

It never mattered what was true.

It only mattered what people believed.

And right now?

For some reason they believed I was a killer.

I squeezed my eyes shut, my fingers curling into my sleeves.

Deep down, I was ashamed.

Not because they were right.

But because it didn't matter if they were wrong.

Because their voices were louder than mine.
And they probably always would be.

56

— · —

NOVEMBER 25, 2024, 4 PM - SOPHIA

31 DAYS AFTER JULIE WENT MISSING

I should have let Jay do this.

Or Eli.

Or anyone else.

But if I let them protect me forever, when would it end?

The cold November air was sharp against my skin as I walked down Main Street, the sky an endless stretch of dull gray. The town felt heavier.

People had been whispering for almost 2 months. But outside of Jessica, and Stephen, no one had actually confronted me.

But today was different.

I could feel it. The weight of their stares pressed against my back stronger than ever, holding my gaze when I dared to look up.

A group of women stood near the florist, pretending not to notice me.

I kept my head down but I heard it.

"Disgusting," one of them muttered under her breath.

My heart shrunk. I walked faster.

Everyone was against me.

Even Abbie hadn't answered my latest texts.

Which seriously, seriously, sucked.

The word on the garage still wasn't gone either.

Jay had tried. He had scrubbed for hours, knuckles raw, sweat dripping even in the cold. But as the soapy water dried, the letters refused to disappear. The **M** had come off fine, but the rest had clung stubbornly to the paint.

...URDERER.

Like the house itself had decided to keep it.

So, I was going into town to buy paint.

Because if I couldn't erase it completely, I'd bury it.

I reached the hardware store and pulled the door handle.

Click.

The lock slid into place.

I froze.

Through the glass, I saw Mr. Thompson on the other side of the door.

Eyes meeting mine for half a second. His face twisted, something between disgust and decision flashing across it as his hand stayed on the lock.

He reached the sign on the door, fingers fumbling, flipping it from OPEN to CLOSED right in front of me.

I stared at him through the glass, my breath sharp in my chest.

I had been coming here since I was a kid. Bought school supplies, duct tape, batteries. I used to run my hands along the stacks of paint swatches while my dad picked out screws for whatever furniture he was putting together.

Mr. Thompson had always been nice.

But now, he wouldn't even look at me.

My hand slipped from the door handle.

Fine.

I turned away. My feet moving faster than my brain. The streets suddenly blurring around me.

The air thinned in my lungs when I saw him.

Up ahead, a guy was walking past the bakery, jacket zipped up to his chin, hands stuffed into his pockets.

Stephen.

No.

It couldn't be.

My body reacted before my brain could.

Every nerve locked up, something sharp and primal surging through me.

My hands shook.

He turned slightly.

A soft and happy face.

Not Stephen.

Just a man.

Just an innocent person.

I stumbled from the relief, my toes clipped the uneven sidewalk.

The impact jarred me back into my body.

God. God.

I was losing it.

When I got my bearings and looked up, I saw Julie's mom standing just a few feet away.

Her eyes bored into mine, looking through me, past me, deep into the places I didn't want anyone to see.

Her hands trembled at her sides.

She took a step closer.

"I know Julie was scared of you."

She wasn't yelling. She wasn't shaking me, demanding answers, making a scene.

She was crying.

Tears streamed down her face, carving lines into her grief, making her look hollow.

Her voice cracked, raw and broken. "I have them, you know."

My stomach twisted. "Have what?"

She reached into her coat pocket, her fingers shaking as she pulled out a crumpled piece of paper.

My chest tightened.

Notebook paper. Torn at the edges. Writing smeared from her tears.

She held it out like a weapon. "Someone left this in my mailbox last night."

Stephen must have put her diary pages in the mailbox.

Even now, even after everything, he was still pulling strings somehow. Still playing games.

I stared at the paper.

If she was confronting me, I already knew what it said.

Julie's words.

Her handwriting.

Her fear... of me.

"She was scared of you, Sophia." Her voice cracked on my name. "She wrote it down. She was afraid of you."

"That's not—"

"What do you know?" she whispered. "What did you do!"

She collapsed in sobs.

The noise was too much. Too raw.

I couldn't breathe.

The only word I could force past my throat—"Stephen."

"I just want my daughter back. I just want my daughter back."

She sobbed into her hands.

Then she reached out. Not to grab me. She was too far away for that. She was just... reaching.

Like she thought I might still have the answers she needed.

And for a second, my body almost listened.

I felt a familiar pull towards her.

But a car horn honked in the distance pulling me back to reality and I turned and ran.

Before I could see her completely unravel.

Before I could hear her voice again.

Before she could tear me apart.

That night I sat on my bed, knees pulled to my chest, staring at my phone.

The screen reflected just *how bleak* things had gotten. No messages back from Abbie. Just one missed call from my dad.

I could leave.

I could pack a bag, grab my dad's emergency cash from the hall closet, and be gone by morning. I could get on a bus to anywhere. A place where no one knew me.

I could disappear.

But then what?

It would follow me.

Even if I disappeared, the story wouldn't.

My name would still be in the headlines. My face would still be online. My past would still be tethered to me, whispering in every new town.

I squeezed my eyes shut. My breath was uneven. I wasn't going anywhere.

I reached for my phone, gripping it too tight. That's when I saw something out the window.

Ms. Tinson was walking down the sidewalk, her coat buttoned up to her chin, one hand gripping a leash. A golden retriever trotted beside her, tail wagging, nose twitching in the cold.

I sat up straighter, heart stalling for a second.

That dog.

The one I found. The one bleeding out in the road. The one I thought didn't make it. Here it was. Healthy. Happy. *Alive.*

Ms. Tinson stopped at the corner, waiting at the crosswalk as little Tommy ran up behind her, throwing his arms around the dog's neck in a full-body hug. She laughed, tousling his hair as he beamed up at her.

The dog barked once, playfully, like it was just as happy to be here.

Something in my chest cracked open.

I blinked fast.

The dog had made it out. Maybe I could, too.

Tomorrow, I was going to walk back into town. Again.

57

— • —

June 2, 2025, 9 AM - Sophia

220 Days After Julie Went Missing

For six months, I'd woken up in the same place I fell asleep. My bed.

No strange places. No damp clothes clinging to my skin. No disjointed flashes of memory leaving me breathless in the middle of the night. Just me, cocooned under my comforter, with the sound of birds chirping outside my window to greet me in the morning.

It felt like a miracle.

I stretched under the covers, my body unusually relaxed. The sun slipped through the curtains, spilling soft golden light onto the walls. Everything looked still, peaceful.

My eyes drifted to the nightstand. The orange pill bottle peeked out from under a paperback novel, its familiar shape both a comfort and a warning. I reached for it, running my fingers over the label before picking it up.

It had also been six months of taking a pill that was supposed to be *as needed*, every single night.

At first, I told myself it was temporary. Just until things calmed down. But now, every night felt like a game of Russian roulette: take the pill and get the sleep I craved, or skip it and risk waking up somewhere I didn't remember going.

I'd started cutting the pills in half a month ago, using a plastic pill cutter I'd ordered off Amazon. It felt like progress, even if I was still too scared to stop entirely. I'd looked up withdrawal symptoms one night when I couldn't sleep, reading horror stories about rebound insomnia, anxiety spikes, and worse. The thought of spiraling again kept my finger hovering over the "place order" button for a refill.

What happens when you stop? The question sat heavy in my chest.

I exhaled sharply and shoved the bottle back under my opened book, like that would somehow make it less real.

Things were normal now.

The version of normal I could have anyway.

The town had moved on, or at least it had found new things to whisper about, new people to side-eye. The stares had faded. The tension had dulled. I wasn't the girl everyone talked about anymore.

Stephen's name consumed the headlines while mine faded away.

And maybe that should've felt like relief.

But sometimes, I wondered if I had just gotten used to the weight of it all. If the worst part wasn't that people had turned on me, but that eventually, they just... forgot.

Like it had never happened.

Like I had never been at the center of it.

And maybe that was for the best.

Because now, I could do things like this. Meet Jay for coffee. Go through the motions of a life that felt steady, simple, real.

Abbie had reached out just a few days after it all went down—apologizing for not texting me back. She'd been filling me with sugar multiple times a week, attempting to make up for it, I guess.

And my dad was home. He had stayed home for the last few months, even if he was still picking up extra shifts.

But in the end, there was always Jay and Eli.

They had been my rocks.

I held onto that.

Even if some part of me still felt like I was waiting for the other shoe to drop.

Jay was standing just outside Grounded, and I was ready for my must-have coffee fix.

It wasn't the caffeine that kept me coming back anymore though, it was the fact that Jay started working there a few months ago. With his 15% employee discount, we'd convinced ourselves we were practically funding a Cancun trip, one $3 cup at a time.

Jay was still wearing his work apron, his dark hair falling messily over his forehead. He was scrolling through his phone, and when he saw me, a grin stretched across his face.

"Finally. I thought you fell into a hole or something," he teased, shoving his phone into his pocket.

"Yeah, I've been real busy with that," I deadpanned. "Sorry to disappoint."

He smirked. "You ready for trivia night?"

I snorted. "Are *you*? Because last time you cost us the win by confidently, confidently, saying that Beethoven was blind."

Jay groaned. "I blacked out under pressure, okay? And to be fair, the guy had something wrong with him."

I rolled my eyes but felt the laughter bubbling up in my chest. With Jay around, the weight on my shoulders didn't feel so heavy.

We walked inside, the familiar scent of roasted coffee beans and vanilla filled the air. A few of our classmates were already there, gathered around tables with dimly lit candles and stacks of answer sheets.

Jay tossed his apron behind the counter, stretching his arm around me. "All right, Whitaker, we need a strategy. No impulsive answers, and if I panic again, just, smack me or something."

I grinned. "Deal. But if we lose, I'm telling everyone about the Beethoven incident."

"Cold," he muttered, leading the way to a table near the back.

The first few rounds flew by, and to my shock, we weren't completely terrible. Jay actually pulled his weight this time, correctly answering a ridiculously obscure question about 90s pop bands that saved us from elimination.

When the final question came up, something about the capital of a country neither of us could confidently place on a map, I expected Jay to crack. Instead, he tapped his pen against his chin, deep in thought.

"This is it," he said. "This is my redemption arc."

I snorted. "You're really going for that?"

"Oh, absolutely," he said, grinning.

He scribbled down an answer, slid the paper to me, and raised an eyebrow. "Trust me?"

I studied him for a second, then nodded.

When the host read off the correct answer, I nearly choked on my drink. Jay had actually gotten it right.

His jaw dropped. "Are you *kidding* me?"

I stared at him. "I don't know whether to be proud or worried that you've been secretly smart this whole time."

He smirked, looking insufferably pleased with himself. "Guess I'm full of surprises."

Jay was still grinning, basking in his trivia redemption, but my stomach twisted for no reason at all.

A girl at the counter glanced at me. Not for long. Not in a way that meant anything.

But for just a second, my breath stuttered. And I hated that it did.

I brushed it off.

After the game was over, we took the long way back to his house, the streetlights buzzing faintly overhead as we walked. The summer night air was cool, but not in a way that made me shiver. It was the kind that was comfortable.

"So," Jay said after a moment, glancing at me. "How's the sleeping thing been?"

I kicked a loose pebble, watching it skip down the sidewalk. "Still solid. No weird episodes. I think the meds are actually working."

"That's good," he said, his voice softer. "I mean, I know it's good, but... I guess how are you feeling?"

I hesitated, choosing my words carefully. "I don't know. I guess part of me wonders if I'm just masking the problem instead of fixing it."

Jay nudged me lightly. "Hey. Even if that were true, does it matter? You're finally getting some peace, right?"

"Yeah..." I said.

Jay shot me a sideways glance. "You still doing the visualization stuff?"

I nodded. "Yeah. Just... not about that night. Not yet."

He didn't push. Instead, he launched into a rant about how a customer tried to pay for their coffee with a handful of Chuck E. Cheese tokens and then got offended when he wouldn't accept them. "Like, sir, this isn't a casino, and you're not cashing out your winnings," he huffed, gesturing dramatically. I let myself get lost in the easiness of it, in the way he could turn the smallest annoyance into a full-blown comedic saga.

His hand clasped mine and I felt the rush of heat within me. Jay was here. And for the moment, everything felt okay.

58

— • —

June 3, 2025, 4 PM - Newton

221 Days After Julie Went Missing

Stephen's trial was three days away, and the case against him for Julie's murder was still circumstantial as hell. I'd been holding out hope that The Circle scandal would break wide open and finally cement everything. But it never did.

The night after we arrested Stephen, I'd gone back to the station. I'd watched the flash drive footage again. What he'd done to those girls, how deep the manipulation ran. It was enough to turn my stomach. But that wasn't the only thing waiting for me.

There was a message in my inbox.

A secure link. An anonymous sender. No subject. Just: "Play this alone."

And below that: "I'm dead the moment I hit general population."

It was from Calloway.

He had sent it the night we arrested Stephen, just hours before the feds picked him up.

I didn't listen. At the time, I still believed going through official channels was the right thing. I forwarded the email. Sent transcripts. Gave everything to the feds, thinking they'd uncover everything while protecting the witness. Thinking they'd protect him.

They didn't.

I clicked the video again, for the thirteenth time in six months. Calloway appeared on screen, hunched, shoulders rigid like he'd filmed it in a bathroom or stairwell.

"I don't know how much time I have," he said. "So, I'm keeping this brief."

His voice was clipped. Flattened by fear. Still trying to sound in control though.

"The Circle didn't start out as what it is now," he said. "Back then, it was about survival. They say it began during the Great Depression. Powerful men building lifeboats while the rest of the world sank."

His mouth twisted slightly.

"But survival turned into strategy. And over time, strategy turned into doctrine.

310

They passed it down, generation after generation. Handpicking young men from elite universities, grooming them not just to survive the chaos... but to control it. To shape what came next. And not just for the few..."

He leaned closer to the camera. "They believe chaos breeds from too much freedom, too many people with too many opinions. And that control is the only cure. That's what I bought into. That's what we all bought into. We told ourselves we were doing the hard thing. The necessary thing. But I've seen what it costs.

I was running a financial operation out of Chicago. Large-scale corporate-level laundering. But there was a lot of heat, too much regulation."

He glanced away from the camera.

"Then they sent me to Ordinance. Said it was a test site. Small town, no press, no real oversight. Just local authorities who could be nudged into looking the other way if needed."

He let out a dry breath. "We set up shop fast. Ghost nonprofits, fake grants, infrastructure bids that were all smoke. I signed off on all of it. We funneled a few million. Clean, quiet, easy."

He hesitated.

"But moving that kind of scale? It wasn't worth it unless we could replicate it. Dozens, maybe hundreds of towns just like this. We were still figuring that out when Stephen showed up."

He gave a humorless laugh. "I didn't recruit him. He came to *me*. Started asking questions no high school kid should've known how to ask. About how money was moving. About the nonprofit boards. Real specific."

"One night, I came into my classroom, and he'd been in my computer. Nothing stolen. Just... rearranged. Little things were moved on my desktop. Like he wanted me to know."

He looked into the camera now, expression sharper.

"That's when I realized what kind of kid I was dealing with. He was dangerous. Smart, but not normal smart. Strategic. Cold."

Calloway's voice lowered.

"Next thing I know, he's making contact with The Circle leadership. Bypassed me completely. And not just that, he brought in crypto. Said it would solve the speed problem. And it did. Suddenly, we weren't moving millions, we were moving billions. In and out. Instant. Untraceable. No more waiting on banks or burying it in paperwork. It was like he lit the whole system on fire."

He closed his eyes.

"They should've shut him down. I should've shut him down. But the numbers were too good. They looked the other way. Hell, I looked the other way."

His voice cracked slightly, "He didn't want to be part of the system. He wanted to use the system to perpetuate his... natural tendencies. He's the reason I tried to get out.

If you're watching this, I'm probably already dead. Don't trust anyone. Don't go through official channels. If you want to bring this down... work with Tessa Sharp."

He glanced behind him, then leaned forward one last time.

"She's the only one who you *can* trust."

The screen cut to black.

I'd watched that message six months ago. And ignored it. Told myself I was doing things the right way.

Calloway had died in transit the next day.

And I'd done nothing.

I'd looked up Tessa Sharp once, just enough to see she was with some small media outlet I'd never heard of. No social media. No interviews. No digital trail at all, which felt strange for a reporter. Almost like she didn't want to be found.

The Cleveland DA had buried the whole case. No one talked about Calloway. No one followed up on the names he gave in custody. And now, with Stephen's trial just days away... I had nothing new. No way to tie The Circle to Julie or Stephen beyond what was in the flash drive. Just the Rachel murder charge. And that might not be enough.

If the Julie charge didn't stick, Stephen would disappear into a padded cell for Rachel—locked up, sure, but the rest of it? The Circle? Julie? That would die with the verdict.

I raked a hand through my hair, pacing my office like it could dislodge the guilt I hadn't shaken since Calloway's death.

Then I looked over at the box.

The last of Stephen's stuff. What was left after the prosecution scraped everything useful.

I opened it.

Same crap. Clothes. Receipts. Loose pages. But near the bottom was his old hoodie. The Student Council one Sophia had been wearing in the footage the night Stephen had... touched her. My stomach turned.

I dug deeper.

"Damn," I whispered. I'd sliced my finger on the edge of something.

It was the black-and-white checkered notebook. The one full of notes about "conditioning" the girls. The Cleveland DA made photocopies and left it here.

I flipped through to the end, then felt something.

There was a ridge behind the back cover.

I peeled it open.

A photo slid free.

Sophia.

Sleepwalking. In the woods.

Timestamp: October 25th. 2:47 AM.

The night Julie died.

My pulse kicked. I'd seen this photo before. Same angle, same expression, but that version had a handwritten timestamp. I'd assumed Stephen faked it. Another manipulation.

But this one... the timestamp was automatic. Printed straight from the camera.

It was real.

She was there.

Right there. Within walking distance of where Julie was buried.

I stared at it, bile rising in my throat.

I wanted to ignore it. Toss it in the trash. Pretend it was just a coincidence.

But deep down, I knew better.

I didn't know what Stephen had done. Not completely.

And I didn't know what he'd done to Sophia *that* night.

Had he used her?

Or worse?

I sat there, the edges of the photo trembling in my hands.

Stephen was the monster. I'd seen it firsthand. But even monsters know how to use people.

Sophia had been through hell. This town nearly broke her once already.

I wasn't going to drag her through it again unless I had no other choice.

But this photo, it could finally tie Stephen to Julie's death. Or...

I didn't finish the thought.

I stood, grabbed my keys.

Just a house call.

Nothing official. No accusations.

But if I ignored this, and it wasn't nothing, I'd never forgive myself.

And I already knew.

It wasn't nothing.

59

— · —

June 3, 2025, 5 PM - Sophia

221 Days After Julie Went Missing

The knock at the door came sharp and fast.

I froze, a glass of water halfway to my lips. No one ever knocked.

Jay or Abbie would've texted first. My dad didn't knock because, well, he lived here... at least for now. And Eli was home.

The second knock came. Harder.

"Sophia, it's Sheriff Newton."

My pulse picked up.

Newton?

I set the glass down carefully. I already knew why he was here. Stephen's trial was days away, and Newton wasn't the type to make casual house calls.

I pulled the door open.

Newton stood there, looking just as exhausted as the last time I'd seen him. But something was different.

"Newton," I said, my voice even. "What's going on?"

Newton didn't answer right away. His gaze scanned over my face. "Mind if I come in?"

I hesitated. My fingers tightened on the doorframe.

"...Sure."

Newton stepped inside, his boots heavy against the hardwood. He looked around, like he was taking everything in. The stacked books on the coffee table. The half-empty mug on the counter.

Like he was searching for something.

I crossed my arms. "Is this about the trial?"

Newton exhaled, reaching into his pocket.

He pulled out a photo of me in the woods, and my stomach dropped.

315

I didn't need to take it. I'd seen it before, in Stephen's locker. I'd handed it over to Newton myself.

Except that one had a handwritten date.

But in this picture, there was an automated timestamp in the corner.

My head buzzed with electricity.

I'd convinced myself Stephen had written the date to mess with me—to scare me. But this...

I was there.

I couldn't move.

Couldn't think.

Newton watched me carefully. "Sophia, this puts you in the woods that night," Newton said. His voice was measured, but soft.

He let the words settle. I felt them land like a punch to the face.

Newton didn't look away.

Neither did I.

After a minute of silence he asked, "Do you remember anything from that night?"

My pulse flooded my ears.

I wanted to say no.

I wanted to tell him this was just another manipulation from Stephen.

But suddenly, I wasn't sure anymore.

The memory of dirt on my hands. Julie's face.

Hadn't I told myself that it wasn't real?

Newton exhaled, sliding the photo back into his pocket.

All I could do was force myself to shake my head no.

Eli must've overheard, because suddenly he stormed in. "Are you really freaking asking her? Hasn't she been through enough? Haven't YOU put her through enough?! You've dragged her into this, the whole town was against her for months."

He was gesturing to me frantically.

"Unless you have something beyond a shadow of a doubt, I would think about what this will cost. To my sister. To Julie's family."

"Kid. Stay in your lane."

"I'm done doing that. You're not doing this to my sister. Over what? This picture?" he laughed, unhinged.

316

Newton's face flashed between rage and remorse. In the end he just sighed then looked at me with the most devastating amount of pity I've ever seen and said, "If you remember anything," a pause, "let me know."

I nodded automatically.

But I didn't breathe again until he was gone.

The door clicked shut, and the silence rushed back in.

I stood there for a long time, the image of the timestamp burned into my brain.

2:47 AM.

I *was* there.

Eli moved to me, wrapping me in a hug out of nowhere. Comfort I didn't deserve. And it was weird. We didn't hug.

He had the same look of pity I saw from Newton. Because he believed Stephen manipulated me.

And he had. I knew that.

But suddenly, that wasn't enough.

Suddenly, I felt like I was missing something again.

Like I had been looking at this whole thing through a fogged-up window.

And now, I wasn't sure what was on the other side.

60

— • —

June 5, 2025, 8 PM - Sophia

223 Days After Julie Went Missing

The house was quiet, but my thoughts weren't.

It had been two days since Newton showed up with the photograph, but I hadn't seen him since. Two days since Eli jumped in to defend me, his voice loud as thunder while mine got swallowed whole. Two days since I'd been able to breathe without feeling like I was running out of air.

Stephen's trial was tomorrow.

That fact sat heavy in my chest, an immovable weight pressing down on me. He was going away, maybe forever. That should have brought some kind of closure.

So why didn't it?

At dinner, Eli had been the perfect version of himself—calm, steady, not a hint of unease in his expression. He made spaghetti, joking about burning the garlic bread like we were just another pair of siblings having a normal night while dad was at work. But I wasn't normal, and he knew it.

I barely ate. I barely spoke. I couldn't stop seeing that picture in my head—me, in the woods, sleepwalking the night she died. In the same woods she was buried in. It didn't matter that I didn't remember. It didn't matter that Eli swore to me up and down that I was home with him, convinced the picture had been manipulated by Stephen. I didn't believe it. I had remembered something in Dr. Patel's office. The doubt was there, clawing at the edges of my mind like something feral trying to get out.

I excused myself early, heading upstairs under the guise of getting rest. I heard Eli clean up in the kitchen, heard the soft click of the TV turning on downstairs. Like everything was normal.

I shut my bedroom door and leaned against it, exhaling shakily.

318

The bottle of pills sat on my nightstand, exactly where it had been every night for the past six months. Staring at them, all I could think about was how easy it would be to take a full one, maybe even 2. To silence the chaos.

But something held me back.

Maybe it was fear. Or maybe it was the whisper in the back of my mind telling me that the answers I needed, the truth I'd been circling for months, never would come if I kept numbing them away.

My fingers tightened around the bottle.

Then, slowly, I set it down.

Instead, I folded my legs beneath me on the bed, closing my eyes and inhaling deeply. In. Hold. Out.

The visualization exercise had become a ritual—something I could control. I pictured the open field, the sky streaked in purple and orange, fading to dusk. At the center, the wooden door. Waiting.

I reached for the handle. It usually gave easily.

But tonight, it didn't.

The weight behind it was heavier. The door stayed stiff beneath my fingers. Like something, someone, was pressing back.

A twinkle in the darkness.

A voice, distant, muffled.

Julie?

My pulse kicked up. I pushed harder, straining, forcing it open.

For a moment, I thought I was getting somewhere.

Then—*bam*—the door slammed shut in my face.

My eyes snapped open.

"Damn it."

I dragged my hands down my thighs, trying to shake off the frustration tightening my chest. The exercise wasn't working. Hadn't been for days if I was being honest with myself. The stress of the trial, the pressure, it was getting to me.

The knot in my throat tightened. Nope—not doing this. I grabbed my phone. Scrolled. Scrolled some more.

TikTok videos blurred past. Faces, voices, white noise to drown out the restless feeling burrowing inside me.

My eyes grew heavy.

At some point, I slid under the covers.

Tried the visualization again, halfway in a dream state already.

Flashes. Disjointed, flickering, chaotic. My pulse still thrumming in my ears. My mind pulling back from the memory, or reaching for it.

But exhaustion dragged me under.

And for the first time in a long time, I drifted into sleep, fitfully, without the medication.

I woke to the sound of muffled sobs, a trembling hand gripping my shoulder, shaking me gently but urgently. My body felt heavy, the damp chill of the ground seeping into my skin. The air smelled of earth—wet and raw.

"Sophia," a voice choked out, raw with desperation. "Please wake up. Please."

My eyes fluttered open, and for a moment, I couldn't comprehend what I was seeing. Eli was above me, his face pale and streaked with tears. His eyes were red, wide with fear, and his hands were shaking as he clutched my arms.

"What—" My voice cracked, barely a whisper. "Eli?"

He let out a breath like he'd been holding it forever. Relief washed over his face, but it didn't erase the anguish in his eyes. "Sophia, you scared the hell out of me. What are you doing here?" His voice broke, trembling. "Why are you laying here?"

His words didn't make sense at first, but then I felt it, the uneven ground beneath me. My hands sank into the dirt, and I realized where I was. The faux burial site where Julie's body was found.

I sucked in a sharp breath, panic clawing at my chest. I scrambled to sit up, but my body refused to cooperate. Eli's hands steadied me, his grip firm but careful. I looked up at him, and a jolt of recognition shot through me.

He was crying.

The way his shoulders shook, the way his hands trembled as he reached for me, it was the same. The exact same as that night. The image hit like a shockwave. My head split open with it.

My eyes slammed shut.

And then, like a floodgate breaking, it came rushing back.

61

— · —

OCTOBER 7, 2024, 1:40 AM - SOPHIA

18 DAYS BEFORE JULIE WENT MISSING

I loved being outside at night.

It wasn't about breaking the rules. It was the quiet freedom, the way the town felt different when no one was watching.

During the day, Ordinance was chatty, alive, too loud in places it didn't need to be. But now?

Now, it was still. Peaceful.

The plastic skeletons on front lawns swayed slightly in the breeze, their grins glowing lights. A few houses had fake cobwebs stretched across bushes, cheap dollar-store gravestones propped against flower beds. The air smelled fresh, I could already taste the faintest scent of fried dough from Honey's.

Pumpkin donuts. *Yum.*

Abbie and I had only done this a few times before, but it was starting to feel like a tradition. A late-night sugar rush, a secret we swore we'd never tell anyone. Mostly so we could eat all of the donuts.

I adjusted the strap of my bag as I cut through the trees, following the tree line toward town square.

The night was perfectly still.

But then I heard a noise. Something low, muffled.

I barely noticed it at first, my mind still picturing the warm bag of donuts in my hands.

Then I heard it again.

A choked sound.

I stopped.

My ears strained. A cat? A raccoon?

But it was too... human?

My eyes darted between the trees.

The glow of a porch light flickered through the branches, casting shadows along the grass. It was coming from a backyard.

I crouched, pressing my palms into the cold earth as I peered through the trees.

Two figures.

I froze.

For a second, my brain didn't catch up to who they were.

Julie?

Stephen?

What were they doing out here so late?

I cupped my hands around my eyes, creating makeshift binoculars, trying to sharpen the image.

Julie jerked.

Not like someone shifting their weight.

Like someone trying to get away.

My hands dropped and I took a step back.

What was going on?

I couldn't see clearly from here. Her outdoor furniture cast shadows under the back spotlight that stretched over them. Stephen's body blocked hers from this angle.

I swallowed hard and crept forward, keeping low, my hands brushed against damp leaves as I tucked myself behind the trunk of a tree.

Julie wasn't moving right.

My breath was shallow, pressing against my ribs. My fingers dug into the bark, but something in my brain wasn't keeping up.

I was watching, but I wasn't understanding.

Julie's legs kicked out, but not like someone playing around. Not a girl flirting, or wrestling, or messing with a guy she liked.

It was sharper. Desperate.

She arched up violently, twisting her body, trying to shove at his chest.

Stephen barely moved. His weight shifted once, adjusting.

Like she wasn't a person, but an object he was trying to get in place.

Julie's hand flew up, smacking against his shoulder.

Her nails scratched down his arm, digging deep, pulling, grabbing—

This isn't normal.

This isn't normal.

The thought looped in my head without fully landing.

I was seeing it.

I knew I was seeing it.

So why didn't it feel real?

Julie's mouth opened.

A choked sob broke out of her throat, barely above a whisper.

Stephen pressed down harder.

Her body jerked, a full body shake. She was trying to throw him off, using every last bit of energy she had left.

And then, in a voice so weak it barely existed—

"Somebody help me."

The moment it left her lips, something inside me cracked apart.

I felt it.

Not just in my mind.

In my body.

A snap.

Like something had gone completely, irreversibly wrong inside me.

I stopped breathing.

Not like holding my breath.

My lungs had just forgotten how to work.

They didn't belong to me anymore.

My vision swam, blurred out, tunneled inward—

I was in my body but also above it.

Like I had been peeled out of myself and left somewhere else.

Like I was floating just outside my own mind.

My legs weren't mine anymore.

They were weights.

Dead, useless weights locked into the ground.

I tried to move.

I told myself to run for help, jump in between them, scream, do something—

Nothing happened.

Nothing.

Nothing.

Nothing.

I was watching the worst thing I had ever seen, and my body wouldn't let me stop it.

I was inside myself and outside myself all at once.

Julie was still fighting.

Her fingers were digging into the ground, trying to pull herself away.

She was still trying to escape, her will was strong.

Stephen pinned her completely.

She was losing.

And I wasn't doing anything.

I felt the tears running down my face before I even knew I was crying.

I didn't feel like me anymore.

The ground slanted.

The sky pulled further away.

My body was somewhere else.

And my mind?

My mind was splitting.

Julie's muffled sobs barely registered anymore.

Stephen's voice, low and pleased, barely existed in my head.

Everything was far away.

Like I was watching it happen through a glass wall.

Like it was already over before it had even started.

My chest convulsed.

I felt my mouth open.

No sound came out.

Nothing came out.

I tried to reach forward, but my arms didn't move.

Julie's legs stopped kicking.

Her arms stopped pulling.

Her body went still.

Not because she got free.

Because she couldn't fight anymore.

Because he had won.

Julie's voice shattered through the quiet.

A whisper. A whimper. A last ditch effort.

"Anybody. Please."

It broke me.

Completely.

I wasn't a person anymore.

A shattered thing.

A broken mind without a body.

I wasn't there.

I was watching, but I wasn't there.

Stephen exhaled.

Julie curled in on herself.

Her hands twitched.

Her sobs were so quiet now.

And Stephen?

He sighed, rolling his shoulders. Untouched. Unbothered.

Like this was nothing.

Like he had just gone for a jog, stretched his legs.

Like he hadn't just ruined her forever.

And then he turned his head.

He looked right at me.

I felt his eyes on me before I even registered the movement.

My brain screamed at my legs to move.

My hands to claw into the earth, push myself up, run—

But... I couldn't.

My body leaned forward, just slightly. Not a choice. Not even a thought.

It was already leaving me behind.

His mouth curled into something that wasn't quite a smile.

And in that moment, I knew he would never forget that I had watched.

That wolfish grin.

Everything went black.

I woke up slowly, my body feeling heavier than usual.

For a second, I thought it was just from falling asleep too hard. Like when you nap in the middle of the day and wake up feeling disoriented.

I blinked against the morning light slipping through my curtains. Stretched. Then kicked off the blanket.

I paused.

There was something on my comforter.

Faint, dusty streaks.

I ran my fingers over the fabric, frowning. Was that... dirt?

The smudges were dry, light brown. Like I'd tracked something in from outside.

My mind immediately tried to make sense of it.

Did I go outside last night?

No, why would I have? I went upstairs to change into warmer clothes so I could meet Abbie. I remembered sitting down to put my socks on. Then... I fell asleep.

At least, I think I did.

I sat up, stretching again, still half-asleep. But as I moved, something else caught my eye.

My hands.

A small patch of dirt on my palm, under my fingernails.

Cold flushed through my body, but not from fear.

Just... confusion.

I ran my thumb over my other palm, rubbing at the dirt. It smudged slightly but didn't completely come off.

What the hell?

I swung my legs over the bed, and the second my feet hit the floor, my breath hitched.

There was more.

Dirt on my knees.

Faint streaks, like I had been kneeling in the yard.

I stared at it, my brain catching up too slowly.

Did I go outside before bed?

No. That didn't make sense.

I would've remembered that.

Wouldn't I?

I frowned. My chest felt tight now. Not panic, just an uneasiness that wouldn't settle. Like my body knew something my brain hadn't figured out yet.

I reached for my phone, flipping it over, still trying to shake the weird feeling off.

10 missed texts from Abbie.

> Abbie (2:03 AM): Hey where are you??

> Abbie (2:05 AM): Did you bail??

> Abbie (2:07 AM): Wtf dude, are you okay?

> Abbie (2:10 AM): I waited for like 15 minutes

Abbie (2:15 AM): Are you dead in a ditch lol

Abbie (2:21 AM): Ok seriously I'm going home

Abbie (2:30 AM): R u asleep??

Abbie (2:42 AM): Dude seriously what happened

Abbie (3:15 AM): Text me when you wake up

Abbie (6:47 AM): Morning loser. U alive??

I stared at the screen.

I never met her.

I never made it to the shop.

I was supposed to, but—

I fell asleep.

That had to be it.

It was so late I must've crashed when I sat on the bed to change.

But...

How did I get dirt all over me?

I remembered watching movies downstairs, then picking out clothes in my room.

Then what?

Why couldn't I remember actually falling asleep?

I swallowed, glancing down at my hands again, rubbing my thumb over my palm. The dirt was still there, sitting in the small creases of my skin.

Why were my knees dirty, too?

Why did I feel like my lungs were sitting too high in my chest, like something was pressing against them?

Something felt just slightly... off.

I shook my head, forcing a breath out, telling myself to shake it off.

But as I swiped to clear my notifications, as I got up to brush my teeth, as I started moving through the normal steps of my morning, the feeling didn't go away.

It settled.

Deep in my ribs.

A weight.

A wrongness.

Something I couldn't put into words.

62

OCTOBER 7, 2024, 11:20 PM - SOPHIA

18 DAYS BEFORE JULIE WENT MISSING

My body led me here.

Julie's house stood in front of me, bathed in silver light, windows dark and still.

I wasn't awake. Not really.

But I was watching.

I was repeating something. Reliving something. Trying to fix something that couldn't be undone.

Protect her.

That thought lived inside me, deeper than memory. I didn't know why, but I knew I had to be here.

To keep her safe.

Or maybe to punish myself.

There was a rustling in the distance.

A shadow moved between the trees.

Something was wrong.

I blinked.

And suddenly, I was in the woods again, but at a different time.

The trees towered around me, stretching like ribs against the sky.

I was standing between them.

My feet filthy with dirt, my breath slow and even. Mechanical. Like I wasn't really breathing at all.

Stephen stood just behind me.

His voice was soft, intrigued.

"You really are gone, aren't you?"

I turned my head slowly, like my body was on strings.

That was the first time he spoke to me.

He studied me, head leaning, his gaze raking over me like I was something to be dissected.

"Fascinating."

A chill curled through me, even though the night was warm.

"What do you dream about in there?" he asked. "Do you even know?"

I didn't answer.

His smirk widened.

"No? That's okay. I know. I see you."

His voice brimmed with awe, like I was something he'd made.

The trees melted around me.

I crouched in Julie's backyard. A different night.

The grass was wet beneath my feet.

The house stood still. Silent.

Stephen's whisper came from behind me.

"Closer."

I moved forward.

"You want to see her, don't you?"

Yes.

No.

I didn't know.

But I kept walking.

The shadows swallowed me whole. My limbs felt foreign. Weightless. My body, a puppet on invisible strings.

I stopped just before the back patio.

Something inside me resisted.

I wasn't supposed to be here.

I was supposed to protect her.

But my body was not my own.

Stephen's fingers ghosted over my wrist.

"You feel it too, don't you?"

"Next time, you'll go inside."

I didn't nod. But I didn't run.

The world went dark.

I was in Julie's backyard again. A colder night.

The wind cut through my pajamas.

"Tonight, you will kill her."

Stephen's voice was soft. Coaxing.

I wasn't going to.

I wasn't.

Stephen unfolded my fingers and pressed the hilt of a knife into my hand.

His fingers lingered. Like it meant something to him.

"Let's go inside, Sophia."

NO!

The word screamed in my mind, but my lips never moved.

My feet moved instead.

The door was open.

Stephen stood beside it. Watching. Waiting.

"Go on."

I tried to stop.

My muscles tensed, just for a second, before the pull dragged me forward.

"Good girl."

The air was wrong.

The hum of the refrigerator filled the silence.

My feet carried me forward.

"You've come this far."

A gasp.

Julie.

She stepped into view, barely illuminated by the dim kitchen light.

Her head turned.

Her eyes dropped to my hand.

The knife.

"Sophia?" Her voice cracked. "What are you doing?"

I didn't know.

Her gaze darted between my face and the blade glinting in my grip.

"What is that? Why do you have that?"

I tried to let go.

My fingers wouldn't move.

Stephen's voice curled in my mind.

"She's afraid of you."

Julie took a step back.

"Get out," she whispered.

Then louder, "Get out!"

A jolt of something hot burned through me.

I turned stiffly, moving toward the back door.

Running mechanically until I reached the trees.

The cold air slammed against my skin.

I turned back, like I was yanked on a string.

Stephen was still inside.

Julie was frozen in place, her terror pinned on me.

She thought I was the one haunting her.

But I wasn't.

Stephen had made her think that.

He'd turned me into the monster in her nightmares.

Julie's house dissolved.

I stood in the woods. The same night.

Julie was scared.

Her breath came sharp. Ragged.

Stephen wasn't there.

But I was.

I watched from behind a large tree.

She was talking to someone.

Eli.

Then I heard a crunch.

Julie's lifeless body lay beside him, her hair fanned out like a dark halo.

His hands shook as he kneeled, breath unsteady, face streaked with tears.

Oh god.

Tears burned down my cheeks, my chest crushing under the weight of my silence.

I wanted to scream.

I wanted to wake up.

But I didn't.

Instead, I watched.

Like I always did.

Then Eli saw me.

And it all went black.

I stood in the blackness, remembering.

I had come back.

Again. And again.

To protect Julie.

But Stephen always found me first.

His voice slithered through the dark.

"You keep coming back, don't you?"

"We are the same."

"You killed her, Sophia. That's why you don't remember."

I wasn't like him.

I wasn't.

I refused to be.

And then, the pull stopped.

My breath slowed.

The smell of damp earth sharpened.

I wasn't in the past anymore.

I was awake.

I looked down.

My fingers were curled into the dirt.

The chill hit me first.

I was in the woods, behind Linworth's house.

I was at Julie's grave.

And Eli was standing over me.

His eyes were bloodshot.

He reached for me slowly.

"You're safe now. You're safe now."

He repeated it like a prayer.

"I'm sorry," he whispered.

63

— • —

OCTOBER 25, 2024, 3 AM - ELI

THE DAY JULIE WENT MISSING

My phone buzzed and woke me up. Crap, I forgot to put it on silent.

> Julie: Eli, meet me. Now. In the woods behind Linworth's. I'm not waiting anymore. If you don't come, I'm going to tell someone. Maybe even the police.

I stared at the message, my pulse kicking up.

Julie had been texting me for days, her messages growing more frantic.

> Julie (7 days ago): We need to talk about Sophia.

> Julie (2 days ago): Eli, I need to talk to you. Please. Don't ignore this.

And now this.

A sick feeling settled in my gut. This was bad.

I stood abruptly, shoving my phone in my sweatpants pocket. Linworth lived close, but it was late, and my mind was still shaking off the remnants of sleep.

I left the house, but my feet felt heavier with every step.

When I got there, Julie was standing just inside the tree line, clutching her phone like it was the only thing keeping her upright.

Her hands were shaking.

"Julie," I called softly, stepping closer. She didn't turn right away. Her posture was rigid, like she was bracing for something.

When she finally faced me, her eyes were wide and hollow.

Just... afraid.

"We need to talk," she said, voice thin and unsteady.

"What's going on?"

She hesitated, glancing over my shoulder. Like she expected someone else to be there.

"Stephen is using your sister," she said.

"What?" I said hoarsely. "What are you talking about?"

Julie exhaled sharply and pressed a shaking hand to her forehead. "Eli, I need you to listen to me. I've been trying to figure this out for weeks, and I—I don't know what to do anymore."

She swallowed hard, gripping the phone tighter. "Sophia is sleepwalking."

I flinched. "I know."

Julie laughed bitterly. "No, Eli. You don't."

She took a slow step closer, her voice trembling. "She's been in my backyard. She was in my house just now, with a knife."

Her words slammed into me, and for a second the ground shifted.

"I don't think she knows what she's doing." Julie's voice wavered, but her eyes burned with conviction. "But she's not acting alone."

I stared at her.

"What are you saying?"

Julie sucked in a sharp breath. "Stephen is leading her to my house. He's done... things to me. There's... something bigger going on, but..." She looked terrified.

She unlocked her phone with shaking hands, nearly dropping it. "I put a camera outside my house," she tapped on a video and held it up.

I didn't want to see it.

But I had to.

The footage blasted to life, grainy but unmistakable. Sophia stood in Julie's backyard. Her face was slack. Her eyes vacant. Her body swayed slightly, as if being moved by something invisible. But that wasn't what made my stomach churn.

Julie tapped the audio button. A second voice crackled through the silence.

Stephen.

"That's it," his voice purred in the dark. "Good girl. Move closer, let her see you."

My skin went cold.

No.

Julie tapped on the next video, this one taken from her bedroom window.

Sophia again, this time holding a knife outside Julie's house.

And Stephen's voice, low and coaxing.

"She's afraid of you, you know."

"Look at her window. She's watching you."

"Don't you want to protect her? Or do you want to watch again?"

Something sharp twisted deep in my gut. My brain tried to make sense of it. Tried to say this was fake, edited, something else. But it wasn't.

Julie exhaled sharply, watching me like she was waiting for the truth to hit.

I felt like I was going to be sick.

Julie's hands clenched into fists, her whole body trembling.

"I tried to tell Linworth," she said, voice cracking. "I told him something was wrong. That Stephen was messing with me, that Sophia was coming to my house now too. You know what he said?"

I shook my head, throat dry.

Julie let out a bitter laugh. "He told me to drop it. That it was too big. Too messy." She wiped her face, jaw trembling. "But I can't drop it, Eli. I can't."

She stepped closer, eyes burning.

"Will you go to the police?" she asked. "Tell them Stephen and your sister broke in. Say you couldn't find Sophia tonight, but that he's using her. Say whatever you have to. Just... please. It can't come from me."

I stared at her, heart hammering.

She'd just shown me a video of Sophia, walking into her house, with a knife.

And now she wanted me to take that to the cops?

No. No way. That video alone could destroy her.

Sophia could be arrested. She could go to jail.

"Wait. Why are you even bringing Sophia into this?" I asked. "She doesn't need to be involved with the police. If Stephen did something, then say he did it. Why can't you just do that? Why drag me into it?"

Julie's eyes darkened. Her grip tightened around her phone like she might crush it.

"I can't," she said, voice raw. "Sophia's in this too. I don't know what else she's done under Stephen's control. But tonight... I think she tried to hurt me. It's not just Stephen anymore."

The words slammed into me like a sledgehammer. *She tried to hurt me.*

I shook my head. "No—she didn't—"

Julie gestured wildly at the phone, the image frozen on Sophia with a knife. "She might not have done it yet, but Stephen is trying to make her, Eli! He's using her. Controlling her. How long until she wakes up with blood, my blood, on her hands?"

My stomach turned.

Julie exhaled, but her voice didn't soften. "I don't want to believe she meant any of this. But I can't risk doing nothing anymore."

"Julie…" I took a step forward, my voice sharper than I intended. "I'm not bringing Sophia anywhere near this. You need to leave her out of it."

She stepped back like I'd hit her. Her face crumpled.

"If you won't help me," she said, tears streaming down her face, "then I guess I don't really have a choice."

She turned.

"I'd rather be dead than live like this!"

She spun back, fire in her eyes.

"I'm going to the police."

I reached for her, heart racing. "Julie, wait!"

She yanked her arm away.

"Eli, let me go!"

"You don't understand!" My grip loosened. "She wouldn't—"

Julie twisted away, her foot catching on a root. Her body lurched backward, slow motion, like a nightmare I couldn't stop watching.

Crack.

Then a thud.

Her head hit a rock. And everything went still.

I stood frozen, breath caught in my throat, like my body already knew something my mind refused to believe. I dropped to my knees, hands shaking so hard they barely worked.

"Julie?" I whispered, inching closer. "Julie, come on."

She didn't move. Her chest didn't rise.

I pressed my fingers to her neck. Nothing.

I think I said her name again, or maybe I didn't. Maybe it wasn't even a word—just a sound, rough and useless in my throat.

She was gone.

I reeled back, crawling, clutching my stomach like I could hold it all in. My scream, my guilt, my whole world.

What had I done?

I had to call someone. 911. The cops.

My hand moved toward my pocket—then I froze.

She was standing there.

Sophia.

Just a few feet away. Still. Her mouth slightly open, tears cutting silent tracks down her cheeks.

I stumbled back, breath catching.

"Sophia?" I whispered, frantically.

I waved my hand in front of her face.

She didn't move, but the tears kept dripping down her cheeks.

"Wake up," I said.

She was... sleepwalking.

Jesus.

How much had she seen?

I looked back at Julie's body. Then at my sister.

Oh god. The video. The knife. Her walking into Julie's house.

And now this.

They'd think she did it. That she killed her.

If I called the cops...

They'd find the videos. All of them. They'd see Sophia. They'd lock her up.

She's all I have left.

I shoved the panic down, hard. I couldn't fall apart now. I had to think.

Focus.

I had to make sure no one saw her.

I gently grabbed Sophia's arm with shaky hands and guided her home. Through the woods, to the patio, through the back door and to the couch.

Crap. What now?

A million thoughts raced through me.

I was thinking about how this wasn't happening.

Thinking about how I wasn't the kind of person who did things like this.

Thinking about how if I just stood here long enough, reality would reset itself.

If I went back to bed, if I woke up again, it wouldn't be real.

But Julie was still in the woods.

Sophia had been there.

And I—I had grabbed her. I had touched her.

The panic tunneled through my ribs, thick and choking.

This isn't real. This isn't real.

But it was.

My body moved on its own.

The next thing I knew, I was in the garage.

The automatic light sputtered on, illuminating the rusted shovel leaning against the wall near the bike rack.

My legs felt weak, hollow when I reached it.

I felt my fingers close around it, but it didn't feel like me.

I wasn't holding the shovel.

I was watching someone else hold it.

Some other version of me stood in this garage. Some other version of me thought this was the only option.

The real me was somewhere else. Screaming at him to stop.

But I wasn't stopping.

This is insane. This is wrong.

But if they found Julie—the videos on her phone, of Sophia—

Those thoughts played in my head over and over.

I swallowed hard. I put the gloves on and left.

The night felt too wide. Too hallow.

Like the woods had swallowed the world whole, like nothing existed anymore except me, the shovel, and the weight of what I was about to do.

I knelt beside Julie. Her hair was wrong. It just laid there, perfectly still.

Something sharp climbed up my throat. I almost expected her to move. To sit up, grab my wrist, and say, "Eli. What the hell are you doing?"

I almost expected this to be the part where I woke up.

But I didn't.

And neither did she.

Vomit pooled in my throat looking at her like that.

What if I just leave her here? What if I tell them she slipped?

But I couldn't risk it. I wouldn't risk it with Sophia.

I buried her face down. I couldn't stand to see her eyes. I didn't want them open when the dirt came.

After the dirt was packed, I stood there with the shovel still in my hand for a minute.

I thought I would feel relief.

I thought I would feel something.

Instead, I just felt a vast emptiness.

Like my skin didn't fit anymore. Like my bones had been rearranged.

The silence wasn't real silence anymore. It was stuffed full of things.

A pulse that wasn't beating.

A voice that would never be heard again.

Julie wasn't here.

Julie wasn't anywhere.

Because of me.

Just then, her phone buzzed. It glowed faintly from the dirt, revealing the last text she sent:

> I might need you tonight. Be ready.

Linworth's reply came now.

> Linworth: Julie, this is over. Don't come here again.

I grabbed the phone, deleted everything. The videos, texts, all of it. I ran through the trees, all the way to her house. I threw the phone from the tree line and watched it roll into her backyard.

I ran home. I didn't look back.

Julie thought she'd found someone who could save her.

She was wrong.

So was I.

— · —

Epilogue: June 6, 2025, 10 AM - Sophia

224 Days After Julie Went Missing

The water was too hot, steam curling around me in thick ribbons, but I didn't turn it down.

I let it burn against my skin—scalding my shoulders, my arms, my hands.

The same hands that had held a knife in Julie's house.

The same hands that had reached for Eli an hour ago, where he had buried her.

The same hands that could pick up my keys right now. Drive to the police station. Tell Newton everything.

The dirt swirled in the water, spiraling down the drain. A ghost of last night, of all the nights before. I watched it go, waiting to feel lighter.

I didn't.

I squeezed my eyes shut. But the memories came anyway.

Julie's voice, frantic, desperate: *"She tried to hurt me."*

Me, standing in her kitchen, holding a knife.

And Eli.

His tear-streaked face. His hands, shaking as he reached for me just moments ago.

"You're safe now."

It wasn't true. We weren't safe.

Eli wasn't safe.

Not really. Not if I told.

I could picture it so clearly, walking into the police station, sitting across from Newton, telling him what I knew.

I could see the way his face would change. The way he'd lean forward, his expression darkening. I could see the way the walls would close in, how everything would lock into place.

Eli wouldn't come home tonight.

No more hearing his voice in the next room, muttering in his sleep. No more teasing me about stealing his sweatshirts, no more eating the last of my cookie dough ice cream just to piss me off.

No more Eli.

No more home.

I'd never hear him say my name in that protective, older-brother way again.

I'd be alone.

Eli had buried a body.

But he had buried me, too. Protected me, hidden me, shielded me, even when I hadn't asked.

I gripped the edge of the shower wall.

Would I still be standing here if he hadn't?

Julie deserved justice.

Eli deserved consequences, but did he deserve to lose everything?

Did I?

No.

Stephen... Stephen deserved the real consequences.

I exhaled shakily, my breath fogging against the tile.

I stood there, waiting, for something. Clarity. A sign. A reason to change my mind.

Nothing came.

I wasn't going to the police.

Maybe some truths were better left unspoken.

The worst part wasn't remembering. It was knowing I might never stop.

I turned off the water.

About The Author

Taylor Jakovina is a writer of psychological thrillers that linger in the shadows between memory, obsession, and fear. She lives in Ohio with her husband and two dogs, Peaches and Cece, who—unlike most of her characters—have never lied. *What She Walked Into* is her debut novel.

THE STORY DOESN'T END HERE

Want to know what Taylor writes next?
Visit www.taylorjakovina.com for book updates,
bonus content, and future releases.
You can also follow her on TikTok @jakovinawrites.